Sign up for our newsletter to hear about new and upcoming releases.

www.ylva-publishing.com

Olivia Janae

The Loudest Silence

Acknowledgments

This book has been a journey and a half. A lot of people worked to put this together, and I have so many people to thank. For now, I think I'll stick with two. Astrid, you didn't have to give me another chance, and you did. It changed my life. Thank you.

Second, Sandra. You have stood by me and helped in every way that you could. This wouldn't be here without you.

Thank you from the bottom of my heart.

Dedication

For Dani, Kel, and the man in the purple hat.

Author's Note

A little information here for my readers before we begin. *The Loudest Silence* has a main character who is Deaf and uses American Sign Language. Throughout the book, I follow the suggestion of the National Association of the Deaf to capitalize *Deaf* when I'm referring to Deaf people as a group with their own culture and language or to members of the Deaf community, while lowercasing *deaf* when referring to the audiological status of not hearing.

American Sign Language (ASL) is a unique language with its own grammar, which isn't based on English at all. When referring to the specific language, I capitalized it. When used generically, *sign language* (*sign* for short) is lowercased, parallel to *spoken language*.

Chapter 1

KATE PAUSED IN THE LOBBY of Chicago's Symphony Center and tried to swallow the lump in her throat. She bounced her shoulders to shift the cello case on her back and popped her neck to relieve the tension yet again. Her hand shook as she reached for the gold-embossed door.

She had been through this first-day thing so many times before. The job with this chamber group was no different than those she'd done with other prestigious groups over the last few years, but the flutter of butterflies never left her stomach.

The annoying voice of reason spoke up in the back of her mind, reminding her that this job was more important than most. It meant she could stop freelancing for two years, a reprieve she was thankful for. Well, a year, anyway.

Taking a breath, she pushed through the doors.

The high warble of violins and the cough and splutter of horns as they teased and joked through their warm-ups were no different than what she heard at any other gig. The welcome familiarity calmed her raw nerves.

Kate paused at the open door, feeling small. In front of her, the stage spread out in a grand half circle, though it was dwarfed by the majesty of the Symphony Center, with its ocean of red velvet seats, tall pillars, double-deck balconies, gold-leaf walls, and huge chandeliers of cloud diffusers.

It wasn't at all like the smaller halls she had often played in, ones with moldy curtains and old 1970s wood paneling, or the hall of some community center. This hall was intimidating, as it was surely meant to be.

Still, Kate smiled. Playing in a hall like this, less than a mile from her dream hall, was what she had been working toward. She walked through the door and started toward the stage.

The world of classical music posted auditions online, and once the job was won, photos and a bio of the new hire were posted as well. Perhaps for this reason, only a few people from the small group noticed her enter.

Kate didn't mind. She hated walking into a rehearsal space and being stared at as if she were a new zoo exhibit. It reminded her of all the first days she had been through at new schools while growing up.

She pushed back the painful memory and climbed the side stairs to the stage. On the far side stood several men and women dressed in professional suits and dresses. Their lofty expressions made it clear that they were board members.

She hesitated. The train had made her later than she'd wanted to be, and she needed time to warm up. But she also wanted to make a good first impression on the board, especially since she didn't have a benefactor, unlike a lot of Chicago freelancers.

She ran the fingers of her free hand through her hair to tame the windblown blonde curls, wishing she had stopped in the bathroom to brush them, and approached the group with a confidence she didn't really feel.

"Hi." She smiled and offered her hand to the nearest board member. "Katelyn Flynn, new cellist."

"Oh, of course. Zachary King, vice chair of the WCCE board." He shook her hand. "I take it your relocation went well?"

"It did. Thank you," she said, smiling politely.

"Good, good." Zachary patted her arm. "Be sure to introduce yourself to the president when you see her."

"Will do." She shook a few more hands, then nodded at the rest. That done, she turned to scan the faces of her fellow musicians, but the face she was looking for wasn't among them. If he didn't get here soon, he wouldn't have any warm-up time. And why did he have to be late on her first day? She wanted to get their reunion over with as soon as possible.

Kate gritted her teeth against the new flutters in her stomach.

She had made her choice. She had taken the job in Chicago despite him being in residence. And it was going to be good, she promised herself yet again. They were both adults. It would be fine.

Despite her pep talk, another lump had formed in her throat

Pointedly ignoring it, she found her seat and shifted the thirty-pound weight off her back. Stretching her neck and shoulders, she pulled out her cello and bow and began warming up.

The still-empty seats gradually filled. Musicians pulled out their instruments and tuned up, then played scales, warming their muscles like athletes before a game.

"Hi! You must be Katelyn."

Kate looked up from her cello at the small woman who had appeared in front of her. "Kate." She forced a professional smile and stood to offer her hand, her cello balanced in the other.

"I'm Mary. We spoke on the phone. It's nice to meet you, Kate."

Kate nodded in recognition. Mary was the personnel manager and artistic director and a violinist. She didn't look like Kate had expected.

Even compared to Kate's own five-foot-four frame, Mary seemed small. Her black hair was styled in a pixie cut. She had the soft yet stony disposition of a schoolteacher—sweet, but with the don't-mess-with-me attitude not far under the surface.

"Are you comfortable getting started right away?" Mary asked. "If you want a rehearsal to sit back and—"

"No, no." Kate waved her hand. "Just throw me in."

"Sink or swim, huh? I like that." Mary smiled and turned to the small group, clapping her hands. "All right, let's get going." After making a few announcements, she added, "As you all can see, our new cellist made it. Kate Flynn, welcome! We're excited to have you!"

Kate looked around to acknowledge the introduction. From the bass section, she caught sight of the lone bass player's familiar brown eyes. Stephen had finally shown up. She nodded to him.

He winked at her and rolled his eyes toward Mary, then the ceiling. The charm that had been so boyish years ago still radiated from him.

Mary continued going over plans for the upcoming season and the first concert. "As you can see from the list here"—she held out a sheet of paper—"we're focusing first on the strings with *Eine kleine Nachtmusik*. It's such a beautiful piece and one we rarely play together. I'm particularly excited because..."

As Mary's remarks continued, Kate's enthusiasm began to wane. *Eine kleine Nachtmusik* was a familiar piece. She had begun playing it at thirteen.

But some of the tension also left her shoulders. The WCCE was well-known in the Midwest, and she'd been worried about the other players being a cut above her. Now she could breathe. It was just another group in another state in another city.

Then a flash of worry went through her. She had been hoping the group would elevate her playing, but *Eine kleine Nachtmusik*... It didn't speak well to the group's supposed cutting-edge image.

Well... She glanced back at Stephen. Maybe there were a few more complications here.

Her gaze dropped to her phone propped on her music stand before Stephen could meet her eye. So far, there were no notifications. She bit her lip, unsure if that made her feel better or worse. Tonight, she had been forced to do something she hated: she had left Max with a stranger, earning her a bundle of bad-mom points. But they had only been in the city for forty-eight hours, so what the hell else could she do?

Thinking of Max with a stranger opened a floodgate of melodramatic thoughts that she had been able to shut down upon entering the hall. But now an image flashed through her mind of Max alone and injured, their apartment emptied of their few belongings, and the ceiling fan still swinging haphazardly. The mental picture appeared in black-and-white, like an old cops-and-robbers movie. The officer who responded to the 911 call would, of course, wear his hat cocked on his head and sound like Humphrey Bogart as he told her there was "very little we can do, sweetheart."

Just as she slipped into another worried daydream, a flurry of motion from stage left caught her eye. She squinted to see past the stage lights.

A medium-height brunette stood in the shadows, her back perfectly straight and her chin held high as she faced down Zachary King. Everything about the woman was fierce, from her shoulder-length bob styled to perfection to the crisp suit and deep-red lips. The woman said something that made Zachary take a step back.

The young Asian woman standing next to her focused on Zachary with her hands dancing as he spoke.

It was sign language. That much Kate knew. She had seen it used on *Sesame Street* with Max. She thought the name was beautiful, that it fit so perfectly with the graceful movements.

What was a person who couldn't hear doing in a chamber rehearsal? Both brunettes were dressed too well to be there by accident. It wasn't as if they had taken a wrong turn at Albuquerque.

The younger and taller of the two finally let her hands fall to her stomach as if in a rest position. She turned toward her companion and waited

The other woman's painted lips curled back. She pinned the man with her gaze, stabbed her finger at him again, and said something that seemed to make him quake in his boots.

He nodded again, turned on his heel, and hurried away too quickly to maintain his dignity. Kate felt bad for him, but then her attention was pulled back to the women.

The younger woman raised her brow as her hands flew into beautiful fluid motion again.

The other rolled her eyes. With quick, stabbing motions, she answered in the same language. The flow of their hands was mesmerizing.

"So, I think that's it for now!" Mary's voice brought Kate back to the moment. "I think we should try a quick run-through."

Reluctantly, Kate turned her attention to the sheet music, ready to play.

The rehearsal had gone as smoothly as she could have hoped for. The group played beautifully, which was great since the first gig was scheduled for only a few days later.

"Well, hello, stranger." She heard Stephen's voice as she pushed through the stage door and stepped outside, eager to save Max from the new sitter—and possible Noir-style burglar.

"Hey." She turned to greet him. "Way to show up at the last minute today."

His smile exuded all his charm. "Eh, I like to get warmed up at home. What can I say?"

She rolled her eyes and forced a smile. "It's good to see you." She hadn't been sure how she would feel talking to him again after so many years, after…well, everything. It was nice to see him, and she hadn't expected that.

"Right back at you, lady." Stephen gave her a slow smile that quickly split into a grin. He held out his arms for a hug. She went to him, far too aware of him to feel comfortable. They ended the embrace quickly, chuckling awkwardly.

"You seem nervous, Flynn."

Kate debated briefly about how honest to be. "It's not exactly nerves. It's more that if there are any mistakes, then it's all me. There's no one else to blame when you're the only cello."

A part of her still wasn't sure if she was supposed to be there. She had won the job, yeah, but had they really meant to pick her instead of some other thin blonde with a cleft chin and a small scar under her left eye?

It wasn't a new feeling either. Kate had never felt as if she fit anywhere. After as many foster families as she had been through, it was impossible not to feel that way.

"We all make mistakes. No one will judge you for them. At least not today," he added, nudging her with his elbow.

Kate snorted and suddenly remembered what it had been like that summer at Tanglewood, sitting in a cabin, sharing a bottle.

She shoved the nostalgic memory back down. "Talk about making the new girl feel welcome!"

His laugh was full-bellied and loud. "Hey, now, don't mistake me for the welcome committee. That's not a roller-coaster I wanna ride."

"You did all right at Tanglewood."

"Yeah, well, I didn't think handing you a shot as soon as you walked in was a good idea tonight."

She laughed. "I don't think I've had one since then."

"How's the apartment? Does it suit you?"

She nodded. The apartment was also something she didn't want to get into just then.

"And little Max?"

Startled that he had asked, she looked into his eyes. Of course he would, but somehow...

"Yeah. Yeah, no." She shoved her hands into her pockets, suddenly feeling smothered. "He's good. Growing like a weed."

"Good, good." Stephen shifted his feet. "Well, it was good to see you. Let's get a drink soon."

"Yeah, yeah." She shivered in the night air.

"Well, uh, you sounded great in there tonight. Seriously." He turned and walked away.

Kate headed down the sidewalk toward the L station. That meeting had gone better than she expected. God, she was glad it was over.

Kate hopped on the train, her teeth chattering in the cool air. If she was this cold now, how would she handle the snow next winter? She badly needed a new coat.

The commute to her apartment in East Rogers Park was fifty minutes—assuming there were no delays. It was long enough for her to lose the feeling in her toes thanks to the poor L car heating. She watched as the train passed the downtown skyscrapers, the lights in the tall buildings twinkling brighter than any stars. She had missed living in a big city. It was nice to be in one again. Who knew where the next job would be? She and Max could next end up in a tiny town in Alaska or even Timbuktu. Everything had an expiration date: jobs, homes, dates, relationships. Even the car she had bought for herself when she was young had finally been retired. It was day one of the job. She shouldn't already be thinking about what was coming next, but it was inevitable. A year went by quickly.

The skyscrapers finally gave way to brick apartment buildings. The outside lights went from bright, warm, and welcoming to dim as the train traveled toward her neighborhood.

She pushed herself deeper into her seat as the train commuters changed from young business professionals to sus-looking teenagers wearing bulky jackets and pants hanging down so low, it was a wonder they didn't fall off.

She made it back to her apartment. "Hello?" she called out softly, picking her way in the dark around boxes littered everywhere.

"Hi, Mrs. Flynn." Stacey appeared from Max's room as Kate rounded the corner into the hallway. The night-light cast an eerie shadow over the babysitter's face.

Max, half-asleep, was draped over Stacey's shoulder. He pulled his thumb from his mouth with a whine and reached for his mother. His half-closed eyes, red-rimmed and swollen, peeked out from under his flop of dark hair.

"I've been trying to put him to bed for two hours, Mrs. Flynn, but he's been really upset."

"Kate. Let's just go with Kate instead of Mrs. Anything. And, yeah, it's all right. It's usually a problem with a new babysitter. Don't worry about it."

Holding her three-year-old—who was getting far too big to be held like a baby—Kate paid the babysitter and maneuvered through the dim light to his bedroom. She laid him back on his bed, rubbed his belly, and gently pulled his thumb from his mouth. "Hey, kid."

"You were gone," he said.

"I had to work, remember?"

He nodded.

"You're sleepy. Close your eyes."

"You home?"

"Yes. I'm home for the night."

Hearing Kate's words, Max rolled onto his stomach, his thumb moving to his mouth. She pulled it out again and rubbed his back gently until his breathing became deep and even. Then she stood up and stretched. He—no, they—were going to be tired in the morning.

As she made her way to her own room, her shins seemed to bang into every box in the apartment.

Kate was tired of moving boxes. She hated them—hated what they represented for Max. At least they didn't have a lot of them anymore. They had moved six times since Max was born. After a while, they had stopped accumulating whatever wasn't absolutely necessary, measuring all things by asking, "Is this worth packing into the car?"

She fell into bed with a sigh. Unpacking could wait for another day. As she closed her eyes, a familiar dissatisfaction crept up her spine: Max had been with a babysitter. She didn't know anyone. She was going to bed alone.

God, she was so tired of this life.

She rolled over and hugged the pillow, forcing herself to sleep before the negative thoughts could fully blossom.

Chapter 2

A FEW DAYS LATER, A teary-eyed Max followed her through the apartment, whining as she pulled on her concert blacks, her usual slacks and professional black blouse, and her heels. When she dressed for a performance, he usually understood that it was time for his mommy to go and play music. Tonight, however, he refused to settle.

"Buddy, look." She pointed at the large pot on the stove. "You get to have soup with Stacey! You like Stacey, remember? You said she's funny."

Max's bottom lip was out, and his huge eyes blinked back tears, making his brown irises stand out until she felt as if she were facing a bereaved Precious Moments figurine.

"But I don't wanna!" he wailed, wrapping his arms around her knees.

She lifted him into her arms and kissed his temple. "Hey, I'll be home soon, Max, and you get to have your soup. Maybe Stacey will put on *Ninja Turtles*." She caught the babysitter's eye, trying to convey that *now* would be a good time to put it on.

Stacey smiled and nodded but didn't move. Whatever message she had just received was not the one that Kate was trying to get across.

"Do you wanna watch *Ninja Turtles*?" Kate pointedly shifted her gaze from Stacey to the TV. "Maybe we can make pizza tomorrow like Michelangelo. Whatd'ya think? You wanna be like Michelangelo?"

Max shook his head, then dropped his face onto her shoulder. She probably had snot on her concert blacks now.

"Okay, buddy, I gotta go."

"No-o-o-o!"

She pulled gently and then harder, fighting to get Max to release his hold. "Jesus, kid, you're getting strong. Stacey, you wanna—?"

"Right! Sorry."

Stacey pulled him from behind as Kate extracted his arms. Finally, she was loose. She scrambled to pick up her things.

"I love you." Kate pushed the mop of hair off his forehead to plant another kiss. She held back the *I'm sorry* that she wanted to say and dashed out the door.

Stomach churning, she hurried down the hall and down the stairs, trying to ignore his screams. With each step, the same thought repeated: *I hate this.* She replayed his flushed, tear-stained face over and over in her mind.

Kate entered the building through the stage door, her cello case hanging from her back.

The WCCE gig was a small one, a fundraiser for a local arts high school. The music was easy, but her fingers twitched, her stomach rock hard.

"Hey, Flynn." Stephen met her at the door. "You okay?"

"What? Oh." She popped her neck, still hearing Max's screams. "Yeah. Max just, uh… He doesn't like it when I leave in the evenings. He really cries and—" She noticed the vacant look on his face. "Uh, never mind. Yeah, I'm good."

Stephen cleared his throat. "You look a little unsteady on your feet. Are you ready?"

"Are you kidding?" Kate swung the case off her back and set it down. "I was born ready."

If he heard the wobble in her voice, he didn't mention it.

"Don't be worried." William, one of the violinists, grinned at her. "This is fun, right? And you only have two pieces today. The others are mostly brass."

"Right." Kate rubbed her moist palms on her slacks.

"You got this. Don't stress." Stephen grinned.

The small group had already assembled on the stage, leaving little time for Kate's nerves to ramp up. She had no sooner set up her instrument than someone announced the piece they were about to play. The room hushed, the eyes of the audience on the players.

The Loudest Silence

It was always at this moment, just before the first piece, that she wondered why the hell she had gotten into this career.

Her hands and fingers were steady even though her stomach spun like a washer. She counted out the beats, then slowly drew her bow across the strings, pulling a low, deep moan from her cello. The sound calmed her nerves, reminding her of the answer to her question. She loved the cello. She loved music. That was why she put herself through this insane career. Love.

As she played, her eye was drawn to a commotion at stage left. She glanced over, and her heart jumped into her throat like an excited bunny. It was same angry woman and her companion that Kate had noticed during her first rehearsal at the Symphony Center. Once again, their hands were flying wildly, and, just like before, it took Kate a long time before she was willing to look away from the mesmerizing movements.

And she wasn't the only one distracted. At least half the children in the audience had turned their heads to watch.

One, two, three, four. She counted the rests, then began to play again.

She did her best to ignore the commotion, but the longer their hands flew, the more her admiration turned to agitation. It was getting harder to look away. In fact, it was getting downright distracting.

The one who had cut into Mr. King so thoroughly was beautiful. Her lightly golden skin, large eyes, and full lips were almost as distracting as the hand movements themselves.

Kate forced herself to look away. God, they were rude! This audience was made up of children! They were learning how to behave during a performance, and the women were setting a bad example.

Finally, the last note of her portion of the program finished. She and the other string players rose from their seats, bowed to the audience, and exited the stage.

"Who are those women?" Kate asked Stephen as soon as they were out of earshot.

Stephen, who was about to go back out to play with the brass ensemble, shrugged.

Finally, the performance was over. Stephen appeared as she was chatting with a stagehand.

"As per tradition, it's time to partake in some bad wine. Whatd'ya say?"

Kate turned at Stephen's sudden appearance.

"You all right?"

"What? Yeah, of course. Wine, yeah, okay. Just give me a minute."

She *had* to speak to those two women, tell them how rude they had been. She had to say *something*. If she were in their shoes, she would want to be told.

Jaw set, she started toward them, remembering the look on the face of the woman who had metaphorically crushed King beneath a designer pump. Perhaps she should have been intimidated, but she wasn't; angry people with authority did not bother her as much as they probably should. She worked through her speech, trying to find a way to say the words politely.

She approached the woman, who was now staring intently at her phone screen, unaware of anything around her.

"Excuse me."

The woman did not look up.

Had Kate really just tried to *speak* to a deaf person? Feeling like an utter genius, she lightly touched the woman's hand. The woman looked up and gazed at her intently. Kate blinked, disoriented. She hadn't seen her up close before, so she hadn't noticed the intensity of her eyes or their rich shade of brown. They were surprisingly beautiful despite their remoteness.

Kate realized that she was staring and blinked. Forcing a smile, she opened her mouth to speak, then stopped. Her face heated. She had no idea how to communicate with someone who couldn't hear.

The stranger forced a smile that said she dealt with this kind of ignorance every day. She drew a circle around her mouth with two fingers and stared at Kate's lips, giving the impression that she could lipread.

"Okay." She pointed to herself. Should she enunciate more? Shaping her lips in exaggerated movements, she introduced herself. "Kate."

"Don't do that with your lips."

"Oh." Kate felt her cheeks go warm and her eyes go wide. The woman had *spoken*. Kate hadn't expected that. Though now that she thought about it, hadn't she seen her speak to King? She hoped she had wiped the surprise off her face quickly.

"Vivian Kensington."

"So, um, I'm the new performer with the WCCE and—"

Vivian Kensington nodded, cutting Kate off. "Yes, the cellist. Katelyn Flynn. Welcome to the group."

Her voice was a bit unusual. While the pitch was perfectly ordinary, if a little deep, it mostly sounded as if she had a bad head cold and made her tone nasal and constricted. Each word seemed to flow just a bit into the next, but otherwise, she was perfectly understandable.

The way she spoke was intriguing. And the way Vivian Kensington stared at her was disconcerting. Kate felt her heart flutter.

"Is there something I can help you with, Ms. Flynn?"

Kate paused, then frowned as she remembered that she had come over because she was angry. *Damn it!* She shifted, her irritation returning. How was it that Ms. Kensington seemed annoyed with her? She had assumed that Zachary King had transgressed in some way, but maybe this woman was just rude. "Uh, right. I just wanted to say that you were really distracting during the performance."

"Excuse me?" Ms. Kensington's voice was cold and flat, dripping with aristocratic venom through the distortion.

"Sorry. That was kind of blunt. What I meant to say was, you were talking through the entire concert, and it was really distracting." The pressure of the woman's glare made Kate shift her stance. "It wasn't just me. The other players were distracted too. And so were the kids. So I thought…"

A pained look flashed across the woman's face before indignation rose to mask it. Her hands began moving in the alien language, fast and quick.

Kate was about to point out that she had no idea what the hand movements meant when a voice from behind supplied her with the answer. "I'm deaf."

Kate looked around.

The woman's younger companion stood with a drink in her hand. "Hi. Charlie Hseih. I'm Ms. Kensington's interpreter."

Kate returned the smile, but Vivian Kensington was having none of their pleasantries. "Tell this—" She scowled, then paused as if reconsidering her words. "Tell *Ms. Flynn*," Charlie read as the woman's hands flew, "that I am deaf, and sign language is my main means of communication. Oh…" Charlie blushed. "Um—"

"Yeah, I got the gist, Ms. Hseih," Kate said, turning to face the interpreter.

"Charlie."

"Charlie. Look, I understand that she's deaf, obviously—"

Charlie opened her mouth to speak, but Vivian snapped her small, manicured fingers in front of Kate's face, drawing her attention back.

"Talk to her," Charlie said. "Pretend I'm not here. Geez, she's really mad. What did you say?"

"I was trying to tell her that, with all due respect, she was drawing attention during the concert." She turned back to Ms. Kensington, refusing to allow her glare to shake her. "Your hands were going during the concert, and it was really distracting to everyone. All of the children were watching you, Ms. Kensington, and not listening to the music."

"And I told you that I am deaf and this is how I communicate!" Charlie read. "What is so hard to understand about that?"

Kate bristled. The woman seemed to be deliberately misconstruing her words. "I get that, but we're here teaching children how to behave in a performance setting, right? So, isn't it rude for *anyone* to talk during a performance, whether it's with their voices or with their hands? I'm just—"

The woman's hands burst into motion so quickly that Kate wasn't sure how Charlie could follow them.

Kate took an involuntary step back as the woman's hands moved, slapping into each other.

"Are we also not meant to teach these children about tolerance and acceptance of those who are different? I apologize"—her face made it clear she was not sorry at all— "if my language was distracting to you, but allowances must be made, just as handicap rails are available on buildings to allow all to enter."

Kate winced. She felt as if she were standing in front of a firing squad. She glanced around.

Yes, people were staring.

"Let us only hope," the woman continued disdainfully, bending a little as her hands bounced sharply, "that people with attitudes such as yours do not spend too much time with these children and that your archaic intolerance will not be passed on to the next generation."

It took Kate a second to recover enough to respond. "Whoa, wait a minute, lady! I wasn't singling you out because you're deaf. I was making a comment about *anyone* talking during a performance! I have a son, and I wouldn't want him to think what you were doing was okay, so I—"

The woman pushed past her. Charlie followed.

"Oh, come on! I meant I wouldn't want him to see someone talking during a performance!" she snapped at the back of the woman's head.

What the hell?

Why had she automatically accused her of discriminating against her because she was deaf? She most certainly had not said that. Why would she even think it?

She considered chasing after her to make sure the woman knew exactly what she'd meant, but before she could react, Stephen stepped in front of her, a cup of wine in his hand. "So, I'm gonna step in here."

Kate snarled.

"I see you met our resident ice queen."

"What?"

He jerked his head toward the retreating back of Vivian Kensington. "Were you two fighting?"

"Yeah, I guess so. I don't know. She was speaking sign language through the entire performance, and it was really freaking distracting. You didn't notice?" She took a sip of the cheap wine, grimacing at the vinegary taste.

Stephen laughed. "Oh, of course I noticed. No one would have the guts to say something to her, though, so *brava* to that."

"Why? Because she's deaf? Does that mean she gets to be as rude as she likes and it should just be ignored?" She knew her anger was making her act out unprofessionally.

From across the room, Ms. Kensington caught her eye and glared.

"Well, no." Stephen shrugged. "But considering her position…"

Kate grabbed his arm. "Oh God, please don't tell me she's someone I should know."

Stephen clinked his plastic cup against hers. "I'm sorry to say it, but good job, gorgeous. You haven't even been here a week, and you've already pissed off the president of the board."

Kate looked down at her empty cup. "Of course I did."

Chapter 3

"Max, hurry! We're going to be late!" Kate picked up the bag that held her cell phone, sunglasses, and the snack she knew Max would want before they even got to the train. "Max!"

He ripped from his room, his ears sticking out from under his baseball cap. His cheeks spread out in a wide grin, making them look as chubby as a chipmunk's. Slamming into her legs, he nearly knocked her over. "For the music?"

"Yes!" she answered. "Let's go!" She leaned down and kissed his cheek.

He squared his cap on his head and pulled her toward the door. "Let's go! Let's go!"

Kate resisted the urge to laugh at the little twig legs sticking out of his shorts, but he gave her arm another tug, and with a promise to herself to stop for coffee, they were off to the Mommy & Me music day with the WCCE.

The last two weeks had been uneventful. Max had been looking forward to their first social event for days. He genuinely loved music.

The community center where the event was being held was large, and Kate was reminded of a happy period during her childhood. It smelled like Play-Doh, apple juice with a side of graham crackers, and construction paper. And it was *loud*. Children of all ages were yelling, laughing, screaming, all of them excited for the afternoon of noisemaking that they had been promised.

Max wasn't shy, but he also hadn't been exposed to many kids his own age, thanks to their constant moving, something Kate felt a never-ending guilt about. Overwhelmed by all the other children, Max pulled on Kate's arm in a silent demand to be picked up.

"Hey, no need to be afraid, Max," she whispered as he buried his face in her shoulder, hiding in her hair. "Should we find the teacher? Yeah?"

He nodded, his hand twisting as his thumb went to his mouth.

"Hey, kid. We've talked about that, right? Mr. Thumb is too big to go in your mouth anymore. You're a big boy, and you don't need it!"

He removed his thumb, his lip jutting out.

Kate moved quickly, hoping to avoid a breakdown. She looked around for someone in charge.

"Ms. Flynn?"

Kate turned to see a casually dressed Charlie Hseih smiling at her. It was strange to see her out of her professional garb. "Uh, Ms. Hseih! Hi!"

"Charlie. Are you here for the event?"

Charlie shot her an easy smile, as if she were inviting anyone who met her to sit back and talk over coffee or a drink. Maybe it was because she wore a pair of worn Converse. Or maybe it was her asymmetrical bob. Or maybe it was the fact that Charlie was makeup free, giving her a relaxed and friendly air. It was easy to smile back at her.

"Yeah," Kate answered. "Are you here for it too?"

"Oh no!" Charlie laughed, waving her hands. "No, I don't have kids. I'm one of the teachers."

"Oh!" She had assumed that Charlie worked privately for Vivian Kensington, but maybe she actually worked for WCCE.

"Vivian didn't tell me you had kids. Who's this?" Charlie asked, flashing Max a grin.

Max peeked out from under Kate's hair, a finger in his mouth instead of his thumb.

"Just the one. This is my son, Max." Kate bounced him affectionately and gently pulled his finger out of his mouth.

"Hi, Max! Oh my goodness, you're so cute!" Charlie squealed. She tickled his side, making him squirm in delight. "He's so handsome."

Kate thanked her. "So, um, how did they rope you into working this?"

"Actually, uh…" Charlie brought her hands up and began moving them as she spoke. "This is something we run every year. This is kind of *our* annual event."

Kate looked at the sign language in panic. "No! You're kidding! Shit. Wait, don't tell her I said that." She slapped down Charlie's hands. Then she felt the air on her back getting colder. Or had she imagined that?

Kate turned to find herself face-to-face with the ice queen. *Oh crap.*

She had dreaded meeting her again. Part of her was convinced that she was going to be fired for having insulted the board president. She hadn't meant to do that. She shouldn't have approached her in the first place. She blamed first-day performance jitters. She told herself it was because she had wanted to make her aware of how distracting she had been, but now, weeks later, she admitted that she had been offended by their rudeness. She hadn't exactly overreacted, but she also hadn't *not* overreacted.

She needed to apologize.

Kate opened her mouth, but the only thing that came out was an awkward "Ah…"

"It's true," Ms. Kensington said with a voice as tight as Kate's back muscles. "We both have a strong passion for children as well as a desire for community outreach." She nodded slightly at Kate and began signing as Charlie translated. "Ms. Flynn, it's very nice to see you." Her words were polite, but her eyes were cold, her chin sharply jutted, her lips a thin line. "Have you signed in yet?"

"Not yet." Kate flinched as the sign-in clipboard was slapped into her hands. Okay, she probably deserved that. She filled it out quickly and handed it to Charlie.

Ms. Kensington looked away from Kate and turned her attention to Max. "And this must be Maxwell." She addressed him in her slightly distorted voice.

"Um, yeah." Kate hooked her thumbs into her back pockets and wondered how the hell this woman knew the name of her son. His *full* name.

Ms. Kensington beamed at him but didn't touch him—something Kate appreciated since most people felt compelled to tousle his hair or pinch his cheek. Instead, she leaned over slightly so that she was level with his face.

At the attention of a new person, he buried himself in Kate's hair.

Ms. Kensington smiled brightly, causing a dimple to appear. "Hi, Max. I'm Vivian."

He peeked out. "Your voice is funny. Are you sick?" He reached out to touch her throat.

Kate felt her face flush. Great. Now Ms. Kensington was going to think that both she *and* her son were jerks.

But to Kate's surprise, Ms. Kensington smiled warmly, staying at his eye level. "No, I'm not sick. My voice sounds different because I'm deaf. Do you know what that means?"

He shook his head and struggled to get down. Kate set him on the ground.

Ms. Kensington kneeled in front of him, not seeming to mind that he stared at her in rapt attention.

"What's death?"

Charlie snorted. Ms. Kensington glanced at her, then laughed too. "No, little prince, *deaf*, not *death*. It means that I can't hear."

"Nothing?" he asked, his eyes wide.

"Nope. Nothing. My ears don't work like yours do." She tugged gently on his earlobe.

Perplexed, Max reached up.

Ms. Kensington leaned in closer, allowing him to look into her ear.

"Max…" Kate didn't know what he had in mind, but she knew her son and—

Max leaned in and screamed as loudly as he could right into Ms. Kensington's ear.

Everyone in the room froze. Everyone except Ms. Kensington.

"Oh my God, Max!" Kate snatched him away and held him against her legs. She was screwed with this woman. There was no hope for an apology. She should just give up now and pick up the want ads on the way home. If she was lucky, she could find a night shift at a McDonald's on the South Side.

Then Ms. Kensington laughed. To Kate's utter bafflement, she *laughed*. "Nope, nothing."

"Wow!" Max had the same look on his face as when they had built and set off bottle rockets. "What are you doing with your hands?" He held one tightly to study it, as if willing it to reveal its magic.

"It's called sign language. That's how Deaf people like me speak. We sign. See?" She signed a few words and Charlie interpreted. "It's nice to meet you, Max. I like your hat."

Max asked several more questions before he fell silent, seemingly satisfied.

Kate had watched the entire interaction in slight horror, unsure if it would be worse to stop his questioning or allow him to continue.

Finally, Ms. Kensington spoke again. "Have you met the other children yet?"

Max shook his head, and when Vivian offered her hand, he took it.

Vivian looked up at Kate, the warmth melting from her eyes.

Kate tried to look as apologetic as possible.

"It's all right." Ms. Kensington spoke before Kate could open her mouth. "Children always have questions, and I don't mind them. Thankfully, children do not have the same prejudices as their parents. *Children* can still learn better."

Kate's mouth fell open. She turned to Charlie as the ice queen took her child across the room.

Charlie whistled and said something in Chinese, her eyebrows high.

"I didn't mean it like that!" Kate wailed.

"Tell her that, then. Make it up to her," Charlie told her. "Take her to dinner and apologize or something."

Kate swallowed and nodded back. It made sense, yet her stomach twisted with nerves at the thought. It didn't matter. She was going to do it anyway.

Every time Kate began to have fun playing with the kids, every time she began to let her hair down, Ms. Kensington would catch her eye, burning her with her stare, her nose wrinkled as if she smelled something bad. Then Kate's enjoyment would dissipate in angry humiliation. It was as though the sight of Kate disgusted the woman.

This was so bad. She had to get this behind her and say something before she left today. She knew better than to think that an apology would make it better; clearly Ms. Kensington hated her. Maybe if she apologized, though, she could move on and feel less guilty.

At the end of rehearsal, she turned to where Max was playing with his new friends. She felt Ms. Kensington's eyes on her back—or maybe her mind was playing games with her. Either way, the sensation was like nails on a chalkboard.

Max was bouncing uncontrollably as the class wound down. At least he had enjoyed himself.

Across the room, Kate looked again at the perfectly presented woman. Part of her intimidation, Kate decided, was how pretty she was. On top of that, the tailored slacks, tight black blouse, and tall heels gave her a too-put-together professional air that told anyone who dressed casually that they needed to stay ten feet away.

As if she knew Kate was thinking about her, Ms. Kensington glanced at her, looked away, then glanced at her again. She all but rolled her eyes before she looked away the second time.

It was now or never.

"Do we hafta go?" Max whined.

"It's over, kid. That means it's time to go home."

"Don't wanna."

"Max, sit right here for a minute, okay? Stay put. I mean it." She eyed him. He could be a loose cannon when he wanted to be. "So, what are you doing?" she confirmed.

He sat down with a sigh, swinging his dangling legs. "Not getting up."

"Good job, buddy."

Kate approached the woman from behind and tapped her shoulder. Ms. Kensington jumped and turned, a scowl on her face.

"So," Kate said, "can I help clean up?"

Ms. Kensington's mouth popped open, appearing ready to say something, but instead she flattened her hand on her stomach and rubbed it as if it pained her. With her face hard, she pointed to the toy instruments and a large plastic bin.

"Right." Kate placed them into the bin and pushed it into the corner with other bins. Ms. Kensington watched the entire time.

When Kate had finished, she returned to face her nemesis. "Anything else?"

Ms. Kensington shook her head and moved to turn away, but Kate caught her arm.

"Look, I want to apologize."

Ms. Kensington looked down at Kate's hand, then back up to meet her eyes with a scathing glare.

Kate dropped her hand and opened her mouth.

Before she could speak, Ms. Kensington held up a single finger, spun on her heel, and walked purposefully away.

Kate stared after her, flabbergasted. "What kind of an adult holds a grudge like this?" she shouted at the back of Ms. Kensington's head, her arms flailing. But of course Ms. Kensington neither saw nor heard her.

"Stomp on the floor!"

"What?" Kate swung around to see Charlie standing next to Max.

"Stomp on the floor! That's how you get a Deaf person's attention. She'll feel it through the wood."

Kate stomped twice on the floor, hard, and the retreating woman spun around as if she had been tapped on the shoulder. She walked back to face Kate, who quickly spoke before Ms. Kensington could leave again. "Give me two minutes. Please!"

Ms. Kensington folded her arms across her chest and lifted a single eyebrow.

"I'm sorry. I didn't mean what I said at the community center to sound the way it did. I didn't mean to insult you."

"What did you mean, then?" Ms. Kensington asked in her distorted voice.

"All I meant was that I thought we were trying to teach the children that all talking, all *communication*, whether with our mouths or our hands, can be distracting to the performers. I was talking about respecting the players and the music." Kate began to gesticulate wildly. "It wasn't about you being deaf. I'm not some evil person who's against Deaf people!"

Ms. Kensington's dark eyes narrowed, and Kate stuffed her hands into her back pockets. This wasn't working at all. Charlie's suggestion popped into her mind, and her teeth ground.

"Look, Ms. Kensington. Let me do *something* to apologize." Then, as if the words had a life of their own, she added, "Let me take you out to dinner."

Ms. Kensington continued to stare but still said nothing.

"Oh, come on, I'm not that terrible! This is silly."

"Dinner?"

Kate gulped. "Yes."

Ms. Kensington's face didn't relax as she considered. Then she dipped her head. "Next Friday."

"It's a date."

Ms. Kensington's eyes narrowed again. "Dinner."

Kate coughed, her mouth suddenly dry. She hadn't meant… She didn't want… "No, no, I meant… No, I didn't mean…"

"Friday," Ms. Kensington said again. Then she turned and walked away.

Subject: Meeting Time
To: kflynn88@wcce.org
From: vkensington@wcce.org

Good afternoon.

I would like to settle on a time and place to meet Friday night. I am free any time after 7 pm.

Cordially,
Vivian Kensington
President, Board of Directors
The J.C. Kensington Foundation
Windy City Chamber Ensemble
2381 South Michigan, Chicago, IL 60604
312-783-4230, ext. 825 | 312-733-7330 (fax) |_www.JC-Kensington.org

Subject: Meeting Time
To: vkensington@wcce.org
From: kflynn88@wcce.org

Ms. Kensington:

Do you have any suggestions about where to go, since you live here?

K

Subject: Re: Meeting Time
To: kflynn88@wcce.org
From: vkensington@wcce.org

I suggest, Ms. Flynn, that you know the details of an engagement before you present it.

Cordially,
Vivian Kensington

Subject: Re: Meeting Time
To: vkensington@wcce.org
From: kflynn88@wcce.org

Let's say 8 pm.

K

Subject: Re: Meeting Time
To: kflynn88@wcce.org
From: vkensington@wcce.org

And where, exactly, shall we meet?

Cordially,
Vivian Kensington

Subject: Re: Meeting Time
To: vkensington@wcce.org
From: kflynn88@wcce.org

I'll let you know.

K

The Loudest Silence

Kate stood in front of the mirror, smoothing her dress. She kept checking her makeup, her hair, and her teeth as though constant inspection would make it better. She couldn't imagine what this evening was going to be like. She had never eaten a meal with someone who hated her so openly.

Her stomach was fluttering, but not with eager anticipation.

They had decided to meet at a small trendy restaurant that Stephen had suggested, and Kate wasn't going to be late.

She checked her outfit again. Her sleeveless silhouette cocktail dress showed off her arms and legs yet was long enough for decency. The plain black hinted at professionalism.

Finally satisfied that she looked as good as she was going to get, she kissed Max and headed to the door, then paused.

What if Charlie wasn't there? She didn't want—for lack of a better expression—a third wheel. If she had to grovel, she would rather do it with fewer eyes on her. But oh God, what if she *didn't* bring her? How could she fully apologize without an interpreter?

She had spent the previous evening watching sign language videos. She tried to learn a few basics but had given up when she discovered that some signs had gone out of fashion or had been updated over the years. Plus there was ASL, English, cued speech, and something mysteriously called "home sign." How did she know which one to use? Wikipedia had said that most Deaf people spoke American Sign Language, but what if Ms. Kensington didn't? Would she laugh at her if Kate used a 1970s version of a sign? What if she offended her again by using the wrong sign?

Oh God.

She grabbed a small notepad from the counter and shoved it in her bag before starting into the city.

Friday night in the Loop, aka downtown, was filled with people making their way to and from functions in every state of dress, from tuxedos to nothing but a tie and black boxer briefs. Kate's black stilettos clacked in time with the pulsing energy of the city around her.

She arrived at the restaurant early and quickly glanced around. When she didn't spot Ms. Kensington, she stepped forward to the hostess station.

"Name?" The young girl barely looked at her.

"Flynn," Kate croaked and cleared her throat.

The girl checked the book. "It looks like your party isn't here yet, and your table won't be ready for another thirty minutes. Would you like to wait here or in the bar?"

"Bar," Kate answered quickly.

The bar was bright with lots of fluorescent lights. Red and deep purple uplighting highlighted the huge oval counter space.

The raven-haired bartender approached her with a slightly flirtatious eye and smiled expectantly.

"Give me a Jameson up, please."

"Liquid courage?" the bartender asked.

"Yup." Kate chuckled. "Something like that."

What if Ms. Kensington didn't show? Would that be a good thing or a bad thing?

Maybe that would be better because then we can just keep glaring silently at each other. At least rehearsals wouldn't be torture.

A warm hand touched her arm.

"I'm sorry I'm late."

Kate turned to find a very different-looking woman than she had thus far seen.

Ms. Kensington waved for the bartender and ordered a glass of wine. She stood beside Kate, looking down at her. "And what is it that you're staring at, exactly?"

"You're smiling." Immediately Kate looked away. That had been so not-at-all smooth.

She rolled her eyes. "It may surprise you, Ms. Flynn, but I *am* known to do that every now and then."

Kate looked down at her drink. So they were still in this icy place where Kate was afraid to take a step.

"Was there something else?" Ms. Kensington asked.

Kate glanced up, squaring her shoulders. "No, nothing. You, uh, you look nice." She was about to begin a long mental list of remarks about how stupid that had been to say when Ms. Kensington nodded.

"As do you."

Kate shivered at the still-frosty tone. "No Charlie?" she asked. Her heart was pounding in her chest again, and while she knew Ms. Kensington couldn't hear it, she wondered if maybe she could read it on her face.

"I gave her the night off."

"Oh."

A minute or so passed in uncomfortable silence. Finally, Kate said, "They said the wait would probably be about thirty minutes."

Ms. Kensington frowned. "Why are you yelling? I can't hear you any better if you yell, Ms. Flynn."

Kate groaned and hung her head. She *had* been yelling. "There's a band playing."

"And this equates to you yelling because…?"

"Right. Because you won't hear me any better even if I yell over the noise. Sorry, Ms. Kensington."

"Just for this evening, let's drop the formalities. Vivian. Please. And it's easier for me to read your lips if you speak normally. When you yell, or overenunciate, your mouth moves differently."

Kate considered that information.

Vivian tilted her head, studying her. "What does that look mean? You're quite expressive, you know."

Kate glanced around, unsure of how to move forward, then blurted out, "I know that you think I'm the enemy, but I just want to make this as easy on you as possible."

"Then speak *normally*, Kate."

Kate nodded. "Okay, then."

They studied each another. The pressure to engage in small talk was making it hard for Kate to breathe.

"So the children were watching me, were they?"

Kate leaned back, relieved. "Yeah, they were."

Vivian's eyes flashed.

"You're still upset."

"Not as much as I was." Vivian sipped her wine. "You don't seem to understand. So many people don't realize that the words they say matter to someone like me. The power of words is so often underestimated. I know you meant well, but the way you spoke was less than kind. It was ableist at the very best. Children learn even when we don't think they're listening. I realize I can be a bit abrasive at times, but what if a child had heard how you spoke to me?"

"I—" She hadn't thought about it that way.

"That being said, you were right. I was being rude."

"And I was being totally insensitive. I'm sorry." Kate swirled her drink to give herself a moment to think before she continued. "What I had meant to say that night was that for those of us who aren't used to seeing sign language, it's impossible not to watch. It's so beautiful." She flushed.

Vivian finally sat on the barstool beside Kate. "So now that we've covered that, may I ask you a question?"

"Okay," she said slowly.

"Why did you invite me here?"

Kate frowned. "Stephen said it was good."

"No, not here to this restaurant. You could have apologized and left it at that. Why did you invite me to dinner? Was it fear for your job? Did you think I would fire you?"

"No. I mean, maybe. But that's not why I invited you. Is it bad that I did?"

"I didn't say that. I was just, let's say, surprised." Vivian's gaze intensified. "So you know Mr. Foy?"

Kate nodded and wrinkled her nose. "Yeah, I do."

"Oh." Vivian smiled politely. "I didn't realize you two were involved."

Kate nearly choked on her drink. "What? No! I didn't mean—no."

"I apologize," Vivian said quickly. "The face you made led me to think... I didn't mean to intrude on your personal life."

Kate snorted. "Don't worry. I don't have much of a personal life to intrude on. We did have a thing once at Tanglewood, but that was about it. He's just...a friend, I guess."

It had been a summer of drinking, hanging out, taking lessons with some of the best musicians in the world, and playing some of the best music she had ever played. Their friendship had developed quickly into something else, then had been cut off abruptly. Maybe they were friends now. It was...complicated.

"Oh, you attended Tanglewood? I must have missed that. How did you like it?"

"It was good."

The Loudest Silence

"Were you there during Andrew Goltich's tenure?"

"No," Kate answered. "This was four years ago, so I studied with Linda Peet."

"I understand she's amazing."

Kate smiled, remembering the experience. "Yeah, she is. I was supposed to follow her to Georgia to work with her a bit longer, but, you know, life."

"I'm sorry to hear that."

Kate shrugged. The loss still smarted, though she had long ago stuffed that loss into a mental box. "But, yeah, Tanglewood was amazing."

"I see. I knew the hairpiece had attended, but I didn't realize you had as well."

"The what?"

Vivian laughed again, and Kate realized that she kind of liked its deep, rich timbre. "Mm. A toupee. Mr. Foy is a walking hairpiece, Kate. That's all he has going for him. His looks are satisfactory, his bass playing is adequate at best, from what I've been told, but his hair always looks like it's fresh from a shampoo commercial." Vivian grinned wickedly over the rim of her glass.

"You're not a fan, huh?"

"If we are speaking off the record, so to speak, I promise the feeling is mutual. A few years ago, he and Charlie dated, and it ended badly. And I have had very little patience for the man since."

Kate had a lot of questions, but it only took one look at Vivian's expression to know that she would say no more about it.

"Flynn, party of two?"

Kate turned to look at the hostess.

"What?" Vivian asked.

Kate turned back and was surprised that, for the first time, the face of Vivian Kensington held neither animosity nor malice. In fact, she was smiling, and her smile was so beautiful that it took Kate a moment to gather her thoughts.

She glanced back at the hostess. "They're calling us. Our table is ready—eep!"

Vivian had gripped Kate's chin and pulled her face back around.

Kate stammered, trying to remember the words she had said only seconds ago, but her brain had short circuited. "I, uh…"

Once again, Vivian traced an oval around her own lips with two fingers.

"Sorry." Kate's cheeks grew hot. "Our table is ready."

"Shall we?" Vivian took Kate's elbow, and they followed the hostess.

They were led to a table and given menus. When the server arrived, he rattled off the specials with his face hidden in his notepad.

Halfway through, Kate glanced at Vivian, who was watching the young man with a blank expression, her chin propped up on her fist.

"Do you need some more time?" He asked, a false grin plastered on his face.

"Yeah." Kate's gaze flicked between him and Vivian.

"Take your time," he said and left for another table.

"Did you get any of that?" Kate asked.

"Very little," Vivian said flatly.

Instead of explaining, Kate pulled the menu of specials from her own menu and handed it to Vivian.

They studied the menu for a few minutes, then Vivian asked, "How do you like Chicago so far?"

Kate looked up "Oh, you know, there are some things I love and some I hate. The city is wonderful, though I haven't seen much of it. And I'm not a huge fan of where we live, but it's what I could find in a short time."

"I'm sorry, will you please repeat that?" Vivian asked.

Kate did.

"Oh? Why don't you care for it?"

Kate had had to work right up until the end of the month before moving and hadn't been able to look for apartments before they moved. She had signed a lease without even seeing the place.

"The landlord told me that it was a very family-friendly neighborhood, but either he was outright lying or he meant it was ideal for a family of drug dealers."

Vivian nodded thoughtfully. "So it's a less-than-desirable location."

"Yeah. When I was moving us in, I met someone in my building who told me that our neighborhood is called the Jungle."

Vivian raised her eyebrows.

"Yeah. So I'm not too sure about where we live."

"Can you not get out of your lease?" Vivian asked.

"I don't think so."

Vivian sighed. "One more time, please."

Kate frowned. "What's wrong?"

"You speak very quickly, and the glare of the candle is—"

Kate blew it out before Vivian finished her sentence.

"All right. I ask again, can you not get out of your lease?"

"I don't think so."

"Are you concerned for your safety?"

Kate opened her mouth and then closed it. How the hell did she answer that? It wasn't her safety she was worried about. She had lived in some sketchy places growing up, but she didn't want that for Max. "Let's talk about something else."

Vivian was studying Kate in a way that made her squirm. Kate thought there was a good chance that the subject of where she lived would come up again. "All right. And how do you like playing with WCCE?"

"It's great! Really great!" Now she was being too exuberant. "The people are awesome. Everyone plays well together. I can't complain."

"It seems that there is something else as well. Your eyes lit up when I asked you."

Vivian held her gaze in that way that Kate was quickly becoming familiar with. Perhaps it was because Vivian needed to study her lips to communicate, but Kate had never met someone with such an unwavering gaze. It was as if Vivian could read all of Kate's secrets through her skin.

"I'm deaf, Kate. I read facial expressions."

Kate shifted. What could she say other than the truth? "It's true. I think I'm pretty happy to be with WCCE."

"Oh?"

"It's because of Max," she admitted with an ease that surprised her. "When I was freelancing, I took any gig that came up, so my hours were all over the place. I like having a steady schedule for him."

"It must have been hard for him to never know when you would be home." Vivian's eyes softened.

"I think it was. I mean, he's still with a babysitter more than I would like him to be, but it's less often than it was before we moved."

"Where did you move from? I know it's in your file, but I can't recall at this moment."

"Gainesville, Florida. Before that, Pittsburgh, Pennsylvania."

"Mm." Vivian sipped her wine. "I was in Pittsburgh once. I got stuck on the expressway for two hours, only to get through a tunnel and realize that the tunnel itself was the reason for the delay."

"Yeah." Kate chuckled. "That sounds about right."

They fell into a thoughtful silence for a few minutes, Kate still thinking about Max. "You know, it's not just the schedule. It's also the fact that I have a contract for longer than eight months. I mean, I know it's only two years, but that's still better. Or maybe it's worse. I don't know."

"Why would it be worse to be settled for two years instead of one?"

Vivian leaned forward in her seat with genuine interest, so Kate answered without reservation. "I think it will probably be okay this time because he's still young. He won't make too many attachments. But the older he gets, the harder it will be to pull him away to a new place. He'll start making friends and wanting to build a life for himself in each new city. I moved a lot growing up, and I never wanted that life for him. Ironic, given my career."

"Why did you move so much?"

"My parents died when I was little. After that, I moved from foster home to foster home."

"Oh?" Vivian leaned in a little more. "I'm sorry to hear that. Why did you move so often, if I may ask?"

"It's how fostering works in this country. A couple has a baby of their own, and back you go. A couple gets a divorce, and suddenly you're unwanted baggage."

"Oh, Kate." Vivian's hand twitched on the table, and Kate thought she might reach out and touch her.

She cleared her throat, a little nervous at the prospect of intimacy. "It certainly teaches you to appreciate things while you have them. Anyway, I want Max's life to be different. I want him to have a permanent home, but that would mean finding a permanent job or changing careers." Kate picked up her glass and took a long drink. Why had she let herself say all of that?

"I'm curious. If you grew up in foster care, especially unstable foster care, how did you find your way to the cello? I find that classical music is something children are typically forced into until they are old enough to decide whether they like it for themselves."

"Yeah, I've been asked that question before, actually. A foster mother signed me up for an outreach program to bring music to underprivileged kids. They loaned me a cello, gave me lessons, and let me join a community orchestra. I loved it. It was the one thing that was constant in my life, you know? I couldn't take my belongings each time I moved, or keep my friends, but I could keep the cello because it wasn't mine. It was the program's. I got so good so fast that I won a few awards and eventually a scholarship to study music. I didn't even know until I got the scholarship that classical music *could* be a career."

"Really?" Vivian's long fingers toyed with the stem of her glass, drawing Kate's attention. "That…" Vivian paused, her eyes moving over Kate's face, "is the exact opposite of my life."

Kate picked up her water glass again and, ready to change the subject, turned the tables on Vivian. "So if we're getting personal, then I hope it's all right if I ask how a Deaf person ended up in the world of classical music."

"I've been asked that question before," Vivian said, nodding coyly. "I come from a large family of musicians. My mother is a harpist; my father was an oboist. My grandmother was a concert pianist, and my grandfather was a flautist. In the Kensington line, the firstborn is expected to take after the grandmother. My grandmother's grand piano was my mother's birth announcement gift."

"That's unusual."

"What's that?" Vivian frowned, her gaze back on Kate's lips.

After Kate repeated herself, Vivian smiled. "Not in my family. Once my family discovered that I was growing deaf, things became a bit difficult for…everyone. They didn't know what to do with me. I was the only one in the family who wasn't a musician. As I got older, I began to work on the executive side. It seemed to be the only way I could be involved in my family's business."

"Is it difficult?"

"Yes," Vivian said simply. "It's hard to be taken seriously when I can't remember what music sounds like."

"So you weren't born deaf?" Kate asked carefully. She was genuinely curious, but she didn't want to cross any lines.

"No. I was hard of hearing from birth, but I didn't completely lose my hearing until I was seven."

The server interrupted at that moment. They placed their orders and fell easily back into conversation.

The dinner was nothing like Kate had expected it to be. Vivian's change from the ice queen was unexpected and welcome. She was pleased to find that Vivian was kind, even funny. She asked questions about Max, demanded stories, and made Kate laugh with her own stories of the ways people treated her once they learned she was Deaf.

"Would you like to take a walk?" Vivian asked as they stepped outside after their meal.

Kate began walking. "Sure, if you want to."

"What was that?"

Kate repeated herself but kept walking.

Vivian caught up to Kate and stepped in front of her, putting her hands on her shoulders.

"Oh, er, sorry."

Vivian smiled and dropped her hands. "Come with me." Taking Kate's elbow, she led her down the busy street and onto another that was bustling with activity.

The scene brought to mind Gershwin's *Rhapsody in Blue*. Pedestrians weaved in and out in a constant frenzy to get from point A to point B. Blue, red, and green lights glared down at them from each restaurant and shop. Music blared from loudspeakers. Their heels clicked along with the nightlife.

Kate glanced at Vivian as they walked. She wondered what it felt like for her. Could she feel the pulse of the city without hearing screaming patrons, car horns, and street performers? Did the energy feel different to her? She decided to save the question for another time.

"This is Michigan Avenue."

For the first time that evening, Vivian's free hand began to move, speaking in her own language.

"If you go that way"—she touched the small of Kate's back to turn her—"you hit what is called the Magnificent Mile. It's the best shopping and probably one of the biggest tourist locations of the city." Vivian took her elbow again, guiding her up a flight of wide stairs and into a huge plaza. "See that building there?" She pointed to a tall edifice shaped by two Vs with a large gash down the center that split the point at the top and the bottom. "A few call it the Diamond Building, but most know it as the Vagina Building."

It wasn't hard to see where the building got its nickname, but she was more distracted by the sign that Vivian had used.

"It's actually the Crain Communications Building, but the nickname makes the locals laugh." Kate watched as Vivian quickly and easily spelled out names with her free hand. "And this"—Vivian pointed in front of them—"is The Bean."

Kate looked to where Vivian had pointed. When she saw the giant sculpture, her mouth dropped open.

It was a huge mirror shaped exactly like what it was called: a bean. It was set on its side so that it bowed in an arch tall enough to walk under. In the daylight, the sculpture probably mirrored the sky and anyone who stood close to it. In the evening, though, it exploded into vibrant yellows, whites, and golds, reflecting every light in the surrounding skyline.

"This is amazing, Vivian." Kate smiled at the reflection of herself and Vivian in the sculpture as Vivian's hand still lightly touched Kate's elbow.

Was it gallantry, she wondered, or was it a need to keep track of her that inspired Vivian to keep touching her? She could feel her warmth through her dress. She caught Vivian's eye in the mirrored sculpture and laughed out loud.

A few moments later, Vivian led them to the walkway under the arch.

Kate grinned like a gleeful child as she looked at their elongated reflections that dissolved into kaleidoscopic patterns.

"It's actually called *Cloud Gate*, though I've never known anyone to use that name." Vivian again signed with a single hand. "It's my favorite."

Kate made a silly face into the sculpture, stretching her lips into something grotesque. Vivian laughed. The sound was so light, so free from constraint, that hearing it made Kate's heart beat faster. She reached up nervously to tuck her hair behind her ear. "I can see why this is your favorite."

"I like it at night, but I like it better when it's about to rain," Vivian said. "The sky turns black, and it looks almost dangerous."

Dangerous. That was a beautiful way to describe it, Kate thought.

When they were through admiring the sculpture, they sat on a nearby bench.

The two fell silent, watching tourists run through the walkway, children making faces, and families taking pictures. Behind them, a trumpet played a muted scat that melted into a soft jazz number. The notes were smooth as silk.

Kate closed her eyes to enjoy the dichotomy of the horn against the loud honking of the traffic on the opposite side of the plaza.

"Are you all right, Ms. Flynn?"

Kate opened her eyes and smiled. "There's a trumpet behind us playing 'It Never Entered My Mind.' It's one of my favorites."

Vivian looked back at the musician. "What does he sound like to *you*?"

"He's pretty good, actually."

"No." Vivian reached out and turned Kate's chin toward her.

Just as before, her touch made Kate's brain fizzle and then slowly power off. Vivian's fingers were warm against her skin, and the warmth spread into her cheeks and down her neck.

"I mean, what do you hear?" Vivian asked. "What does it sound like?"

How did one explain what music sounded like? What could she say that Vivian might understand? "Blue."

Vivian looked off into the distance, and Kate was again struck by the beauty of her eyes, the soulful richness of them.

Kate blushed. "That was stupid."

"No." Vivian closed her hand on Kate's wrist. "Please. Continue."

Vivian smiled encouragingly, and Kate no longer cared if she sounded stupid. She closed her eyes and let her mind drift to the music, the car horns and the screaming children falling to the background. The music took over, reminding her of how much she loved her career. "It sounds like water. It's…it's rich and smooth, like swirling, like steam that twists up from a cup of coffee or the way the Chicago River twists through downtown. Only, they're using a mute, so there's a different tone to the sound, like a pressure, a desperation. It's like, I don't know, maybe a cobalt, only darker at the edges. It sounds…it sounds like how the color blue makes you feel: warm and relaxed, yet sad and alone." She opened her eyes and looked at Vivian's face.

Vivian was watching her lips move so intensely that Kate wanted to paint a better picture.

"It feels like Chicago, you know? The way the city feels when you... when you're lonely."

"Are you lonely, Kate?"

She answered automatically. "Isn't everyone?"

There was understanding in Vivian's eyes, and Kate knew in that moment that Vivian was every bit as lonely as she was. The realization was somehow soothing.

She smiled at Vivian, who smiled back, the corners of her deep-red lips curling upward. Then breaking their gaze, Vivian looked down at her lap. "Thank you, Kate. That was...that was beautiful."

The silence between them was different now, comfortable and easy. Yet, static ran through her blood, making Kate a little jittery.

The trumpet sang out its last few notes. "Max would love this."

Vivian studied her for a moment, then said, "Let's bring him."

"What?"

"The day after tomorrow. Let's bring him here. We can have a picnic in the park."

Kate's heart picked up its pace again. If this had been a romantic outing instead of an apology date, she would have thought she was being asked out again.

"Are you sure? I mean, Max can be a handful. He's very good, awesome even, but he's, you know, three."

Vivian nodded firmly. "Max is adorable." She moved her hands in a sign that Kate imagined meant *adorable*.

Kate pressed her lips together, then asked, "Will you show me something?"

"What do you mean?"

"In sign language. I've been watching you speak it since we left the restaurant, and it's beautiful."

Vivian looked a little bashful. "What would you like to see?"

"How about my name?"

Vivian flexed her hand, her index and middle fingers standing straight in the air with her thumb in between. Then she bounced her middle finger under her eye.

"That means Kate?"

"In a way, Ms. Flynn. It means *you*."

Kate shifted on the bench. "Explain."

"Well, every Deaf person has what's called a sign name. It saves us from having to spell the person's name out each time, and it shows familiarity."

"How do you get one?"

"Typically, a Deaf person has to give it to you. They choose a characteristic of yours and base the name off of that."

"What's yours?"

"I have two. I have a professional one that I most commonly use." She spread her index and middle finger and softly bounced them off her jaw. "That one is very generic."

"What's your other one?" When Vivian looked away bashfully, Kate laughed and said, "You have to tell me!"

Vivian sighed, made an V with her fingers, and tapped it to her chin.

Kate stared at the sign that was a universally known gesture. "What does it mean? 'Cause it kind of looks like…"

Vivian squirmed. "I know!" she groaned. "It does indeed mean something wholly inappropriate that refers to my sexuality. I've tried to change it more than once, but I cannot break Charlie of the habit."

"So you're—?"

"A lesbian, yes."

Kate wasn't surprised. She got a subtle sense whenever she met women who liked other women. She gestured to herself. "Pansexual."

Vivian nodded as she studied Kate's face.

"Show me again," Kate said.

"Ms. Flynn!"

"Show me."

Vivian made the sign again, and Kate copied it, giggling, then asked Vivian to show her how to sign her name again.

Vivian scooted in closer and took her hand gently. Molding her fingers, Vivian shaped them.

"Wait, what does that mean?" She was positive Vivian had used a different sign than previously.

Vivian smiled. "It refers to your eyes."

"My eyes?"

"Yes."

"Why?"

The Loudest Silence

Vivian stared at Kate intensely. "Because you have the purest green eyes I have ever seen. They always sparkle. They're beautiful."

By now, Kate's heart was tap-dancing. Maybe Vivian had said that to gauge her reaction, but she wasn't sure what she was looking for. Finally, she said, "Show me something else. Something simple."

"Shall we try the alphabet?" Vivian leaned in again to shape Kate's fingers. Her hands cupped hers as she worked, her arm and shoulder pressing lightly against Kate.

When they finally started back toward the train platform, it was later than Kate had planned. "Do you take the L?" she asked.

"Actually, I only live a few blocks from here, just off Grant Park, right off the Loop." Vivian nodded back toward where they had been sitting.

They stood together by the L stop. Kate tried to think of something to say.

Vivian broke the silence first. "Sunday?" She leaned against the post for the Red Line train, her arms casually crossed.

"Yeah. That would be fun."

"A few of the WCCE players are playing a concert in the park that afternoon. Do you think Max would like that?"

"He would love it!"

"Good."

"Okay. Well, I, uh—"

"Thank you for inviting me out tonight, Kate." Vivian was scrutinizing her as if to give her words some deeper meaning. "The effort meant a great deal to me."

Unsure of how else to respond, Kate merely nodded, though her skin was tingling.

"And thank you for the song."

"No problem."

Vivian continued to study her.

"O-okay," Kate stammered. "I guess I'll see you, then. Wait, do you have my phone number?"

Vivian laughed. "Katelyn, I'm the president of the board. Of course I do."

"Right. Duh." Kate groaned inwardly. "Okay, well..." Kate shuffled backward, beginning her descent to the train. "Good night."

"Good night, Ms. Flynn."

Kate gave Vivian a half smile and disappeared into the underground.

After she arrived home and paid Stacey, she collapsed onto the futon in a daze. She touched her stomach, aware that it was still fluttering an hour after she and Vivian had parted company. The entire evening had turned into something unexpected.

As a rule, Kate didn't date, not since Max was born. If Kate was going to do that, she wanted to feel something. She wanted an over-the-moon, knock-it-out-of-the-park, head-over-heels connection. That made it almost impossible to find someone worth leaving her son with a sitter.

She stared up at the patterns on her ceiling. This night—even though it hadn't been a date—had been absolutely out of the park.

Chapter 4

Before Kate was even fully awake the next morning, she smiled and touched the smile on her lips. The night before had been... *Wow* was the only way she could think to describe it. She had... Her smile faded.

The night before had felt romantic. The way the city lights reflected on The Bean, the way they had sat together, Kate studying Vivian's hands. It had all been so...*good*. The evening had carried her away to the point of feeling intoxicated.

"Goddammit, Kate!" she moaned to her empty room.

She was attracted to Vivian Kensington. The transformation over the evening from angry stranger to beautiful and bewitching woman had been enthralling. But an attraction didn't have to mean anything. It wouldn't mean anything.

She didn't date for a reason. What was the point when life was so transient? Even when she did, she rarely dated to the point that the person met Max, and she never dated anyone Max was already fond of. It was too sticky, and Max was the one who got hurt. They had learned that the hard way.

And Vivian... She wasn't Kate's boss, but she was as close as it got. That was *all* she needed in this brand-new job.

She couldn't have another night like last night, a night filled with romantic possibilities. And that was all right. She was good at being alone. In fact, she preferred it in some ways. It was less complicated than relying on someone else. She liked her TV time in the evenings after Max went to sleep. She liked her solitary living room workouts. She liked being able to spend weekends practicing and spending time with Max. They had a good life, just the two of them: Kate and Max against the world. If she sometimes couldn't watch romantic movies, that wasn't a huge deal. And if sometimes all she wanted was to watch romantic movies—and, okay, sometimes she cried—so what?

She didn't need to date Vivian, even if she was attracted to her.

She could, however, be her friend.

A friend she found attractive.

Her phone went off somewhere under her pillows, and Kate reached for it.

Ms. Flynn, here is the setlist for the park concert. Shall we meet at noon? – V

Despite all of the promises she had just made to herself, she smiled.

"Hey, buddy, do you remember Ms. Vivian?" she asked Max when she entered the living room.

Max looked up from under the blankets on the futon. It took a lot to pull him from his morning cartoons, but that seemed to do it.

No surprise there; he had spent the day after the Mommy & Me event talking about Vivian.

"Yeah!" He grinned and shot up, the blanket falling off his shoulders.

"She wants to take us to the park tomorrow to hear a concert. What do you think?"

"Yeah!" he said again, jumping up and down on the futon as though on a trampoline.

"It's time to go! It's time to go!" Max bellowed by the door, bouncing as if he had springs for legs. "Hurry up, Mommy!"

She had wanted to dress Max in a clean polo shirt and jeans, but Vivian had insisted that Max wear swim trunks and that Kate bring a change of clothes and a towel. She also insisted that there was no need to bring any food. Kate wasn't surprised by the food thing since there were vendors all over the place, but she couldn't imagine why Max needed swim trunks in a downtown park. She would have to take Vivian's word for it. She dressed him in a blue tank top and his favorite orange trunks, hoping the sunny June day would keep him warm enough.

"I'm coming!" Humming "It Never Entered My Mind," she checked her hair again, making sure it flowed in wild adventurous waves.

She caught a glimpse of her green eyes in the mirror. What was she *doing*? Her hands dropped from her hair and she admonished herself, pointing a finger at her reflection. "Listen, lady. Knock it off."

It didn't matter how beautiful and intriguing Vivian was. She wasn't... She didn't...

She raised her hand to fix her hair again.

"Ugh!" With a growl, she shook out her hair, letting it land however it wanted to.

Max appeared in the doorway, hands on his hips. "Mo-o-m!"

"Sorry, kid." Kate's heart pinged. That had been the first time he had used "Mom" instead of "Mommy." "Okay, come on."

Hand in hand, they left the apartment and headed to the L.

Kate craned her neck this way and that, searching the crowded plaza. Max was on her hip, gripping her shirt and swinging his feet. His excitement was making her own heart beat harder.

She and Vivian were to meet south of where they had sat the night before last so they could bring Max to The Bean together.

Max spotted Vivian first. One moment they were standing in the bustling crowd, trying to resist the tide of people, and the next Max had grabbed a handful of her hair, screaming as if Wonder Woman herself were walking through the plaza.

"All right, *all right*!" Kate released the squirming boy, letting him fly toward Vivian.

Vivian smiled when she saw him and waved with both hands. He flew into her, and she scooped him up, hugging him tightly.

Kate didn't know what surprised her more: the fact that Vivian had picked her son up as if she had known him for years, the fact that as soon as he settled on her hip she began to sign to him, or the fact that Max signed something back. When had Vivian taught him to sign?

Vivian shifted her large bag to her other shoulder, and together they looked around until Max pointed her out. Vivian winked in greeting.

Kate fought through the tourists until she made it to them. "When did you teach him sign language?"

"At Mommy & Me. What did I teach you, Max?"

Grinning proudly, he moved the fingers of one hand, pursing his lips in concentration.

"What does that mean?"

"It means Max!"

"What else did I teach you?"

He opened his hand and jabbed his thumb into his chin. "Mommy!"

"And what did I just teach you?"

He signed a full sentence, translating with gusto: "Where's your mommy?"

"Look at you, buddy! How did you get so smart?" Kate laughed, bubbling over with maternal pride. She high-fived him, and then, because it seemed like the natural thing to do, she high-fived Vivian as well. When she did, their fingers ensnared, and though their hands dropped, Vivian hadn't let go. She didn't even seem to realize what had happened.

Feeling a rush of warmth, Kate pulled her hand free to push the hair out of Max's eyes. "Show me something else?" Kate asked.

"In sign?" Vivian grinned, seeming pleased by the request. "All right." She demonstrated a small series of motions.

"What does that mean?"

Vivian shifted Max on her hip. Her sunglasses were large and darkly shaded. Despite that, Kate could feel Vivian's intense gaze on her. "It means 'Your hands are very soft.'"

The heat started at Kate's belly and spread in both directions like wildfire, simultaneously moving down to her feet and up to her cheeks.

Damn it.

"Right." Kate laughed, staring in the opposite direction to let her cheeks cool. Her hands were anything but soft, given the deep calluses she had developed on her fingers from years of playing the cello.

Kate looked back at Vivian and saw that she was still watching her.

"I'm happy to show you more," Vivian offered and began signing her words whenever she spoke.

"So where are we going?" Kate asked.

"You ready to get wet?"

The Loudest Silence

Kate nearly choked, but thankfully Vivian didn't seem to notice. She was busy getting Max settled on his feet.

"Ready!" Max copied her sign with a grin, and the three set off.

The downtown Chicago plaza opened into a wide space where children, teens, and parents skittered and slid across the water-laden tiled floor. On each end were giant rectangles where digital faces appeared and disappeared. On one screen, the faces puckered their lips, pouring a fountain of water onto giggling children.

Max's eyes turned into saucers as he tugged at Kate. "Did you see? Did you see, Mommy? It spits water! You're not uhsupposed to spit!"

"Tell you what, kid. We'll cut it a break just this once."

Vivian explained. "It's called the Jaume Plensa Crown Fountain. The water doesn't run in the winter, but in the spring and summer…" She gestured to the children.

"Mommy, can I go? Please?"

"Promise not to run, okay, Max?" Vivian said.

"Mommy, please?"

"Okay, Max. Max! Did you hear Ms. Vivian?"

He nodded solemnly, so she pulled his shirt off and watched as he sprinted away.

"Well, that promise didn't last long, did it?" Vivian laughed.

"No. I didn't expect it to. But even if he skins his knee, he'll be fine."

They watched him for a while, then Kate asked, "So how do you know about all these awesome places?"

Vivian was unaware of Kate as she watched a torrent of water fall onto Max's head. He sputtered and giggled happily.

"Yo, earth to Vivian." Kate pulled on her arm.

The smile fell from Vivian's face. "I'm sorry. What did you say, please?"

Her intense reaction surprised Kate. She raised her hands. "Whoa there, lady. It's okay."

"I'm sorry," Vivian repeated. "I try to stay aware of everything happening around me. Please repeat what you said."

Kate repeated her question, smiling reassuringly at Vivian.

Finally Vivian understood. "I've lived here most of my life."

"Your family brought you here as a kid?"

Vivian snorted. "I doubt they did," she said without further explanation.

Kate nodded and looked back at Max.

"Viv'n! Come on, Viv'n!" Max called from the puddles, waving both arms. "Viv'n! Viv'n!"

"Max, she can't hear you when you call her like that. You have to come over here and talk to her, remember?"

He rolled his eyes and continued to wave his arms over his head until he caught Vivian's attention. "Come on!"

Vivian shook her head.

Kate wondered what Vivian would do if she grabbed her and ran through the water with her. Would she be angry or would she laugh? It probably wouldn't be appropriate. Still, she had to bite down the impulse.

They watched Max from a nearby bench as he screamed and ran, making friends with other children and splashing in and out of the water until there was a distinct tint of blue to his lips.

"Max, come get warm for a bit!" Kate called out.

Instead, he swooped under the spout of water again.

"Max!" Kate stood with her hands on her hips.

"I believe he's calling you out, Ms. Flynn." Vivian leaned playfully against her shoulder.

Kate looked at Vivian, surprised by the touch. "I think you're right." She walked to the edge of the water and called him again.

He spun around, grinning, with mischief in his eyes.

Kate knew exactly what was coming next.

Sure enough, Max shot off through the crowd. Kate raced after him. Being chased was one of his favorite games and had been since he was old enough to walk.

"You can't catch me! You can't catch me!" he shouted over his shoulder. "I'm the gingerbread ma-a-an!"

Kate laughed in spite of herself, then called in a mock monster voice, "I'm going to squish the life out of you!" His disobedience should have frustrated her, but she could hear Vivian laughing and cheering Max on from the sidelines.

Max giggled, running with his arms out like an airplane when Kate caught up. She reached out to grab him. Just as her fingers brushed his arm, icy water poured down through her hair, her back, and into her shoes, soaking her instantly.

The Loudest Silence

She shrieked like a banshee that had stubbed its toe. In chasing Max, she hadn't paid attention and had run under the waterspout just as it spewed. It reminded her of the ice bucket challenge that had been everywhere online a few years before. Howling, she jumped in place as she tried to catch her breath against the arctic chill.

Max looked over his shoulder at her, his eyes popping. He stopped running so suddenly that he tripped and landed on his butt.

Behind her, she heard a giggle.

She turned to see Vivian laughing into her hands at the edge of the water. "Think it's funny, do you?"

In an instant, Vivian's demeanor changed, and she turned back into the icy president Kate had first met. "Absolutely *not*! Defiance should never be rewarded with laughter." Then she snorted and the facade was ruined.

Sheepishly, Max approached. Kate kneeled by him and pointed toward Vivian.

At first, he looked confused. Then the realization hit, and he pounded toward her, Kate not far behind.

Vivian's eyes widened. She jumped back, screaming in protest, and hurried to put a bench between them.

The obstacle stopped Max in his tracks, but Kate vaulted over the top of the bench and grabbed at Vivian as she dodged out of the way.

"No, no, no!"

"I'm gonna getcha!" Max shouted, catching Vivian from behind.

Kate caught her in a bear hug, soaking her thoroughly.

Vivian wailed, her body going slack against Kate's. Vivian's short hair tickled the side of Kate's face, and she breathed in the scent of perfume, a scent she hadn't noticed on Vivian before; light, smooth and—

Then she realized she was still holding on and let go sheepishly. She probably shouldn't have wrapped her arms around someone who was essentially a stranger.

"Uh, I know you're the president," Kate said, hooking her thumbs in her back pocket and scuffing her shoe, "so don't fire me for this, okay?"

"Oh, you've been terminated! Effective immediately!"

Kate laughed, throwing her head back at the simple pleasure pouring through her. "Can you do that?"

"Not at all," Vivian said. "There would need to be a majority agreement by the board. But I have influence!" She glared at Kate, but for once, it wasn't at all scary.

"You're all wet, Viv'n!"

"That's right, I am!" Vivian leaned down to bop him on the nose.

Vivian wrapped Kate and Max in the fluffy towel she had brought and then moved them into the sun.

Once they were as dry as they were going to get, they headed toward the bench that she and Vivian had shared just the other night. Vivian and Max walked hand in hand a few steps ahead. They were really cute together.

She pulled out her phone, knowing Vivian would be mortified if she saw, and snapped a picture, then snapped another, getting the perfect shot of Max's face lighting up when he first saw the sculpture.

Max brought out the parental instinct in most people that met him, but he seemed to draw a whole different level of affection from Vivian. Their eyes were bright together, and Kate wondered what had captured Vivian so thoroughly. Max was adorable with his pixie features and dark hair and possibly the best child ever, but Vivian acted as though each smile swept her off her feet anew.

Max let go of Vivian's hand and ran to the mirrored metal, smashing his nose against it so hard that the tip flattened entirely.

"He's having fun?" Vivian paused to let Kate catch up. Vivian drew her brows together as one hand played nervously with her necklace.

"He is. Stop worrying."

Vivian smiled back. "Come on, then." Her hand wrapped around Kate's body, settling on her opposite hip.

Kate's heart flipped happily.

"Table?"

Vivian showed Max the sign.

"Tree?"

Vivian showed him the sign.

"Ice cream?"

Vivian showed him the sign.

"Okay, dude." Kate pulled him into her arms and kissed his head. "Let's give Vivian a break now, okay? The concert is going to start soon."

Vivian smiled and lay back on the grass.

Their picnic, it turned out, was not from a hot dog vendor or gyro booth. Instead, Vivian had brought nuts, cheese, fruit, French bread, and deli meats. The trio dived in, polishing it all off within minutes.

Max climbed onto Vivian's lap, his face furrowed in thought. He pulled her chin toward him. "How come we at a concert if you can't hear?"

Vivian had abandoned her sunglasses, and she studied Max's face. "Lie down. Both of you."

Max rolled onto his back, still on Vivian's lap.

"Plug your ears and just feel."

Max shoved his fingers into his ears.

Beside them, Kate put her fingers into her ears as well. She could still hear a little, but as she paid more attention, she began to notice other things: the soft cooling breeze across her face, the grass that tickled under her arms, the warm sun against her skin. Above her, a bird flew, a smaller bird sailing behind it. The clouds were white and fluffy. Yeah, she knew exactly what Vivian meant.

"See? Even though you can't hear what's around you, you can see the grass, feel the sunshine, and watch all the people having fun. It's relaxing." Vivian caught Max against her body and tickled him until his flailing legs got to be too much. She set him down, and he began to spin, his face tilted toward the fading sun.

"I'm sorry." Vivian turned to Kate, frowning. "I just realized I've been handling Max without your permission. I didn't mean to overstep."

Kate smiled and rolled onto her side, her head propped up on her arm. Vivian rolled toward her in mirror image. "Actually, yeah, that is kind of a thing. He's cute, so people like to touch him. How could you resist? He's the cutest, most awesome, smartest, bestest kid in the world."

Vivian smiled, her eyes crinkling. "You say that like it's a joke, but he is."

"Oh, I know." Kate rolled her eyes, then said, "You're really good with him."

"I like being with children. Though he is specifically wonderful, isn't he?"

"Well, I think so."

They watched him spin until he was dizzy, then get up and spin again, chuckling every time he landed on his butt.

"Do you want one of your own?" Kate asked. She was almost sure that she did: she could see it in the way Vivian held his hand, in her attentiveness, in the look of longing in her eyes.

Vivian nodded quickly as if she didn't need to think about it. "But I suppose I need to find the woman before I get the child, don't I?"

"Or maybe not." Kate shrugged. "It doesn't take two to tango these days. I'm raising him on my own."

Vivian looked back at Max. "And you're doing a very good job."

"Thanks." Kate smiled.

"Max's other parent? You haven't mentioned them."

Kate played with the blades of grass with her free hand. His second parent… "I, uh…" She swallowed, digging into the ground with a finger. "He doesn't exactly have one. Not really, anyway."

"May I ask what happened?"

Kate paused. It wasn't her favorite story to tell.

"Oh, I'm sorry. I'm being nosy, and you probably don't want to discuss it in front of Max."

Kate reached out to reassure her. "No, no, don't worry about that. Max and I have talked about his biological father. It's important to me that I'm honest with him. He knows the story, or at least a kid-safe version of it."

"Oh."

"I just kind of—I don't know." The story seemed so much more complicated now. When they were in Florida, it had been no big deal. It was so much more complicated now that they were in Chicago.

"What?"

Shaking her head, Kate said, "It's a long story." Then she laughed. "No, actually, it's not a long story at all." She had done what countless women in their early twenties had done.

Vivian watched her, an expectant look on her face.

It was amazing how much Vivian said with just her expression. Was it because she was deaf, or was it simply who she was? She wondered if it was possible to hold a whole conversation with her eyes alone.

And there was something wildly sexy about Vivian as she lay in the grass, focused on Kate.

"Max's father isn't involved?"

Kate cleared her throat, unsure how to answer. How honest did she want to be? She glanced at Max, who was now playing with a dandelion. "No. He knows about Max and all of that, but we were never anything serious."

"Oh?"

"Yeah. I mean, I liked him." She had liked him a lot. They had clicked as friends in a way that she had rarely experienced before. But everything had turned on its head when that little stick had come up with two lines. It was par for the course, but it had come as a terrible blow. And that feeling was one she knew well: abandonment.

"When I got pregnant, he told me that he wasn't ready for kids. He didn't even know if he wanted them. I did, so we agreed that I would have Max and he wouldn't be involved."

"That doesn't bother you? That he didn't want to be in Max's life?" There was no judgment in the question.

Kate shrugged. She had struggled with his answer for a long time, sure that she should have been angry with him. "No, not really. He was honest with me. He supported me doing what I wanted and didn't try to throw money at me for an abortion. I think we're both okay with how things turned out."

"But to not know Max when you could be a permanent part of his life and watch him grow up on a daily basis…" Vivian signed with one hand, and she looked at Max again.

It really was beautiful, the way her hands danced. *She* was beautiful. Kate looked away, not so far that Vivian couldn't read her lips but far enough to break the spell. "Not a great story about me. A drunken one-night stand."

"A one-night stand four years ago?"

There it was. "Yeah."

"Four years ago… You were at a music festival, correct?"

"I…was."

Kate waited while Vivian processed the information.

"That was the music festival you attended with Mr. Foy?"

"Yup."

Vivian blinked. She seemed to be studying Max's features, and Kate wondered if she saw things she hadn't noticed before. "So his father...er, his biological father..."

Kate nodded. "Max doesn't know his father at all. He's never met him."

"I see. And he doesn't want to meet him? His father, I mean."

"It hasn't come up."

Vivian silently brushed a bug off Kate's hand. "Well," she said carefully, "I think on the list of mistakes we all make, bringing Max into the world was not one of them."

Kate smiled. The tension in her shoulders released. "I can't argue with you about that."

"Do people know?"

Kate shook her head.

"But now you're all here. Does that mean...?"

Kate shrugged. "I don't know yet."

Vivian studied Kate's face.

"So, Vivian," Kate said after a few moments of silence, "each time I've heard you introduce yourself, it's always as Vivian. Are you ever Vivi?"

Vivian cringed. "Are you always Kate?"

It was Kate's turn to shudder. "On occasion, I go by Katelyn, like in auditions."

"Well, on occasion, I am Viv, thanks to Charlie, who is on occasion Charlotte. However, I am more comfortable as Vivian."

The loudspeaker crackled as mics switched on and a man's voice welcomed the crowd.

Kate sat up. Max scurried back to her and crawled into her lap.

"Did it start?"

Kate glanced at Vivian and nodded.

Vivian rolled onto her back, put her arms under her head, and closed her eyes. She dozed through a good part of the concert. When the music finished, Kate realized that Max had also fallen asleep.

Kate woke Vivian up. "Is it over?" she asked, her hand over her eyes to block the sun.

Kate nodded.

"How did they sound?"

"Good! The quality of the mics wasn't the best, though."

"What?"

Kate was surprised by the sharp expression on Vivian's face. "It was just sort of distorted is all."

Vivian stood and, brushing off the grass, shouldered her belongings. She looked agitated. The fierce woman Kate had first met lurked in her eyes. "I told those idiots to fix that. Damn it! How many complaints do we need before they take the issue seriously? If you'll excuse me for a moment, I need to catch them before they leave."

"Hold on. I'll come with you." Kate tried to get up, but her sleeping son was too heavy.

"Is he asleep?"

"Completely."

Vivian waved her hands toward herself and, assuming she was offering to help her up, Kate reached out with her free hand. Instead, Vivian carefully transferred Max to her own shoulder.

His head lifted just enough for him to smile and say, "Hi, Viv'n." Then he put his head back on her shoulder and drifted off again.

Kate gaped. She was fairly certain that, in all the years he had been alive, he had never willingly slept on anyone besides her. She reached for him, but Vivian shook her head.

"You sure? He's pretty heavy."

Vivian nodded and headed toward the stage.

When they reached the amphitheater stage, Vivian went over to the small sound booth, leaving Kate to greet her colleagues. She was surprised to find Stephen still on the stage, putting his bass back into its gig bag. She hadn't even noticed his presence. Had she really been that wrapped up in her afternoon? "Hey."

Stephen grinned. "Hey. What are you doing here? Come to hear us play?"

"Well, as much as I would love the brownie points..." She jerked her head in the direction of Vivian, who was speaking to the sound technician with Max hugging her neck. It looked as if she was trying to yell at the man without waking Max, which meant she was probably screaming in a whisper.

Vivian looked back at Kate and Stephen, but instead of smiling as she had done all day, she quickly neutralized her expression.

When Kate frowned at her, something else flashed across Vivian's face. She shifted her arms under Max, then turned back to the sound engineer.

Stephen straightened, zipping the bass into its bag with a jerk. "Oh, you're here with the ice queen, huh?"

Kate rolled her eyes. "You do realize that she isn't actually an ice queen, right?"

"And you're defending her. What's up with that?"

"Oh, shut up."

He laughed.

"You guys sounded great, except we could barely hear the strings. The mics were super screwed up."

"Yeah. Uh-huh. Right."

She looked at him, crossing her arms. He wasn't listening to her at all. He was staring at Vivian. "Yeah, it was weird," she continued. "And then out of nowhere zombie cows attacked us. It was like Night of the Living Zombie Cows out here."

"Right…" His voice sounded distant. "Hey, Kate, is that Max there with the ice queen?"

"Yeah," she said slowly. "Yeah, Stephen, that's Max."

"Oh." He continued staring. It was eerie how much he looked like Max when he was blindsided by something.

"Yo, earth to Stephen," she said, nudging him.

Stephen shook his head. "Yeah. Sorry."

"Hey, do you want to meet him? I can introduce you as my colleague. I bet he'd think your bass was cool."

Stephen didn't move, staring down at his shoes. Whatever was happening in his head seemed to have rendered him unable to function. "Oh. Actually, I better go if I wanna make my train."

"Okay. You sounded great," Kate said again banally.

"Thanks."

She made her way to Vivian, who by then had wiped all evidence of emotion from her face.

Vivian threw her a sign that Kate had to think about for a minute. "Oh yeah, I'm ready," Kate said.

"Was he checking for frostbite?" Vivian asked as they headed out of the park. She seemed grumpy now.

"Huh? What does that mean?"

"Ice queen."

"Um..."

"People assume that because I'm deaf I don't know what they say around me."

"Oh God." Kate groaned. "That's terrible. I'm sorry."

Vivian shook her head as if to feign indifference. "It's better than other nicknames I've had. Why was he so upset?"

Kate shook her head. "I'm not sure. He seemed..."

Though she didn't finish the sentence, Vivian nodded. "He did. Then again, anyone would be a fool not to want to be in this little prince's life. Do you think you'll let them meet?"

It wasn't a question with a simple answer. "I don't know. I just offered Stephen the chance to meet Max, you know, as my friend and not...you know. But he seemed like he really didn't want to."

"Uh-huh."

"That was weird, wasn't it?" He had never once shown any interest. Was he put off that she had offered?

"And if he did want to?"

And if he did...

"I have no idea," she said. "Max gets attached to people and then doesn't understand why they disappear from his life." It occurred to her that she was probably going to have that problem not with Stephen but with Vivian. How would he handle it when, for whatever reason, Vivian disappeared? "I think he really just wants a second parent."

"It must be hard to meet new people or date when a child is involved."

"Yes, very."

They had come to a crosswalk, and Kate turned to press the crossing signal button. When she turned back, she said, "Have you ever done it? Dated someone with a child... I mean, someone with kids?"

"No, not in a very long time. In truth, I don't date much. I have to confess: in the past, I broke up with women when I found out they were parents. It is one of the two guidelines I follow."

"Oh." Kate shoved a hand into her pocket. "Can I ask why? You said you love kids and you want them."

"I do. I do. That's the problem. It's similar to what you were saying, isn't it? It's difficult enough to go through a breakup with someone, but when you have also grown close to their child, well, you lose two people, don't you?"

"I've never thought of it that way." They fell silent again as they crossed the street.

"In truth, between that and how small the Deaf community is, I don't date much at all."

"Oh?" Kate glanced at Vivian and then looked away quickly. "You only date in the Deaf community?"

Vivian sighed and shifted Max to her other shoulder.

"I mean—" Kate fumbled with her words, feeling as if she had intruded. "I didn't mean… I mean—"

"No, I suppose that's right."

"Oh," Kate said, then felt stupid for saying it. She didn't understand. Vivian had seemed… Had she imagined Vivian's interest? She felt like a sixteen-year-old girl again. She could have sworn…

Vivian cleared her throat. "I suppose it's just less complicated."

"Oh." She really needed to come up with something better to say than "oh." "What is the other guideline?"

Vivian's lips twisted, looking away from Kate's face. "Generally speaking, I avoid dating hearing women."

"Uh-oh." Why did that feel like a personal insult? She wasn't…they weren't… "Why?"

Vivian pushed her hair back and sighed. "It's difficult for them to connect with me. We're from different worlds."

Kate nodded, a sour taste in her mouth.

Silence fell between them.

"So *are* you going to introduce Max to the hairpiece?"

Kate chuckled. "Hey, just like he needs to stop calling you 'ice queen,' you need to stop calling him 'hairpiece.'"

Vivian removed one hand from Max and held it up in mock surrender. Max stirred, looking up at her. "Hi, Viv'n."

"You want to get down, buddy?" Kate asked.

He shook his head and tightened his grip around Vivian's neck.

"Do you want a ride home?" Vivian asked.

"Sure."

Chapter 5

KATE DIDN'T SEE VIVIAN AGAIN until July, but in that month's time, their friendship grew. They texted four or five times a day

Max-o-million says 'hi, Viv'n.' I keep trying to get him to say Vivian, but so far, no luck. I think you're stuck being Viv'n. Which I think you would be okay with it if you could hear him because it's adorable when he says it. – K

I think the lunch vendor was trying to ask me on a date a few days ago, but I was looking for change in my purse and I missed half of what he said. Now I am uncomfortable whenever I pick up my lunch, and I'm not sure how to address it. – V

Every now and then Charlie threw herself into the mix as well. She and Kate were becoming friends as well.

Do you think ants feel it when we step on them? – C

In no time at all, their first formal chamber concert was upon them.
Kate was sweating heavily in her concert blacks as she pulled her hair back into a ponytail. She knew there was no reason to be this nervous, but she couldn't seem to calm down. One minute she flashed hot and the next she chilled cold. She groaned and wiped the moisture from her upper lip.
Kate was sure she was going to vomit: too much stress and she turned into Linda Blair.

"Buck up, Kate." Stephen pounded her on the back, making her wince. "You'll be fine."

Kate tried to smile. She took a few deep breaths, but her heart insisted on doing the tango. Just as she got enough air into her lungs, she heard the click of high heels behind her.

She looked up, forgetting to play cool and casual.

But Vivian blew by her, deep in discussion with another board member. Charlie flanked her, hands flying.

Kate did her best not to stare, but this time it wasn't the hand movements that made it hard. Vivian wore a tight single-diagonal-strapped black dress that trailed all the way to the floor. A slit up one side exposed a toned calf and hinted at more. Even Charlie had given up her jeans for a slinky blue dress.

"Have you ever noticed how happy she looks when she's yelling at someone?" Stephen was still hovering nearby.

"What? Oh. I guess so." Kate felt like a child on the playground watching the popular girls and hoping that one day she could play with them. She tried putting her hands into her pockets and was thwarted by the unbroken seams. She crossed her arms instead, but that wasn't satisfying either. She popped her neck and dropped her hands to her side, not knowing what else to do with them.

She realized with a jolt that her gaze had settled on Vivian's exposed leg.

This wasn't helping her preconcert focus. She closed her eyes, reaching for the mental state she liked to be in before she walked onto the stage. Calm. Cool. Ready.

"It's the hall, isn't it? That's why you're nervous." Stephen nodded. The look on his face said he knew exactly what her nerves were about.

He wasn't exactly wrong either, at least not about that part of it.

"The first time I played here, I felt that too," he continued. "I think it's all the gold." He stroked his chin, glancing at the stage through the curtain.

"It is a lot of gold."

"I mean, look at that, Flynn. Is that a golden cherub? Nothing says grandeur like flying golden babies."

Kate snorted.

"Good. I got you laughing."

"Don't let it get to you." Mike, the trumpet player, worked the valves on his instrument. "It's just a hall."

She nodded, but she still couldn't swallow the lump in her throat.

"Think of it like diving into a pool. No hesitation." Mike grinned.

Kate rolled her neck and reached up to stretch her back. Almost involuntarily, she glanced back at Vivian, who was still arguing with the other board member. Should she go over and say hello? She didn't want to assume a friendship when there wasn't one. She had never been very good at making friends, and she wasn't sure she knew how to do it.

She hadn't even realized that she was watching Vivian again until Vivian caught her eye, then snapped her gaze away again.

Kate could have tangoed across the room. Vivian *had* noticed her. Maybe there *was* a relationship—a friendship—developing between them.

Someone tapped her shoulder, making her jump. She turned her head so fast that her forehead nearly collided with Charlie's.

"Jesus, Kate!"

"Sorry. You scared me. What's up?"

Charlie whispered in Kate's ear. "We're going out for drinks after the concert. We'll wait for you."

It wasn't *Do you want us to wait for you?* or *Do you want to come?* but *We'll wait for you*, as though they assumed she would join them.

She didn't have to think twice. "Totally." She could send Stacey a text to let her know she would be late. Stacey was always hinting that she needed more hours.

When Vivian glanced her way again, Kate grinned. Vivian dropped one eyelid into a wink, then her face returned to its mask as she turned her attention back to the board member.

When Kate picked up her cello and walked out, she barely noticed the stage lights or the waiting audience.

Stephen caught her as they exited. "So, Kate, I was thinking we should get a drink and catch up."

Kate craned her neck, trying to track down Vivian and Charlie in the crowd milling around the enormous hall.

"I'm sorry, but I can't tonight. I'm going with Vivian and Charlie. Do you want to come?"

"With the president of the board and my ex-girlfriend?" He smiled sheepishly. "You know Charlie is my ex, right?"

"Yeah. Vivian told me."

"Of course she did."

"Rain check?"

"One of these nights, Flynn, I'll get you to myself, but I won't fight it."

"Have fun."

"Don't get frostbite."

Kate found Vivian and Charlie in the lobby in the middle of a group of people. She waited for a pause in the conversation before softly touching Vivian's elbow and whispering to Charlie that she would wait by the stage door. Charlie signed and Vivian nodded.

The change in Vivian was obvious as soon as she appeared outside. It was like a mask dropped away. Her shoulders were relaxed, her jaw unclenched. She pointed up the street and signed, letting Charlie speak for her. "There's this great little hole-in-the-wall down the street that Charlie and I like. Amazing martinis."

"Wait," Kate said, looking from Charlie to Vivian. "Go back. What's the sign for *Charlie*?"

Vivian cupped her hand for the letter C and made an obscene gesture. "Why?"

Charlie rolled her eyes. "Vivian thought it was funny to give me that name when we were kids. It was fine until my parents started picking up some sign. Then it got me grounded."

"To be fair," Vivian said, "it was in response to the name that Charlie gave me."

"So neither of you feels comfortable using your names in public, and yet you both keep them because you gave them to each other?"

Vivian and Charlie exchanged amused glances.

"Right," Kate said slowly. "And follow-up question: you grew up together?"

Vivian chuckled as Charlie threw her arm around Vivian's shoulder. "Charlie and her family lived a few houses down from mine," she explained through Charlie's voice. "We were best friends. As Charlie got older, she became the only person in my life to learn sign for me. When she was good enough, my parents hired her. It's as simple as that."

"How long have you known each other, then?"

"Twenty years or so," Charlie said.

"Wow. I've never had a friend longer than a few weeks. Months at best. Jesus, twenty years. That's amazing."

Vivian and Charlie exchanged another glance.

"Never?" Charlie asked softly.

Apparently Kate had said too much. "So, where are we going again?" she asked quickly to hide her embarrassment.

The bar was loud and surprisingly filled with people whom Kate recognized. They found a booth, and Charlie ordered three dirty martinis.

"Wait. Are we eating or are we just drinking?" Kate looked back and forth between Vivian and Charlie, concerned for her sobriety. She had to at least be able to make it home on a train that often smelled of urine.

Vivian smiled and playfully batted her long eyelashes. "A little of this, a little of that."

I would like to taste that smile.

The thought had appeared out of nowhere, and it startled her so badly that she jerked involuntarily, slopping water down the front of her concert blacks.

"Are you all right?" Charlie asked.

"You mean aside from being a complete klutz?" Kate mopped herself with a napkin.

What was wrong with her? Vivian might be the biggest flirt ever, but Kate didn't want to date her. They were friends. Even if there was a magnetic pull between them, it couldn't happen.

But God, I want it to happen.

She scooted over to put more space between her and Vivian. When she looked up, Vivian's face still held the coy and all-too-knowing smile that had caused Kate to spill her water in the first place.

Vivian turned her smile up to a megawatt level of brightness, making it impossible for Kate not to smile back.

Charlie held out her glass in salute. "The group sounded amazing tonight."

Kate nodded a courteous thank-you, a professional knee-jerk reaction, but she couldn't tear her eyes away from Vivian.

"Uh, guys? Guys? Hello?"

Finally, Vivian turned away and smiled at her best friend.

Charlie's eyes narrowed, her hands moving fast.

Kate had no idea what she had said, but Vivian only shrugged in response.

"Right," Charlie said.

"So, Kate," Charlie said, halfway through their first drink. "How's Max?"

"He's good." Kate smiled as she always did whenever someone talked about Max. "He's getting excited for his birthday."

"When is it?" Charlie nibbled on an olive.

"Next month. We're going to the public pool. He can't wait to swim. I hope you two will come. He might just die if he doesn't see this one again soon." She nodded toward Vivian.

Vivian beamed and, with her hands flying, told Charlie about how she had carried him through the park.

"He loves you." Kate shook her head. "He can't stop talking about you. I don't know what you did to my son, but he's bewitched," she said, although she understood entirely where the kid was coming from.

"Aw-w!" Charlie pouted. "I want Max to love me! Do you think if I buy him some candy, we might be friends?"

"If you give him candy, you have to take him home with you and deal with the sugar high."

"You don't stand a chance," Vivian told Charlie, wrapping her arm around Kate's shoulder. "I think he likes me best."

"I think he might like *me* best," Kate teased right back. "You're just a shiny new toy."

Vivian laughed, winking at Kate as she pulled her closer. "The public pool? You mean at the Y?"

"Mm."

"Why not just have it at my penthouse? I have a pool."

Kate scoffed. "Yeah, sure." She could picture chocolatey handprints everywhere.

"I'm serious. Think about it."

They powered through three drinks quickly. Everything took on the foggy haze of inebriation, and she loved every moment of it, relaxing for the first time in what seemed like months. She needed to go out with friends more often. She needed to go out with *these two* more often.

Kate was laughing so hard, her sides hurt.

Vivian was telling them about a man she had met earlier that night. "He was telling his friend in graphic detail exactly what he would like to do to me. He was only five feet away! Did he not understand that I could see him?" Vivian's face was twisted in in a look of disgust.

Kate's eyes filled with tears of laughter. Vivian's animated facial expressions and noises were too much for her. "So what—he thought because he was to the side of you that you couldn't know what he was saying?"

"I assume so, yes."

"Well, that slit is pretty intense," Kate said. "You can't blame him totally."

Vivian raised her eyebrows. "How kind of you to notice." She crossed her toned legs, exposing smooth golden skin.

Kate gaped at the exposed thigh, heat rising to her face. Whatever she had planned to say next flew from her head. "Oh my God! That was rude!" Kate slapped her hand over her eyes. "I'm a little drunk. I'm sorry."

"You have a point, though." Charlie laughed. "Look at those things. Yeow! Kind of makes me wish I enjoyed *The Vagina Monologues*."

"Kate!" Her name cracked through the noise in the bar.

She tried to straighten, her legs flailing in her haste to remove herself from Vivian's casual embrace. As she did, she knocked over the empty martini glasses and smacked her knee on the table leg. When had Vivian put her arm around her shoulders? When had Kate leaned in so closely?

She glanced up to find Stephen standing at their booth. "Hi," she said and scrambled to stand up.

"You didn't hear me calling you?"

"You were?" She swallowed back a laugh at the look on Vivian's face. Her cheeks were flush from drink, but she had slipped on her hard mask again, her upper lip curled, her nostrils flared. She looked as though she would snatch Kate away if Stephen got too close to her.

Stephen looked between her and Vivian. "Are you okay?"

"Yeah." She smiled. "Totally okay."

Out of the corner of her eye, Kate caught Vivian's hands flying. She turned and glared at her.

Vivian raised one eyebrow innocently.

"Charlie?"

Charlie pretended she hadn't heard Kate speak, though her eyes shone with laughter.

When Kate looked back at Stephen, his jaw had tightened. "She's talking about me, isn't she?" he asked.

What the hell was she supposed to say to that? She didn't know for sure, but somehow she didn't think Vivian had asked Charlie for the time.

Vivian's hands flew again. Charlie burst out laughing, then tried to hide her smirk behind a napkin.

"That's real polite," Stephen said, "talking about me when I can't defend myself."

Vivian's lips curled into a snarl as Charlie translated. "My, that's a bold assumption, Mr. Foy."

"It's not an assumption if it's true."

"I'll give you that." Vivian said, nodding politely. "All I said was that the more I learn about you, the more I find to dislike." She glanced at Kate and then back to Stephen.

Stephen blanched.

"Guys! Hey!" Kate waved her arms in the air. "Can you two knock it off?"

Vivian's mouth snapped shut, though she looked as if she would rather keep arguing.

Stephen glared at her. "Right. Can't ask them to behave like adults, can we?"

"Hey, you too!" Kate said, feeling like a ref in a fight that had started before the bell. She pulled him away from the table. "What's up?"

The Loudest Silence

"Nothing, really. I just thought that since we were in the same place, maybe I could get you that drink."

"Sure." She smiled at him, but he answered it with a glare. "What?"

"What are you doing, Kate?"

"Huh?"

"With *her*. With *them*."

"We're friends." She tilted her head at him.

"Is that smart?"

"Is what smart?"

"You know what? Never mind. Not my business. What's everyone having?" he asked, his mood still obviously sour. "You, Vivian, and Charlie. I'll buy the next round."

"Thanks, but you don't have to do that."

"I want to," he grunted, acting very much as if he didn't.

"Hey, Stephen." She touched his arm lightly. "I'm sorry about what just happened. I'll talk to them, okay?"

He looked at the floor. "Yeah. No. What you don't know is that I deserve it." He looked back up at Kate with a forced smile. "So," he said, "what'll it be?"

She placed their drink orders and glanced back at the booth, expecting to find Vivian and Charlie chatting. Instead, Vivian was staring at her intensely, her arms crossed over her chest.

"So I was thinking…" Stephen began.

Her head whipped back around.

"Now is not the time, of course, but do you think we could chat soon?"

"Sure. Of course."

"Good." He smiled.

The silence stretched awkwardly between them until the barkeep announced, "Three dirty martinis."

"Let me help you with those." Stephen took two of the glasses from the bar and, with a flourish that was at once charming and dorky, handed Charlie one of the drinks.

She accepted it with a glare.

"Is it poisoned?" Vivian muttered in what Kate supposed was meant to be a quiet voice.

"Viv!"

Stephen shrugged. "Hers isn't. I'd be careful of yours, though."

"Guys!" Kate threw up her arms in defeat.

Vivian conceded. "I'm sorry. That was rude. Thank you, Mr. Foy, for the drink," Vivian said between obviously clenched teeth.

Ignoring her, he touched Kate on the back. "I'll see you, Flynn. Don't be stupid."

"Thanks for the drinks," she said as he walked away. *What did that mean?*

"So how was that?" Vivian asked a little too innocently.

Kate glared. "You're really not helping the situation, you know."

Vivian's gaze shifted to something on the other side of the bar.

"Hey!" Kate moved into Vivian's line of sight. "It's fine that you don't like him, but you can't expect him to treat you better than you treat him."

"You're right. I don't know why I did that. I'm sorry."

Kate relaxed a bit. "Thank you."

"So what did he want?"

"Nothing. He just wants to talk at some point."

"Oh?" Vivian's tone was neutral, but her face said otherwise. "And you're okay with that?"

"Okay with what? Oh." Of course. Why hadn't it occurred to her right away? She had thought he just wanted to hang out, but he had said *talk*, hadn't he? He probably wanted to talk about Max. What else could it be about?

Charlie glanced between them. "Okay, what's happening right now?"

Kate blinked, releasing Vivian's gaze. She wasn't ready to let more people in on the secret she shared with Stephen. "What I want to know is what you said before I went to the bar."

Vivian looked away, but her eyes were twinkling.

"Charlie?"

"I'm not getting involved in this one."

Kate waved her hand to draw Vivian back into the conversation. "What did you say?"

Vivian looked away again.

"Hey!" Kate reached for her jaw, turning her face back.

Kate narrowed her eyes. "What did you say?"

Vivian fluttered her eyelashes. "Nope."

"What did she say?" Kate looked at Charlie again.

"What did who say?"

"Charlie!" Kate demanded.

Vivian's smile died on her face. "I said, do you think he knows that she's not interested?"

"Oh." Kate had expected a quip or a joke. She released Vivian's jaw. "But he's not interested."

Vivian raised her eyebrows again. "I've seen the way he looks at you, Kate."

"What?" She laughed nervously. *No way.* Hell, they had barely spoken since she had gotten into town.

Wait. Why did this feel like an accusation, or maybe like a question that wasn't being asked? She could feel both Vivian and Charlie watching her intently. Vivian sat so close that if Kate leaned in an inch she would probably feel Vivian's breath on her cheek.

She gazed down, noticing how perfect her line of lipstick was, how smoothly it transitioned into her golden skin.

"I just wonder if he knows that you're interested in…someone else," Vivian said softly. She brushed Kate's hand lightly again before settling it on her thigh. Her thumb rubbed in gentle circles. "Kate…"

The contact snapped her out of her fog. She was a little drunk. She glanced at Charlie, who pointedly looked in the other direction as though to appraise a group of men at the bar.

She was too drunk to be an adult about this, but she *had* to be an adult about this. She wasn't going to get involved with someone who didn't want to date someone with kids! In fact, she wasn't going to date anyone.

Kate stumbled from the booth, nearly taking out a waiter in the process. "I, uh, I gotta go. I gotta get going."

Visibly startled, Vivian reached for her arm, but Kate pulled away.

"I'll see you later, yeah?" Kate dropped a few bills on the table and was moving before she even finished her sentence.

The night air seemed to clear her head. She walked briskly down the sidewalk, the sticky summer air making her sweat.

"Kate! Slow down! *Katelyn!*"

She whirled around. Vivian was hurrying toward her, her hands flying as she ran.

"I don't understand what you're signing!"

Something passed across Vivian's face, frustration as she opened her mouth to speak. "I'm so sorry." Vivian's voice came out as a croak. "That was rude. I shouldn't have…" She shifted her weight as she caught her breath. "That was inappropriate. I'm sorry." She reached out for Kate's arm.

Kate shook her off. "No need to apologize. I just realized it was getting late, and I, uh, need to relieve the babysitter."

I really want you.

"You're upset."

"No, I'm not upset," Kate said, though she was pretty sure Vivian knew she was lying.

"Are you sure you should go alone? I should go with you to make sure that you get home safely. It's late. You've been drinking, and your neighborhood—"

"No, I'm okay. Really. But thanks for tonight. I had fun."

"Kate, talk to me, please." Vivian took Kate's hands in hers.

What could she say? She didn't understand Vivian at all, but her skin where Vivian touched it felt on fire.

"I was jealous, Kate. I'm sorry."

Kate looked back at Vivian. "What do you mean? Jealous of–"

"Flynn!"

Kate jerked her head up to look over Vivian's shoulder. Stephen was walking toward them.

Vivian, following Kate's eyes, glanced behind her. She released Kate's hands.

"Are you headed home?" Stephen joined them, nodding briefly at Vivian.

"Um, yeah."

"Oh. Well, let me head back with you. It's on my way."

"Yeah, okay." She forced a smiled at Vivian. "See? I'll be fine. Stephen will take me home. He lives a few stops before mine, and you live, what, five minutes from here? You would have to go all the way there only to come all the way back."

Vivian glanced at Stephen disdainfully, her face etched in dislike. Kate softly touched her chin, drawing her attention back to her. She looked her squarely in the eyes. "I'll be *fine*."

"Come on," Stephen said. "If we go soon, we should make the next train."

Vivian studied Kate's face, frustration flicking across her features.

"You gotta turn around," she said to Stephen. "Otherwise she can't tell what you're saying."

Stephen frowned. "But I was talking to you."

The ice on Vivian's face solidified.

"Stephen!"

"Text me when you get home, please, Kate," Vivian said over Kate.

"I will."

"Don't forget."

"I won't."

She saw the hurt in Vivian's eyes, and she wanted to hug her, speak to her, make it better. Her mouth opened, but no words came out.

With a barely perceptible nod, Vivian turned and started back toward the bar.

Stephen took Kate's arm and started moving toward the train platform. When she glanced back, Vivian was watching them. The lights of the city behind her made it seem as if the ice queen was on fire.

"So," Stephen said, "it looks like I have you all to myself."

"Yeah," Kate said. "It looks like you do."

Chapter 6

KATE SHIFTED IN HER SEAT on the train, wishing Stephen wasn't sitting so close to her. His arm rested against hers.

She got it. He had no idea what it meant to be around a Deaf person. She was only learning herself. And Vivian had acted like a petulant teenager most of the night when it came to Stephen.

That didn't erase the resignation she had seen on Vivian's face, the hurt.

Stephen reached into his pocket for his phone, his elbow pressing into her side.

"Dude, can you give me some space?" she snapped.

The people sitting close to them glanced their way.

Stephen's mouth dropped open.

"Sorry. I'm sorry." She sighed.

"Sure. Okay." Stephen sat back and looked at her. "You wanna tell me what's up?"

No, she didn't. She didn't want to get into the way their fight had made her feel or how the look on Vivian's face haunted her or the way Vivian's arm had felt around her shoulders.

What the hell did Vivian have to be jealous of? Didn't Vivian know…

She wasn't going to tell him, and yet her mouth opened, disobeying her orders. "Do you remember when you were talking to me outside of the bar?"

He let out his breath, his shoulders dropping. "Man, she just… She gets to me, you know? She acts like I'm this horrible asshole when she—"

"I know." Vivian wasn't innocent in this situation. Not at all. "But you get that your comment about talking to me was next-level rude, right? And kind of ableist."

The Loudest Silence

He stared at her, looking genuinely mystified. "I meant... Wait! What?"

She grew more annoyed. "Think! You were talking with your back to her."

He still looked blank. "I, uh..."

"Do I have to spell it out for you? She couldn't see what you were saying! It was like you were purposely taking advantage of the fact that she can't hear."

"But I wasn't."

"And then when I pointed it out, you said that you were talking to *me*."

"But I *was*. I was talking to you, not her."

Kate ran a hand through her hair. He still didn't get it. "Okay, so think of it this way. Imagine that you're having a conversation with a group of people. Two people split off and start talking to each other in another language, leaving you completely out of it. It feels like shit, right?"

His mouth dropped open as realization dawned. "Oh shit. So it looked like—"

"Like you were purposely hiding what you were saying from her. Like, purposely leaving her out."

"Oh shit," he said again, his cheeks turning pink "I didn't mean... I'm sorry. I didn't even think... It wasn't on purpose."

"You owe her an apology."

He swallowed. "I guess I do."

"And she owes you one too. Is there anything I can do to resolve this feud between you?"

"I don't know. It's been like this ever since Charlie and I broke up. But I'll try, okay?"

She sighed. "Thanks."

They sat quietly the rest of the train ride, Stephen looking shell-shocked. Kate stared out the window, processing everything that had happened: the desire she felt, the look in Vivian's eyes when she said what she had about Stephen, and her anxious apology outside of the bar.

As they walked from the L to Kate's apartment, Kate asked, "You're not interested in starting something up with us again, are you?"

Stephen stopped walking. He looked as though he had stepped into a bear trap.

71

"I'm not saying *I* am," she clarified. "God, we haven't even really talked, have we?"

He let out his breath, and Kate couldn't help laughing at his relief. "Jesus, Flynn! What was I supposed to say to that?"

"Yeah, I guess you were kind of cornered there, weren't you? My bad."

"Talk about giving a man a heart attack." But he smiled good-naturedly, reminding her of that guy from all those years ago.

The memory made her smile. It hadn't been all that long ago, but everything before Max felt like a different lifetime. She glanced at Stephen. Did he feel that too? Probably not. His life wasn't centered around the tiny creature she had brought home from the hospital.

The thought made her sad. Max was often a lot of work, and more than once she had sobbed through the day or night. Still, there was so much Stephen had missed. Did he care? She supposed if he ever had, she would never know, and the thought made her sad.

"Come on."

They started down the street again, the mood a little lighter.

"So I'll take that as a no?" she asked playfully.

Stephen wrapped an arm around her waist and pulled her in tight to his side. "It isn't that you're not beautiful and funny and all of that…"

"The unplanned pregnancy kind of put a damper on that, though." She had felt the same way. There was nothing like the stress of trying to decide whether to keep an unexpected baby and what it would mean for the future of the two parents.

"Why do you ask?"

"Oh, something that Vivian said."

"Of course." He rolled his eyes.

They reached the foul-smelling hallway outside her apartment. Stephen dropped his hands into his pockets. "So, Flynn, I was wondering. Can I come in and talk for a few minutes?"

She paused. "Sure. Come on in."

Thankfully, the apartment was quiet, which meant that Max was asleep. She paid Stacey, who left quickly.

"Beer?" Kate asked.

"Sure."

The Loudest Silence

"Take a seat." She sat on the opposite end of the futon from him. "Cheers."

Stephen looked around. "It's not a bad place." His gaze lingered on the framed painting of blotches and squiggles on the wall, made by Max.

"Yeah, it could be worse."

He took another drink from his beer. "So what did you think of the Mendelssohn the other day?"

They talked shop for a while. When they had finished their beers, Kate sat back. As nice as it was to talk about chamber dynamics and the pieces they would be playing soon, it was getting late.

Stephen put the empty bottle down on the coffee table and clapped his hands. "All right."

She shushed him immediately. Max wasn't a bad sleeper now, but he had been a light sleeper when he was younger, and she still worried that any loud noises would wake him.

He grimaced. "Sorry. Did I wake him up?"

"Probably not," she said.

"I'm making messes all over the damn place tonight, aren't I?"

Kate shrugged. "What were you going to say?"

Stephen shifted in his seat. "Did you want to finish—"

"No, it's okay."

"Right. I, uh, was wondering…" His gaze flicked to the painting again and then back to Kate with a nervous laugh. "I'll just cut to the chase."

His anxiety was starting to get to Kate. What the hell could—?

"I want to meet him." With these words, Stephen fell silent, his stubble-covered jaw clenched. He stared down at his clasped hands.

"Yeah, sure. Of course you can meet him. I'm sure he'll be at a concert—"

"No, Flynn," Stephen said, looking up to meet her eyes. "I want to meet him as my son."

"You do?" she asked, not quite believing what she was hearing. Stephen had always been content to keep his distance. He had never commented on photos of Max on Facebook. He had even turned down meeting him at the park.

"Yeah."

She got up from the futon and began pacing. "Why now?"

He rubbed at his chin, the sandpaper sound grating on Kate's nerves. "What do you mean? He's here. You're here."

"Yeah, but you said you didn't want to meet him."

"Come on, Kate. I was young. I didn't think I was ready."

"No! The other day. You said you didn't want to meet him." She hadn't thought much about this possibility, but when she had, she'd thought she would be open to it. So why did it feel as if her fist were closing tighter, hiding Max away?

Stephen lapsed into unbearable silence, staring at the floor between his knees. Finally, he looked up and said, "I just…" He sighed and ran his hand through his hair. "I don't know. I think I panicked. I mean, I haven't let myself think about him at all, you know? He was just *there, but now he's right here.*" He reached out as if Max were resting on Kate's shoulder. "He was right there. He's the spitting image of my brother at his age."

"So you want to be a parent now?" She stopped pacing long enough to look at him, sticking her hands into her back pockets.

"What?" Stephen nearly choked on the word. "No. I mean, I don't think so. I don't know, Kate."

She frowned. This wasn't a choice like whether to buy a diet or regular soda. "Are you ready to get up every morning at six? To cut your practice time in half?"

"Whoa, whoa," Stephen waved his arms.

"To go home after dates without sex because the sitter needs to go home?"

His eyes had grown wider as she spoke. Now he chuckled. "Well, I don't know about that."

She ground her jaw. "But that's what it's like, Stephen."

"Jesus, Kate! Can't I start with meeting the boy?"

"No! You can't walk in here and tell him that you're his father if you don't know whether you're going to be around. He's three! Do you know how much that would confuse him?"

Stephen sat back, scrunching his eyebrows. "The kid looks just like me, Kate."

It was true. She hadn't noticed it until she came to Chicago. Stephen's face was so much like Max's, it was alarming. "I don't even know you anymore, Stephen. Damn it, I barely did then! It's been years. We were just stupid people who got drunk and had some fun. And now I'm supposed to trust you with my kid?"

"Then get to know me."

"I mean..."

"He's my son."

Anger flared through her. "No! No, he isn't! You signed away your rights. I don't owe you anything, especially something that might hurt him!"

"I don't want to hurt him, Kate!"

"Coming into his life and then leaving him again would hurt him!"

"Right." He picked up the bottle again, then realizing it was empty, set it back on the coffee table with a thud.

Kate waited. It had always been her and Max against the world, just the two of them. What would happen if there was someone else?

His face was pinched, but as he sat with his hands clasped between his knees, he began to relax. "He looks so much like me, Kate."

She didn't smile back at him. "I know."

"Just promise me you'll think about it, okay?"

She doubted her answer would change. "I will."

"Okay. I'm gonna go. Thanks for the beer."

"Night."

She closed the door behind him and leaned against it. Her breath was tight in her chest, catching as if in panic. Why hadn't she prepared for this?

She heard a chirp from the pocket of the jacket she had lain on the futon. Sighing again, she retrieved it and read her text messages.

Did you make it? Or did Mr. Foy lead you off a cliff? – V
I'm becoming quite worried about you. – V
Kate? – V
You're going to get a phone call in a second. – V

Surprised, Kate typed: *How can you call me? Is Charlie still with you? And where are there cliffs in Chicago? – K*

But before she could hit Send, her phone rang with an 800 number.

"Hello?"

"Hi, this is Adrika translating for Vivian. Is this Kate?"

"Yeah. Hi."

"Are you ready?"

"For what? Oh. Yeah, of course."

"Okay. Vivian says: what the hell, Kate? It doesn't take you over two hours to get home! I was worried something happened to you."

"I, uh…" Kate's sputtered, thrown by the phone call and hearing Vivian's words being voiced by a stranger. "I'm really sorry. I only just got Stephen out the door."

There was silence for a while, then: "Are you all right? I can still come over."

"What? No, I'm okay. Don't come. It's late."

Silence again.

"Vivian?"

"I just wanted to be sure you were okay. The thought of you walking through your neighborhood at night often worries me."

Stephen's face as he asked to meet Max floated through her mind. She wanted to tell her, but somehow it felt strange having a middleman. She swallowed the impulse back down. "I am. I'm good."

"All right, then. Good night, Ms. Flynn."

"Um…good night."

"No, really." Kate sat across from Vivian's desk, one leg over the arm of the chair. "It's too much."

"Did you not tell me you were planning on having his party at the public pool?"

"Yeah, but—"

"Well, then, I have a pool."

Kate glanced at Max in the chair beside her as if he could help her explain. Did Vivian have any idea at all what she was signing up for? Had she ever been around a group of hyped-up toddlers? Kate supposed she probably hadn't, which only made her more insistent. "I don't know, Vivian. I mean, who offers their place for a kid's birthday party? It's going to be messy and dirty and loud, and—"

Vivian's lips twitched. "Well, it's a good thing the noise won't bother me."

Kate rolled her eyes, slumping back in her seat. "Okay, yeah, but do you have any idea how much frosting kids can spread around? You'll have chocolate on your ceiling."

Vivian laughed, her eyes crinkling around the edges. "And I have a cleaning service."

"But..." Kate searched in vain for another argument.

"It seems silly to have the party at the Y, Kate. It will be close to the end of summer by then, and Max has been asking to swim in my pool since June. We're running out of time, and his birthday is a perfect opportunity."

Kate shook her head.

"Besides," Vivian finished, "who is going to be there besides you, Max, Charlie, and me? Who else do you know in this town?"

Max put down his *Highlights* magazine, climbed down from his chair, and rubbed his face against Kate's thigh. "Mommy, do you have Monkeyz?" Monkeyz was the stuffed brown monkey he had had since birth.

She rubbed Max's back, pulling him up so he was standing again. "He's waiting at home, but don't worry, we're leaving soon." To Vivian, she said, "I'm not sure. He's had playdates with a few kids that he met at the Mommy & Me thing."

"Mommy." Max pulled on her sleeve and reached up. Kate picked him up and put him in her lap.

Vivian came around the desk. Crossing her arms, she leaned against it and rubbed his back.

Kate shifted her eyes away from Vivian's pantyhose-covered legs. Breathing in Vivian's perfume, she licked her lips. "I don't know, Vivian. It's a lot."

"It's not a lot. It will be fun." Vivian smiled.

"Mommy" Max whined and pulled himself into her lap. Usually when they rode the L, he pressed his face to the glass like a puppy on a road trip.

Kate ran her fingers through his hair, enjoying the warmth of him in her arms. He had grown out of the cuddle phase too quickly.

"Max?" Kate prodded him lightly as they approached their stop. He had fallen asleep, which was unusual. Unless... She lifted his shirt and flattened a hand across his back. It was hotter than it should be. "Hey, kid, are you not feeling well?"

He shook his head sleepily.

Kate swore to herself. She hated when he got sick, imagining disaster after disaster. She had no significant other, no family. What would she do if one day he got sick and it turned out to be a serious illness? "What feels yucky?"

"Tummy."

She licked her lips. She had rehearsal that night, and she couldn't miss it. She hated when Max was sick and she had to leave him with the babysitter.

She carried him home, ignoring the whistles from the men on the corner.

She struggled up the five flights of stairs. Once inside, she settled him onto the futon and walked away to find a blanket.

"Mommy!" He burst into tears the moment she stepped away from him.

"I know, I know." She covered him with a blanket and gave him Monkeyz.

He hugged it to him and opened his mouth for the thermometer.

It was 101.2. She swore. She would bet if she checked his temperature again in an hour, it would be higher. Stress curdling her stomach, she gave him some baby Tylenol, then watched as he fell asleep.

What to do, what to do, what to do.

She stroked his forehead, her mind working. Max was going to need more medicine. Maybe Stacey would be willing to stop on her way over.

She pulled out her phone to call and saw she had several text messages and voice mails. They must have come through when she was underground on the train.

Ms. Flynn, I can't make it tonight. I think I have the flu. I'm sorry to tell you so late in the day. – Stacey

"No, no, no, no, no. Fuck, fuck, fuck, fuck. No," she muttered, then read the message twice more.

She looked around the room, trying to come up with a solution but failing.

Playing classical music was not like other jobs. There was no calling in—ever—for anything. There was nobody to pick up the slack for you, no stand-in or double to take your place. Come hell or high water, bleeding, vomiting, or losing an appendage, you were at work every day, no matter what. The show must go on.

She wracked her brain, considering who she knew in the city, and quickly checked each one off. Vivian, Charlie, Stephen. All three would be working with her that night. Why hadn't she sought out a second babysitter before now?

She called Mary, who was sympathetic but firm. "I'm sorry," she said. "I really am. Trust me. I understand the sick kid thing, but we need you here, Kate. The concert is in less than a week. Can you bring him? I'm sure someone in the audience can sit with him."

Reluctantly, she dressed Max, who cried when she pulled him away from his warm futon. Despite the heat, she stuffed him into his favorite hoodie, then checked his temperature again.

It was 101.7.

"Shit," she muttered.

"Mommy, that's a bad word."

"You're right. I'm sorry. Did you go potty?"

He nodded.

"Do you have Monkeyz?"

He nodded again.

"All right, then, let's go. You get to come with Mommy to work tonight."

He smiled weakly.

Before they even made it to the L stop, Max was dragging his feet. "Mommy, pick me up."

Kate glanced down at him. "I can't right now, kid. Do you remember why?"

He nodded. "'Cause you got your cello."

"That's right. Come on. We don't want to miss the train." She gently pulled his arm, but he dug in. "Mo-o-my-y-!" He dropped his head back and wailed.

Relenting, she picked him up, shifting her cello case to her back, and hurried to catch the train.

She made it to rehearsal with five minutes to spare, gasping for breath and sweating profusely under all the extra weight.

Stephen greeted her at the door. "What's wrong with Max?"

With a groan, she handed Max to Stephen and put down her cello case. Max immediately began wailing again. Their meeting, *if* it was going to happen, should have been a bit different, but dear God, her back hurt.

She tried not to notice the shock on Stephen's face as he held the child who had his eyes and hair.

"He's sick."

Stephen all but tossed Max back into her arms. "Now you tell me! I can't afford to get sick right now. We have a concert coming up. We have, like, ten concerts coming up!"

"I know!" she snapped, shifting Max to a more comfortable position on her shoulder. "I hear you, Stephen. But I need you. His sitter is sick. I need you to take him. Please. You're going to be sitting in the auditorium until your piece is up to rehearse, right? I'm asking for your help."

"I can't get sick, Kate!"

She shifted Max again. Her back was starting to really hurt. "I'm sorry, but I don't have anyone else, and this is what it's like to be a parent."

Stephen opened his mouth, but Kate cut him off.

"He's too young to sit by himself! Please, just keep him with you in the auditorium until you play. Oh, and keep him away from everyone else in case he's, you know, contagious." She smiled at him hopefully. "Stephen, if you don't help, I don't know what I'm going to do. *Please.*"

He looked from her to Max and back again. "Okay. Come here, buddy." He pried Max's arms from around Kate's neck.

"Thank you. Max, this is my friend Stephen. Can you say hi?"

He shook his head, reaching for Kate.

She brushed his hair back and kissed his damp forehead. "Okay. Well, I have to go play. You're gonna sit with Stephen for a while, okay?"

"No-o-o-o!" Max wailed, his eyes filling with tears.

"I know, buddy, but I need you to, okay? Can you do that for me?"

Max sniffed and wiped his nose on Monkeyz. "Hi, Steph'n."

"Hi. You, uh, you can call me Steve, okay?" Stephen patted his back.

"Stephen, thanks. I know this isn't…ideal."

Stephen nodded and swallowed, his Adam's apple bobbing. "I, uh… We'll be fine."

Kate sprinted up to the stage, took her seat, and pulled out her cello and bow just as Mary tapped the stand with her baton and held up her hands.

Kate leaned her cello against her, still trying to catch her breath, and looked out into the auditorium. Stephen had taken Max to the middle seats, but instead of holding him as Kate would do, Stephen had put Max in the seat next to him.

She set her bow on the strings and waited for Mary to drop the baton. Who didn't want to cuddle Max? There had been times when he cried in public, and random people had stopped to coo at him.

She was being overprotective, her internal mama bear on full alert. Max had Monkeyz, and Stephen was new at this. Still, she felt helpless.

Kate tried to concentrate as they began to play, but she couldn't relax, not when Max was sniffling so close by.

"All right," Mary said, "let's try the second movement."

In the auditorium, Kate heard Max's sniffles turn into outright crying.

It was everything she could do not to get up and go to him. She glanced at Stephen meaningfully, silently begging him to hold Max.

Instead, Stephen patted Max awkwardly on the back. When Max continued to cry, Stephen took him by the hand and led him from the hall.

Kate's heart twisted. She didn't like not being able to see him.

"Don't worry, sweetheart," the viola player sitting next to her said. "He's okay with Stephen. We all do what we have to. You're a good mom for coming into work and making sure he has food on the table."

She blinked back tears. "Thanks."

When they had finished rehearsing the second movement, Mary called for a two-minute break to allow Kate to check on her son.

She exited the stage and entered the hallway outside the auditorium, then stopped short.

Max sat on the carpet. Stephen was bent over the trash can, losing whatever dinner he had eaten.

"Oh my God. What's wrong?" She scooped Max up.

After a long moment, Stephen lifted his head. "I don't…do well…with vomit," he finally managed to say. "He threw up…on me."

"He what?" Kate looked at Max's pale, blotchy face. "You threw up?"

He nodded, looking as if she had rescued him from being tortured.

"I'm so sorry. I've been there." Kate had never been good with vomit herself. When Max first had the flu, she was barely able to stop herself from being sick with worry.

She held him closer, intending to return to the stage and insist on leaving. But at that moment, she saw some of the board members enter the auditorium.

From the stage, Kate could hear Mary tapping the podium to signal that break was over.

Kate reluctantly handed a screaming Max back to Stephen and forced herself to return to the stage.

By the second hour of rehearsal, Kate could no longer focus. She misplayed passages, missing notes left and right, but she no longer cared. She wanted to comfort her sick son.

Her nerves were like a rubber band stretched too tightly. She couldn't do this. It was ridiculous.

No, she wouldn't put a job before her child.

Just as she was about to get up and leave mid-rehearsal, the screaming cut off. Every head turned toward the door, their instruments stumbling for a moment before continuing on, as if they had all hit the same pebble in the road.

The door flew open, and Vivian marched through, holding Max and shooting stern signs at Stephen with her available hand.

For his part, Stephen looked murderous as he ducked this way and then that, trying to find a way to take Max back, reaching over one side of her and then the other.

Relief cooled the stress headache that had been pounding on Kate's temple like a drop of ice on sizzling skin. *Vivian.* He would sit quietly for Vivian. He would be comforted by Vivian. Thank God for Vivian.

Vivian and Charlie, followed by Stephen, found seats. Vivian signed to Max as she rocked him in her lap.

Charlie turned to Stephen and began arguing in a low voice until, with an exasperated look on his face, he stood, his seat folding with a loud smack. He stomped off into the backstage area.

Kate caught Vivian's eye and mouthed, a *thank you*. Vivian nodded and smiled.

The rehearsal continued. Kate was still distracted. She shifted her eyes continually from the sheet music to the auditorium. She knew she needed to focus, but each time she determined to return to the music, she found herself looking at Vivian again.

There was nothing quite as beautiful as Vivian sitting with Max against her chest.

"Kate." She jumped as Mary called on her. "We're ready to begin rehearsing the fourth movement."

Kate felt her cheeks grow hot. "Sorry guys. I'm a mess tonight."

"That's okay. Let's try again."

Kate picked up her bow, glancing back out into the auditorium once more.

Vivian shook her head and signed something that Kate thought might be about not paying attention.

"Right," she muttered to herself and returned her focus to the music in front of her.

Stephen entered the stage a few minutes later, his expression dark. His shirt had been cleaned, a large water spot on the front. He sat a little more aggressively than need be, his foot tapping.

"What's wrong? Why are you so mad that you got help?" Kate whispered, once again not paying quite as much attention as she should while she was watching Vivian and Charlie bustle around Max.

"I just can't see why you didn't ask your girlfriend to sit with him in the first place!"

"She's not my girlfriend! Don't be a dick!"

"Fine!" He looked around the room, everywhere but at her and at the trio in the audience.

Kate sighed. This dynamic between all of them was starting to feel confusing.

Chapter 7

As the musicians packed up their instruments, Kate overheard some of them talking.

"Are you sure she isn't going to eat him?" Mary asked William, the first violinist.

William laughed. "It's not as though she's the nicest person in the world. I'm surprised she knew how to get the kid to settle down."

Kate looked up, realizing that they were talking about Max and Vivian.

"I think it just proves that there is a real live woman somewhere inside the ice queen." Mike, the trumpet player, sneered.

Kate snorted, picturing the grin Vivian usually had when they were together.

"Do you have a counterargument, Kate?" Mike asked. "I mean, it's your kid she has, so—"

"None of you know her very well, do you? Have you ever tried to talk to her at all?" Kate asked, doing her best to keep her tone civil.

The three looked at each other uncertainly.

"I mean," Mary began, "I've talked to her, of course."

"Look." Mike laughed, jerking his head toward a man who was now talking with Vivian in the auditorium. "That poor guy thinks he's going to change her mind about next season's selections. She's going to rip his soul out through his testicles."

Kate flushed. She had thought Stephen's attitude toward Vivian was personal, but they *all* were talking about her as if she were some mythical villain. What the fuck was their problem?

The Loudest Silence

"I don't know why anyone bothers with that mute. She's as stubborn as a mule," Mike continued, then added with a smirk. "Maybe she slipped the kid some gin."

Stephen had packed up his bass and sat next to Kate. "What are you all talking about?"

Mike was wiping down his trumpet. "Feeding time at Queen Elsa's castle."

"To be fair, Vivian's not a mute," Mary said. "She does speak."

"Who cares? Look at her, singing to him like he was her own little animated snowball. You're right, William. She must actually be a woman."

"Well, that's not what I was saying," William answered.

Kate heard Mike say to the person next to him in a stage whisper, "Do you think she'd go out with me? I like those ball crusher types."

"I wouldn't have said it before, but after tonight, I'd say you might have a shot, friend!"

William interjected. "She always brings women to events. I don't believe she dates men."

"The ice queen is a lesbian, huh?" Mike asked.

"Yup."

Kate shook her head in disbelief. Mike was young, still in college, but what about everyone else? They were too old to be this insensitive. She was trying to keep from responding, but how could she not defend the person who was holding her sick son in her lap?

Finally, she spoke up. "So, I'm new. I get that." Her voice wobbled slightly. "And you all have been very nice about my kid tonight. But I want to point out that just because she can't *hear* you does not mean that it's okay to talk about her as if she's a robot. She's a person, and she can read lips. And you're *so* wrong about her."

Everyone stared at her. Kate looked back, ready to throw away the little bit of professionalism she was trying to hold on to.

The clarinet player whooped. "I guess we're all learning that tonight!"

"Knock it off!" Stephen spoke up, his face etched with fury. "She's helping a sick child."

Kate stared at him. He was defending Vivian?

Mike laughed nervously. "I never thought I'd see the day when Stephen Foy defended the ice queen."

"She's a person!" Kate snarled.

"That's right." Stephen jumped in again. "This is completely unprofessional."

"It was just a joke," Mike muttered.

"That's enough, Michael," William said.

Mike looked around. "No one can take a fucking joke now? Fine."

At that moment, Kate understood why Vivian was so outwardly cold. Any sign of humanity and she became a target.

She glanced at Stephen. He still looked as angry as when Vivian had taken Max from him.

Kate finished packing up her cello and stood up.

"Kate," Stephen said.

She turned and softened, wrapping Stephen in a hug. "Thank you."

He hugged her back uncertainly. "Yeah. I mean, that was…" He released her and puffed out his breath.

"Yeah, it was. Thanks for defending her."

He scratched the back of his neck, grimacing.

"You okay? What was wrong with you earlier?"

Stephen merely grunted.

"Were you jealous before Vivian took Max? Is that it?"

"Jealous?" Stephen smirked. "Jealous that she's holding Max and he isn't screaming? Or that she doesn't mind being covered in puke?"

Kate stared at him, astounded by the sudden attitude change. "So you are jealous that she calmed him down when you couldn't."

The anger drained from his face, making him look like a hurt little boy. "I'm sorry. You're right."

"About?"

"Vivian. You're right. I shouldn't have said that. I tried to calm Max down—I did—but I couldn't. He just…" Stephen looked at Kate with sadness in his eyes. "He just really didn't want to be with me. Of course I'm jealous."

"He doesn't know you."

And then his anger was back. "Yeah, well, whose fault is that?"

Kate looked at him, startled. "Are you saying—?"

"No! God, no! It's my fault he doesn't know me. I'm supposed to be his father, and I couldn't even hold him after he…"

"Hey, don't beat yourself up, okay?"

Stephen nodded once.

"I gotta get back to him, but thank you, Stephen. Seriously."

"I hear you defended my honor." Vivian said the moment Kate sat beside her.

"Huh?"

Vivian smiled. "My vision is twenty-twenty. I could see what they were saying," she said, adding under her breath, "I always can."

"Stephen did too. Defended you."

Vivian looked startled. "Mr. Foy?"

Kate nodded, her gaze drifting to her son. "Thank you for taking him," she said, taking Max from Vivian's arms. He sighed deeply, his thumb never leaving his mouth.

She stood watching Vivian, waiting for her to speak. It was clear she wanted to say something.

Kate had an idea of what was on her mind. She reached out and touched the back of Vivian's hand. "You're my friend, Vivian." Kate felt a spark when she touched Vivian's skin.

"Yes, well, thank you." Vivian uncrossed and recrossed her legs. "And please thank Mr. Foy for me as well."

"This is why you keep your professional face on all of the time, isn't it? It's because people talk about you like that no matter what you do."

Vivian studied Kate's face. Finally, she began to sign, speaking in a whisper at the same time. "Talking with my hands"—she held them up—"it's unusual. It's unwelcome. People don't know how to respond. Not only am I a woman in the workplace but I'm a vulnerable woman, a woman with a disability."

Kate opened her mouth to protest, but Vivian silenced her with a hand on her wrist.

"If I don't prove them wrong, they'll walk all over me. They'll exploit my vulnerability, as has been proven time and time again."

Kate reached for Vivian's hand. "I get it. I hate it, but I get it."

Vivian's fingers danced lightly over Kate's hand as if looking for a landing spot.

The moment was broken when Kate noticed the large splotches of vomit on Vivian's white blouse. "Oh shit, Vivian!"

Vivian chuckled. "Every time I tried to get up to wash, it woke him."

"Oh my God! I'm so sorry!" She covered her face with one hand.

"Don't be." Vivian reached over to stroke Max's head. "I'll go clean up now, then I'll give you two a ride home."

"What? No, your car!"

"We can get him something to be sick in, if he needs it."

Kate opened her mouth to protest again, but Vivian held her hand up. "Would you rather he be sick in a bucket in my backseat or on the L?"

"Really, you don't have to," Kate said as she climbed out of the car, holding her son and the Ziploc bag he had thrown up in.

"I found a parking spot. That alone is proof that I should come up and help you."

It was true Vivian had found a parking spot, but it was six blocks away from her apartment. She wasn't sure that counted as fate. The truth was, she was reluctant for Vivian to come with her. Five minutes in this neighborhood and the crisply dressed woman would run away screaming.

"Seriously, Viv—" Her lips smacked shut at the chilling look Vivian gave her. "Okay, then. This way." She retrieved a can of pepper spray from her bag and gripped it in one hand. "I've never actually needed it," Kate said.

They walked silently for a block, Vivian surveying the area. "You know," she said, "perhaps I've been unduly influenced by movies and television, but I always thought the harder neighborhoods of Chicago would be more intimidating. You said that this area was rough, but I find it to be quite charming."

Vivian was looking into the courtyard of the apartment building they were walking past. The grass was green and trimmed, flowers were blooming on the bushes, and lamps lined the walkway.

"Yeah, *that* place is cute."

In truth, Kate's neighborhood wasn't as bad as some—not by a long shot. The hardest parts of the city had few redeeming qualities. Walking through one of those would be a nasty shock to Vivian.

As they walked, the neighborhood began to change. Flower bushes in front of apartment buildings disappeared, giving way to Styrofoam cups, broken beer bottles, and empty chip bags. The glowing streetlamps turned into halogen lights and police surveillance boxes. Empty sidewalks filled with groups of sullen teenagers who looked as if they were itching for a fight.

At last they arrived at Kate's building. "This is it." Kate felt heat rise to her cheeks. "It's fine during the day, but at night—"

"Hey, Snow Bunny," a familiar voice called out. One of the usual men and his friends were crowded around the entrance to her building. "Whew, you stink, girl! Usually you smell so pretty! Let me help you with that boy. He looks heavy. I don't mind playing daddy for a while."

The man's bark was probably worse than his bite, but she squared her shoulders and pushed Vivian through the crowd to the door, averting her gaze to avoid eye contact.

"Damn, Mama! Look at those titties!" One of the other men whooped.

Kate realized that he was talking about Vivian. Her white shirt strained at the bosom, and when Vivian had cleaned up Max's sick, it left the blouse damp and see-through. Frowning, she pushed Vivian firmly into the security doors, grateful that Vivian couldn't hear them.

As they moved down the hallway to the stairs, Kate saw Vivian's nose twitch.

She laughed. The hallway smelled strongly of mold and decay, which even the odor of marijuana, fried fish, and rotten food could not overcome.

She led Vivian up the creaking stairs. Rounding the landing to the third floor, a large cockroach skittered across. She hoped that Vivian hadn't seen it. Most Chicago buildings had roaches, but Kate was willing to bet that there were none where Vivian lived.

Stepping over the bug, Vivian took Max so Kate could open the door to the apartment.

"You're right, Kate. The area is…perhaps less than desirable, but your apartment is cute."

"I think the city is trying to rejuvenate the area," she answered lamely. Turning away from Vivian, Kate pulled off her soiled shirt as quickly as she could—Max had vomited again on the walk from the L—then turned her back to her guest, who had settled with Max on the futon.

"What was the…gentleman downstairs saying to you?"

"Oh. He always offers to help me when I have groceries or I'm carrying Max. I haven't figured out if he's trying to hook up, if he wants to case my apartment, or if he's just trying to be nice."

"I see." Vivian's voice was flat.

"It's not so bad, Viv. I promise."

Vivian clasped her hands in front of her. "Perhaps I can do something. It's possible your lease could be broken."

"No, it's okay. I just spent most of our savings to move here. Plus, where else are we going to find rent this cheap?"

"Kate, surely—"

"I'm good." She pulled on a tank top. "We're good."

"Mommy!" Max sat up suddenly on the futon. Kate had just enough time to grab a pot from the kitchen before he heaved again.

Vivian rubbed his back while Kate wiped his face clean. "Maybe we should have taken him to the ER. Surely this much vomit isn't normal."

Kate chuckled. "You'd be surprised. Let's see how he is in the morning." She retrieved a bottle of Pedialyte and poured him a cup, but Max was buried under his blanket again.

Kate joined Vivian on the futon, Max curled up between them. "Are you heading back home?"

"I'm sorry?"

"I said, are you heading back home?"

"Oh. No, I think I'll stay and help for a bit, if you don't mind. Why don't you change the rest of your clothes?"

Kate hurried into her bedroom, shucking her stained pants and cleaning up as best she could. She pulled on a pair of pajama trunks, then brought a pair to Vivian. "You should take a shower and change. Seriously."

Vivian glanced at the clothes, then at the large windows that faced the street. Even though they were three flights up, the crowd of thugs was visible at the front of the apartments across the street. It would only take one of them to look up and see inside.

Kate closed the blinds.

"Take a shower. You're safe here, Vivian. Look." She pointed at the door, which had a deadbolt, a lock, and a swing guard. "The back door has three locks too."

"I'm being silly, aren't I?" Vivian took the clothes and stood. "Truly, I'm not worried about myself. I'm worried about…" She gave a tight, small smile and disappeared into the bathroom.

It took only minutes for her to emerge with damp hair, a face clean of makeup, and soiled clothes in the plastic bag that Kate had given her.

Kate stared. Vivian wore one of Kate's tank tops and a pair of pink cotton pajama bottoms that hung loosely off her hips. It was Kate's first full glimpse of Vivian Kensington without designer labels and makeup, and she wanted more.

"Is he sleeping?"

Kate nodded as Vivian settled onto the futon on the other side of Max.

"Kate, I'm sorry if I made you uncomfortable before," Vivian said.

"It's okay. I just hate that I can't help him."

"You are helping him." Vivian wrapped an arm around Kate.

Kate sighed and rested her head against Vivian's shoulder. She tilted her head up so Vivian could see her lips. "Not in any real way. I guess—"

But just then Max woke up, ready for his next *Exorcist* re-creation.

———

Groaning sleepily, Kate wiped at a tickle at her nose. She wiped again, but when she opened her eyes, she found that the thing tickling her was a wisp of brown hair.

She and Vivian were leaning back against the cushions with Max curled up between them, but their shoulders and heads had shifted together until they were touching.

What was it about Vivian? She had said that she wanted children of her own, but then she said that she wasn't interested in being involved with someone who already had a child. It was clear that she had latched on to Max. It was obvious when you saw them together that Vivian was getting as much out of her relationship with Max as he was getting out his relationship with her. Kate wasn't sure if this was something she should encourage or if she should limit their time together. She had rules about dating as long as she had Max. How had they bypassed the actual dating and stepped into a quagmire where Max could get hurt?

Kate shifted, groaning, her back still sore from lugging her cello and Max to rehearsal the previous night.

Vivian stirred, yawning as she stretched.

"I guess we fell asleep."

Vivian nodded.

"Mommy?" Now Max was awake too.

"Hey, kid. How are you feeling?"

He wiggled off the futon. "I want *brekfast!*"

Chapter 8

Two weeks later, Kate had lived through the bug that her son had given her...as had Vivian, Charlie, and Stephen. And they had come out of it in one piece.

Illness behind them all, they turned their attention to the next big event: Max's birthday.

The summer had flown by, and now it was three days to September. Max was yanking hard on her arm to get her to hurry up, excitement bubbling over and spilling everywhere. "Mommy, come on!" he pleaded, trying to run despite her not moving fast enough. "We're gonna be late to my birfday *party*!"

"Max, wait! This can't be right." Kate checked the address on her phone again.

Google Maps identified a huge warehouse on Wabash one block from Michigan Avenue as the location of Vivian's apartment. not far from where Vivian had taken her to see The Bean. Vivian had said the building was still under renovation, but this one looked abandoned, and there was a homeless man sleeping in the doorway.

Kate had the impression that Vivian not only made a great deal of money but also came from a wealthy family. She must expect a certain standard of living. But where was the doorman? Where was the valet?

Shoving her phone into her pocket, Kate carried Max past the sleeping man.

The lobby was sparsely furnished yet gave the impression that the building would be beautiful when it was finished. The exposed brick walls looked new, and the wood flooring shone like a jewel. The chandelier hanging from the middle of the ceiling was a spiral of clear-blown glass sticking out at sharp angles, equal parts art and light fixture.

On the far wall was an architect's drawing of something called "K Lofts" with the promise that they were coming soon. Beside the large poster, two security guards watched her from behind a counter.

She smiled awkwardly and moved past them but stopped when she realized the elevator required a key. She chewed her lip nervously and turned around to approach the guards. "We're here to see Vivian Kensington." She put Max down, shifting her bag on her shoulder. He clung tightly to her leg, awed by the uniformed men.

"Name?"

"Kate Flynn," she squeaked.

One of the men consulted his clipboard, then without saying a word, led her to the elevator and turned the key.

Inside the elevator, mirrored silver walls reflected the black marble flooring. A small table to the right held a vase of white and lavender lilies. But what really convinced her that they were in the right place was the small handmade sign that read *Max Flynn's birthda – PNTHSE.*

"All the way to the top," the guard's voice boomed in a deep bass.

As the elevator rose, so did Kate's nerves. Vivian was obviously well-off. She wore designer suits that she had probably picked up in the Magnificent Mile shopping district, where Saks was nestled along with high-end boutiques like Armani, Versace, and Coach. It wasn't as though Kate hadn't known that already.

When Vivian had said that her building was under construction, Kate never considered that she meant the building she owned. *K Lofts—K for Kensington.* It seemed pretty obvious now. Vivian was *rich*.

Most of the foster homes Kate had passed through had consisted of two people who used the subsidies from fostering as their main source of income. She had spent her early teen years slinging burgers, and when that wasn't enough, she stole food and clothes for herself and her foster siblings. She and Max were comfortable, even well-off compared to some, but no one went into classical music expecting to earn enough for a penthouse with two security guards. *How* was she supposed to let ten kids run around in a fancy penthouse? Things would get broken; she just knew it.

The elevator doors slid open, and Kate led Max from the elevator onto a high catwalk on the second of three floors.

The catwalk followed the length of the space, giving way on either side to large, suspended rooms.

The living room, with a TV and a set of couches, was to the left at one end of the catwalk. Along the back wall, a set of industrial-looking stairs led up to an open space on the third floor. To the right was an office with a desk, a computer, and a treadmill.

The far wall was built of glass bricks that let in filtered daylight. Along the entire opposite wall were floor-to-ceiling grid windows from which Kate could see a rooftop patio with a pool, some table and chair sets, and a barbecue grill. The panorama of lights along Lake Shore Drive, Grant Park, and Lake Michigan could be seen in the distance.

To the left below the catwalk was a huge kitchen with a stainless-steel island and matching appliances. To the right, black curtains were half drawn over a pair of glass doors. Just visible through the space in the curtains was a bed. The middle space of the room was a sparsely furnished sitting area containing a couch set and some side tables.

As Kate looked around, taking everything in, she heard an iPhone ringtone. Simultaneously, purple lights flashed in the corner of each room. Kate spotted a device on the table in the room below with a screen and keyboard on one side and a long cord connected to an iPhone on the other.

"Viv'n!" Max squealed, pointing out toward the patio. He ran down the stairs to the left of them, but Kate was frozen in place.

Vivian stood on the patio, her hands on her hips, still unaware that anyone had arrived. She was looking down at a table littered with birthday supplies. Her eyes were hidden behind a pair of huge *Breakfast at Tiffany's* sunglasses. She wore a seafoam-green bikini. Two gold chains crisscrossed from her waist and over her hips. Her arms and legs were sculpted, and her stomach was flat and tight. Her bronze skin glowed in the afternoon light.

Kate swallowed through a suddenly dry mouth.

Vivian caught sight of Max running toward her and smiled, her hands moving quickly.

Kate spotted the sign for "mom" and knew if she didn't move, Vivian would find her still standing mesmerized by the elevator. She headed downstairs to join her son. "Wow, this place doesn't look like you at all. It's so cluttered and unorganized. How can you live in this mess?"

Vivian smiled. "I like structure."

"Yeah, well, you do realize that all of this black and white is in serious danger of being ruined by sticky three-year-old hands. And there's going to be a cake later. *Chocolate.* Do I need to say this again?"

Vivian scoffed. "I'll have you know that Max is four now."

Kate laughed.

Behind them a bright yellow light flashed twice. Vivian made the sign for "door."

"Who is it?" Kate asked.

"I don't know," Vivian said coyly. "This is your party."

Vivian turned her attention back to Max, her hands moving again.

"What did she say?" Kate asked him. The gold belly chains had distracted her, and she had completely missed Vivian's hand movements.

"She told us to go to the bathroom and change," Max said.

Kate waited to greet the new arrival, who turned out to be the parent of a recent playdate, followed by Charlie storming in as if she owned the place. Then Kate slipped into the downstairs bathroom to change.

She had spent days debating over what to wear for the occasion. That morning, she had shaved and manicured everything that could be shaved and manicured, telling herself that it had nothing to do with Vivian or the fact that this would be the first time Vivian saw so much of her.

She pulled her hair back into a ponytail, then stripped down and pulled on her black swimsuit. As much as she wanted to wear something like the little red number she had just spotted Charlie in, she knew a full day of chasing Max would threaten the life of something so flimsy.

When she stepped out of the bathroom, Stephen was standing on the floor above, just outside the elevators. She called up to him.

He looked thankful to see someone he knew and came barreling down the stairs in his swim trunks. "Hi! Where's the birthday boy? Swimming with the ice queen?"

"Stephen," Kate warned.

He laughed good-naturedly. "I'm sorry. I'll be good. I'm just excited to be here. Thanks for inviting me."

"Relax. It's just a kids' party."

"Right." He nodded and thrust a package toward her that was wrapped in red and green. "Sorry. Christmas paper was all I had."

"It's okay." Kate was touched by his obvious nerves. "You okay?"

Stephen shifted on his feet. "Yeah, just, you know, a little nervous meeting him when he's actually aware of his surroundings."

Kate was nervous too.

She pushed the thought away. "Let's add your gift to the pile and go find Max."

They found Max exploring the various pool toys. "Hey, kid," Kate said. "Do you remember Stephen?"

Max looked up, studying him, one eye closed against the sun. His shorts hung low on his hips, his belly hanging over them.

Stephen smiled. "Happy birthday, little man."

Max continued to stare.

"Max, what do you say?"

He looked at his mother, then looked back at Stephen, still wary. "Thank you."

Stephen nodded. It was clear to Kate that he couldn't think of anything else to say.

Finally, unable to take the awkward silence, Kate said, "Max, why don't you see if Charlie needs any help."

"Okay!" he shouted and dashed off.

Stephen rubbed a hand over his face. "He hates me. Did you see that? He remembers puking on me, and he hates me."

Kate snorted. "No, kids are just like that with people they don't know well. Give him time."

She handed him a beer and showed him to a chair. Then she approached Vivian, who was busy blowing up balls for the pool. "Anything I can do?"

Vivian pulled off her sunglasses and bit the earpiece, scanning Kate's body from top to bottom.

Kate felt her face flush, the heat radiating down into her toes and back up again. She swallowed, then said again, "Is there anything I can do?"

Vivian shook her head, still nibbling on the glasses, her gaze never leaving Kate.

"Oh, stop it." Kate playfully pulled the glasses away and dropped them on a nearby table. Then she went to find Charlie and Max.

"Okay, line up!" Kate called to the children by the shallow end of the pool.

Max was prancing with excitement, raising first one foot and then the other as though the ground was too hot to stand on.

"All right, Jamal. Come here. Let me check." She checked the nozzle on his water wing to be sure it was closed and tight. "No drowning on my watch, okay, soldier?"

"Yes, ma'am!"

Kate gave him a high five and he turned and threw himself into the pool with reckless abandon. "Shelby? You're up! All right, kid, no swim gear for the expert swimmer. Gimme a high five. All right!"

She checked each child, giving them high fives and sending them into the pool until she got to Max. "Okay, Mister Birthday Boy!"

Max grinned and pushed his chest out proudly. He had finished his beginner's swimming certificate the year before.

Kate pretended to check him anyway, squeezing his arms as though they were water wings.

"Mommy!" He laughed, pulling away from the tickle. "Those are my arms!"

"They are?"

"Yeah!" He rolled his eyes, imitating Kate perfectly.

"Okay, you're good. Have fun."

"Yay!" Max leaped into the pool, splashing happily.

Once the kids were all in the pool, Kate's attention was drawn to Vivian on the other side. She had finished putting out the plates and napkins and now looked back at Kate over the table, rubbing her stomach with one hand.

Kate waved her hand. "I know that pose. What's wrong?"

Vivian shook her head and said something back.

"I can't hear you!" Kate called out.

"What?"

Kate cupped her hand to her ear.

Across the pool, Vivian signed.

"I can't—" Kate shook her head. "What?"

The Loudest Silence

Vivian's hands dropped, her face pinched in annoyance. She looked around as if looking for Charlie.

When Kate caught Vivian's eyes again, she said, "Okay, I'm coming to you."

Vivian nodded.

Kate had just started around the pool when she felt something cold grab her ankle. The next thing she knew, she was in the water. "Stephen!" she garbled when she broke the surface. "You are *so* lucky that I didn't have my phone!"

He laughed. "Look, Flynn, look. Hey, Max." He smiled at Max and sang the first line of "Baby Shark."

Max dove under the water, lifting his hand like a fin at the back of his head.

Kate groaned. "And here I thought we were finally done with that song."

Max swam to her and tried to climb up onto her shoulders, nearly pulling Kate under in the process.

"Jesus, kid!" Kate gasped. "Hold on, hold on."

"Flyyyynn," Stephen whined.

"Hold on! I need to talk to Vivian, okay?" She kissed Max's cheek and let him swim off, splashing Stephen and sticking out her tongue as she went to the side of the pool where Vivian stood waiting for her.

"How's the water?"

Kate reached a hand out for Vivian's. "Why don't you come in and see?"

Vivian shook her head.

"Oh, come on."

"Oh, no. I don't think so." Vivian winked, holding Kate's gaze.

The pool suddenly felt warm.

With a hum, Vivian turned and walked away. Kate stared at her swaying hips.

"Hey, Kate. You okay?"

The voice jerked Kate out of her daze, and she looked up guiltily at Charlie.

Charlie looked at her curiously. "You have this really weird look on your face. Do you need resuscitation?"

Instead of responding, Kate dove back under the water.

As she swam and played with Max and the other children, Kate found her gaze returning again and again to Vivian in her seafoam-green bikini. Vivian was in constant motion, attending to every detail of the party, hugging Max and smothering him with kisses whenever he got out of the pool.

Kate got out of the pool just before lunch, grabbed a towel, and sat next to where Vivian had finally settled to watch the kids. "This is all amazing. Thank you."

"It does seem like he's having fun, right?"

Kate reached over and touched her arm. "Are you kidding? He's having the time of his life."

"Good. That's good," Vivian said, still watching the children in the pool until, sensing Kate's gaze, she looked back at her.

Kate quickly looked away, returning her attention to the kids.

Vivian signed something to Charlie across the pool, and Charlie signed back with a roll of her eyes.

"Are you two talking about me?" Kate asked.

But Vivian was frowning in the direction of the pool. She followed Vivian's gaze.

Stephen was holding Max on his shoulders. Approaching them was a teenage boy with a child on his shoulders.

"Are they... are they playing Chicken?"

Kate exchanged a look with Vivian and didn't feel better about the fact that she looked as nervous as Kate felt. "Uh, Stephen?"

Without warning, the other child pushed Max over, and he went flying backward.

"Shit!" Kate scrambled to her feet, running with outstretched arms as Max fell headfirst toward the stone alongside the pool.

Just in time, Stephen spun and caught Max. "I got him! I got him!"

Max began to cry.

Her mind showed her blood and broken bones. Kate took him from Stephen and ran her hands over him, frantically looking for injuries. When her hands collided with Vivian's, she realized that Vivian was doing the same thing. She looked up to meet Vivian's eyes, then looked quickly back down at her son.

The Loudest Silence

When Kate was sure he was unhurt, she laughed, her voice wobbling. "Look at you!" she said. "You went freaking flying, kid!" She knew from experience that the more upset she was, the more Max would be. She nudged Vivian. "He's a superhero, isn't he? He just flew through the air."

Vivian played along, plastering on a smile.

"Did you get a superhero cape for that stunt?" Kate asked

Max's tears slowed. "No."

"You didn't?" Vivian laughed nervously. "Well, we must fix that! A fall like that deserves a cape!"

With that, Max seemed to forget his fright and giggled. After a cuddle, Kate sent him back to the pool.

Vivian touched her arm. "Are you all right? You're shaking."

Kate nodded. "Yeah. Just scared."

"Me too."

Stephen pulled himself out of the pool. "Kate, I'm sorry. I didn't realize…" he started.

Vivian rounded on him. "Surely you have more intelligence than what we just witnessed, Mr. Foy! If you cannot play responsibly, then perhaps you should not be allowed near the children at all."

The worry in Stephen's face evaporated. "He was pushed. I didn't mean to let go of him. He's okay, though, yeah?"

"By pure coincidence only."

Stephen's mouth opened and then closed. Without another word, he headed over to the cooler of beer.

Kate took a deep breath, trying to get her stomach to unclench. "That scared the crap out of me."

Vivian squeezed Kate's hand. "Well, he's just fine. Look," she said, nodding toward the pool. "See? He's okay."

She nodded, her eyes moistening. "He's just all I have, you know?"

"I understand." Vivian had her fingers wrapped around Kate's palm.

"I have to go to the bathroom!"

Vivian let her hand slide away. Kate looked down at the little girl standing in front of her. "Okay, sweetheart, I'll take you."

"That's all right, Kate. I'll take her." Vivian looked at the child. "Thank you for not going in the pool, missy."

"My mama says that's dirty."

Kate watched as Vivian took the girl's little hand and led her inside.

After lunch, Charlie put music on to enforce the thirty-minute wait rule. The children began jumping up and down in their three- and four-year-old versions of dancing. Charlie reached down and picked up Max, spinning with him as they laughed together.

Vivian and Charlie were both so good with Max. He loved them too. As usual, a sliver of sickness passed through her stomach. Was it wise to let them get so close to him? The season would end in January. One more season after that and it would be over. Would Max remember them once they had moved on?

"The kid's a natural," Stephen said, coming up behind her.

"He is. I've thought about putting him in dance classes. Maybe I will next season."

"Does he take after his mother?"

"I don't know. I think all of the family talent went to him." Kate watched as Max signed to Vivian, who nodded and signed back, taking him from Charlie and making her way to one of the speakers. Vivian took one of his hands and gently pressed it to the speaker grill. Max squealed and nodded, then began to jump and spin again. Vivian moved her hips in perfect time to the music.

Kate watched Vivian dance, her hair bouncing as she moved. She imagined running a hand down Vivian's hips and nuzzling her glistening collarbone.

Vivian looked up straight at Kate and beckoned her with one finger.

"Be right back," she told Stephen, never dropping her gaze from Vivian.

Max ran toward her and, grabbing her hand, pulled her to where Vivian still danced. Charlie joined them, completing the circle.

Kate had always been a sucker for a woman who could dance. Who knew that Vivian would be so good at it?

"Mind if I join you?" Stephen moved tentatively to join the small circle.

"Sure." Kate made room for him.

After more swimming, the cake was cut and Max opened his gifts. Soon after, parents began to gather their children to leave.

Kate wrapped Max up in a towel. "Did you have fun?"

"Yeah!"

"I'm so glad, my big birthday boy!" Vivian said, appearing beside them. "Why don't you help pick up those paper plates, okay?"

"Okay!" Max said exuberantly, too high on his big day to argue.

"My, my. That is something I never expected to see."

Kate turned to follow Vivian's gaze. Stephen and Charlie were standing on the other side of the pool.

Vivian crossed her arms. "I didn't think they would ever speak civilly again after he cheated on her."

"Cheated on her?"

Vivian looked at Kate. "Why do you think I dislike him so much?"

The dirty plates had been picked up, the trash taken out, and the furniture returned to its original position. Soon Kate and Max would have to leave for the train.

Stephen cornered her as she was gathering up their things. He shifted his weight uneasily, looking at the floor.

Kate spoke first. "What's up, Stephen?"

"I had fun today." He looked up at her.

"Well, that was kind of the—Oh. You want to do it again." Max had seemed to enjoy Stephen's company. And other than Max getting pushed off Stephen's shoulders, their meeting had gone well.

"Yeah. Yeah, I do."

She nodded slowly, processing.

"I don't want you to feel like I'm stepping on your toes, okay? I don't. This is all new. I don't know what I want. But I know I want to try to connect with the boy."

"Right."

"And we did well today, didn't we?"

"Yeah. Yeah, you did." She studied Stephen's face. His dark features were so much like her son's.

"I can tell that this throws you, so I'm gonna go. I just...I just want the chance, okay?"

She nodded.

"Okay. I'll see you at rehearsal, yeah?"

She nodded again.

As he turned, a lock of his hair fell into his eyes. He dragged a thumb across his forehead to push it back.

The move hit her like a punch. How many times had she seen Max do exactly that? How was it possible for Max to have mannerisms from a man he didn't even know?

She reached out to stop him from walking away. "Stephen."

He turned back to her expectantly.

"You can't."

His face fell.

"What I told you before is still true. Just because today went well doesn't mean that Max is less vulnerable."

"Wha—"

Kate held up her hand. "I know you don't understand, Stephen. I know. But you have no idea what it's like to be a dad."

Stephen leaned in. "Well, how the hell am I supposed to learn, Flynn?" he asked in a rasping whisper.

"I know. But if you start showing up and then disappear, it will break his heart."

He opened his mouth to protest, but she interrupted, needing to get the words out. "If you decide you want to be his father and then you decide it's too much, it will damage him in ways you'll never know. If you're going to be in his life, you have to mean it. Trust me, I went through it over and over again when I was a kid."

The color drained from his face. He nodded.

"Think about it. Come over in a couple of days, and we'll talk. Okay?"

He nodded again, working the muscles in his jaw, then turned to leave. She watched him go.

"What was that?"

She turned to Vivian. "He wants to spend time with Max."

"Oh? Are you going to let him?"

Kate opened her mouth, but she didn't have an answer. Finally she shook her head. "I don't see how I can say no. If he wants to be involved, how can I deny that to Max? At the same time, if he doesn't follow through…" She trailed off. Then without thinking, she reached for Vivian and pulled her into a hug.

Vivian returned the embrace, burying her face in Kate's hair, then turned to rest her head on her shoulder.

The moment Vivian's arms closed around her, Kate's skin tingled. She was vibrantly aware of Vivian's cheek against her collarbone and her hair tickling her chin.

Feeling suddenly awkward, Kate abruptly released Vivian.

As if stung, Vivian turned away fast and headed down the stairs.

"Vivian?" Kate followed her, placing a hand on Vivian's shoulder. She pulled it back immediately. She shouldn't have touched her. What had she been thinking? When Vivian turned to face her again, Kate asked, "Are you okay? Was that not okay?"

Vivian stared at her wordlessly, her thoughts hidden behind her sunglasses.

Kate caught the set of her jaw. "Oh. You're *mad* at me!" she blurted out. "Why are you mad at me?"

"Hey, Max, you want to show me your new basketball?" Charlie appeared, breaking up the tension. "We could play some one on one."

Kate watched the two go, wishing she could leave with them.

"I'm sorry. I wasn't thinking. I shouldn't have touched you like that."

"I'm not mad at you, Kate! I'm frustrated. Can't you see the difference?" The words tumbled out of Vivian's mouth as if she had held them back for a very long time.

Kate frowned. She had clearly missed something. "What?"

Vivian took a step back, her hands on her hips. "You're just going to let Stephen into Max's life? He humiliated my best friend in front of her colleagues. He cheated on her at a work function."

That was news to Kate. "That's horrible. But, Viv, the situation with me and Stephen is different. This isn't about Stephen's history with Charlie. This is about Max and his biological father."

Vivian scoffed. "Then what about the fact that he left you, Kate?"

"What?"

"He found out you were having a baby, and instead of staying around to be in Max's life, he left you to raise him all by yourself!" Vivian was shouting now, her hand shaking as she pointed at the door Max had disappeared through with Charlie.

"Whoa!" Kate raised her hands, ignoring the sting of Vivian's words. That was something she tried not to feel if she could help it. Where was this coming from? "That's not—"

"He has missed every day of this boy's life, and you're going to let him walk in and be his father because it's convenient now?"

"Hey!" She reached forward to grab Vivian's flying hands. It was beginning to feel as if Vivian was upset about something else. "What's really going on here?"

Vivian's hands twitched in Kate's. She stared at her, her lip curled in a sneer.

Tentatively, Kate reached forward and pulled off Vivian's sunglasses, expecting to see fire in her eyes. Instead she saw hurt.

"I don't want him to be the one in Max's life, Kate."

"What does that even mean?" she asked.

Vivian gently removed her hands from Kate's and balled them into fists at her side. "*I* want to be in your lives, yours and Max's! You deserve more than a man who is known for his bad deeds."

Kate stared, her mouth hanging open.

"How long are we going to do this, Kate? How long are we going to pretend?"

"What do you mean?"

"Kate!" Vivian said, exasperated.

She looked at Vivian, her head already shaking. They didn't talk about this. They never had, and that was probably good. "It's not that simple, Vivian. You know that."

"But we both know what we want."

Kate snorted. "Oh yeah?" she asked. "How can you know what I want when I don't even know what I want?"

When had they moved so close together? She could feel the heat of Vivian's body.

"Are you sure?" Vivian's voice was gravelly even as she whispered. "Are you sure, Kate? Because I can tell you exactly what you want."

"And what's that?" Kate asked and bit her lower lip. Her skin tingled as if every cell were on fire.

Vivian reached up and gently squeezed Kate's cheek. She threw her head back and laughed, acting like the answer was the most obvious thing in the world. "Me. You want *me*."

Chapter 9

"Come out with me tomorrow night." Vivian said it as though it were the simplest thing in the world.

"Yeah, okay." They went out all the time. No reason not to go out with her again.

"No. Come out with me on a date."

"What?" Vivian wanted a date? "But, Vivian, you don't date women with kids, and you don't date hearing women. You were very clear about that."

Vivian's eyes flashed, exciting and terrifying Kate at the same time. "I think we're past that, aren't we?"

All right, if Kate were honest and they were talking about things they didn't normally talk about, then they probably were. But Vivian had told her she didn't date women like her. And Vivian was still president of the board. Didn't that matter now?

"Come out with me. Let's go dancing."

"Vivian…" She so wanted to, but she needed to be convinced.

"Kate." Vivian took her hand and squeezed it gently. It felt so warm and so soft that it distracted her from her arguments.

She loved Vivian's hands. She had since the first time she had seen them dance. She liked seeing them against her skin. She laced her fingers with Vivian's. When she looked up to meet her eyes again, she was beaming.

"Viv, there's so many… How can we…"

"Whatever obstacles there might be, we're already past them or in them. I'm not asking for anything except a date, okay?"

Kate swallowed. She shouldn't. She knew she couldn't. It went against her rules. She nodded. "Okay," she said. "Yes."

The Loudest Silence

She was jittery when she got up the next morning, so she decided to skip breakfast and lay off coffee for the day. She sat down with her cello to give her fingers something to do. Besides, practicing was a good way to process when she couldn't make up her mind about something.

She practiced longer than usual, reveling in the musical vibration that massaged the stress from her limbs, her own at-home sound therapy.

Thankfully, Max was happy to play with his new toys. He was especially fond of the set of superhero action figures that Vivian had given him. Vivian could do no wrong when it came to her son.

Me. You want me. The words shivered up her spine.

Maybe the truth was that Vivian could do no wrong with both of them. She would pick Kate up this evening, giving Kate all day to wrap her head around the situation.

When Kate had first become aware of her attraction to Vivian, she had decided not to get involved with her.

Could Max handle losing Vivian if—when—their relationship ended? Even if things worked out, her contract would be up soon. Max already loved her so much. Was Kate being selfish to put him through another separation? Because separation was coming either way. Either she and Vivian wouldn't work out or the contract would end.

She pulled on her bow, soothed by the moan of the strings.

Vivian was president of the board, and WCCE was a small group. What would happen if it ended badly? She didn't think Vivian would fire her. Even if she wanted to, she couldn't legally. But it could still be awkward.

And Kate…was hearing.

And Max. Really, Max.

But this was *Vivian*: beautiful, complex Vivian. The woman who held her sick son and smiled as if she had a secret that Kate would want to know.

Kate wanted this date with Vivian. She was all in. *Max* was all in.

She dropped her bow arm, letting it fall to her side. She had a date with *Vivian*. And she knew her decision; it had been made already.

Kate threw on a favorite going-out dress and heels. She ruffled her hair a bit, refusing to spend much time in front of the mirror. Then she planted herself onto the futon, twiddling her thumbs and tapping her toes. The moment she heard a knock, she shot up and threw the door open, wincing as it slammed against the wall.

"The downstairs door is not very secure. Every time I come over, it's unlocked and—what?"

Vivian ran her hands up and down the tight maroon dress that accentuated her skin and eyes, twisting to check that nothing was amiss before looking back up at Kate, frowning.

Kate snapped her jaw shut and picked up her keys and wallet. Immediately she began to fiddle with them.

Pretty, She was very pretty.

Charlie had picked up Max a few hours earlier for a sleepover.

Vivian offered a hand to Kate, and they started down the stairs.

The men were hanging around outside as usual, cigarettes hanging from their lips.

Kate didn't usually dress up like this when they were around, not willing to bring unwanted attention to herself. When she was by herself, she often slipped out the back door into the alley. But that was risky too, and it smelled of mold and urine.

Kate pulled her hand away from Vivian, watching the men peripherally as she and Vivian crossed into the courtyard. The men turned as they passed, openly appraising them. They walked a little faster, hurrying to the train stop.

It was dark by the time they had got off the L. They worked their way down Halstead to Boystown, holding hands and grinning at the purple-haired passersby and half-naked men. Kate smiled up at the men hanging out of windows, enjoying their catty remarks. The music, the rainbow striping on the street, the slightly sleazy ads—everything reminded her of her time in New York City.

A man passing them on the sidewalk said something to Vivian. Kate tapped her shoulder and pointed at him.

The man snapped his fingers over his head. "Look at you! Get it, girl! You go!"

Vivian laughed, swaying her hips with a sass that would have put RuPaul to shame, and gave him a high five.

They continued to the club Vivian had in mind.

"Dancing, huh?"

Vivian gave her a pull. "Come on, you."

The bar had been built from a huge warehouse. The dancefloor, already full, was dead center with a bar to the left and right. Strobe lights flashed to the rhythm of the music.

"Are you ready?" Vivian signed as she spoke, already swaying.

Kate watched her, still grasping her hand. The lights reflected off her hair and sparkled in her eyes. She pulled Kate into the throng of dancers.

For the first time since Kate had met her, Vivian looked free: free from the chains of her job, of her deafness, of all the judgment others put on her. Her shoulders were relaxed, her smile easy. She was radiant.

"What does that look mean?" Vivian asked, pulling Kate closer and moving against her.

"What is this like for you? How can you hear it? Or is it rude to ask something like that?"

Vivian signed a few words, but all Kate caught was the word *music*. "Can I show you?" she yelled over the music.

Vivian beckoned her to the farthest corner of the dance area, where the beat pounded through the floor. "What're you—?"

But Vivian simply covered Kate's eyes with one hand, cutting her off, and placed her other hand on Kate's breastbone.

Her heart beat harder at Vivian's touch, matching the music vibrating around them. Vivian moved to the beat and, with a finger on Kate's sternum, tapped out the rhythm.

"I can't hear it. But I can *feel* it. I can also feel it in my feet," she said. "The floor vibrates."

When the music segued to a different rhythm, Vivian pulled Kate to the bar and ordered a round of drinks for them.

They finished their first quickly. They drank the second much more slowly, leaning on the bar, their shoulders and hips touching, sending bursts of static between them.

After the third drink, they were back out on the dancefloor, their hair flying, their bodies twisting to the beat. People bumped into them, but they stuck together, tittering each time someone else's body pushed them closer together.

Kate watched Vivian dance, watched her full red lips, all too aware of how little space was between them.

She didn't know if the drinks were to blame for this feeling, but she knew if she wasn't careful, if she saw Vivian smile hungrily at her one more time, she would lose control.

With each song, the space between them grew smaller until, with a twist of hips and a spin, their bodies brushed. Kate lost the rhythm when she realized she was only a breath away from Vivian's exposed neck. She could smell her skin, feel her warmth, see a bead of sweat trailing down the curve of her neck. She ached to touch her, to pull her close.

Without giving herself time to think, she let her hand fall to Vivian's waist. Vivian shivered against her touch, and she rolled her hips closer until they were touching.

Vivian smiled, her eyes twinkling. Kate pulled back, embarrassed by her bold move. Then Vivian pushed her, forcing Kate to turn in a half circle, and Vivian's hips were brushing in a circle over her rear while her arms wrapped around her waist.

Kate leaned back against her, and Vivian pressed tighter, whispering in her ear, "I told you that you wanted me, darling."

Kate tried to regain her equilibrium, to steady her racing pulse. She could feel Vivian's warm breath on her neck, igniting a fire in her core.

She pulled away from Vivian's arms and turned around, but Vivian kept her grasp. Finally, she smiled coquettishly and made as if to remove her arms.

Reflexively, Kate held them in place against her. She opened her mouth to tell Vivian that she didn't want her to let go, that she wanted to feel her hands on her, but no words came out. Vivian pulled Kate against her again, holding her possessively. Kate groaned.

Kate dropped her head onto Vivian's shoulder, breathing into Vivian's neck, but Vivian pushed her away just enough to look into her eyes.

At that moment, something clicked into place for Kate. She needed Vivian. She needed to touch her, to taste her.

Vivian ran her hand through Kate's hair and down her neck, then caressed the lips with her thumb. She moved her lips. Although there was no sound, Kate understood her perfectly. *"Let's go."*

She nodded.

A few minutes later, they were sitting together on the train, their thighs touching. As they walked to Kate's building, their hands brushed. There was no need for words.

They reached Kate's door. She fumbled with the keys, in too much of a hurry, until finally, using all of her concentration, she unlocked each of the bolts.

The door had barely closed behind them when she felt Vivian's arms close around her waist, felt her soft lips brush against her neck. She reached around and took the keys from Kate, dropping them on the coffee table.

Kate hadn't felt this level of intensity in a very long time. She wasn't sure of what to do next, so she stepped away from Vivian's embrace, kicked off her heels, and ran her hand through her hair. Vivian leaned against the wall, her eyes glowing, never leaving Kate. She smiled, basking in the feeling of desire coming off of Vivian in waves, feeling sexier than she had in a long time. She clicked off the light and turned toward her bedroom.

Then Vivian was there with her, and she reached behind her, unzipped her dress, and pushed it off her shoulders. She ran her hands down Kate's arms and then back up until she cupped her face, gently lifting it until their eyes met.

Vivian's eyes were full of emotion when Kate looked into them, surprising her. Under the sensual smoldering that Vivian was so good at, what Kate saw was raw. It was pleasure, pain, possession, apprehension, and joyous happiness. It made Kate's breath catch in her throat as the realization came: if they did this, it would be so much more than sex. It would be the start of a relationship, a serious one even.

With that Kate slowly leaned forward and brushed her lips lightly against Vivian's, touching, but not kissing; the rest would be Vivian's choice.

She waited.

Vivian parted her lips just a bit, and a small sound rose from her throat: a little whimper, perhaps a moan, that sent shivers through Kate's body. She wanted to pull her close and hold her, to hug her close in the way that Vivian had held her at the club—tightly and possessively.

Her stomach gave a clench as Vivian pulled her in by the small of the back before her ghosting lips closed the distance, fitting to Kate's, and Kate accepted them willingly. There was a quick hiss of warm air as Vivian's breath left her in a rush, making Kate's hovering hands close on her arms.

The kiss only lasted a few seconds before Vivian pulled back.

Kate didn't know what was on her face, but she could feel how tightly she was holding on to Vivian's upper arms.

A small smirk drifted across Vivian's face, and then she was there again, with her lips traveling over Kate's, making Kate marvel over their softness, over the taste of her lipstick. At the press of Vivian's lips, Kate's parted automatically. She slipped her hands down to Vivian's ribs, hovering high, forcing herself to stop there as, with a skill that had her weak, Vivian met her tongue and gently brushed against it.

The kiss was agonizing— in the way Vivian moved, her lips constantly distancing and then reshaping with Kate's, in the light brush of her tongue along her own as if she knew exactly what would make Kate's head pop. Maybe she did; sometimes it seemed as if Vivian were looking into her soul. Maybe she really could read Kate like a book and took pleasure in unveiling her secrets.

"Mmmm," Vivian hummed with obvious relish, as if she had been thirsty for months and was finally able to enjoy a sip of the finest wine. She ran one hand up the back of Kate's neck and into her hair, clutching tightly.

Kate shivered and pressed into her, walking her backward toward the bed, kissing Vivian's slender throat until, with a final push, she and Vivian tumbled onto the bed, their foreheads very nearly colliding as they landed.

Kate pushed herself up until she was straddling Vivian so that she could take in her breasts, the line down her stomach, her hips.

"God, you're beautiful," she whispered.

She leaned down and slowly traced a path up Vivian's stomach with her tongue

Vivian shuddered, and she reached up to fold her hands into Kate's hair again.

In response, Kate trailed fingers over Vivian's breasts and then cupped them firmly.

That made Vivian pull Kate's head down for another kiss. She pressed against her until Kate's hips began to move against Vivian's, until Kate pushed her thigh between Vivian's legs.

Vivian's head fell back, and she made a loud, coarse sound.

The sound was startlingly different in timbre and volume from Vivian's normal speaking voice, and Kate froze. For only a brief second, her lips moved away from Vivian's and her body hesitated, but that second was all it took to break the connection.

Vivian crossed her arms against her chest, and her face flushed. Her eyes went from melted chocolate to ice, reminding Kate of the terrifying woman she had met at the first rehearsal. "What?" Vivian demanded.

"Nothing!" Kate protested.

"Don't you lie to me, Katelyn Flynn!"

Kate leaned down and gently took Vivian's bottom lip into her mouth, sucking until she emitted another coarse sound, smaller this time. "I like the way you sound," Kate whispered, lifting her head so Vivian could see her lips move.

"Oh. I… Well, it takes a certain amount of…*control*…to keep my voice…normal," Vivian explained. "When I lose control, the hearing women that I've been with have told me that I sound"—Vivian looked away—"quite strange."

Kate frowned. Why would someone say that to an intimate partner?

"It's why I haven't been with a hearing woman in a long while." Vivian looked back at Kate. "I'm sorry if—"

"I said I *like* it."

Vivian searched her face as if trying to determine whether Kate was lying.

"How long is long?"

"How long is long what?"

"Since you've been with a hearing woman?"

"A few years at least."

"Are we really so different?"

Vivian looked away again as if considering how honest she could be. "Yes," she said at last.

Kate kissed her again, long and hard, wanting Vivian to respond. She moved her mouth down Vivian's neck until she reached her chest, then uncrossed Vivian's arms and buried her face in the cleavage underneath.

Vivian's fingers traced around Kate's back, moving to under Kate's torso, and she pulled her so that one of Kate's breasts fell into her mouth.

Kate moaned. The sensation of Vivian's mouth on her skin, after she had wanted the woman for so long, made her head feel as if it might explode.

Kate slid back down until they were breast to breast again. Vivian's hips rose to meet her thigh, their bodies moving in synch until Vivian cried out. Then slipping her head between Vivian's legs, she kissed a trail along Vivian's inner thighs.

Vivian whimpered, then twitched when Kate touched her clit. She clutched the back of Kate's neck and gasped her lover's name.

That took any self-control Kate might have had. She buried her finger into the moist folds of Vivian's flesh as Vivian raised her hips to take her in, bucking faster and faster until she cried out, rising up as her orgasm pulsed around Kate's finger. At last, she lay still.

"Oh my God! I'm sorry. It's been so long, and I've wanted—"

Kate slid up to meet her lips, kissing away her apology, still moving her hips over Vivian's body. They rocked together as though they were back on the dancefloor. Then Kate peppered Vivian's jaw with kisses, moving over her temple, down her chest, across her breasts, and back up to her lips again, loving the way Vivian tasted, the way she moved, the way her lipstick had smudged down her lips. Soon, Vivian was holding her tightly again, crying out loudly, calling out her name breathlessly as she flew over the edge, rolling and writhing, her hand twitching as if she were trying to speak until at last she went limp in Kate's arms.

Kate kissed her over and over. Then, Vivian reached up, and before Kate knew what had happened, she was flat on her back with Vivian at her side, playing her body as if it were a piano, signing poetry into her skin. She hesitated, then dipped her fingers into Kate's mouth before sliding them across her ribs, sinking them into where Kate needed to be touched the most. She gasped at the sensation.

Vivian touched her lightly, drawing Kate closer and closer to the edge before pushing her away again and again. Just as Kate finally exploded, Vivian touched her face, gently turning it until their eyes met. Kate was fully exposed to the gaze of her new lover.

When they had finally exhausted their passion, they lay together under the covers, kissing and caressing each other until at last they faded into sleep.

Chapter 10

THE BENEFIT OF KATE'S APARTMENT building was the same as that of having a deaf lover: when you woke in the middle of the night and decided to practice your cello, you woke no one.

Kate pulled the bow across the strings, basking in the deep, seductive, almost mournful sound of one of her favorite pieces: the prelude to Bach's "Cello Suite No. 2."

Normally, Kate sat stiffly as she played, without the theatrical swaying that some cello players seemed to associate with their instrument. Tonight, though, with her body more relaxed, her head clearer than it had been in a while and filled with simple happiness, she gave in, her eyes closed, lost in the music.

As she played the final note, soft hands slid over her shoulders and down to her breasts. Vivian kissed her neck. "You're beautiful."

Kate turned her head and accepted the kiss.

"Will you play some more?"

Kate chose another piece of music. She closed her eyes as she played, taking in the notes as Vivian's arms draped over her shoulders, grateful for a few moments of beauty in a life filled too often with loneliness.

Vivian let the blanket fall to the floor, her palms gently resting on the cello's face, her face settled against Kate's neck. Kate felt a small smile form on Vivian's lips as Kate deepened the groan of the cello, making it shake under her fingers. The small smile blossomed because for that one moment, Kate and Vivian were speaking the same language.

When she had finished the piece, she set her cello down and turned to face Vivian, who caressed her cheek, then wordlessly led Kate back into the bedroom.

Kate woke late the next morning with Vivian's body intertwined against hers. When she swept the hair out of Vivian's face, she stirred and signed something before burying her face into Kate's chest again.

Kate frowned, unsure of what she had said, and prodded her in the shoulder.

Vivian shifted her head onto the pillow and spelled the words out for her, her long fingers dancing.

Still Kate didn't catch the meaning. It was like doing math in her head, trying to keep up with the movement of letters she thought she had learned.

"That one I thought you would know," Vivian said.

"What did you say?"

"I said"—Vivian pulled the covers down to her waist, baring her breasts—"Good morning, lover."

Kate leaned down to meet her lips, straddling her as they kissed. Vivian moaned.

Kate covered Vivian's mouth with one hand and smiled. "You're really loud!"

Vivian scowled and turned away from Kate. "I'm sorry. I didn't know. I can't always tell when my voice is louder than normal," she mumbled. "As a matter of fact, sometimes I can't tell if I'm speaking at all."

"Hey." Kate reached for her, pulling her back and kissing her again. "Don't be sorry. I like it."

She began to stroke Vivian's body, prepared to continue the previous night's activities, when she heard the patter of little feet in the kitchen.

"What's wrong?" Vivian asked.

"Charlie must be back with Max."

"Do you need to let them in?"

Kate shook her head, getting out of bed and pulling on underwear and a T-shirt. "There's a key in Max's overnight things. Come on."

Max jumped into her arms as soon as he saw her. She smothered him in kisses, then greeted Charlie.

The woman took in Kate's attire and ratted hair. "So, how was your night?" she asked innocently, but before Kate could answer, Vivian emerged, dressed in similar fashion. Charlie clicked her tongue. "Uh-huh. Only a date, right? Nothing's gonna happen, right?"

Vivian glared at her before giving Kate a quick kiss and taking Max from her arms.

Kate froze. She hadn't expected anything so public in front of her son and Vivian's best friend before they had talked about it. She glanced at Charlie and giggled, her face growing hot.

"Did you have a sleepover without me?" Max asked.

"Yeah," Kate answered, "but you had a sleepover with Charlie."

"Don't worry, Max. I'm sure they'll let you come to the next one," Charlie said.

"So," Kate asked, changing the subject, "who's hungry?"

Kate prepared breakfast while Vivian and Charlie sat at the kitchen table talking. Her ears perked up when she heard Vivian mention Lyric.

Kate spun around, a knife clutched in her hand. "What's happening with Lyric?"

"I assumed you already knew," Vivian replied. "You're a cellist, after all."

"But I'm new to the area. I don't know anyone who would have told me anything." Lyric Opera of Chicago was one of the best-known opera companies in the country. More importantly, it was Kate's dream job. Lyric was known for its edgy and modern interpretations. Plus, unlike WCCE, where the contract was only two seasons, it was a full-time tenure-tracked job with a union contract. Kate had dreamed for years about an audition, but someone literally had to die or retire for a spot to open up.

"Well," Vivian said, "you know the Rendells?"

"The husband and wife in the cello section, right?" Charlie asked.

"That's right. Well, it appears that Mr. Rendell has been sleeping with someone in the flute section while married to someone in the cello section."

"That's the older man with the huge bald spot, right? The one that always has food on his shirt?"

"Right."

"Ew." Charlie scrunched her face in disgust. "He's a creep."

"Well, I guess now that his wife knows, she might be leaving."

"What?" Kate dropped the knife on the counter. "So, um, is Lyric going to audition for a cellist?"

Vivian smirked. "Maybe."

"Maybe?"

"They don't know yet," Vivian said. "His wife—I can't remember her name—hasn't told the board officially what her decision is. There's an audition tentatively scheduled for the new year, but they don't know yet if they'll actually need to fill the position. Kate, are you okay?"

Kate blinked. "Uh, yeah. I'm good." But she was rattled. It was silly to hope, but the thought of a permanent job with Lyric meant a lot of things. Like staying in one place. Like staying with Vivian.

She picked up the knife and continued chopping.

After they ate, Charlie excused herself. She had a sign language lesson to teach. Vivian said she should go too, but when Max whined, she decided to work from Kate's living room while Kate practiced.

When Vivian was done with her work, she pulled Max into her lap and showed him how to feel the vibrations while Kate played.

That night, they made dinner together. After putting Max to bed, they made love until it was long past time for sleep.

Chapter 11

"Just one?" Max kicked his legs under the covers. They had been trying to put him to bed for thirty minutes. He had ramped up and set off into a game of chase until they wrestled him, squealing and laughing, into his bed.

"Hey, what did I just say, kid?" Kate tucked the blankets tighter around him. "You run around like that and you lose your reading time."

He screwed up his face as if trying to decide whether he should scream, kick, or cry. Instead, a huge tear slipped down his cheek.

Kate gave him her best don't-mess-with-me expression, but Vivian interceded with a pout of her own.

"Oh, you're so weak!" Kate wrapped an arm around her waist. "All right, one," she told Max, "if you promise that tomorrow night you go to bed without a fight."

"Promise!"

"If you don't, then you have to eat Brussels sprouts every night this week. Deal?"

"Deal." He stuck out his hand for her to shake.

Kate selected a book and took a seat at the edge of the bed.

"No! You." Max pointed at Vivian.

"Me?" Vivian asked. Then to Kate, she said, "See? I told you he likes me best."

Kate rolled her eyes. "Yeah. We'll see, lady."

Scooting in next to him, Vivian began to read aloud. Max stared at her, then he reached up and pinched her lips closed. Vivian slipped into sign.

From the doorway, Kate snapped a picture and texted it to Charlie.

Vivian's reading him a bedtime story. – K

Max watched Vivian's hands swirl and dance until his eyelids began to droop. Just before he fell asleep, he said, "Love you, Mommy. Love you, Viv'n."

Vivian looked at Kate questioningly.

"He said he loves you."

Vivian turned back to Max and kissed him on his forehead. "I love you too, sweetheart."

If this woman isn't careful, she's going to make me fall in love with her. The thought drifted unbidden through Kate's mind along with another: *be careful, Kate. All good things come to an end.* She pushed it away.

Vivian got up from the bed, wiping away a tear.

"What is it?" Kate asked as they clicked Max's door closed.

She looked at Kate. "I've never had anyone accept me so completely before. He might be a child, but that acceptance is a powerful thing."

Kate caught her around the waist, giving her a long and soft kiss before releasing her to take a shower.

While Kate was in the shower, she heard something slam in the living room. It was probably nothing. Vivian often didn't realize how many things make noise: the refrigerator door closing, setting down a glass, footsteps.

She dried off, wrapping her hair in a towel. Maybe she shouldn't bother to get dressed. How would Vivian react if she walked into the living room naked? She had decided to find out when she heard voices.

It wasn't the TV. Maybe Max was up and pushing Vivian to read him another story.

"No!" The word was a shout.

Kate's heart jumped into her throat when she next heard a series of high squeals and sobs. She hurried to Max's room but twirled in a one eighty when she heard Vivian's voice coming from the opposite direction. "Absolutely not! You may not come in!"

When she reached the living room, she froze.

Vivian was clutching a sobbing Max against her shoulder with one arm, the other arm straight out to block Stephen, who stood in the doorway.

"Stephen! What are you doing here?"

"Oh, look." Stephen extended his arm in a grand gesture. "There's the woman of the hour!"

The Loudest Silence

Vivian turned toward Kate, looking like a mama lion. She clutched the wailing boy as if she would lunge for the throat of anyone who came too close.

"What the *hell* is going on?"

Stephen opened his mouth to respond, but Vivian spoke first. "I answered the door, and he attacked me!"

"No, I didn't!"

"Okay. Let me take Max and put him back to bed." Kate reached for Max, but he clung even tighter to Vivian.

Vivian's hands flew in a noiseless rant.

"What's she saying?" Stephen demanded. "What's wrong with Max?"

Kate threw up her hands. This was getting out of hand. She turned to Vivian. "What happened?"

"He woke Max when he pounded on the door, and Max came and got me." Vivian glared at Stephen.

"He called Viv'n names!" Max said into Vivian's shirt. "He's a bad man!"

Kate rounded on Stephen. "You yelled at her until you made my four-year-old cry? Are you *serious*, Stephen?"

Stephen's eyes flashed. "I didn't mean to! She just… She won't let me come in." He gestured to Vivian, who was still blocking his way. "Can I please come inside?"

"Yeah. Of course." She put a hand on Vivian's arm.

Vivian snarled and took a step back. "I'll put Max back to bed."

Kate nodded. "Thanks."

Vivian glared at Stephen once more before disappearing into Max's room.

"Okay." Kate gestured Stephen inside. "What the hell was all that about? What are you doing here?"

Stephen looked at her, puzzled. "We were supposed to talk tonight."

"Oh shit!" She had completely spaced their conversation at Max's birthday party. "That was tonight?"

"Yeah, you seem a little distracted." He stepped into the living room and flopped onto the futon. "Jesus Christ. I knocked, and she flat-out refused to let me in when she saw it was me. And I got mad. I'm sorry. I just… I'm so tired of her acting like I'm a virus."

123

What could she say? He wasn't wrong—that was exactly how Vivian treated him. But he wasn't much better.

"Is that what's wrong?"

Stephen clenched his jaw. "Look, I just didn't expect it to be this hard, okay?"

"You didn't expect what to be this hard?"

"You two being here!" he said loudly.

She stared at him as she processed his comment.

"And Jesus wept. *Vivian*. Vivian being a part of your life! I didn't sign up for my son to be raised by a woman like that."

"Like *what*?" she asked.

"She hates me so much. She's going to poison Max's mind before I ever get to know him."

"Well, you did cheat on her best friend." She had meant it playfully, but Stephen was not in the mood to laugh.

"I know! *Trust me*, I know. But if Charlie can forgive me, why can't she?"

Kate shrugged. Whatever had happened between Stephen and Charlie was before her time in Chicago.

They both looked up when Max's door clicked. Vivian barreled into the living room, fire in her eyes. "Isn't it rather late to want to be part of his life?"

Stephen jumped to his feet. "This has *nothing* to do with you, Kensington!"

Vivian wagged her finger in his face. "I care about Max! I love him! *I* wouldn't have *abandoned* him!"

"I did not—"

"Hey! Hey! Whoa!" Kate jumped up and forced herself between them. "I can't keep doing this!" She shoved Stephen back onto the futon.

"This isn't fair!" he cried. "How is it that *she* gets to know my son but I can't?"

"You forfeited that right," Vivian snarled.

"Stop!" Kate held up her hands and looked between the two of them. "You two have to find a way to not kill each other."

"He cheated on my best friend!" Vivian snarled.

"That's none of your business!" Stephen muttered, looking down at his feet.

Vivian's eyes flashed in that way that Kate had come to learn meant she hadn't understood and didn't want to admit it.

At that, Kate stepped in. "Stephen, she doesn't know what you say unless you look at her when you're speaking."

Stephen looked up and repeated what he had said.

Vivian pressed her lips together.

"Listen," Kate said before either one could speak again. "You're both going to be around me and Max, and you're both going to be around each other. You can't fight in front of Max. Did you not see how upset he was? In fact, you can't fight in front of me either!"

Vivian relaxed her scowl. "You're right. I'm sorry."

"Me too. It's just not fair that *she* gets to know him and I can't."

"Stephen, I never said that you can't get to know him." Letting him be a part of Max's life would be hard, but if he wanted to get to know Max, she wouldn't stop him.

"I want him to get to know me as his father." He glanced between her and Vivian as if daring them to say something negative. "How am I supposed to know what it's *like* to be his parent if I don't act like his parent? Spending a few minutes with him at his birthday party is easy, but that's not what we're talking about here, is it?"

"It's not that easy. This is about Max, right? Having a trial run as a daddy isn't how it works. You can be his friend, okay? Let's start there."

"You mean it?" His face lit up.

She glanced at Vivian for a hint of approval, then looked back at Stephen. "Come over next week, and we'll take him to the park together, okay?"

Stephen grinned and stood up, throwing his arms around Kate. "This is going to be good. You'll see."

Kate nodded. "Yeah. I think so too. Just don't use the F word in front of him."

"Kate, I would never swear in front of him."

Kate snickered. "I meant *father*, Stephen."

"Well. That settled..." Vivian excused herself with a tight smile and headed into Kate's bedroom.

"She *really* doesn't like me," Stephen said as he watched her disappear down the hall.

"It seems that way."

"I get it." He leaned back in the futon. "I really hurt Charlie."

"You sound like you regret it."

Stephen nodded. "She was pretty great. I was young and stupid. I've done a lot of growing up this past year." He stood up. "All right. I'll get out of your hair. But next week?"

"Next week."

"You're sure?"

She laughed and playfully shoved him toward the door. "I'm sure."

But she wasn't sure. Part of her was ready to give him this chance. After all, she had told him he was welcome in Max's life. And yet she had a sense of foreboding too.

She would ask Vivian what she thought.

She opened the door to her room to see Vivian leaning back against the pillows in the middle of the bed, a book in hand. She wore one of Kate's T-shirts that was too big for her, a lock of hair draped over her face.

"I thought you would be awhile," Vivian said as Kate crawled into bed with her.

Kate pulled off her shirt and settled beside her. "You want to tell me what that was about?"

Vivian frowned.

"It's not just about Charlie, is it?"

"No," Vivian admitted with a sigh, "it isn't." She looked at Kate. "I just… I don't understand how you can forgive him for not being there for you. He got you pregnant and then he left you to raise Max on your own. It's just one of the reasons I dislike him."

Kate sat up to face her. "You can't judge him for an agreement he and I made."

"Like hell I can't, Kate!" Vivian's cheeks turned pink with anger.

"No, you can't." Kate shot back, meeting anger for anger. "You can't judge him for my arrangement with him, okay? You weren't there, so you don't get to add it to the list of why you don't like him."

"It tells me who he is as a person. Surely you can see that."

"Actually," she snapped, "I see the opposite. He wasn't ready to be a dad, so instead of being a shitty one, he stepped away. I respect him for that. And it was the right thing for us at the time."

Vivian shook her head. "Children are meant to be loved no matter what! They are meant to be wanted and loved whether they were planned for or not."

Kate looked at her, realization dawning. This wasn't about Max at all. But this wasn't the time to probe. "You're right." She picked up one of Vivian's hands and kissed the knuckles. "*All* kids deserve to be loved. All of them."

Vivian looked down.

"Hey." Kate reached for her chin and tilted her face up. A tear sat in the corner of Vivian's eye. "Can you do something for me?"

Vivian nodded.

"Can you give him a chance? For me? I mean, I'm not really comfortable with the situation either, but I think he deserves the chance."

Vivian sighed. "All right. I will. But I still do not approve."

Chapter 12

Max tugged excitedly on Kate's hand as they walked into Lincoln Park. It spanned for miles along Lake Shore Drive with a zoo, a nature museum, a soccer field, and picnic areas. On the other side of the park, Lake Michigan lapped at the shore.

She sipped her coffee while Max drank a hot chocolate.

She asked herself for the hundredth time whether this was the right thing to do. She had created so many boundaries to keep Max from getting hurt, and yet here in Chicago, the boundaries seemed to dissolve. First Vivian had snuck into Max's life, and now Stephen was knocking on the door.

"I'm done," Max said, holding his cup out for her to take.

"Hey, kid," she said, nudging his shoulder. "I see trash cans all over the place."

He rolled his eyes but went to the nearest can and dropped his empty cup in.

She watched him with amusement. He really was growing so fast.

"Are we waiting for Viv'n?" Max asked, looking up at his mother hopefully.

"No, buddy. Remember? We're waiting for Stephen. Remember him from your birthday?"

He drew his eyebrows down, then brightened. "Oh yeah!"

"Great!" She raised her hand for a high five. "Come on. Let's go find the playground, huh?"

Max meeting his father was a good thing, she reminded herself yet again, especially if it worked out. Max needed people, and if making connections made it harder for him the next time they moved, well, she would have to figure it out then.

"Mommy, my hand."

"What? Oh." Kate loosened her grip.

"Hey, Max!"

They turned to see Stephen making his way through the crowd smiling broadly. Maybe a little too broadly, Kate thought.

"You made it." Kate felt a little better at the sight of him. He had cleared the first hurdle: he had shown up. "Max, you remember Stephen?"

Max stared up at him, his eyes narrowed.

Stephen looked from Max to Kate, then back to Max. "Hey, Max. You remember me?"

Max continued to glare.

"I brought you something." Stephen held out the football-shaped package. "I hope it's okay," he said to Kate.

"Max?" Kate prompted.

Finally Max spoke. "You were mean to Viv'n."

Stephen looked at her, the gift still in his outstretched hand. Kate shrugged.

Stephen dropped his arm. "I, uh—You're right."

"Get on his level," Kate whispered.

Stephen squatted down so he was face-to-face with Max. "You're right, Max. I was. And I'm sorry."

Max crossed his arms. "You gonna say sorry?"

"I will. I promise, okay?"

Max shifted his attention to the package. "Is that for me?"

Stephen beamed. "Sure is."

Max examined the wrapping. "Dinosaurs! Look, Mommy, it's dinosaurs!"

"I see."

Max ripped off the wrapping and, with barely a pause for permission, dashed off onto the play area, tossing it into the air and running after it. A minute later, two other little boys joined him.

Stephen breathed a sigh of relief. "It's a hit," he said, turning to Kate.

"It is. And I like the paper."

Max shouted, and they both turned their attention back to the field. One of the bigger boys had snatched the ball away from Max.

"Why, you little—"

"Hold your horses there, buddy." Kate said, touching Stephen's arm to keep him from going after the bigger boy. "He'll work it out."

"He just took the ball from Max!"

"Sounding like a dad already."

As they watched, Max convinced the older boy to give up the ball, and the kid ran off, leaving the younger boys to their game.

"Mommy! Come play wif me!"

Kate smiled. "Why don't you teach him how to throw it?" she said to Stephen.

"You sure?" he asked.

"Go for it."

The game of catch quickly turned into a game of chase as Stephen ran away from the kids, the ball in his hand, zigzagging until they finally caught him. Max pulled him onto the playground equipment. Stephen paused for a moment before joining him in the sea of kids, looking like a giant in a land of little people.

Kate laughed as she watched them play. If Stephen was willing to make an ass out of himself for Max's amusement, that was half the battle.

"You've got yourself some potatoes," Kate called out a bit later as Stephen approached with Max slung upside down over his shoulder.

"I'm not potatoes!" Max said through his giggles.

"Yup, that's right," Stephen said as if he hadn't heard Max. "Just a big ol' sack of taters."

"Hmm. Have you seen Max?" Kate asked.

"Oh, yeah. He told me to tell you that he had to go to work."

"Oh no!"

"Yeah. He had an emergency, so he had to split."

"I'm here! I'm right here!"

Stephen put Max back on his feet.

"Steph'n is taking us for ice cream!"

"Oh, he is, is he?"

Stephen grinned at her hopefully.

"Okay, okay."

"All right!" Stephen snapped his hand to his head in a stiff salute. "Soldier, march!"

Max marched off down the sidewalk. Stephen and Kate followed.

They walked in silence for a while. Then Stephen said, "I can't believe that I walked away. He was out of sight, out of mind, you know? I mean, you unfollow a person on Facebook, and that's that."

So that was why he had never commented on a picture of Max. "I've never been mad at you, you know." The night she had told him she was pregnant, it was a short conversation, little more than Kate holding out the pregnancy test while Stephen stared at her with eyes the size of golf balls. Then he had mumbled that he needed time to think. Even when he gave her his decision, there had been very little conversation.

Stephen glanced at her, one eyebrow raised.

"Okay," she admitted with a laugh. "There were moments, but overall, I understood why."

"Flynn, I'm sorry."

As they walked to the ice cream shop at the other end of the park, Kate hung back, listening as Stephen told Max about his time in Cub Scouts.

"You went camping? Overnight?"

"Yeah. And we went hiking and made s'mores."

"Wow. I wanna be a Cub Scout."

Stephen grinned. "You do?"

"Yeah! Can you take me?"

The two stopped at the door to wait for Kate. Stephen looked back at her. "Well, maybe. If your mom says it's okay, then yeah, we can figure that out."

"Cool!"

Stephen scooped Max up so that he would see the ice cream choices. "What'll ya have?"

Max didn't hesitate. "The pink one!"

"All right, pink it is." He ordered a strawberry cone and a mint chocolate chip for himself. "Come on, Flynn, what'll ya have?" Stephen looked at Kate with a grin, his eyes shining.

"I'll have a chocolate cone, please."

"Okay, here you go, son." The man behind the counter leaned over to hand Max his cone. "And one for your girlfriend." He handed Stephen a chocolate cone.

Max screwed up his face. "Nuh-uh! Charlie says that Viv'n is my mommy's girlfriend. She came outta Mommy's bedroom and she wasn't wearing any pants."

"Okay!" Kate quickly turned Max around. "Let's find a place to sit."

Stephen grinned as they settled around a table. "So you and the ice queen, huh?"

She glared at him over her cone. "No, me and Vivian."

"Right. Sorry. So you and Vivian, huh?"

Kate smiled. "Yeah, I guess so."

"Ha! I knew it. No wonder she wouldn't let me into your love nest last week."

"Yeah, yeah, yeah." She rolled her eyes in a vain attempt to suppress the smile spreading across her face.

They ate in silence for a few minutes. Then Stephen spoke again. "So, Flynn, are you going for it?"

"Hmm?"

"The audition."

It didn't really surprise her that Stephen knew about it. That was how the classical music community worked.

"I mean, who knows if there even will be one, but, yeah, I'll go for it."

"Go for what?" Max looked up from his ice cream, his face pink from nose to chin.

"An audition, sport. Your mom has a big one coming up."

Max's face dropped. "We're leaving?" His eyes filled with tears.

"Oh, no, no, no!" She scooped him up, ice cream face and all. Of course Max would assume they were moving. They had moved so often in his short life.

Stephen looked from Max to Kate. "What's wrong? What happened?"

She held Max close, running her hand through his hair soothingly. "He hears 'audition,' and he thinks we're moving."

"I don't wanna to go," he keened. "I like it here!"

Kate kissed his tears away. "No, Max. The audition is *here*. We're not leaving."

"No! Don't do it!" Max shouted and threw what was left of his cone on the floor.

"Kid, it isn't like that. I promise."

She wanted to explain to him that if she won this audition, they could make a real home with couches instead of futons. He could be in one school district for his entire childhood. They wouldn't have to live out of boxes. This audition, if she won it, could change everything for them. But even if she could explain all of this to her wailing four-year-old, she couldn't guarantee anything. It was a million-to-one shot. So she held Max until he cried it out. Then she set him on his feet and bent to his level. "Max, I can't promise you that we won't have to move again, but I'm going to do my best to make sure that if we do, it will be the last time."

But the damage had been done.

The year was passing too quickly.

And this time…

This time, she didn't *want* to move. She didn't want to leave this city. She didn't want to leave Vivian.

But how long would that last, anyway? Eventually she and Vivian would break up. Max would lose Charlie in the breakup.

And now Stephen…

What the hell was she supposed to do?

Chapter 13

"I just don't get it! How is it already October?" The weeks since her trip with Stephen and Max to the park had flown by. The leaves on the trees were changing color, stores were filled with Halloween decorations, and everything smelled of pumpkin spice.

"To be fair, you might have missed it with everything else going on," Vivian teased as she held open the door to another Halloween-decorated shop.

Kate couldn't argue. She had performed in a concert, taken Max bowling with Stephen, and, of course, spent a lot of time with Vivian.

"So what is it again?" Kate asked, plopping a witch's hat on Vivian's head.

Vivian laughed, modeling it for Max, who frowned and shook his head. "It's the annual All Hallows' Eve Gala. My parents' foundation is a huge donor, so every year someone from my family has to go. Since my mother refuses to *mingle*, as she calls it, and my father passed away, I always go."

"And you want me to go with you?" Kate asked skeptically.

Vivian kissed her hand.

"What about Max? I thought we would take him trick-or-treating."

"Of course we will. The gala doesn't start until eight. We can take him trick-or-treating in this nice neighborhood that I know. Then, afterward, we can have a sitter come to my loft."

"Oh yeah?" Kate frowned as she rifled through the makeup kits. She was fairly sure that no amount of money would convince Stacey to babysit on Halloween instead of going out with her friends.

As if reading her mind, Vivian said, "I assume Stacey will be occupied. I thought I would go through a babysitting service."

"A service?" There was no way Kate could afford a service on Halloween night.

"Yes. I hear there's one that caters specifically to the tenants in my building."

Kate snorted. "And by 'hear,' you mean you know, right? Since you own the building, you probably contracted with the service."

Kate was going to have to tell Vivian that she simply could not afford to hire a babysitting service unless she picked up an extra gig. She and Vivian had very different experiences around money. Vivian never seemed to think about what things cost—ever. She never checked the price tag on something she wanted to buy and she never flinched when she handed her credit card to a server or a bartender.

"Kate, just because I'm deaf doesn't mean I can't hear the cogs whirling in your head."

"What?"

Vivian squeezed her hand. "I was planning on covering the cost for the sitter as well as the makeup artist."

"Wait, there's a makeup artist? What the hell? I can't—there isn't—Viv!"

"I was planning on covering the cost because you're coming to my event as a favor to me."

"Yeah, but—"

"Kate, if you don't feel comfortable, you don't have to come. But if you do, I'm not going to put you out financially."

Just as Kate opened her mouth to protest, Max pulled on Vivian's arm. "Can I go as Deaf for Halloween?"

With that, the tension was broken as Kate and Vivian laughed.

"Is it time to get dressed?" Max burst into Kate's bedroom on Halloween morning and jumped onto her bed, planting his knees firmly into her gut.

"Not yet, kid." Kate groaned and rolled over, sending him back out to watch cartoons. She had been working gigs nonstop over the last few weeks, playing for gothic-themed weddings, and even signing up to help the stagehands before and after rehearsals and concerts.

Fifteen minutes later, Max was back. "Is it time to get dressed now?"

That was all it took for Kate to drag herself out of bed. She helped Max put on his cape and watched as he ducked and weaved throughout the apartment, laughing his best evil villain laugh.

That afternoon, as Max splashed away in the tub, Vivian knocked at the front door wearing a pair of tight jeans and a cotton T-shirt. Her face was clean of makeup and her short hair slightly frizzy. It was the first time Kate had seen her dressed in anything but Chanel skirt suits, Armani slacks and blouses, or Gucci dresses.

Kate stood with her hand frozen on the doorknob, her face growing hot.

"What's wrong?" Vivian took a step back.

"Nothing." Kate reached for her hand and pulled Vivian straight into the bedroom, leaving the door open a crack in case Max needed anything. She pushed Vivian against the wall and pressed her mouth onto hers, her hand cupping Vivian's crotch through her jeans. "I don't think I've ever seen you look so sexy," she gasped between kisses.

She dropped to her knees and softly bit Vivian's inner thigh.

Vivian whimpered, grabbing Kate's hair and pulling her back to her feet. She sank her tongue deeply into Kate's mouth, her free hand fumbling with the zipper of her jeans. "Have I told you lately," Kate asked, her hand pushing Vivian's jeans down around her knees, "how much I love doing this with you?"

"Right now, you're...making yourself...abundantly clear."

"You know, I don't think I am. Let me try again." Kate worked with focus, using every bit she had learned about Vivian. Behind her hand, Vivian gasped. And gasped again. And again.

Then she began to shake, her hands in Kate's hair, pulling hard but not too hard. Kate slowed enough that Vivian whimpered. She stood, clutching Vivian's jaw and kissing her roughly before pulling away to check her face and hair in the mirror, pretending not to notice Vivian gaping at her, still trying to catch her breath. Then, with a wink and a smile, she left the bedroom.

"Oh my God, you're so cute!"

Max groaned. "Mommy, I'm supposta be scary!"

"Well, you don't have your makeup on yet."

He had finished his bath and pulled his costume over his head. He stood in front of the mirror in his room, trying to comb his hair to the side. He scowled in concentration.

"Look at you! Good job, buddy! You're so handsome! Got your sleepover bag?"

He nodded briefly and returned to styling his hair.

Vivian stumbled into Max's bedroom, tripping over a stuffed animal, her eyes glossy and her hair a mess. "I don't think that's ever happened to me before," she mumbled.

"What happened?" Max asked.

"Viv'n had too much Halloween candy!" Kate teased.

"Viv'n!" Max put his hands on his hips, "You're not supposta eat that many!"

When Max was finally satisfied with his hair and after his makeup was applied, they drove to Evanston, a suburb of Chicago. The streets were bustling with costumed children and their parents traveling from house to house.

Max stared out the window, gaping at the lights covering the houses and the animations on the lawns.

Finally they pulled into a neighborhood a block from Lake Michigan.

Max shrieked and flew from the car the moment they parked, but before Kate could give Max another lecture on trick-or-treating safety, Vivian grabbed her by the arm, pulling her ear close to her lips. "Don't think I won't get you back for what happened earlier, Ms. Flynn. I can barely sit down."

"Oh, please do, Ms. Kensington. Please do."

It was a beautiful area with grand old houses and trees lining the sidewalks. Their autumn colors stayed vivid even in the dimming light. Max ran from house to house, shouting "trick or treat" loudly and opening his pillowcase to receive the treats. Kate and Vivian followed behind.

As Max grew tired, he fell in step between them, lugging his full pillowcase.

"We need to go." Vivian said as the sun finally disappeared behind the large houses. "Our appointments are in an hour, and I assume you want to check his candy before giving him any."

Kate stiffened at the mention of the makeup appointments. She had never had her makeup done professionally. She wasn't sure what her costume was going to look like, but she decided she would give the makeup artist full artistic license She was anxious to see what the woman came up with.

"Okay, Max, Are you ready to go back?"

He stifled a yawn. "Can I have a candy?"

"I get to sleep here?" Max asked, his eyes wide at the size of the guest room.

After weeks of dating, somehow they had never gotten around to a sleepover at Vivian's. As a matter of fact, other than the birthday party, they had only gone over when Vivian needed something before heading to Kate's apartment.

"You sure do!" Kate swung him up in the air and tossed his giggling form into the middle of the bed.

"It's so big!" Max stretched out his arms and his legs, reaching for the edges of the bed. "It's as big as a house!"

Kate tickled his tummy one last time and went to the kitchen to dump the pillowcase of candy onto the island counter, shuffling through until she found a bite-sized Snickers.

"Tsk," Vivian said as she passed behind her.

"I'm checking it for poison!" Kate sputtered after her, her mouth full of chocolate and caramel, knowing full well that Vivian hadn't been facing her.

The yellow light flashed in the corner, and Kate pushed the button on the intercom. "Who is it?"

"Kate? It's Amy."

"Come on up!"

"Makeup," she mouthed to Vivian, then dished out a small bowl of candy for Max to snack on that evening. The rest she put into a large bowl and placed it on top of the fridge. No doubt she would be dipping into it just as much as Max.

Kate put *The Little Vampire* on the TV in the downstairs living room, then kissed Max's head.

The Loudest Silence

Amy arrived at the penthouse with Michael, the man who had planned Vivian's outfit and makeup, and they split up into separate bathrooms with their clients, Kate and Amy upstairs, Vivian and Michael downstairs.

"So," Amy said, looking at Kate as though she were a blank canvas, "you should get into your costume first. Go ahead and take everything off, and put this on." Then she began her work.

The process seemed to be taking a long time, and Kate was just beginning to wonder exactly how long it was going to take when, with a satisfied nod, Amy stepped back. "Take a look."

Kate stood to face the mirror and gasped.

Her skin, which was pale at the best of times, was now white, making her glow. There were shades of blue that reminded Kate of her first night with Vivian, but the blush on her cheeks and the rouge on her lips made her look healthy, vibrant, and beautiful.

The angles of her nose, cheeks, and jaw had been accentuated, giving her the look of a classic pixie, while her ears had been delicately pointed. Her shoulders, cheeks, and eyebrows wore a delicate dusting of something that looked very much like snow had frozen in place on her skin. Her hair, pulled into a loose chignon with curls framing her face, was tinted with fine dust, creating a soft, shimmering white.

She was dressed in a light cream-colored top that gathered over a single shoulder. Her ribs peeked out through the light lace trim that hung just past her hip bones. Long, white gloves covered the length of her arms. A pair of iridescent bluish-white tights encircled by a sash completed the costume.

"Amy! I can't believe it!"

"I have to say, I'm quite proud of this work." Amy grinned and began to snap pictures with her phone.

"Who am I?"

"Jack Frost. Genderbending is *very* in right now."

Kate checked herself in the mirror again, then asked, "Is Vivian ready yet?"

Max rolled his eyes. "She's been ready forever! She's scary, Mommy!"

"Oh yeah?"

She stepped into her white ballet-style slippers and, taking a deep breath, headed downstairs.

Vivian wore a simple, elegant white dress that looked as if it were sewn to her body. The arms extended all the way to her fingers. The front was designed to look like snow caught in the wind, and it shone with a pearly luster.

Her hair was brushed back and to one side and dusted like Kate's so that it was completely white. On top, she wore a crystal-clear crown.

Vivian's usually golden skin had been turned into ivory with a soft dusting of pale white. Shards of reflective ice trailed down the side of her face. She wore contacts that made her eyes silver, which contrasted sharply with her eyelids and lips that were painted in black matte.

"If I'm Jack Frost, then who are you supposed to be?" Kate asked.

Vivian laughed. "Why, darling, you can't tell? I'm the ice queen."

Chapter 14

THEY TOOK PICTURES. KATE SENT Stephen one of Vivian, her face void of expression, save for one slightly raised eyebrow.

Here's your ice queen.

Stephen responded immediately: *The ice queen lives! Hide your children and wives!*

Kate showed her the text, which sent Vivian into peals of laughter. "Just because I refuse to back down in the face of opposition I get called cold, whereas if I were a man I would be considered strong."

Vivian pulled Kate into her arms.

"You look…"

Vivian slid one hand down Kate's hip, her eyes hooded. "Just wait until you see what's underneath."

Just then, the lights flashed, signaling that the babysitter had arrived.

As they stepped out of the elevator and into the car, Kate fretted. Why had she agreed to come to such a formal event? She wasn't an executive or any other kind of important person. She was just an awkward single mom who wanted to make her girlfriend happy. What if she made an ass of herself or Vivian?

In the car, Vivian rested her hand on Kate's thigh, gently fluttering her fingers up and down.

Kate closed her eyes, welcoming the distraction.

The beautiful and iconic Chicago Cultural Center had been converted from its original use as the city's first public library, and the ballroom had been transformed into a glamorous nightmare with cobwebs and other decorations. At the entrance to the ballroom was a sign declaring *The J.C. Kensington Foundation and Altman Enterprises present: Chicago's 25th Annual All Hallows' Eve Gala.*

Kate tugged Vivian's hand to catch her eye. "You didn't tell me that it was *your* foundation putting on the whole freaking event!"

Vivian cleared her throat. "It's silly to say *my* foundation. I hold the position of president of the board for WCCE, but I am a mere board member at the foundation."

"Oh. Right. Of course." This information didn't make Kate feel any better. In fact, she was now convinced she would do something that night to embarrass herself or Vivian. It was too late to fake an illness or claim a broken leg. If she stood any chance of getting through this event unscathed, she needed to fake her way through. She stepped from the car with her chin held high, a polite smile on her face, as she held on to Vivian's arm like a lifeline.

The room was filled with people who seemed to have stepped off a movie screen. Frankenstein's monster appeared to have real metal bolts embedded in his neck. Elvis looked to be alive again. And mummies were rotting from the inside out. It was as if they had stepped into the land of make-believe.

"Ms. Kensington." A man called to them as they entered the grand lobby.

Kate glanced at Vivian, then gently bumped her elbow into Vivian's side and nodded toward the silver-haired man walking toward them. Kate stepped away slightly, but Vivian placed her hand on Kate's forearm and said, "Stay close."

Then her face hardened into its usual indifference. "Mr. Altman, how good to see you. May I introduce my companion, Katelyn Flynn? Ms. Flynn, this is Carlyle Altman of Altman Enterprises. He is also the general director of Lyric Opera."

Kate stiffened.

"Ah yes. The cellist." He reached for her free hand, openly appraising her. His long, white hair, expensive suit, and gold-handled cane gave him the air of a wealthy and powerful man. "I've heard good things about you."

"Thank you, sir," Kate finally croaked out.

He turned back to Vivian. "How is your mother, Vivian?"

"She is doing very well, thank you."

"Will she be gracing us with her presence tonight?"

Vivian chuckled. "Now, Mr. Altman, you know my mother is a very busy woman."

"Of course. Well, I must say, you two look lovely in your costumes."

Vivian nodded politely, and Kate watched him go, wishing she could have been dashing and charming with the man who held her dream job in the palm of his hand. *So much for good first impressions. Damn it, Kate!*

She didn't have time to dwell. Once Mr. Altman had left, a line of people formed to greet Vivian. It only took her a few interactions before she understood why Vivian hadn't brought Charlie. An interpreter would have sullied the executive persona she had wrapped herself in. Vivian would work hard tonight, doing her best to catch every word so that no one would remember that the representative of the J.C. Kensington Foundation had a hearing disability. It was impressive, Kate thought. But why was it so important?

As they slowly made their way to the bar, stopping every few steps to smile and greet people, Vivian slid a hand across Kate's lower back.

"Ms. Kensington."

Kate looked up, surprised to see Mark Carry, the WCCE's resident flautist.

Vivian greeted him. "Mr. Carry. I apologize. I received your call this afternoon, but it's been a very busy day. Has everything cleared up?"

Mark glanced at Kate before responding. "Actually, ma'am, no."

"All right. Find me before you leave, and I will see what can be done."

Mark nodded vigorously, his face flushing. "Thank you, Ms. Kensington. Thank you." He disappeared into the crowd.

"Everything okay?"

"Oh yes." Vivian waved a hand. "He just needs an advance on his paycheck."

"WCCE does that?"

"Not exactly, but I can cut him a check myself, and the office will reimburse me."

At the bar, Vivian took two glasses of champagne and handed one to Kate. "I promise the night will become more interesting. The more these old codgers drink, the more excitable they tend to be. As long as you are not the target of their attentions, it can be quite funny. Though"—Vivian looked Kate up and down—"I don't know if I can stop them when you look like that."

"I don't know about the old codgers, but there seems to be one person who can't keep her hands off me tonight."

"Mm." Vivian pulled Kate in tighter to her side. "And who would that be?"

"Oh, I don't know," Kate said, her eyes lingering on Vivian's matte black lips. "Just someone."

"Ms. Kensington."

The impassive look returned to Vivian's face as she shook hands with the next person who approached.

Over the next hour, Kate tried not to yawn, but she was bored to tears, and it was obvious that Vivian was just as bored. When there was a lull in the traffic, Vivian turned and whispered in her ear, "Soon. Soon I will have you back home and I can *get you back*."

That woke Kate instantly, but before she could respond, a woman approached wanting Vivian's attention.

Kate used the interruption to take a break. Taking Vivian's empty champagne flute from her hand, she said, "Will you excuse me, please?" and went to the bar.

After ordering a cocktail, she turned and watched Vivian as she mingled.

She was beautiful, especially in her costume. How had Kate managed to be her date?

As Kate gazed at her, Vivian glanced around the room, looking for her. When she spotted her at the bar, she frowned.

"I was thirsty," Kate mouthed slowly.

Vivian glanced away briefly. Kate slipped away, leaving her empty glass on the bar. Just before she slipped out into the hallway, she caught Vivian's eye again. "Wanna make out?" Kate mouthed as she disappeared through the door, looking for the nearest restroom.

Seconds later, Vivian burst in, then suddenly halted as a white-haired woman shuffled to the sink next to Kate.

Vivian moved around to the sink on the other side of Kate, leaning across to check her makeup. Kate shifted her weight until her rear bumped into her. Kate caught Vivian's eye and held it until her insides began to boil. When Vivian's eyes flashed, Kate looked away, biting her lip lightly.

When the older woman headed for the door, Kate followed, matching her pace.

She needed to find someone to talk to so she could keep Vivian from dragging her back to the bathroom—or perhaps out to the car.

The thought made Kate's breath catch.

"Hey, Captain Hook. That's an amazing costume." The man looked like a cross between Dustin Hoffman and Johnny Depp. His dark hair was arranged in deliberate tangles, and his paper-thin mustache was curled on both ends.

"Why, thank you, lass." He bowed theatrically, sweeping his hat off his head.

From the corner of her eye, she watched Vivian emerge from the bathroom, doing her best to look casual and failing entirely. She hesitated when she saw Kate speaking to the pirate. She pressed her lips into a thin line. "Ms. Flynn." She nodded as she approached, then looked at the pirate disdainfully. "Mr...?"

The man lifted his fake silver hook in salute. "Mr. Hook."

Then, moving past them both, she muttered, "Nice eyeliner."

Kate excused herself from Captain Hook and followed Vivian to the bar and leaned in next to her. "Can I help you, Ms. Flynn?" Vivian asked, her voice a low velvety rumble.

She blew lightly across Vivian's ear. "Just getting a drink." Then, with her fresh drink in hand, she was off again, moving away before Vivian could respond.

"May I have this dance?" A man dressed as Napoleon had appeared silently beside her.

"Oh. Sure." The man lifted her arm onto his shoulder, then grasping her firmly around her laced middle, spun her out onto the floor.

"That is quite a costume, miss," he said.

"Uh, thank you."

As they twirled, she glanced at Vivian again, who was now openly scowling. Kate felt Vivian's jealousy, frustration, and excitement burning into her. The flirtation game that had started as a diversion was working on her as much as it was working on Vivian. Her heart pounded harder.

When the song finished, she nodded politely to the man and crossed the room before turning around to meet Vivian's eyes again.

"Have you ever noticed that you get jealous?" she mouthed.

Vivian scoffed and looked away. She was sitting at the bar, watching Kate as though she were a rabbit she would like to pounce on.

A tall, beautiful woman stepped into her line of vision. "Hello."

"Oh! Hi!" She smiled.

"May I?" The woman held out a hand, and, not thinking twice, Kate accepted it.

As the woman swung her around, Kate saw that Vivian was watching like a child who had caught another child playing with her favorite toy. She quirked one eyebrow, and Kate flashed a bright smile as if daring her to come and take what was hers.

When the dance was over, Kate retreated to the opposite side of the room. When she turned back, Vivian had followed her with her eyes. "This game you're playing. You won't win," she signed, though Kate only caught "won't win."

Kate licked her lips seductively. "Are you having fun now?" she mouthed.

Before Vivian could answer, Kate slipped through the doors and into the hallway, walking slowly, hoping Vivian would follow. She smiled when she heard the door open behind her.

"I thought you said I wouldn't win," she teased, turning to speak before turning away again.

"And who says you have?" Vivian's voice rang in the hall.

Kate turned around when she felt Vivian close behind her, and the moment she did, Vivian attacked, her hands cupping Kate's ass and breast, her mouth a breath away from Kate's in barely controlled restraint.

"I am *not* jealous." Vivian snarled, her eyes flashing. "I do not get jealous."

Kate pushed herself against Vivian until she whimpered.

When another door to the ballroom opened, Kate broke away from Vivian and stepped back inside.

She made her way through the crowd, nodding politely at people she passed. She glanced around again. Vivian had disappeared. She accepted another dance, but the longer Vivian remained absent, the more distracted

Kate became. She took another glass of champagne from a waiter and began to circle the room, searching for her.

Finally, Vivian reappeared and, catching her eye, signed, "Phone."

Kate lifted her phone from beneath her sash and saw she had received a photo from Vivian. In it, Vivian stood with her back to the mirror, looking over her shoulder. One hand held her dress up just enough to show one side of her round ass sans her usual lacy panties.

She looked up.

Vivian smirked, now in control of their game, then turned her attention to speak with a woman standing next to her.

Kate stood rooted to the spot for a moment, then handed her glass to a passing waiter and strode past Vivian into the hallway again.

She didn't have to wait even a second after reaching the bathroom. Vivian was so close behind her, they might as well have been attached.

Kate marched into the last stall before turning on Vivian, locking the door behind her, and slamming her into the stall door. She brought her mouth as close to Vivian's as she could without touching so that she wouldn't smear off her black lipstick, but it turned out that holding back drove Vivian mad. She strained forward, her lips reaching toward Kate's, and moaned when Kate instead ran the tip of her tongue up the side of Vivian's neck. Kate pressed her hips into Vivian's, sliding up and down, rubbing her body against her.

"That wasn't fair, you know?"

But Vivian's eyes were closed as she kneaded Kate's rear, her fingers digging into her skin.

Reaching for Vivian's wrists, Kate raised them up and slammed them into the wall above Vivian's head.

Vivian whimpered, writhing as Kate nipped at her neck, trying to pull out of Kate's grasp so she could touch her. Kate transferred Vivian's wrists to one hand and reached down with the other until her hand grazed the front of Vivian's dress. She moved her head back so Vivian could see her mouth.

"Do you want me to touch you?"

Vivian's eyes were unfocused, so Kate asked again.

"Do you want me to touch you?"

Vivian smiled. "All day."

Kate grinned wickedly, but instead of slipping her hand under Vivian's dress, she thrust it down her own tights, pressing against Vivian's body so she could feel her moving.

Fast and hard, Kate caressed herself while she pressed against her lover, gasping while Vivian thrashed under her.

Kate leaned her head against Vivian's shoulder as she rocked. Then quickly, perhaps a little too quickly, the spike rippled out in waves from Kate's belly. "Oh God," she cried and dropped her face onto Vivian's shoulder.

Vivian moaned as Kate exploded, their hips still moving together. "Oh, Kate," she breathed. "Oh, I adore you."

The orgasm that was meant to be for Vivian left Kate's knees shaking. Kate pressed hard into her, struggling to stay upright.

They heard the bathroom door open. "Can you even?" one woman said, and the other replied, "Did you see that guy at the punch bowl?"

Without another sound, Kate released Vivian and exited the stall, washed her hands, and hurried out of the bathroom.

As the door closed behind her, Kate smiled. She replayed the look on Vivian's face until, not paying attention, she walked into an older woman.

"Oh, I'm so sorry, ma'am. Are you all right?" she asked, reaching out to steady the person she had bumped into.

"There you are, Ms. Flynn. I've been looking for you. Wherever have you and my daughter been?"

Chapter 15

KATE WOULD HAVE RECOGNIZED VIVIAN'S mother anywhere. She had the same high, chiseled cheekbones, pointed chin, and golden skin. Only the thin lips and the silver peppering her black hair were different. Vivian's mom was just as beautiful as her daughter. She also had the same stare that reached into the bottom of one's soul. It said that she knew exactly what Kate and Vivian had been up to. Kate felt like a child who had been caught sneaking into her Halloween candy in the middle of the night.

"Mother!" Vivian's voice brought Kate back to the moment. "What are you doing here?"

Mrs. Kensington pulled Vivian in for a hug. "Hello, my darling. How are you?" Then, without waiting for an answer, she asked, "Have you danced with Mr. Altman yet?"

"I will soon. Mother, this is Kate Flynn, my date."

"The cellist. Jacqueline Kensington." Mrs. Kensington extended a hand, smiling warmly.

"It's a pleasure to meet you, ma'am."

"Please call me Jacqueline." She stepped back to appraise them both. "My, these costumes are wonderful. Vivian, I love what they did with your makeup. It compliments your looks so well. As you can see, this year, I simply wore something from my closet."

Kate glanced at Vivian. She had a vacant look on her face, as though she couldn't understand what her mom was saying. But then why didn't she say something? And why wasn't Jacqueline signing?

As Jacqueline continued talking about previous galas, Kate tried to sign a few words here and there for Vivian but quickly got lost.

Jacqueline paused, her eyes drawn to Kate's hands. "Oh, sweetie, you don't need to do that," she said, an arctic freeze in her words.

Vivian reached out and touched Kate's hands. "It's all right, Kate. Thank you."

"Excuse me. May I borrow Ms. Kensington for a moment?"

Jacqueline beamed at the newcomer. "There are two Kensingtons here. Which one would you prefer?"

"Vivian, if you please."

Jacqueline nodded as Vivian was pulled away. She turned back to Kate. "Care to escort an old lady outside for a cigarette?"

"Uh, sure," Kate responded and led Jacqueline outside.

"So, Katelyn," Mrs. Kensington said, pulling a cigarette from her clutch purse and handing the lighter to Kate to light it, "I know I've seen your biography, but I can't recall the details."

Understanding the comment to be a request for information, Kate listed the orchestras and conductors she had played with.

"I've also heard you have a child."

Kate pulled her phone from her sash and proudly showed the home screen photo of Vivian and Max looking out a window together.

Jacqueline squinted at the image. "My, my! You must have taken quite a liking to my daughter." Her eyes traveled over Kate. "Though that seems rather obvious." Jacqueline studied her face, then smiled and changed the subject. "How old is your son?"

As Kate told Jacqueline about Max, she felt as if her legs were on two different slabs of ice drifting slowly apart. There was nothing amiss in Jacqueline that she could put a finger on, yet something was not right, something beyond asking her not to sign.

"Ah, Mr. Altman." Jacqueline produced a long, thin cigarette from a small purse on her hip and handed the lighter to Kate.

It took her a second before she realized that Jacqueline was waiting for her to light the cigarette for her. Kate switched on a polite smile and acquiesced, handing the golden lighter back to her once it was done.

"Ladies. Enjoying the party?"

"Of course," Kate said.

Mr. Altman pulled out a cigar and lit it. "Gallantly polite, Ms. Flynn. Though I did notice you were the bell of the ball for a while. Please save

The Loudest Silence

a dance for me." Then, turning to Jacqueline, he said, "And how are you, my lovely?"

"Carlyle." Jacqueline extended her gloved hand for him to kiss. "When is this secret audition no one is supposed to know about?"

"The new year. Why?"

Jacqueline looked at Kate. "Katelyn, you will be auditioning, will you not?"

Kate felt the blood drain from her face. "Isn't it by invitation only?"

Jacqueline blew smoke from her nose, making Kate think of a dragon. "Consider yourself invited."

Mr. Altman drew on his cigar, studying Kate, then nodded.

Kate wanted to scream, jump up and down, and vomit all at the same time, but she smiled graciously. "Thank you, Jacqueline, Mr. Altman."

Shuffling sounded behind her, and Vivian appeared. "Where did everybody go?" She glanced at Kate, and her eyes widened.

"What?"

Vivian shook her head quickly and smiled, slipping into her professional mask as she turned back to the group, her eyes owlishly large.

"Seriously, what?" Kate mouthed.

"Ms. Flynn." With an exasperated huff, Jacqueline dug through her purse and handed her a compact. "Allow me to explain since it appears no one else feels comfortable."

"Really, Mother?" Vivian growled.

Nervous, Kate looked into the little mirror and searched her face. Her makeup wasn't quite as flawless as it had been, that was true, but what did they expect? She glanced up quizzically.

With an embarrassed huff, Vivian moved Kate's hand so that the mirror reflected the long black smudge across her throat.

Kate gasped. When had that happened? She didn't remember Vivian's lips touching her when they were in the bathroom. She rubbed the smudge but only smeared it, transferring some of the stain onto her glove in the process.

She had two choices: keep rubbing it while Vivian's mom and the general director of Lyric watched or run for the hills.

She nodded in what she hoped was a casual manner. "If you will excuse me, Mrs. Kensington, Mr. Altman, Vivian."

Kate walked as quickly as she could without running into the bathroom and looked at her neck in the mirror. There wasn't much to be done.

"My mother invited you and Max to an early lunch next Sunday."

Kate and Vivian stood waiting for the valet to bring the car around.

"What? Why?" Kate wasn't sure she could face Mrs. Kensington again.

"I think you impressed her."

"You mean with the lipstick hickey?"

Vivian shook her head. "Perhaps she liked the way you handled yourself, or she sees that we enjoy each other. There's really no way of knowing."

"She invited me to the Lyric audition."

"I know."

"You know?"

"I do. I was the one who recommended you."

That explained why both Jacqueline and Mr. Altman knew her by name.

The car arrived, and they settled in. "I'm still surprised she invited us, though," Kate said.

"I think she's just interested in getting to know my girlfriend."

The word hit Kate's ears with an electric crackle. "Girlfriend?"

Instantly Vivian dropped her smile. "Oh. I guess I just thought… Do you not—"

"No, no!" Kate held up her hand. "It's just that we hadn't talked about it." She wrapped an arm around Vivian's waist, pulling her closer. "I'm your girlfriend, huh?"

"Aren't you?"

"Well, duh."

"So I suppose," Vivian said with a smirk, "that you liked my photo."

"Clearly," Kate said.

"You're quite an intriguing woman, you know."

"Is that code for you liked my reaction?"

"Very much."

Kate grinned. "I *so* won."

"Oh, trust me, Kate. You may have won the battle, but I will win the war."

Chapter 16

AFTER THE GALA, KATE AND Vivian fell back into simply being together. Kate had never known this type of happiness with a significant other before. The relationship was so…easy. Looking around the loft and seeing Max's stuffed animals, toys, and dinosaur-print tighty-whities filled her with contentment. But Sunday morning, the day they were to have lunch with Jacqueline, Charlie and Vivian were like animals anticipating a thunderstorm.

Kate brushed her hair into a ponytail for the third time, then groaned. It was no better than the previous two styles she had tried.

"Seriously, you look fine," Charlie said from the bathroom doorway. "Everything will be fine."

Kate snapped back. "Dude. When she saw me, I had a huge lipstick hickey from her daughter that was roughly the size of Canada."

"Yeah, but—"

"This?" Max appeared at the doorway dressed in a polo shirt and jeans.

"No, buddy, I think we need something a little fancier. Charlie, would you please go and help him find a pair of slacks?"

"Whatever you say, boss."

Vivian noisily opened and closed drawers in the bedroom. "Goddamnit!" she barked. "Kate, have you seen my grandmother's pearls?"

Kate leaned her head out of the bathroom. "Did you look on the dresser? I put them up there yesterday so Max wouldn't get them."

Vivian had spent the morning scrutinizing every part of herself. She had combed and combed and combed her hair until it flared perfectly. Her dress was black and fitted but not tight, and she wore a cream and black Chanel suit jacket over it. Her nails were freshly polished, and her makeup was flawless. Next to her, Kate felt like the messy kid sister. But it would have to do.

Vivian pushed past to check her hair in the bathroom once more, but Kate caught her and held her still. "Viv, you look beautiful. You always look beautiful. Your hair, your clothes, your jewelry—it's all perfect, okay? Why are you so nervous?"

Vivian stiffened. "My mother tends to be very disapproving of me. Let's just say that."

"What do you mean?"

But Vivian had already broken out of her grasp and turned toward the bedroom door, where Max had reappeared, finally dressed appropriately, his hair wet and flattened. Charlie stood next to him, looking sour.

Kate sighed. "Are we ready?"

Vivian drove them straight to Evanston, where they had taken Max trick-or-treating.

Kate looked out at the large houses as they drove by. "Okay, why didn't you tell me this neighborhood was your mom's? Which house was hers?" She answered the question before Vivian could. "Oooh, the one you made us skip, wasn't it?"

Vivian pulled into the front gates of the huge Georgian mansion, conforming Kate's thought, and parked at the top of the U-shaped driveway. She glanced at Charlie's moving hands in the rearview mirror. "To be fair, my mother doesn't give out candy anyway."

"You could have told us," Kate grumbled.

"Oh, you guys came out here for trick-or-treating?" Charlie asked. "Max, I bet you got a lot of candy."

"It will be fine. Everything will be fine. It might even be fun," Kate muttered.

They parked and walked up the steps to the front door. Vivian gave Kate half a smile and knocked, glancing at Charlie.

Jacqueline opened the door. "You made it," she said kindly, and Charlie's hands flew.

"Of course we did, Mother." Vivian leaned in to give her mother a peck on the cheek. "How are you?"

"I am very well, dear, thank you." She turned to look at Kate, smiling warmly.

"Mrs. Ke—Jacqueline. It's good to see you again. This is my son, Max."

"Max!" Jacqueline smiled down at him. "It's very nice to meet you."

"It's nice to meet you, ma'am," Max said, signing as he spoke.

They followed Jacqueline into a huge sitting room where a large fire roared in the fireplace. Max ran to it, stretching out in the nearby chair.

"Max! Manners!" Kate snapped. "I'm sorry," she said to Jacqueline. "He's excited."

Jacqueline held her hand up. "It's nice to have a child in the house again." She glanced at Vivian.

"I'm working on it, Mother."

"I know you are, dear."

Vivian glanced at Charlie, who rolled her eyes.

"Something to drink? Coffee?" Jacqueline offered. "Max, would you like a glass of juice?"

"Yes, please," he said politely.

"Leigh!" Jacqueline called, and a woman stepped into the room as if she had been waiting for the summons, bowed her head briefly, and stepped back out.

Kate glanced at Vivian, looking for an explanation.

"Leigh is my mother's assistant. She also serves drinks, cleans the house, and cooks on the rare occasion that the cook is off."

"Coo*k*," Jacqueline said, clipping the K to emphasize it. "Coo*k*. Sometimes I wonder if those speech therapy sessions did anything at all for you."

Vivian flushed, clearly mortified as she repeated the word, capturing the K clearly.

"Yes," Jacqueline continued as if she hadn't just humiliated Vivian. "Leigh is a great comfort to me now that my husband is gone."

They chatted until lunch was served. Once seated, Jacqueline asked Max, "So what do you play, Max?"

"Oh, he doesn't play anything yet." Kate answered. "I thought I would start him on piano when he turned five."

Jacqueline frowned. "I started violin when I was three. He should really be a year into his studies by now. And piano, of all things. I mean, really."

Kate shrugged, then changed the subject. "I understand you play the harp."

Max looked at Jacqueline, his eyes wide. "You play the harp? Can I see?"

"After lunch, yes," Jacqueline said with a wink, then turned to Kate. "Katelyn, do you think you will be ready for the audition with Lyric?"

Kate laughed nervously. "Well, my calluses are getting calluses, so I guess so."

Jacqueline nodded approvingly. "Wrap your fingers in tiger balm and gauze at night, and that should help the cuts heal quickly. Are you wearing wrist guards when you practice?"

"No." Kate frowned.

"Do you want tendonitis, dear?"

"Mother knows every trick of the trade," Vivian said.

"Oh. I'll have to look into that."

Jacqueline pushed her plate away and lit a cigarette. "It's so nice to have another musician in the family."

Kate glanced at Vivian, who was looking out the window.

"What is your practice routine, if you don't mind me asking?"

By the time coffee was set out, one thing had become clear. Jacqueline spared few words for her daughter and none for Charlie, but she was absolutely taken with Kate and smitten with Max. This should have been a win for the new girlfriend, but Kate felt as if she had been drafted to the wrong side of a war she hadn't known existed.

"Excuse me, Mrs. Kensington?" Max asked, his hands flying.

"Yes, dear?"

"Will you show me your harp now, please?"

Jacqueline took Max's hands in hers and kissed his knuckles. "Max," she said, "I want to tell you something."

Max looked at her attentively. "Okay."

"When you're in my house, you don't have to do that."

"Do what?"

"With your hands. In this house, we don't do that."

"You mean sign?" he asked, looking at his hands as if they had been acting on their own.

Jacqueline nodded.

The Loudest Silence

"But then Viv'n won't hear us! She won't know what we're saying. You're supposed to sign when someone deaf is in the room."

"Oh, but she will. We don't have to use sign language with her because she was taught to get along without it. See, Vivian and I made an agreement when she was young. Outside the house, she can use an interpreter and sign language, but in here, she's to work on what she was taught growing up. Isn't that right, Vivian?"

Vivian stared at Jacqueline before answering. "Right, Mother."

Kate jumped in. "Wait. I don't und—"

Vivian gripped her thigh, her fingers digging in.

Max furrowed his brow, as if he had been given a math problem that even a college student couldn't solve.

Jacqueline stood up from the table, took Max's hand, and led him from the room.

As soon as they left, Kate turned to Vivian and Charlie. "What was that about?"

Charlie made a few vague gestures, then gave up and looked out the window. Vivian shrugged, finished her glass of wine in one swallow, and stared down at the table.

It appeared that Kate was lost in a sea of family secrets without a life jacket.

They drove back to Vivian's apartment in complete silence. Max was probably confused about Jacqueline's reprimand for speaking the language that he spoke at home. Kate was confused about—everything. Why had no one warned her? Why had Jacqueline been so *nice* to her and Max, yet horrible to Charlie and Vivian too?

"Nap time?" Max asked as soon as they entered the loft.

Kate nodded, ruffling his hair. "We'll talk after nap time, okay?"

He disappeared into his room. Kate found Vivian and Charlie sitting silently at the kitchen island with a bottle of wine and glasses. Whatever had happened, it was clear that they knew what was going on in the other's mind.

Kate sat with them in silence, unsure how to navigate the landmines. "Vivian, what—"

Charlie let out a loud, obvious sigh, putting her empty glass down on the counter, silently communicating something to her best friend with her eyes. "I'm going to get going." She kissed their cheeks before wordlessly slipping out the door.

Kate watched her go. "So am I not welcome in this part of your world? Should I just accept that?" She waited for a response, but Vivian remained silent. "Vivian, please. I'm just trying to understand."

Vivian got up and moved to the couch. When Kate joined her, she held out her arms.

She leaned back, pulling Kate on top of her, and found her lips. Her kiss was desperate and full of sadness, full of hurt that went so deep that there were no words. She pulled Kate deeper and deeper into the abyss.

So Kate helped her escape into it.

She made love to her, softly and sweetly, trying to heal the wounds she couldn't see and didn't understand, soothing them with all the adoration for Vivian she had.

Afterward, Kate held her in her arms.

She kissed her forehead, then shifted so Vivian could see her speak. "Your mom doesn't sign to you."

Vivian stroked Kate's jaw, then shook her head.

"Never?"

"She can't speak ASL at all. In fact, she forbids it."

"But how is that possible? It's your *language*."

Vivian laughed, the bitterness like ice. "At first, I had enough hearing that if you were very loud, I could hear you. So my parents spent the first five years of my life yelling everything at me until my mother complained that it was damaging her vocal cords. She used to sing as well as play the harp. She even toured with Lyric once."

"And she blames you for her career ending."

"You know her so well already." She sniffled. "From what I was told, she was always rough on her voice, even before I came along, but there's no way of knowing. Either way, growing up, my life consisted of pantomime and raised voices. When I was around five, they noticed that yelling was not working as well anymore. I think my mother thought I wasn't trying hard enough."

"What about your dad?"

"My father wasn't overly involved. When he was there, he was busy with work. But often he wasn't there at all." Vivian lapsed into silence again.

Kate held her for a long while without speaking. Then she said, "It's funny. Growing up, I always thought that any parent would be better than not having one at all. I guess you never really know, do you? I mean, I was always alone, and it sounds like—"

"I was too."

Kate shook her head. "I don't get it. She just seemed so nice until that moment when suddenly she wasn't."

"That's my mother. She loves me; I know she does. I am simply the wrong child for her."

Kate picked up Vivian's hand and kissed it.

"I remember the day I lost my hearing completely. I had just turned seven. My mother and I had had a fight, and I went to bed crying. When I woke up in the middle of the night, my ears were completely clogged. I thought it was because of the crying."

"Up until then, I only heard the loudest sounds. Then I started hearing a high-pitched buzzing in my ears. One night I got up, and suddenly I felt this little pop, and my hearing was completely…gone. It was the loudest silence I had ever heard. I ran to my mother, and she screamed herself hoarse trying to make me hear. She put headphones on me and turned up the stereo to full volume, but I could only feel the vibration. I couldn't hear anything.

"After the doctor confirmed that I was deaf, they hired an interpreter as my nanny. She taught me sign language, and after that, everyone in the family spoke to me through her. When I was eleven, Mother learned of this aggressive type of speech therapy. The idea was that, if I worked hard enough, I could live a normal life. I was put in one of the most prestigious speech therapy programs available that taught me to use my voice and read lips.

"In truth, though, even at a young age, I never spoke well. I quickly learned to stop speaking at all because I could see my mother cringe when I did. It took a lot of work and therapy to speak as well as I do now, but it was a grueling process.

"Finally, my parents decided that I had gotten as good as I was going to get at speaking and reading lips. They fired the interpreter and forbade me from using sign at home. I think the idea was to force me to live hearing. Then my mother started me on piano, which was pointless, and she seemed to be more and more disappointed in me as time passed. As I've told you, my entire family are musicians, and no one knew what to do with me once it was clear that I could not be like them.

"I felt like the unwanted family pet. They would pat me on the head, put me on a chair in the corner, then go off to discuss music. I think I finally got involved in the only way I knew how just to stop feeling so left out. I couldn't play their music, but I could help to run the organizations. And I proved early on that I could run their organizations far better than they could."

Kate stroked Vivian's cheek. "You must have been so lonely with no one to talk to."

"I was. People assume that it's simple to read lips, but it's not. Following a whole conversation, especially in a group, catching emphasis and inflection, is almost impossible. Even now, I don't understand as much as I pretend to. My mother would get frustrated at any indication that I was deaf, whether it was using sign language, not understanding what was happening around me, or a vocal slip, so I learned to fake it. For years, I was unable to really communicate with anyone."

"How did Charlie end up as your interpreter?"

Vivian smiled. "Languages come naturally to Charlie, as I'm sure you noticed. She liked it, so she learned it. On the very rare occasions that circumstances required an interpreter, we hired her until she made it her career path. She's devoted her entire life to helping me. She's been a godsend. I don't know what I would do without her."

"So why is your mom still so angry?"

"Sign was never good enough for my mother. She wanted me to understand *her when she spoke*. But my mother barely moves her mouth when she speaks. She thinks it's unladylike. She always thought I was pretending I couldn't understand her to get back at her."

"Is that why Charlie came today? To interpret for your mom?"

"Yes. Once I got old enough to realize I would never have her love anyway, I started bringing Charlie with me."

"You had a lonely childhood. I know how that feels. I was always wrong too."

The Loudest Silence

"What do you mean?"

Kate sighed. "People always saw me as temporary, even couples who were looking to adopt. I always found myself back with the social worker, waiting for the next place. I always felt different, always felt unwanted."

"Oh, Kate."

Kate shrugged. "A lot of the people I stayed with were nice people. In fact, I thought I found a home once with Sheila and Don."

"How long were you with them?"

"Almost two years," Kate said, smiling at the bittersweet memory. "It was the longest I had been anywhere. They were so happy to get me. They had been looking for someone to adopt for years. I even started to call them Mom and Dad."

"What happened?"

"They had just bought me a new backpack, one of those clear ones that were so popular for a while."

Vivian laughed. "They were entirely impractical, but I loved mine."

"When I got home from school, I found out that Sheila had died of a heart attack. Don wasn't prepared to adopt on his own. I begged him to try, promised I wouldn't get in the way. But two days later, I was back with the social worker.

"It happened over and over and over again. I was the trial kid. It made me a little jaded, like, why am I not good enough for a forever family? And I learned that nothing ever lasts, especially relationships."

"Oh, Kate, I'm so sorry. You deserved so much more. They were simply horrible people. Do you understand that?"

Instead of answering, Kate wrapped Vivian in her arms, and they sat in silence until Max woke up from his nap and crawled into Vivian's lap.

"Viv'n?" he asked.

"What, sweetheart?"

"If I want to sign to you, is that okay?"

Vivian smiled, her eyes filling with tears. "Of course it is."

"Okay. Viv'n?"

"Yes, Max?"

"Why are you crying?"

Vivian laughed, a tear escaping from her eye. "Well, because I love you, and I am so, so lucky to have you and your mommy in my life."

"Mommy!" Max launched himself onto the bed.

Kate bolted upright from a sound sleep and groaned. The light coming in through the window seemed brighter than usual. She and Vivian had stayed up late talking, and it seemed far too early to get up.

"Mommy! Mommy, come on. You have to see!"

He bounced off the bed, pulling Kate with him. She shivered as her feet hit the cold wooden floor.

"Look!" Max pulled her to the window, grinning up at her. "It's snowing, Mommy!"

At some point in the night, the sky had opened up and delivered their first Chicago snow.

Snow was one of her favorite things. Kate had experienced it for the first time when she moved to New York for school, and the big, fluffy flakes still filled her with wonder.

Still in their pajamas, Kate and Max flew down the stairs and, throwing the patio door open wide, ran outside.

"Mommy, I'ma catch it! Watch me!" Max turned his face up to the sky, his tongue out.

Vivian appeared in the open doorway, smiling at them. When Kate spotted her, she and Max exchanged mischievous grins and, scooping up snow as fast as they could, began pummeling her with snowballs. Vivian screamed and tried to close the door, but Kate caught her around the waist and tossed her into the snow.

Vivian sat up, shook her head, and, getting to her feet, pointed a finger at Kate and said, "You're fired, Ms. Flynn."

Kate's laughter was cut off when one of Max's snowballs hit her in the head. "Why, you little!" She grabbed Vivian and swung her around for a shield.

They continued heaving snow at each other until Vivian noticed that Max's lips were turning blue. That prompted Vivian to insist in her best mom voice that everyone should march their butts inside before they all froze.

They wrapped themselves in blankets and stood together at the guest room window, looking out over downtown Chicago. Everything was covered in a thick white blanket, making the usually dirty city seem magical.

Kate sighed, utterly content. She pulled her son in closer to her and kissed Vivian's head. "Our very first Chicago snow."

Chapter 17

"You want to come with me to an all-Deaf event?" Vivian asked in disbelief. "You do understand, Kate, that almost everyone there will be deaf, correct? I've been told that can be quite intimidating." They had just gotten home from a late rehearsal and were getting ready for bed.

"Why would I care that it's all-Deaf? I just want to meet your friends." Kate swung her legs up onto the bed.

Vivian looked at Kate in the mirror as she removed her earrings. "But I haven't seen most of them since I was at Gallaudet."

"That wasn't *that* long ago!"

Vivian rolled her eyes. "While flattery will get you everywhere, my dear, it has been eleven years since I finished my undergraduate degree!"

Kate had seen Vivian's diploma from Gallaudet hanging over the computer in her office. She had never heard of a university for the Deaf and hard of hearing before meeting Vivian. "Think of it as Harvard for the Deaf," she had explained.

"Why shouldn't I want to go? It obviously means a lot to you."

"It's just a school."

Kate gazed levelly at her.

"All right. It does mean a lot to me. I'm a donor, and I attend many alumni events. Gallaudet was my first experience of living in a community of people like me."

"Couldn't have put it better myself. That's why I wanna go."

Vivian crawled into bed and snuggled up against Kate. "Actually, that does sound rather nice. But there's no need to dress up since we're just going to a Chinese restaurant."

"Are you sure you're ready for this?"

Kate pulled Vivian's hand up to kiss it. "Why wouldn't I be?"

But the moment they walked in together, Kate understood why Vivian had asked.

It turned out the Gallaudet University Alumni Association had rented out the entire restaurant for the evening.

As soon as they got in the door, a sea of people with hands flying came at them, swarming like excited bees.

Kate's mind went blank. She recognized a few signs like "how are you," but for the most part, it was like being an English speaker in a room full of Mandarin.

She glanced at Vivian anxiously, but Vivian, grinning broadly, didn't seem to notice. She pulled her hand away from Kate and began signing along with everyone else.

Kate squared her jaw. She could do this. Being here in Vivian's world was awesome.

But despite her efforts, she felt out of place.

She followed Vivian, thankful that she was always introduced vocally because her sign comprehension had dropped to zero.

Vivian pulled Kate toward a tall strawberry blonde and signed as she said, "Kate, this was my college roommate, Kristen. Kristen, this is Kate, my girlfriend."

Kristen smiled as she signed in response. Vivian tapped Kristen on the shoulder and said, her hands still moving, "Voice."

Kristen nodded and said something that sounded like a jumble of vowels. Kate flushed. "I'm sorry. I didn't understand."

Kristen looked briefly annoyed, but she quickly covered it with a smile and spoke again. "Hearing?"

"Oh. Yes." She flushed. "I am."

Kristen patted Kate's shoulder condescendingly. "Well, good for you for trying to learn." She might as well have said, "Our language is far too complex for a silly hearing person like yourself."

She wanted to respond, wanted to defend her intelligence, but instead she faked a smile and shoved her hands into her pockets.

And now it was even more clear why Vivian had questioned whether Kate really wanted to go to this event with her. She had explained it to her before, how sometimes the Deaf weren't comfortable with hearing people, that being forced to fit into the world of the hearing made them resentful, even cliquey. Vivian had told her stories of being bullied, of people assuming she was stupid because she couldn't hear, of people trying to take advantage. She imagined everyone else in this room had similar experiences with hearing people.

Vivian led her around the room, moving from flying hands to flying hands, until Kate felt as if she were on a never-ending teacup ride at Disneyland. She felt lost, useless—and completely invisible. People tried to talk to her, then realizing that she didn't understand, returned their attention to Vivian while she stood by silently.

Finally, overwhelmed and needing a break, she found her way to a table and ordered a beer.

It *was* fascinating to be here, Kate thought as she looked around. Other than the odd sound here and there—a cough, a sneeze, or the sound of a hand slapping another hand—the only consistent sound was the tape of pop songs that the restaurant played as background music that no one but her and the servers could hear. If she closed her eyes, she could pretend the room was empty, but the moment she opened them again, she was met with a visual explosion of hands and facial expressions.

Was this what Vivian felt when she was in a room full of hearing people?

She took a long pull from her beer. They hadn't been there long at all, but she was already exhausted.

Across the room, Vivian smiled and talked, for once completely in her element.

Vivian caught her eye and waved her over. Kate smiled back and made her way to her. She felt like a fool. People wanted to know about her, about what her life was like, yet she couldn't hold up her side of the conversation. Vivian answered most of the questions.

"I was just talking to Orin here about the Gallaudet football team," Vivian explained when Orin's hands stilled. "They kicked Notre Dame's ass this year."

Kate smiled weakly. "Go Bisons," she said, which made Vivian and Orin both laugh.

"Where did you go to school, Kate?" Orin asked, clearing his throat before speaking and rubbing his throat.

Kate's hands twitched in her pockets. She knew this sign. Vivian had shown it to her. Kate pulled her hands out to try, but Kristen was watching her across the room, smirking.

Orin nodded her on, so she quickly and clumsily signed, "New York University."

"Ah, I see!"

Kate smiled, feeling a little less foolish.

Then Vivian reached over and moved her fingers into the correct shapes.

Kate glanced at Kristen, who was laughing behind her hands.

Kate felt like a child being corrected by her teacher and wished that this one time Vivian had let the incorrect sign slide.

Kate stuck her hands back into her pockets, but neither Vivian nor Orin seemed to notice. Her cheeks were still burning when she felt her phone buzz.

How's it going? – C

Vivian seems to be having a great time. – K

My first Deaf event was hard too. Don't worry, you'll get there. – C

I feel like a gorilla in a room full of scholars. I want a hole to open up and swallow me. – K

Cut yourself some slack. It's your first event. – C

I can't. Not when this blonde woman keeps following me around and laughing. – K

Oh God. That's Vivian's old roommate and girlfriend. She's always hated me. She said it was because I was rude to her, but I'm pretty sure she thinks only Deaf people are worth knowing. Stay away from her. – C

Yeah, I figured that out. Also kind of mad at—

Kate felt a subtle change around her. She looked up to see everyone watching her. She shoved her phone back into her pocket.

"I was asking," Vivian said with ice in her voice, "if you were ready to eat. Orin has invited us to his table."

The evening did not improve. She did her best to focus on the conversation as they ate, refusing to ask anyone to slow their signing. Despite her efforts, though, she knew she was in trouble when she reached to take the bill and Vivian brushed her off.

She could smell the upcoming fight in the air the way she could smell rain.

They walked back to the car and drove home in silence.

Max greeted them as soon as they entered the loft, but instead of picking him up as she usually did, Vivian asked Stacey to take Max out for a hot chocolate.

Max bundled up quickly, and they were out the door in seconds. Kate looked after him helplessly.

Irritated, Kate sat at the kitchen counter. "Hey, could you not send my kid off for sugary snacks right before bed without asking me?"

"My, my." Vivian's eyes flashed. "You are *full* of surprises tonight."

"What's that supposed to mean?"

Vivian narrowed her eyes. "You've never cared before when I help that way."

Kate opened her mouth to respond but closed it again. Vivian was right, She did parent-like things for Max all the time.

Kate ran her hands through her hair. "You're right. I'm sorry. That was rude."

"And tonight?"

And tonight.

She didn't know how to explain how she felt about that night. It had been amazing and inspiring but also terrifying and humiliating.

"Well, first, I'm sorry about the phone thing. I got a notification, thought it might be Stacey, and then I got into a conversation with Charlie. I'm sorry. It won't happen again."

Vivian's face didn't soften. "It wasn't just that, Kate. I can't believe your behavior tonight."

"What?"

"Before this evening, I would not have believed that you could be so rude in a room full of Deaf people."

"Rude?" She blinked in confusion. "Because I couldn't under—"

"Kate, you spent the entire evening checked out. After a while, people stopped talking to you because you weren't responding. Did you know that Orin invited us for cocktails tomorrow night?"

"He did?"

"Yes, and he suggested I bring an interpreter."

"Why would you need an interpreter in a room full of—" She stopped abruptly. "Oh. He meant for me, didn't he?"

"Yes, he did. Kate. It's like you didn't even try to sign or keep up. You just saw that it was hard, and you checked out."

"What do you mean, I didn't try? I tried all freaking night. I have a killer headache because I was trying so damn hard!"

"To do what? Daydream?"

"To understand, Vivian! I was completely lost most of the time. And the one time I tried to communicate something, you fucking—"

"You didn't try, Kate! You didn't try to communicate at all. Everyone would have understood that you're a new signer and would have helped you, but you retreated."

"You're really selling me short here! I did! And the one time I signed, your old roommate laughed at me. Then you had to point out that I had done it wrong!"

"Isn't that how you learn? You try and you fail. Sometimes you make a fool out of yourself. You were in a safe environment to practice signing."

"You're not listening to me!" She jumped up from the kitchen stool and began pacing the room.

"You going with me went exactly as I feared it would. I'm sorry about Kristen. She's always been an elitist jerk, but you should have talked to me."

"Bullshit, Vivian! You're the one who made me look like an ass!"

Vivian snarled at her. "You looked like an ass anyway, Kate. In fact, you made me look like an ass when you didn't try to communicate."

"That's not fucking fair, Vivian! I tried to keep up, but I'm new to this! And frankly, I didn't think anyone would have the patience for my amateur signing, especially after you pointed out to everyone how bad I am at it!"

"And what should I have done, Kate? The sign was wrong!"

"Literally anything but what you did!"

Vivian's eyes rolled, dismissing her point. "Stop acting like a child, Kate!"

"I'm not the one acting like a child, Vivian!"

"I told you that it would be hard, Kate. I told you it would be intimidating."

"You're right. I didn't understand. I didn't understand how terrible I was going to feel, especially when people used their voices for me. Even then, I couldn't understand them half the time. It's not like they're used to trying to communicate!"

Vivian stared at her, then turned to the sink to fill a cup of water.

"In that way," she tried to tack on, but Vivian's back was to her.

Kate stomped on the wood floor. "How the hell am I supposed to talk to you when your back is turned?" she yelled futilely. She walked to the sink and gently turned Vivian to face her. "You're not being fair."

Vivian sighed. "I'm tired. I'm going to bed."

"Vivian!"

"No, Kate." Vivian said, brushing her off like a fleck of dust. "I think we've said plenty tonight." She started up the stairs to her bedroom.

Kate watched her go, then marched up the opposite stairs and climbed on the elliptical, her legs pumping away her anger.

She hadn't planned on working out. She wasn't wearing the right clothes, but she cranked up the resistance and pushed on until she began to sweat.

Max found her there a few minutes later. His cheeks were pink and he had snow in his hair. "Mommy, I ate hot chocolate with extra whipped cream!"

"You did?" She slowed her steps and got off the elliptical. She glanced up toward Vivian's bedroom. The bedside lamp was on.

Maybe she should apologize, though she wanted to keep fighting, to point out that she wasn't the only one who had made mistakes that evening. But if she were being honest with herself, she really hadn't tried hard enough. She had let herself retreat from a difficult situation.

She took Max to bed, then started up the stairs, mentally rehearsing what she would say.

Vivian had a book on her knees and didn't look up when Kate walked in.

Kate sat next to her and gently pushed the book down. "Hey."

Vivian looked at Kate without expression.

"I'm sorry, Vivian." She reached for Vivian's hand and squeezed it. "Really. I'm sorry tonight went so badly."

Vivian relaxed her face. "Thank you, Kate."

She leaned forward and kissed Vivian's cheek. "I'm going to shower."

When Kate got out a few minutes later, Vivian was curled up under the blanket. She turned off the light and climbed into bed beside her, resting her hand on Vivian's hip. Vivian pushed back, pressing her body into Kate's.

She wrapped her arms around Vivian and sighed, glad that their first real fight was over.

Chapter 18

MAX SQUINTED AT THE TURKEY. The skin was black on top and smelled like charred rubber, but Kate was grinning. A burnt turkey wasn't that big a deal. What was under the skin was more important.

"Oh, come on, kid. You don't need to be scared."

He wrinkled his nose. "It's burneded, Mommy. I don't think you did it right."

Kate scowled. "It's supposed to look like that!"

"Nuh-uh."

Kate laughed and lightly smacked his butt with a wooden spoon.

"All right. Who's ready to eat?" Vivian asked, eyeing the burned turkey.

"Me! Me! Me!"

They sat around the Thanksgiving table and loaded their plates, then raised their glasses.

"To Thanksgiving! May it be one of our best!" Kate said with a wink at her son. "And this year I'm thankful for"—she glanced around the table—"my life, right here and now. I'm in really good playing shape. I have a roof over my head, plenty of food, and wonderful people to share it with. What are you two grateful for?"

Max scratched his chin thoughtfully. "Chocolate pie!"

"Chocolate pie?" Vivian feigned shock. "Not Mommy or your food or Superman?"

He giggled. "Yup! Chocolate pie! Now you." He pointed at Vivian.

"Me? Well, I…" Vivian looked around the table. "I'm thankful for the turn my life has taken recently."

Kate smiled. "So, like, how recently? Did you meet a cute girl at the store or—"

"Oh hush, you!" Vivian threw her napkin at Kate.

"Let's eat!" Kate picked up her knife and fork. She had never cooked so much in her life. She had always believed that if you added good spices to a dish, then it would come out well. But as she bit into the turkey, the meat turned to sawdust in her mouth.

She took another bite, avoiding Vivian's and Max's eyes.

After the third bite, she tossed her napkin on the table. "Also I'm thankful your mom will have food at her house. Whose idea was it for me to cook the turkey?"

Vivian laughed.

They filled up on stuffing and gravy, then lounged on the couch to watch *A Charlie Brown Thanksgiving*, dozing off and on through the thirty-minute special. When it was over, they went to change their clothes.

"Why does your mother want me to bring my cello?"

"She always plays something after dinner, and she will probably ask you to play a piece with her."

"Oh God." Kate felt the blood drain from her face.

"Don't worry about it. Remember, it's a compliment."

Kate pulled on her shirt, puffing out her belly. "I'm so full I feel like I did when I was pregnant with Max."

Vivian had leaned over to lace her booted heels. "What?"

"I said, I'm so full I feel like I did when I was pregnant with Max."

Vivian looped her fingers through Kate's belt and pulled her closer to kiss her belly. "You know, I've never seen pictures of you pregnant with him."

Kate reached to her dresser and took a photo from the top drawer. "You have to promise not to make fun of me."

"I promise no such thing!"

"Well, then, you can't see it!"

Before Kate could react, Vivian snatched the picture from her hand. "Oh my God!"

In the photo from four years ago, Kate was dressed in her concert blacks, her hair pulled back in a ponytail.

"Your belly is huge!"

"I know. I put on thirty pounds."

Vivian returned the photo and went back to lacing up her shoes. From the way she avoided eye contact, Kate could tell that she had something to say.

Finally, Vivian looked up. "Would you want to get pregnant again?"

"What?"

"Do you think you would ever want to get pregnant again?"

Kate frowned. "Why are you asking?"

Vivian finished lacing her boots and stood up. "We've been dating for a while now. We're both in our thirties—"

"Uh, not yet thirty, thank you," Kate said.

"And I'm a few years *past* thirty. Things are different when you're dating in your thirties than when you're in your twenties."

Kate nodded. She had been raised with no family whatsoever and knew by the time she was fifteen that she wanted enough children to create her own sports team—provided she had a significant other to help referee. "Does that mean you would want more kids than Max?"

Vivian smiled. "Don't you think Max wants brothers and sisters?"

Kate's heart pounded in her chest. "I don't know. Why don't we ask *him*?"

"We could."

"How many more do you want?" Kate asked.

"Three."

Kate bit her lip. "Do you want to get pregnant?"

"Yes. Would you like that?"

"Or maybe we could foster."

A beautiful smile stretched across Vivian's face. "Or maybe we could foster Deaf children. There's a huge need for that in our community."

Warmth blossomed in Kate's belly.

Just then, Max stomped in, his tie in his hand and tears on his face. "I can't *do it*!"

Vivian beckoned him over. "Turn around."

Kate smiled. It was dangerous to plan too far into the future, but this agreement had been as easy as sliding into a warm bath. She and Vivian were good together, and that felt better than anything.

Chapter 19

Leigh greeted them at the door to the Kensington mansion. "Jacqueline is in the library. Charlotte got here a few minutes ago."

"Charlotte?" Kate whispered as they walked across the long foyer. "I didn't know anybody was brave enough to call Charlie by her full name."

Vivian sidestepped into the kitchen to grab a glass of wine. "Only one. And her assistant, I suppose. My mother says it's from knowing her as a child."

Kate nodded, understanding. It was just another way that Vivian's mother asserted her dominance.

Jacqueline beamed when they entered the room. "There they are!" The whole room turned to watch them enter.

She kissed Vivian's cheek and then, to her surprise, Kate's before leaning down and planting a smudge of lipstick on Max's forehead.

"Sorry, kid." Kate laughed and grabbed a napkin. "You're surrounded by women. That means lipstick kisses."

Charlie chuckled. "Don't worry. In a few years, he'll love that."

Jacqueline guided Kate and Max toward a group of people standing by the shelves. Kate recognized some of them from the Halloween gala, and she smiled graciously. Beside her, Jacqueline preened as if Kate were her personal discovery.

Mr. Altman stepped forward, his hand outstretched. "You are becoming a regular occurrence, Ms. Flynn."

Jacqueline pulled Max forward. "And this is her son, Maxwell."

Max stared at him. "What happened to your leg?"

Kate flushed. "I'm sorry. Apparently, he was raised by wolves."

"Are you the wolves in this situation?" Charlie muttered beside her.

"It's quite all right," Mr. Altman said, then excused himself.

Kate leaned down and turned Max to face her. "I know I raised you better than that."

"Charlie said he's part Borg!" Max said in a loud whisper. "Is he gonna assimiate us?"

"Charlie!" She rounded on her friend, who was laughing behind her hand.

"Careful, Max," Charlie said, winking at Kate. "You're going to get your mama in trouble with her future boss!"

Kate and Vivian stuffed themselves into a love seat with Max between them. Charlie perched on the arm.

Jacqueline tsked as she walked by. "Really, Charlotte. There are plenty of chairs."

Kate waited for Jacqueline to pass out of hearing. "You two really don't get along, do you?"

Charlie scoffed. "We just don't agree with each other's methods. For example, I think Vivian is a *person*."

When dinner had been served, they filed into the dining area, politely interacting, then afterward returned to the library.

Max fidgeted in his seat, but Kate pulled him back and, with a stern glance, made him settle down.

"I'm sorry you're bored, Max," Vivian spoke as she signed. "Just remember that chocolate pie is coming soon."

From the other side of the room, Mr. Altman's voice rang out. "Jacqueline, when are you going to bring out your harp?"

Jacqueline looked shocked at the request, as if it had never occurred to her to play for her guests. "Oh, Carlyle, should I?" Then she beamed. "Well, if you insist." She nodded to Leigh, who disappeared and then returned, rolling in the giant harp.

The guests milled around the room finding seats while Jacqueline settled behind her harp.

Vivian leaned in to whisper in Kate's ear. "This is the part where she thanks everyone for wanting to hear her play as if she hadn't played for them a hundred times already."

Jacqueline cleared her throat, and the conversation stilled. "Thank you, everyone, for joining me again this year. I hope you enjoyed the meal.

Dessert will be served shortly, and Carlyle Altman has asked me to fill the time by playing my harp."

Vivian yawned.

Kate glanced at her girlfriend. Vivian seemed to be a little drunk.

"As always, thank you for listening." Jacqueline leaned the huge instrument back, balanced it on her shoulder, and began to play.

Kate watched in awe as Jacqueline stroked the strings. The cello took quite a bit of dexterity, but that was nothing compared to what she was seeing now. One hand moved rhythmically over one side of the strings while the other plucked at the instrument like a spider weaving a web.

The longer Jacqueline played, the more agitated Vivian became. She bobbed and shifted in her seat. Kate took her hand, but Vivian pulled it away.

It was probably moments like these that had been the loneliest for Vivian as a child. Kate looked at her, imagining the child version sitting in the corner, watching her mother play music she couldn't hear, surrounded by people enjoying something Vivian couldn't share.

Kate reached for Vivian's hand again, and this time she didn't pull back.

With a final glissando, Jacqueline returned the harp to its resting position and stood up, her face radiant with the applause of her listeners.

"We'll take a short break," Jacqueline announced, "and then I would like to invite Katelyn Flynn, the newest member of our musical family and star cellist, to join me in playing 'Romance for Cello and Harp in D minor' by Johann Strauss."

Vivian rose, her lips pinched. "Here's your chance. I know you will play wonderfully."

Kate laughed nervously. "Does it bother you that she's pushing me forward like this?"

"Well, we all know she values music above all else." Vivian turned away and, without another word, walked out of the room with Charlie.

"You're a little green, dear."

Kate turned to see that Jacqueline had appeared behind her. "Excuse me?"

"I said, you're looking a little green. We're going to have to work on your poker face."

Kate laughed. "It's never been my strong suit."

"Don't worry." Jacqueline patted her arm. "I know a few tricks. I'll share them with you another day."

Kate nodded, surprised. "That's…that's kind of you."

"Did you see which way my daughter went?"

"I think she and Charlie went to get more wine."

"Oh my." Jacqueline sighed. "She really does hate coming here, doesn't she?"

Not sure how to answer that, Kate decided she would stay silent.

While the guests filtered back into the study, Kate set up her cello, and Jacqueline handed her the sheet music. Thankfully, she had played the Strauss piece before.

Jacqueline tapped her glass and spoke to the room again, but Kate didn't hear a word she said. The next thing she knew, Jacqueline was seated behind her harp and, nodding to Kate, they began to play.

Kate focused on the music in front of her, transposing as she went. Her head swayed with the motion of her bow, and, despite her racing heart, she breathed with the rhythm of the music.

When they finished the piece, she looked up. Jacqueline's eyes were shining.

Kate looked out into the audience and caught Vivian's eye.

Vivian nodded and winked in reassurance.

When Kate glanced back at Jacqueline, the woman had returned the harp to the resting position and nodded to her. Kate understood that she was to play by herself. Without giving herself time to think, she chose a piece she knew well and began to play from memory.

"I thought I was going to throw up." Kate hadn't been able to escape from the library fast enough. As soon as she had finished playing and Jacqueline announced dessert, she ran to find Charlie in the kitchen, Vivian right behind her. Max had stayed with Jacqueline, still fascinated by the harp. "It was like an audition, but so much worse. Oh God."

Vivian purred against Kate's neck. "You did wonderfully. I could tell. I was watching my mother's face."

Kate leaned her head back. "Oh yeah?"

The Loudest Silence

"Yes." Vivian kissed her, then said, "She was testing your ability, and you rose to the occasion. She clearly loves you."

"She seems to. But I don't get your mom. Is it a trap?"

"It very well might be."

"I thought I was going to fall flat on my face. Altman will be the one overseeing the Lyric auditions, right?"

"I don't actually know that." Vivian looked Kate up and down. "Would you like to go somewhere and make out, Ms. Flynn?"

Kate took Vivian in her arms. "I think you're drunk, Ms. Kensington."

"Mm, I think I am, Ms. Flynn. That does not change the fact that I would like to see you in the downstairs bathroom, please."

"And that's too weird for me. I'm officially off duty." Charlie started toward the door but was intercepted by Jacqueline's appearance.

Kate jumped away from Vivian guiltily, but Jacqueline didn't seem to notice. She asked her daughter, "How much wine have you had, Vivi?"

Vivian looked to Charlie to interpret, then said, "Don't worry, Mother, I won't embarrass you tonight."

Lips pinched, Jacqueline turned to Kate. "Katelyn dear, would you follow me, please? I have something I would like to show you."

"Um…"

"Come along." Jacqueline turned to leave, and Kate followed, knowing she didn't have a choice.

"Katelyn," Jacqueline said as they ascended the staircase, "I would like to confer with you about a Christmas gift for Vivian."

"Oh? I'm not sure how much I can help you. I'm not sure what to get her myself."

Jacqueline opened the door to a private study and motioned for Kate to sit in front of the cherry wood desk. "All the better, then." She sat behind the desk like a dean of some high-priced university. Eyes narrowed, she retrieved a pamphlet from the top drawer and handed it to Kate.

Kate looked at the pamphlet. "Cochlear implant?"

Jacqueline nodded.

Kate looked at the pamphlet again. The images were labeled "sound processor," "hearing nerve," and "internal implant." "I don't understand. What is it exactly?"

"It allows the deaf to hear, Katelyn."

Chapter 20

"I don't...I don't understand," Kate stammered.

"This is something I've been looking into for a while now. It's a device that, once implanted, sends sound directly to the brain. Or something like that. I admit I don't understand it entirely myself. But I spoke to the best otolaryngologist in town, and she assures me that this could improve Vivian's life exponentially."

"Wait." Kate shook her head, trying wrap her head around how the device would work. "This little thing here"—she pointed at the image of the implant—"attaches to her brainstem and allows her to hear? Isn't that kind of invasive? That's—that's brain surgery!" The thought of anything being implanted made her skin crawl.

"No, no, it's not, and you're missing the point, Katelyn. Vivian will be a normal person after this is done."

"She *is* normal."

"And yet there is so much she is missing out on."

Kate wanted to argue, but she had seen sadness in Jacqueline's eyes when they were performing. "I just—"

"She struggles, Katelyn. You of all people know that. If I can do something to help my daughter have a happier and better life, then why would I not want to?"

They were interrupted by a knock at the door. Leigh popped her head in. "Ms. Kensington, Mr. Keen would like to speak to you."

Jacqueline nodded, then looked back at Kate.

"Please think about this. Think of how it could change Vivian's life." She stood and walked to the door, waiting expectantly. "And not a word to Vivian. Hide the pamphlet for now, please."

"Don't you think—?"

But Jacqueline held up her hand. "Not a word. I will see you on Christmas Day."

"Oh, so we're coming over—"

"For Christmas dinner. Yes, dear."

"Is this another big Kensington event?"

"No, just a family get-together."

The thought of spending another holiday in Jacqueline's mansion, with its servants and formal dining, made Kate balk. Christmas was supposed to be a happy day. She and Max, wherever they were, always felt at home because they were together. "Why don't you come to us?" she blurted out without thinking.

"I'm sorry?"

"Come spend Christmas with us. That would mean a lot to Vivian."

Jacqueline blinked, her eyelashes fluttering. "Oh. I suppose I could. All right."

Kate drummed on the steering wheel as she drove them back to the loft that night.

"Are you all right?" Vivian finally asked.

"What? Me? Yeah, of course." She glanced at Vivian. "Why wouldn't I be?"

Vivian studied her. "You've been behaving strangely ever since my mother pulled you aside. What did she say to you?"

"Nothing! Well, she told me about an audition in Louisville." It wasn't a lie. On their way back downstairs, Jacqueline had mentioned the audition and said she thought Kate should take it to help her get in better shape for the Lyric audition.

From the back seat, Charlie scoffed, muttering in Chinese before she switched to English. "Of fucking course she did."

Kate glanced at Charlie in the mirror. "What do you mean?"

"Of course Jacqueline would tell you about something that would—"

Vivian reached back and slapped Charlie's leg.

"Whoa, whoa, whoa! Is there something I need to know?" Kate asked.

"My mother just likes to control lives a bit too much," Vivian said.

They drove the rest of the way in silence. When they got to the loft, Charlie waved them off, then got into her own car.

Inside, Vivian poured herself another glass of wine in the kitchen as Kate helped Max into his pajamas and tucked him in.

Kate closed Max's door and made her way to where Vivian sat at the kitchen counter. "I've never seen you drink this much," Kate said.

"Are you asking if I'm okay?" Vivian asked.

"Yes."

"Tonight was fairly typical in the land of my mother."

"So you always have that much fun, huh?"

Vivian snorted. "Let's call the drinking a survival tactic. I usually drink a little more at my mother's. I'm sure she thinks I have a drinking problem. After I have a few drinks, I miss all the little side comments, so I consider it worth it."

Kate sipped from Vivian's wine glass. "She's an interesting woman," she said carefully. "I don't know if I get her." She was beginning to suspect that Jacqueline was more than the cold bitch that she appeared to be.

Vivian leaned against her with a sigh. "It makes me nervous that you think she's interesting instead of abhorrent."

Kate stretched her arm around Vivian's shoulders. "Why? I mean, I get it—well, no, I don't get it. I don't get her thing with ASL. But she loves you, Vivian. She loves Charlie too."

Vivian tilted her head up for a kiss. "It's cute that you want to see the best in her."

They showered and went to bed, but after Vivian had drifted off to sleep, Kate slipped away, tiptoed to the downstairs office, and opened Vivian's computer. She typed two words into the search engine: *cochlear implant*.

She studied late into the night, reading about the procedure and how the implants worked. She watched online videos of people hearing for the first time.

The longer she watched, the more she thought about how Vivian's life might have been different. What if cochlear implants had been available when Vivian first lost her hearing? Would she have studied music like the rest of her family? Would she be the pianist in the symphony instead of the board president? If Vivian got the implants, what would she look like when she heard her name for the first time since she was a child? Would Kate be the one to say it?

It wasn't until early morning that Kate noticed something at the bottom of the search page that alarmed her: *cochlear implant controversy*. She clicked on the link and read: *The cochlear implant is still controversial. The procedure is considered a miracle cure for deafness, but many recipients are overwhelmed and fearful at the sudden flood of sensory stimulants. These reactions are seldom seen on YouTube.*

Despite the drawbacks, Kate loved this idea. The implant would eliminate so many of Vivian's problems, so much of Vivian's pain, all of the times that she felt different or unhappy. There would be no more fighting with her mom, no more pretending she understood what was happening in a room full of people. Vivian would be a hearing woman again.

She crawled back into bed and studied Vivian's face. "Vivian," she said softly. Then she said it again louder. Vivian did not react. She began to hum her favorite song. Still nothing.

She stroked Vivian's cheek with her thumb. Vivian's face twitched.

What would it be like to help bring this woman she cared for so much out of her own personal silence?

It took exactly one week for Kate to break her promise to Jacqueline.

Max was over at Charlie's, playing with her new gaming console. She and Vivian had spent the afternoon in bed until Kate had to get dressed for the evening's concert. Vivian got up too, pulling a robe on over her naked body.

"Why'd you get up?"

"Bed wasn't as warm after you left it."

"Come here." Kate pulled her into her arms.

Vivian let out a sound like a purr. "I wish you didn't have to go. We never have an evening where Max is gone." "You could come with me." Kate regretted the words as soon as they were out.

Vivian raised her eyebrows. "Do you want me to come with you?"

"No, I just…"

"What is it? What are you trying to ask?" Vivian asked.

"Sorry. I guess that's dumb."

Vivian stared up, waiting.

Kate wasn't sure if it was okay to ask a Deaf person this, but she had to know. "Do you ever wish that you could?"

Vivian pulled away and sat on the bed. "What are we talking about here, Kate? Do I wish that I could hear, or do I wish that I could hear you play?"

Kate turned back to the mirror, sorry she had asked.

Vivian stood and wrapped her arms around her from behind. "It's all right, Kate. I'm not mad. Of course I wish I could hear you play."

"You do?"

"Of course. There are many things I wish I could take part in."

"Would you change things if you could?"

Vivian kissed her lightly on the lips. "Sometimes. Sometimes I think I would."

"What the hell did she mean by that?" Kate asked Stephen as she packed up her cello. "Leave it to Vivian to give me an answer that isn't an answer at all."

Stephen leaned with one shoulder against the wall, his arms crossed, his brows furrowed. "She said 'sometimes'?"

"Yes!" She swung her cello so hard onto her back that she stumbled. "I just… I want to get into her mind. Like, does she even know about implants? She wasn't raised in the Deaf community, so maybe she doesn't."

"And you feel like you can't go along with Jacqueline's Christmas gift unless Vivian actually wants it?"

"Of course! I've *seen* how she struggles. This could be a really good thing. And why does her mom want to do this? Is it because she would love to not have a Deaf daughter anymore? Or is it for Vivian's benefit? And even if she is trying to *fix* Vivian, does it matter if in the end it helps her become a happier person?"

They pushed out into the cool night air, cinching up their coats, and stood facing each other to finish their conversation.

"Well, she's her mom, right?" Stephen said. "My mom always knows what's best for me."

"Right."

"And they might have an awkward relationship, but she knows Vivian better than anybody else. That's her job. No mom ever means their child ill will. That isn't in the job description."

Kate laughed. "All right, mama's boy."

Stephen grinned. "Hey, what can I say? I like my mom."

Charlie came bounding out of the stage door. "What are you two talking about?" She bounced up beside them, breathing into her hands.

"Nothing at all." He glanced meaningfully at Kate. "See you soon, Flynn."

"What was that about?" Charlie asked.

They started toward the L. "I saw this thing online the other day, and I was wondering about it."

Charlie grinned and shoved her shoulder. "Have you been doing something on the internet that you shouldn't?"

"Shut up! I was talking about this thing called a cochlear implant."

Charlie looked out across the avenue, studying a crowd of college-aged students. "Oh. Yeah, I know about those."

"Why doesn't Vivian have one? I mean, it could be a really good thing, right?" Kate watched Charlie, frustrated with her inattention. "Char?"

"Hmm? Oh, no, yeah, they can be great. We've never really talked about it."

"Oh."

"I'm gonna be late for my train. Chat later, okay?" Charlie hurried off.

If Kate had been confused before, she was even more so now.

The next morning, Kate paid Jacqueline a visit. Leigh showed her into the office.

"Katelyn, what a surprise. To what do I owe this honor?"

She sat in the chair across from Jacqueline's desk. "Why?"

Jacqueline's lip twitched. "Why *what*, dear?"

Kate leaned forward, resting her elbows on her knees. "*Why* do you want to do this for Vivian? Is it because you hate that she can't hear?"

Jacqueline shuffled the papers on her desk. "Contrary to popular belief, I do not hate that she can't hear. She is my daughter. Despite what she thinks of me, I have always and will always give her everything she needs and wants. That is my job."

"But why now? The implant has been available since the nineties. Vivian could have been hearing all this time."

Jacqueline didn't smile. "If Max had a disability that a new and controversial surgery could solve but he could live with the disability, would you do it? Or would you wait, let the technology advance, and consider it at a later date?"

Kate stared at Jacqueline, her mind working. She heard the honest pain in the woman's voice, believed that the decision had been difficult for Jacqueline. "I would have done the same thing that you did."

"Thank you."

"But I still think you should talk to her first."

"What do you mean?"

"You know, talk to her before you make an appointment with anyone, and see what she thinks."

Jacqueline nodded. "Well, I'm going to go ahead and book the date. That way there won't be any further delay."

"No, I'm saying you should talk to her before you schedule anything."

Jacqueline waved her hand in the air. "Oh, don't be silly. We can always cancel if she doesn't want to do it."

"Don't you think—"

"Have you been scheduled for the Louisville audition yet?"

The audition. She had hoped to avoid the subject until she had made up her mind. "No, I—"

"Katelyn. Take the audition."

"All due respect, ma'am, but shouldn't that be my choice? Besides, the Louisville Orchestra is my unicorn."

"I'm sorry?"

She shifted in her seat. "You know, my unicorn. The unreachable thing. I've auditioned for Louisville a number of times. I always make it to the final round, but I never win."

"You want to build a reputation for yourself in this town, correct?"

"Of course I do." She tried to keep her voice from wavering.

"Then how would it look, dear, if an audition was available to you and you did not take it simply because, as you say, it's your unicorn?"

Kate pressed her lips together. She hated being told what to do, but Jacqueline made a very good point.

"It's a full-time position, Katelyn. One that is below your abilities, yes, but one not to be ignored."

Kate sighed. Okay, she'd audition. It wasn't as if she was going to get the position anyway.

Chapter 21

Kate had told Vivian she was taking the Louisville audition, but she didn't tell her it was because of her mom. She refused to be the cause of any more animosity between them.

On the surface, everything was fine—they did their Christmas shopping, they cuddled, they made love—but Vivian was always a little distant, no matter how many times Kate insisted she was taking the audition for practice.

"What about your position here? Louisville won't want to defer a year while you finish next season," Vivian had asked when Kate first informed her about her plans.

"That depends. Are you asking as my girlfriend or as the board president?" Kate thought the comment would make Vivian laugh.

Vivian's expression didn't change. "Both."

"Viv, I'm not going to win. I've never won an audition there. And I don't want to move there at all. No one fits in unless they have an unnatural love of horses. But I should probably take the audition. Think of it as a warm-up for Lyric."

"That isn't until the new year."

"I know, I know, but stop worrying, okay?"

"What about Max?"

Kate shrugged. "I thought it might be a good excuse for a sleepover at Stephen's, you know?"

Vivian's face fell. "You're sending him there?"

"Yeah. Max seems to like him. I mean, I'd leave him at the apartment by himself, but I'm a little worried he would invite friends over for an apple juice kegger."

Vivian finally cracked a smile. "I meant, why don't you leave him with me? We'll have fun."

"Vivian, Max should spend some time with Stephen. Isn't that the point of all of this? We're trying to see if it works."

Vivian pressed her lips into a thin line.

Kate smiled to herself. Vivian *wanted* her to leave Max with her. She saw it in her face. "Look, why don't you two split the time?"

"Excuse me?" She looked as though the thought of sharing anything with Stephen was off-putting.

"Why not?"

Vivian sighed, but she nodded in agreement.

"Just don't come crying to me when he gets into your apple juice."

The time came to go, and Kate had to admit that she didn't want to, not with that shadow on Vivian's face. She had decided not to tell Max why she was going out of town for the day, worried that he wouldn't understand; not that it seemed that even Vivian really understood.

"I promise," Kate said yet again. "I am coming back. I can tell you're worrying. I'm not going to win."

Vivian gave her a brittle smile and pushed her toward the elevator. "You'll be late if you hit any traffic."

Kate wrapped her in a tight hug. "I'll be back before you know it."

Vivian's huge brown eyes blinked slowly, and this lack of a reaction worried Kate more than the evasive shrugs.

"Okay," Kate finally said, unsure, and took a step toward the elevator. "I'll see you tomorrow night at the latest. And Stephen should be here to pick up Max for the afternoon in like an hour. Be nice, okay?" She eyed her.

It seemed like Vivian, despite her cool look, was all but shaking.

"I'll see you soon," Kate said and reached for the button that would close the elevator.

Vivian reached out, shooting a hand in front of the elevator sensors. "Kate."

"Hmm?"

Vivian pushed her hand away from the button and cupped Kate's face, bringing their lips together quick and hard.

Kate gasped, feeling the pull of Vivian as she carefully slipped past Kate's lips.

Vivian wrapped an arm around her waist, holding her so tightly that Kate's back bowed backward a little.

"Mmmph," Kate grunted, turning into a puddle. She pulled her close, both reveling in and fearing the feelings that were flowing over her like a tidal wave.

Vivian slid her hand to the back of Kate's head, clasping it hard in her hair, making Kate grunt again. Then, just as suddenly, Vivian released her.

With clouded eyes, Kate pushed the button for the lobby and stepped out. Kate grinned, listing over like Jell-O against the elevator wall. Her thumb traced her own lips, pleased with the sendoff.

Vivian smirked, seeming proud.

Kate grinned. "I'll be back before you know it."

"I'll be waiting," Vivian said. Her smile was wide and suggestive, making Kate feel as if she could fly.

The doors began to close, but still Kate didn't look away, which was why she saw that beautiful smile on Vivian's face drop, disappearing just before she was gone from view.

Kate debated turning around the entire five-hour drive. Vivian didn't want her to take the audition. She clearly didn't want Kate and Max to leave. Kate had never been with someone who was afraid to lose her before.

And Jacqueline would not take away the Lyric audition—would she?

But it didn't matter, right? She already knew that Louisville was not the place for her. And Jacqueline was right: any audition she *could* take was one she *should* take. Auditions kept her name out there.

She parked and pulled out her cello. At a previous audition, she had been told that her sound didn't blend well with the section, which was a polite way saying that they hated her playing. This audition wouldn't be any different. She wasn't going to win. She was barely even going to try.

So when she heard someone call number seventy-four as the other three finalists sat waiting, she didn't even look up.

He called the number again. "Seventy-four? Congratulations."

Kate looked at the woman sitting next to her.

"You won."

Kate whipped her head around. "What?"

His smile turned into a frown. "Of course, if you don't want the job—"

"No! I mean, I don't know. I'm in the middle of a contract with the Windy City Chamber Ensemble right now. Do you need an answer today?"

"No, Ms. Flynn, though we need a commitment before the next season starts in May."

Fuck.

Chapter 22

KATE DROVE HOME IN A daze. What was she going to do?

She had finally caught her unicorn, and now she didn't want it.

The trouble was, she couldn't exactly ignore it.

The job wasn't the best paying, nor was it in an area she wanted to live, but it was a step up from the job she had now. It was a full-time orchestra job with salary and honest-to-God *benefits*. Lyric was the dream job, but it would be a cutthroat audition in which only the best in the *world* would advance to the final round. The odds of her winning were a million to one. If she turned down the Louisville offer and failed the Lyric audition, she'd be back on unemployment and panicking daily about where her next paycheck was coming from.

She would have to accept the offer.

But what about Vivian? How could she leave her? How could she take her away from Max?

And Stephen. He had texted her the night before, elated at the time he was spending with Max. He had even asked if Max could meet his mother when she came to visit in the summer. It had made Kate's stomach tie itself into knots. She had been so focused on whether Stephen would stick around, she had never considered that *they* might not.

Kate wished she had never auditioned.

The moment the elevator doors opened into the loft, she wrinkled her nose. The apartment that usually smelled of Vivian's perfume—and most recently a Christmas tree—now smelled strongly of paint.

Max greeted her with a loud "Close your eyes!"

She obediently slammed her eyes shut, her shins colliding with the metal catwalk. "Ow! What's wrong?"

"Why would you assume something was wrong?"

Vivian's deeply sensual voice, followed by the click of heels on the metal stairs, brought a smile to Kate's face. She pictured Vivian climbing the stairs in her black pencil skirt, her favorite burgundy wraparound top, and spiked black suede heels.

Vivian's soft lips brushed hers. "Welcome home."

"Ew! Stop kissing! You're gonna get cooties!" Max grabbed Kate's arm and pulled her toward the stairs.

Kate gasped. "Who told you about cooties?"

"Charlie! She said that you gets them from kissing girls!"

"I'll have you know, Max, that I do not have cooties," Vivian said.

"Wait, does that mean I do?"

"Come on!" Max tugged on Kate's arm again and led her down the stairs where the smell was even stronger.

When he released her, she opened her eyes. Max had led her to the guest room, the room where he slept. The black curtains that had once covered the three glass walls had been changed to a deep rusty maroon. The fourth wall had been repainted from white to Max's favorite shade of Superman red. The comforter on the bed had been changed to one of royal blue. The room that had always been so black-and-white had exploded into a large reflection of the Superman logo that hung over the bed.

Kate turned to Vivian, and when she did, she realized that more had changed than just his room. The entire loft, once so black-and-white and geometric, had evolved into a rich and warm home. The black-and-white area rug that had once covered most of the downstairs living room had been replaced with a swirling earth-tone design that set off a single maroon wall. The black-and-white living room couches were gone, replaced with wine-colored couches. The wall of the upstairs office was a deep cream, and the wall above Vivian's bed was now midnight blue. Even the stainless-steel appliances had been replaced with counterparts of mustard yellow.

"We brought color!" Max jumped up and down as if he were on a trampoline.

Kate looked down at her son. "Max! Your hair!"

When she had left the day before, Max's hair had been a shaggy mop. Now it was cut and styled into a fashionable forelock.

"I gots it with Stephen!"

"You…"

"Apparently he had an appointment yesterday for a cut," Vivian explained. "They got the same style."

"Do you like it?" Vivian asked, leaning against her.

"The haircut or the paint?"

"You can deal with Stephen about the haircut. I meant the paint."

"You painted your room blue." Her voice sounded weak.

"I did. I have grown rather fond of that color over the last few months."

"How did you do this so fast?"

"What, this? It only took a few phone calls to hungry contractors." She was obviously proud of the makeover.

Vivian had had the spare bedroom painted for her son. She had painted her bedroom a color that would remind them both of their first date. Kate's head was spinning, and perhaps that's why she blurted out, "I won."

Vivian looked like someone had stuck her with a pin. "Oh."

"Yeah. Not first runner-up, but actual winner. In Louisville."

"Con-congratulations," Vivian cleared her throat, her hand rubbing at her stomach.

She tried at a smile and failed. She knew that she was avoiding Vivian's eyes and that it wasn't going to help anything so she reluctantly looked up. What she saw on Vivian's face upset and surprised her.

Vivian was still smiling, her lips drawn into a too large grin, but her eyes were intense, and the vein in her forehead that showed whenever she was stressed had popped out under her skin.

"Viv—"

She was interrupted by a blood-curdling scream. "We're moving?" Max's face had turned as red as the new wall in his room. "No! You said—you said you wouldn't! No!" He threw down Monkeyz and ran into his room, slamming the door.

Kate looked down at the abandoned lovey, then looked up at Vivian.

"You're leaving?" Vivian whispered.

Kate opened her mouth to speak, but no sound came out.

"I see," Vivian said, and retreated behind her mask.

"I don't know yet." Kate reached for her hands, but Vivian pulled away. "But hey, even if I take the job, it's only five hours away. Things don't have to change too much."

Vivian scoffed, turned away from her and, dropping onto the couch, folded herself up.

Kate squatted before her. "I don't know what to do."

"What is there to do, Kate? This is part of the job. You know it and I know it."

"My position here has always been temporary. I have to think about Max. I don't want to go, but I'm not sure I can say no to this job."

Vivian stared at the wall behind Kate.

"Viv, please. Take that look out of your eyes. Come back to me."

Vivian laughed. "Am I so transparent?"

"You are to me."

Vivian's face softened as she caressed Kate's cheek.

"I don't see how I can turn down a steady paycheck, Viv, as much as I want to stay here." She got to her feet, then sat next to Vivian.

Vivian took Kate's hand. "If the only reason you're considering the job is because of the financial aspects, then please reconsider."

"And do what once this contract ends? What if nothing else comes along?"

"There are plenty of contracts around here, Kate. This is Chicago. There is always work for an artist. I am happy to help as well."

"So, what? If I don't have a job when this one is over, you'll float us?"

"I didn't mean it like that. I just meant that money doesn't need to be your only motivating factor."

"That's really easy for you to say." Kate pulled her hands away and sat back.

"Kate, what's mine is yours. After all, being with you has given me so much."

Now it was Kate's turn to stare at the wall.

"All right, so you don't want my help." Vivian said. "Then what about this? We have never discussed your finances, but you have said enough that I think I understand the picture."

Kate pulled her legs up under her. "I'm listening."

"I can't help but think, Kate, that the way you live life now means that you're always catching up from the last move only to begin preparing for the next move. It seems to keep you in constant debt."

Kate pulled a throw pillow onto her lap.

"If you settled in Chicago and simply gigged, you would be as financially secure as you are now. There are endless gigs here in town, once you get on the sub lists."

"Viv, it's not that simple. Every time I move, the next job is more prestigious than the last. That's the idea, right? To get better and better jobs? Otherwise there's no point in picking up and moving."

"You could further your career just as easily by staying here. And until you can make that happen, I can help."

Kate shook her head in an effort to clear it. It was a kind offer. So why did it make her feel as if she were just a lowly person on Vivian's staff? Why did it make her feel as if she were being bought? She shifted in place, rubbing her face. "I get it, and I appreciate it. Thanks. How did Max seem after he came back from his day with Stephen?"

Vivian didn't flinch at the abrupt change of subject. "He seemed to have a good time, as much as I don't want to admit it."

"Good. I'm gonna go check on him."

Kate got up and went to his room, but when she grasped the doorknob, it refused to turn.

"Okay." She gave a dry laugh, turning to Vivian so she could see her speak. "How did I not know this room had a lock on it?"

Vivian's eyebrows shot up. "It has never even occurred to me that it did."

She knocked. "Max, unlock the door. Max!"

Ten minutes later, after threats of Santa only visiting good little boys, Max opened the door, still sniffling.

Kate led him to the couch. "Max, I understand you're upset, but *that*"—she pointed back toward his room—"is not how you behave! Do you understand me?" She felt Vivian's steadying hand on her shoulder and took a deep breath. She didn't want to be in this position. She was angry with Max, but she was angrier with herself and the career choice she had to make. And she was angry at Vivian for not understanding the world she lived in.

When she looked at Max again, he had folded his arms across his chest.

"Max." She tried again in a softer tone. "Do you hear me?"

"Max," Vivian said gently, "why don't you sit on the couch for a few minutes and cool down?"

"No time out!" he shouted.

"No, not a time out." Vivian crouched down to meet him on his level. "I know you don't want to leave but even if you do, Max, you'll see me again. Okay?"

Max's little lip trembled. "Next day?" he asked hopefully.

"Maybe. I'm not going anywhere. Now, remember your deep breaths? Why don't you do that for a few minutes?"

Kate walked her son over to the couch and set him down with a kiss that he angrily wiped away.

Tears were beginning to prickle in Kate's eyes.

They left Max on the couch and continued their discussion at the kitchen island. "Kate," Vivian said, "when I said 'float you,' I simply meant help you, and I meant only until the next job came along."

"It's just... I'm not some charity case. You're right that I'm still in the hole from the last move. And even if I weren't—" The thought of asking Vivian for money to get by sent a wave of nausea through her stomach. How could she look Vivian in the eye if they ever broke up, knowing what she owed Vivian? What would she do if Vivian disappeared one day, leaving her stranded?

"I can see I hurt your pride, but would you not do the same for me? If I lost my position tomorrow, would you not do all you could to help? Would you not take me in?" She stood and wrapped her arms around Kate. "Or does this mean it's over?"

Kate shook her head. "No, it's not over. Louisville is only a few hours' drive. But, Viv, I have to put Max before anything else."

"And yet you have a viable option. Let me help!"

"No, Viv! Just no!" Kate pulled away and jumped off the stool. "The problem is I'm not completely sure what the right thing for Max is," she admitted.

Vivian sighed. "Fine." She moved in to hold Kate again. "You're a good parent, so I have to accept that you might take this job."

Kate pulled away when she felt her phone vibrate. It was a congratulatory text message from Jacqueline Kensington. How did she know?

"Who was that?" Vivian asked.

"Your mom. Congratulating me."

Vivian shook her head. "She always knows."

"Also I might as well tell you now. I invited her over for Christmas dinner."

Chapter 23

THE ATMOSPHERE OVER THE NEXT two weeks was weighted like a heavy blanket The possibility of Kate moving loomed over them, the elephant always in the room. Vivian was silent, speaking only when necessary. For now, the silence was preferable. It meant she could put off thinking about the prospect of a move until after Christmas.

What she did think about was the cochlear implant. Kate had begun to picture Vivian's face as the doctor prepared to activate the device, Vivian waiting to hear a sound for the first time since that pop all those years ago.

Would she and Max even still be around to teach her how to navigate the hearing world, or would that job fall to Charlie?

She knew that in the end, it didn't matter who was with her as long as Vivian was happy.

Then there was the planned dinner with Jacqueline. Kate had begged Vivian to cancel, but Vivian refused, insisting that it would be much worse to cancel than to go through with it.

They shopped for hours in preparation, visiting every organic food store in town for the Christmas meal that Vivian would cook. Kate was the penitential pack mule, silently carrying bags of groceries up to the loft, dragging the fancy chinaware from the basement, and wrapping the presents to put under the tree.

Finally, on Christmas Eve morning, Vivian thawed, and they made love in the light of the early dawn.

Classical musicians tended to feel one of two ways about Christmas music and Christmas concerts: either they saw it as a way to pass along the holiday spirit through their love of music, or they wanted to crack their instruments over the head of every single concertgoer. Normally, Kate was in the latter group. After all, there were only so many traditional Christmas songs, and by high school graduation, every musician could play them by heart. If she had to play "Sleigh Ride" one more time, she would launch her bow into the percussion section.

Today, though, as she walked through the bustling streets of Chicago, Christmas music flowing from each little shop, she smiled as she stepped over a large pile of snow and went through the stage door.

Stephen grinned when he saw her enter. "Merry Christmas, Flynn."

"Hey, Foy." Kate put her cello down and fell into his hug.

"How's Max?"

"Excited. His hair is already getting shaggy, though." She reached up to tussle the forelock on Stephen's head that matched her son's.

Stephen dodged her hand. "Whoa! Don't mess with the 'do."

"You know, you got Max's hair cut, so I think you need to be in charge of upkeep," she teased.

Stephen beamed. "You mean, like, be in charge of his hair?"

Kate opened her mouth to tease him, but he looked so excited by the idea of something so simple. And Max was warming to Stephen more than she had thought he would. It might be time soon to tell Max the truth about him.

Her smile faded. But how could she if they were about to leave?

"Yeah, he seems to really like it," she said with a little less enthusiasm. "Why don't you take him after Christmas for a trim?"

Her feet left the ground as Stephen picked her up in a bear hug. "Oh my God! Put me down. Put me down!"

He plopped her back down and kissed her forehead. "Thanks, Kate."

She smiled at him. "You're welcome, Stephen. What are we—"

Too into his phone, Stephen didn't seem to hear her. "Hey, do you think Max will like this?" He turned his phone and showed her images of superhero costumes. "You know…for Christmas."

Kate grinned. "I think he'll love it."

"Yeah?"

"Yeah." She didn't have the courage to bring the topic she had wanted to ask about again.

They moved to the stage to set up their instruments and warm up. The hall was louder than normal, filled with excited children, parents, and grandparents. Kate smiled as the music began and the crowd sang along.

"That was a lot of fun," Kate said as she packed up her cello.

Stephen had packed up his bass and turned to walk off the stage. "It was. I usually—"

Kate turned to see what had caught his attention. Max stood at the edge of the stage, his hair slicked down, looking very dapper in a black suit with a red shirt and green tie.

Stephen greeted him. "My, my! You clean up well, Max. You're a regular lady-killer!"

Max dropped the smile from his face. "I don't wanna kill any ladies."

Kate set her cello down and dropped to one knee to clutch Max to her chest. "Oh my God, Max! You're so cute. You're killing me with your cuteness."

"Mom, you're so silly!"

Vivian was five feet back, her face bright and warm as she laughed, her hips swaying as she approached, grinning with pride. She was beautiful, and the way she was looking at Kate's son, the way she loved him, made her all the more striking.

"What are you doing here?" Kate asked, getting back on her feet.

"We heard you play!"

"You did?"

"We did." Vivian had appeared like an apparition behind Max.

"Did you like it?"

Max nodded, then began to sing his favorite carol.

"We thought," Vivian said, "you might want to get some hot chocolate and look at Christmas displays."

"I would love to get hot chocolate and look at displays!"

"Stephen?"

Stephen blinked. "You're inviting me?"

Vivian smiled warmly. "I am."

"Yeah! I'd love to! What do you think, bud?" He offered his hand to Max.

"Yeah!" Max said, then pulled Stephen toward the stage door.

"You know," Vivian began, "I think that there might be—what?"

Kate shook her head. "Thanks."

Despite lukewarm hot chocolate and displays wilted by heavy snow, the four walked the Chicago streets for a couple of hours. Finally, when their noses and fingers were red with cold, they decided to call it a night. Besides, Santa's cookies were yet to be made. They stopped to say their goodbyes.

"Um, before you go…" Stephen shuffled his feet in the snow. Kate put her hand on Vivian's shoulder to get her attention.

He looked at Vivian. "I know in the past… What I mean is…" He blew out and watched his breath form a cloud in front of him. "It was really good of you to invite me. And, um, I—"

Vivian reached out and rested a hand on his arm. "Charlie told me about your talk." She squeezed his arm. "Merry Christmas, Mr. Foy." Then she took Max by the hand and began walking toward the L.

Stephen turned to Kate. "Does that mean she forgives me for all of the shit between us? Because that's what I was trying to say."

Kate shrugged, crossing her hands in front against the cold. "Looks like she's trying."

Charlie was already at the loft when they arrived. Max squealed when he saw her.

"Are you ready to make cookies, Max?" she asked.

"Not until you change your clothes and hang up your suit," Kate directed.

Minutes later, flour and sugar covered the counters and the floor in the kitchen. Kate and Charlie had created a decorating station on the far side of the kitchen island with sprinkles, frosting and a few Red Hots.

Max, his dark hair completely dusted in flour, inched toward the frosting.

"Uh-uh, mister." Kate moved the frosting out of his reach.

"But the cookies!"

The Loudest Silence

"We can't decorate them while they're still hot or the frosting will melt."

"Put them in the 'frigerator. Then it won't melt!"

"Maybe you and Charlie should go out to the patio," Vivian suggested. "You haven't shown her your superfast curveball yet."

Charlie grumbled, but the two threw on their winter coats and gloves and headed out into the cold.

"Smooth one." Kate wrapped an arm around Vivian, and they watched as Max nailed Charlie with a huge snowball. "Ten bucks on the kid."

"I'll take that bet. Charlie has a competitive streak."

"You're on, lady."

When Charlie and Max came in, trailing snowy footprints, they were greeted with warm blankets. Kate hustled Max off for a bath.

Finally, with Max in his pajamas and Charlie in a pair of Vivian's sweatpants and a sweater. they gathered around the kitchen island to frost the cookies. The news had begun reporting sightings of Santa's sleigh in various locations around the world. Max spread frosting faster and faster, often missing the cookie entirely.

"Relax, Max. You have time."

"It's important to be in bed, Viv'n!" Max insisted, glancing at the TV screen again to be sure Santa hadn't been reported in the Loop yet.

"I don't know, kid. I think he's getting pretty close," Kate teased.

Max's eyes widened. "But I haven't finished his cookies!"

Vivian glared at Kate. "I think you have plenty of time. They just said he was in England. That's nearly four thousand miles away."

Max studied his handiwork. "Do you think Santa will like them?"

Vivian ran her hand through his hair. "Santa will think they are the best cookies ever because they are extra-special Max cookies."

A flash made them all look up.

"Oops," Charlie said with a grin.

"Take anover one, Charlie! Take anover one!"

"Okay, okay, okay."

They paused for a photo session, then Max hopped down from his stool and grabbed a plate, choosing what he thought were "the bestest of the bestest" cookies, and scattered them haphazardly on the plate.

"So what happens now?" Vivian asked.

"Well," Kate said, pulling out a glass. "We pour the milk."

"Right." Vivian took the glass that Kate handed her and followed Max and Kate to the living room area.

"Max, where do you want to put Santa's cookies and milk?"

Max looked around the loft, finally deciding on the window ledge closest to the tree. Then he frowned. "There's nothing for the reindeer."

Kate pulled a large carrot from behind her back.

"Yeah!" Max dropped the carrot onto the edge of the plate. "Ima gonna go to bed now."

Kate and Vivian bade Charlie good night and followed Max to his room.

"Where do you think he is now, Mommy?" Max asked, settling under the covers.

"I don't know, kid. Could be anywhere."

"Next door?"

"Could be. That's why little boys have to go to sleep. He could be here any minute."

Max squeezed his eyes closed.

"Good boy." Kate kissed his head and slipped from the room. Vivian closed the door behind them.

They returned downstairs to finish preparing the room for Christmas morning.

It was late when they finished. Vivian took Kate's hand and led her upstairs. Vivian slipped out of her clothes and, smiling slyly at Kate, stepped into the bathroom. Quickly, Kate pulled off her clothes and stepped into the shower behind Vivian, wrapping her arms around her.

She kissed the hollow of her shoulder. Then taking the shampoo bottle from Vivian's hands, she poured some shampoo into her palm and began to gently work it through Vivian's hair. When she had done a thorough job, she turned Vivian around and gently pushed her head back to rinse, leaning in to kiss her wet throat.

When she was done washing Vivian's hair, she lathered soap onto her hands and explored her bare skin, starting with her arms, traveling down to her stomach, then between her legs. Afterward, Kate closed her eyes, enjoying the feel of Vivian's hands against her skin. Washing someone and being washed in return was so intimate, so satisfying.

They wrapped each other in bath towels, kissing and stroking until Vivian stepped back, falling onto the bed and pulling Kate with her. Kate kissed Vivian's stomach, sliding her lips over the ribs and chest until her face was nestled under Vivian's jaw. She breathed in her scent, relishing the closeness of their bodies, wanting, *needing* to be even closer.

With their arms wrapped around each other, they breathed in unison, faster and faster. Kate reached for Vivian just as Vivian reached for her, and they began rocking together, their fingers sliding in the slippery wetness.

Vivian nuzzled her face into Kate's throat. "I want to hear you."

Kate nodded, and as Vivian thrust deeper, Kate cried out. Vivian gasped and pushed again.

Kate lifted her face. "Can you feel my voice?"

Vivian nodded. "I can. Oh, Kate, I can."

Soon, Vivian began to shudder as they moved melodiously together, her gasps tight and growing ragged. A large quake passed through Vivian as her hands danced over Kate's back and through her hair, holding her tighter to her. It was something that Kate didn't recognize, something new. She felt a leak of something warm run down her nose from the cheek pressed to Vivian's and she gasped, understanding as another quake rocked through her lover. She hugged her tighter as yet another sharp shudder wracked Vivian. A few more tears slid from her eyes, landing lightly on Kate's cheeks.

"I love you," Kate said. Comfortable, Kate quickly followed her, knowing that no magical world she could find in slumber would be better than the one she had while she was awake.

Chapter 24

"Mommy! Mommy, Mommy, Mommy! Wake up!"

Kate awoke with a jolt. The screaming voice came from the guest room downstairs. Kate had made him promise to wait there until they were awake.

"Okay!" she called back. "I'm up! I'm up!"

She glanced at the clock. It was only six thirty, an hour earlier than he had woken her the year before. There was no hope of him going back to sleep, and, in truth, now that she was awake, she was excited.

She leaned over Vivian and brushed the hair back from her face, stroking her cheek until her eyes fluttered open.

Vivian watched her. She seemed to be looking for some type of reaction, as if she were vulnerably nervous about the tears she had shed as they'd made love the night before.

Kate smiled down at her, not wanting her to look so afraid, and kissed her again.

Vivian's eyes slowly closed as the kiss continued until finally Kate pulled away, enjoying the way that Vivian had melted, seeing her go limp, her lips parting as she let out a long sigh. Her eyes opened again, warm and bright, and Kate grinned. Her heart beat hard in her throat. She could feel that sense of new again.

"Max is up."

Vivian reached her arms around Kate's neck and pulled her down to kiss her, slow and deep. When she at last released her, she was grinning sheepishly. Kate leaned in and kissed her again, then pulled away. "If we keep making out, my son's head is going to explode."

The Loudest Silence

Vivian nodded, and reluctantly they crawled out of bed and threw on their holiday-themed pajamas. That was all it took to engage in the thrill of Christmas morning, and they hurried downstairs.

Kate had been hoping for the last two weeks to get some insight into whether Vivian might want to be part of the hearing world. Finally, the night before they were going to bring it up, she had her answer.

I want to hear you.

Vivian sat on the couch across from Max's room and lit the tree again. Then checking that everything was in place, Kate plopped down next to her. Vivian curled up under her arm.

"Are you ready?"

Vivian nodded.

Kate leaned in for another long kiss, then called for Max to come out.

He stepped into the room, his eyes bulging. "He came! He came! Santa came!" He launched himself at them, an arm around each neck. He looked overwhelmed.

"Don't know where to start?"

"Stockings first?"

It was tradition in the Flynn household that they opened stockings first, but this year they had others to consider. "Maybe let's wait for stockings until Charlie gets here."

"So…" Max coiled like a tiger ready to spring.

"So…" Kate teased, holding him back for another second. "Go!"

And Max was off, tearing through paper and ribbons. He examined each present carefully before setting it aside and picking up the next one. When he had opened every gift, he plopped in the center of the crumpled paper, looking stunned.

"You must have been a very good boy," Kate commented. "Do you know which of your toys you're going to give back to Santa's helpers this year?"

Vivian looked at her, startled. "He has to give some back?"

"Since we move a lot, we always give away some of his old toys after Christmas."

"Right, because you move a lot."

Kate glanced up at the tone of her voice. Vivian stood up abruptly and disappeared into the kitchen. "I'll get a trash bag!" When she returned, there were pink blotches on her cheeks as if she had just wiped away tears. Together she and Max stuffed the torn wrapping paper into the plastic bag.

Kate switched on a big Christmas smile, accessed the camera on her phone, and called out, "Hey, guys, turn around."

Max spun, grinning, but Vivian continued cleaning up.

Oh crap. I'm talking to the back of a Deaf person again. Then she realized that tonight was the night she got to tell Vivian that awkward moments like this never had to happen again. There would be no more missing when someone called her name, no more staring in the wrong direction, unaware that someone was talking to her!

Kate hopped up to make breakfast while Vivian and Max sorted the still-unopened packages into piles.

They ate quickly, barely taking time to chew their food before Max returned to the living area and sat in the midst of the still-unopened packages. Kate and Vivian returned to their places on the couch.

"Who goes first?" Vivian asked.

"Age before beauty," Kate said.

Max chimed in. "You, Viv'n!"

"Me? So I'm *old* then, am I?"

"Yeah!" Max said, giggling behind his hands.

Vivian picked up one of the boxes next to her and carefully peeled the paper back.

Max rolled his eyes. "You're supposed to rip it."

"I am?"

"Yeah! Come on, Viv'n!"

"Yeah, come on, Viv'n," Kate echoed.

"All right, here I go!" Vivian dug a finger under the wrap and pulled, ripping through it.

They each took a turn opening packages until Kate lifted the last box from her pile.

It was a small box. Kate could almost feel the velvet cover under the wrap. She knew this box. It was a box that every little girl dreamed of from a young age, influenced by movies, TV, and books. Her mouth was dry, and she felt her pulse beating in her temple.

She stared at the note on top that said simply "My love" in Vivian's elegant scroll. This box couldn't be for her. She had to be wrong. It couldn't be... Vivian, she wouldn't...couldn't...wasn't... Kate couldn't get her thoughts to stop fumbling over themselves. Her fingers convulsed on the tiny box. "From you, I assume?"

Vivian nodded.

Kate blinked and gripped the box tighter, finally ripping the paper to reveal a small Tiffany Blue box. She gaped at it.

Vivian was...

This was happening...

She had no idea what she was going to say. Should she say yes? Did she want to?

They had moved pretty quickly as a couple, going from friends to lovers who all but lived together. That talk about children awhile back—maybe it had been more significant than she thought.

She knew she would say yes. A thrill of fear spiked through her as she realized she could see it. She could see a whole future as she looked down at that little box.

With one last glance at Vivian, she opened the lid.

Nestled in the plush lining of the *Tiffany and Co* gift box were two large glittering diamond earrings.

"Oh my God." Kate touched the cold stones that seemed to glitter unnaturally in the morning sun. So many things were swirling through her mind, and she resisted the urge to laugh nervously.

She felt naked, as though everyone in the room could see what she had been thinking. She wanted to cry.

Of course it was earrings. And they were beautiful classic solitaire diamonds.

"What is it, Mommy?" Max's voice broke through her stunned silence, and she turned the box to show him.

She was elated by their beauty.

She couldn't meet Vivian's eyes.

"Do you like them? The idea was to get you something simple, something you could wear daily, if you wanted to, something that made you think of me." Her hands twitched nervously as she signed to match her words.

Kate pulled Vivian to her, kissing her fervently. "I love them."

"You do?"

"I really do." It wasn't a lie. Kate put them on. "How do they look?"
"Perfect."
Kate smiled and said, "You're perfect" and kissed her once more.

Charlie showed up in the early afternoon, shaking off bits of snow. Ten minutes later, flashing lights announced Jacqueline's arrival. The four assembled at the foot of the stairs, standing in a line like the Von Trapp children in *The Sound of Music*.

Jacqueline glided into the loft as if she were carried by a cloud, a bag of gifts in one hand. She descended the stairs, critically appraising the apartment as she approached. Kate felt Vivian stiffen beside her.

"Vivian!" Jacqueline set the bag down and wrapped her daughter in a perfunctory hug.

Vivian returned the embrace with about as much warmth, patting her mother's back. "Mother. Merry Christmas. Welcome."

"Thank you. It's so nice to *finally* see where you're living." She turned to Charlie and planted a kiss on her cheek. "Ah, Charlotte." Then she turned to Kate. "Katelyn! I hear congratulations for Louisville are in order."

Vivian looked away.

Kate smiled tightly. "Thank you, Jacqueline. May I get you a glass of wine?"

"Yes, dear. Thank you."

Jacqueline took Vivian's arm. "You must show me around. The colors are so vibrant!"

By the time Kate brought glasses of wine to the decorated room, Jacqueline had settled next to Max and was listening to him rattle off a list of the gifts Santa had brought him.

"And now shall we open my presents?" Jacqueline asked.

"There's *more*?" Max's eyes widened.

"There's more!" Jacqueline laughed, rubbing his back. "Do you think you can handle it, sweetheart?"

Jacqueline clearly wanted a grandbaby to love. Still, it surprised Kate how much kindness this woman showed her son compared to the coldness she showed for others.

Jacqueline rose and retrieved the bag of gifts from under the tree. She handed Max a large, long box and gave Charlie and Kate each a small, thin one. She handed Vivian a small envelope.

Charlie opened her box first. She gasped, pulling tickets from its lining. "Season tickets to the opera? You got me season tickets to Lyric?"

Jacqueline smiled. "You used to be quite fond of the opera. Kate told me you still listen to it in your car. The upcoming season promises to be a very good one."

Charlie looked mystified. "You knew I liked opera?"

"I have known you for twenty years, Charlotte. I introduced you to opera. Have you changed your mind about it?"

"No, but..." Charlie got up and wrapped her arms around Jacqueline. "Thank you."

Jacqueline broke free and turned to Kate. "And how about you, Kate?"

Kate pulled off the wrap from her box, revealing a handwritten card. "Ten sessions with a massage therapist?"

"A massage therapist who specializes in string players, dear. She's been known to alleviate tendonitis as well as muscle fatigue. We all need it at times, and you have a big audition coming up."

It was true. Tendonitis was a huge problem for string players. "Thank you," she said, blushing at the thought of the gifts she had purchased for Vivian and Jacqueline that now seemed so inadequate.

"Have you decided that Kate needs a benefactor, Mother?" All eyes turned to Vivian.

Jacqueline laughed. "I *am* her benefactor, Vivian."

A benefactor. Not only that, but Jacqueline Kensington said she was *her* benefactor. The thought made her head spin.

"And why not?" Jacqueline continued. "We all could use a helping hand now and then."

"Did you even bother to ask her if she would like to have you as a benefactor, or did you simply skip that step and spread the word of your latest music project to all of your friends and colleagues?"

"Oh, *really*, Vivian."

Vivian parried, her face a blank slate once again. "Max, what do you have?"

"Wow!" Torn wrapping paper lay at his feet, and on his lap was a polished violin case. He unbuckled it and stared at the violin. "This is for me?"

Kate took in the curve and coloring of the instrument. It looked like a… "Max, can I see it?" Kate took the violin from him and peeked through the F-hole.

This brand, this model wasn't something you gave to a four-year-old kid. Kate had looked into getting Max a student piano with an upgraded keyboard, and it would cost around two hundred dollars. If she had decided that Max should begin on the violin instead, she could have found a quarter-size student violin for around the same price. The maker of this violin had made perhaps only three hundred his entire career, and it was especially made for a child. This instrument had to have cost at least eight thousand dollars, though it had more likely been inherited from one of the Kensingtons.

Kate looked up. Vivian's expression of surprise matched her own, but there was also a look of pleasure.

"But this isn't for playing, right?" Kate asked

"What does this say?" Max handed Kate the envelope that had been covered by the instrument in the case.

Kate took the card with her free hand and read out loud. "'This voucher entitles the bearer to weekly lessons with Victoria Chinn until June of next year, at which time the parties will reevaluate—' *Victoria Chinn*?" Kate looked up at Jacqueline. "Victoria Chinn, the former concertmaster of the Chicago Symphony?"

Jacqueline beamed. "Ms. Chinn is a magnificent teacher. She will get him on track to a brilliant career."

"If you'll excuse me, I need—" Kate handed the violin to Vivian, then she turned and rushed through the patio doors, moving until she was out of sight of the living room. Her nerves were like a jumble of electrical wires.

Victoria Chinn? Kate had recently attended one of her workshops during which the woman stated that she charged two hundred dollars an hour for student lessons, when she took on students at all.

She felt a hand on her arm and turned. She had been so lost in thought that she hadn't heard Vivian approach.

"Did you see that thing?" Kate bellowed at her. She dropped her head in her hands, covering her face. "Who does that?"

Vivian pulled on her arm to get her attention. "I can't be a part of this, Kate, if I can't see what you're saying."

Kate looked up and repeated, "Who does that?"

"My mother. Well, the Kensingtons in general. She cares for Max, so she got him the best, even if it is a little ridiculous."

"That's an understatement."

"If it makes you uncomfortable, Kate, you don't have to take it."

The words felt like a dig. "Gee, thanks."

"And what is that supposed to mean?"

Kate's retort was hot. "I don't need your permission to refuse it, Vivian!"

"I didn't mean to make it sound like you did. It's a bit much, and he's so young. Without meaning to, he could break it. We should buy him a student violin."

"But I wanted him on piano!" Kate threw her arms in the air. "Why do I suddenly have no choice about that? I'm *not* your subordinate, Vivian!"

Vivian pulled her shoulders back and tightened her lips. "When did I enter into this equation, Katelyn Flynn?"

"Okay, your mom, then!" Kate snapped.

"Kate." Vivian reached out and touched her hand. "We're not making choices for you. My mother just wants…" Vivian's cheeks flushed. "She wants a grandchild. She got carried away."

"But you both make decisions for me like I have no choice and throw money at me like I can be bought."

Vivian met Kate's anger with a glare. "Do not yell at me, Kate, and do not blame me."

Kate took a deep breath and tried again in a softer voice. "Don't you understand? Offering him things like an expensive violin and lessons with Victoria Chinn, it's so"—she searched for the right words—"humiliating! It's embarrassing that you and your mother think I can't offer him anything, so we have to take whatever it is you offer. God! What if one day you decided to stop being so generous? We would be screwed."

"Kate, listen—"

"I can take care of him, of us. I can! I always have!"

"Of course you can," Vivian said, though she shook her head as if she didn't understand at all. "I know you can, Kate. All we are offering is something different. Don't you want the best for Max?"

Kate felt as if she had been slapped. "I can't believe you just said that to me. Of course I want the best for him. But it feels like you think the less fortunate should gratefully take all your handouts."

"It's not a handout if it's from my mother to you."

"Of course it is." They stared at one another. Finally, Vivian spoke. "You think there's an imbalance between us."

"No, but it's like you want to create one."

"Again, Kate, this was my mother, not me."

"But it isn't just your mother."

"What does that mean?"

"I feel like there's an imbalance whenever you offer me money. I feel like I'm an obligation, someone to be taken care of, like you don't think I can do things for Max without you."

"Is this about the fact that I offered to help you financially?"

A long silence followed, and Kate felt as if she were trying to breathe through a heavy fog. She closed her eyes and inhaled deeply before speaking again. "I do what I need to do to take care of me and Max. I don't want to be someone's obligation."

"But we're supposed to be family, Kate. We aren't throwing money at you. We're offering help to our *family*. It's not our fault if you don't know what that looks like."

Kate gasped.

"I'm sorry, Kate. I didn't mean—" But then her eyes widened as if she had just registered what Kate said. "Oh. So you're going, then."

Kate hadn't made that final decision, but as the statement had come out of her mouth, she realized it was true. She had to go. She didn't have a choice. "What the hell else can I do?"

Vivian turned away, facing out to the city. "So many things, Kate."

"I get that you want to help. And, really, thank you. But…" She trailed off. Vivian hadn't seen anything Kate said. Kate gently pulled on Vivian's arm, but Vivian continued gazing outward. Finally, she turned to face her again. "You're right, Kate. We shouldn't be treating you like family."

Kate winced at the words, stung. Then she touched Vivian's hand. "I'm sorry. It's not that I don't want to be part of your family. It's that I don't need your family to take care of us. I've always managed. This was a hard decision, but it doesn't have to mean the end for us."

Vivian dropped her gaze. "I'm cold."

"Yeah." Kate took her hand. "Let's go inside."

They reentered the apartment to see Jacqueline placing Max's fingers onto the neck of the violin.

Kate stopped in her tracks. Vivian looked at her, then turned back to Jacqueline.

"Mother, we are going to talk about this later. But right now, dinner is ready. Max, put the violin away, please." Then she walked into the kitchen.

They ate dinner in silence. No one seemed to know exactly what to talk about. Kate did her best to lighten the mood, but after every attempt she made to bring up a topic of conversation, they lapsed back into silence. At least whenever she smiled at Vivian, Vivian smiled back.

Finally, they finished dessert and began gathering up the plates to be washed.

Max pushed himself away from the table. "Can I play with the violin again?"

"No!" Kate said at the same time that Vivian snapped her fingers sharply in a silent no.

Max's eyes went wide.

Kate hugged him to her. "I just meant, we're going skating now, remember?"

Vivian signed Charlie to tell her to go ahead with Max so they could speak with Jacqueline. The moment they were out the door, Kate opened her mouth to tell Jacqueline that the violin would not be coming home with them. But Jacqueline spoke first.

"Talented students require the best equipment and the best teachers, Katelyn. We can argue until we are blue in the face, but I have the means to do this for him, and you will not challenge my decision."

"Your decision? *Your* decision? For *my* son?"

"I have the means—"

"I know you have the money, Jacqueline, but you have no right to decide anything about Max. Your gift was inappropriate."

Jacqueline's eyes narrowed, and in that moment, she looked like an older version of her daughter, ready to spring and rip out the throat of her prey. "Max deserves to have the best."

"Don't you think I know that?" Kate struggled to keep her voice at a civil tone. "But it doesn't have to be the fucking concertmaster of the CSO to be good enough!"

"Watch your mouth, young lady!" Jacqueline pressed her lips together until they almost disappeared.

Young lady? Jesus Christ! "I know you think you're doing what's right for him, but Max is *my* son!"

"Kate, you will—" Jacqueline began, but Kate interrupted her.

"No, Jacqueline! We won't be taking the violin."

"Fine!" Jacqueline's voice cut like a cold whip through the warm loft air.

Vivian had looked back and forth between them during this entire conversation in a vain attempt to keep up. Finally, she said, "I'm calling Charlie back here."

"No." Jacqueline put her hand on Vivian's phone to stop her.

"Fine. Then let's go catch up with them."

Kate grabbed her coat, but neither Jacqueline nor Vivian had moved. "Are we going?"

But Vivian was looking at her mother, who had said something. "What is it, Mother?"

"I said, before we go, we should discuss the doctor's appointment."

Chapter 25

Vivian stared at her mother. "Mother, are you ill?" She reached out and touched Jacqueline's hand.

For the first time, Kate saw worry for her mother in Vivian's face.

Jacqueline smiled. "Oh no, not for me, dear." She took Vivian's hand in both of hers.

"Then what…?"

Jacqueline looked at Kate expectantly.

Kate pulled out a kitchen stool from the counter and sat. "So Jacqueline and I had an idea."

"Oh, you did, did you?" Vivian looked at her lover warily.

Kate pulled out her phone to pull up the website she had saved. "There's this thing called a cochlear implant that can help the deaf hear. Have you heard of it?"

"What?"

Kate glanced up and, realizing she had been facing her phone, repeated herself. She turned her phone so Vivian could see and reached for her hand. "It's a page for a local otolaryngologist."

"I'm sorry, it's a *what*?"

Kate slowly and clumsily finger-spelled the word she had practiced for the last week. She had thought the little bit of sign would please Vivian, but Vivian's face didn't change.

"Viv? An oto—"

Vivian snapped her hand out of Kate's grasp.

Confused by Vivian's reaction, Kate tried again. "Vivian, have you ever heard of this technology? It's totally *amazing*! And you have an appointment with the best otolaryngologist in the country!"

Kate waited for Vivian to smile, for any look of happiness, any hint of excitement, but her face remained blank. She tried again, bouncing two fingers behind her ear in the sign for the implant.

Vivian grabbed Kate's signing hand. "I *know* what you said."

"Um, ow."

Vivian glanced down at Kate's hand and released it.

Kate eyed her warily. "What's going on?"

"How did you find out about this?"

Kate's hand still stung, but Vivian's ice-filled tone stung more. "You knew about it, then?"

Vivian smacked her hand down on the counter. "Answer me!"

"Your mom! Jesus! What the hell, Viv? Your mom told me about it. We've been talking—"

Vivian clenched her jaw and her eyes hardened. "I see."

This surprise was not going at all how Kate had seen it in her head. She forced a laugh. "Okay, so you know how sometimes you think one thing is happening but something else is really going on? I thought this would make you happy. You'd be able to *hear*. Viv, what am I missing?"

"Goody. Another person who thinks they've found the key to fixing me."

Kate flinched. The key to fixing her? "No. God, no. It isn't about *fixing* you. I just thought, well, no more pretending to understand what people are saying in a large crowd. No more dancing to the beat instead of the music at clubs. No more needing Charlie to communicate with the hearing world. No more fighting for respect." She paused. "So you knew about this already, huh?"

Vivian let out a rude snort. "Oh yes. My mother has been after me for fifteen years to get the procedure."

Kate's mouth fell open. *Fifteen fucking years?* She spun around to face Jacqueline. "What the hell? You didn't tell me that!"

Jacqueline looked at her daughter. "Vivian, dear, I just want you to be happy!"

Vivian pulled her lips back. "If that were true, Mother, then you would have done things differently over the years."

Kate stared at Jacqueline in disbelief at how she had been used. "Jacqueline, why didn't you tell me this wasn't a new idea?"

Jacqueline shrugged. "I just thought she might listen to you."

"Shame on you, Mother!"

Kate's hands went up like a crossing guard. "Somebody catch me up, *please*. Vivian, you don't want this. I get it. But I don't—"

"No, Kate, you're right," Vivian said. "I don't want this. Why would you ever think I would? Do you have *any* idea who I am as a person?"

Kate reached for Vivian's hand. "But what about last night? You said—"

"That's not what I meant, Kate!" She yanked her hand free. "I cannot believe you don't know this about me."

"Vivian, wait! You're mad at me? You don't want it, fine. But why don't you? Being Deaf makes you miserable."

"No, Kate," Vivian said, her voice dripping with venom, "my being Deaf makes *others* uncomfortable. Being Deaf is who—I—am. How is it that you don't know this about me?"

"But you could understand your mother! You could understand me. You could speak to Max—"

"I *do* speak to Max."

That brought Kate up short. "Of course. I just meant—"

"I told myself after the Deaf event that you were still learning about my community. I told myself again and again that your behaviors were because of your ignorance and that you were learning. But you really don't know anything about me at all, Kate."

"Vivian, I think you're being—" Jacqueline's mouth snapped shut when Kate turned to glare at her. Seeing Kate's head move, Vivian turned her head as well. "All right," Jacqueline continued. "I'll just go and find Charlie and Max." And with that, she left.

Vivian barely missed a beat. "I see now that I was right. You simply can't handle that I'm deaf."

"What? No! I thought this would be a good thing. I thought I was helping. I just want you to be happy."

"Of course," Vivian said dryly. "You thought you would ride in on your trusty steed and save me from my life. How original."

"I know it sounds like you think I pity you, but I—"

"Being Deaf is not all that I am, but it is a huge part of who I am."

"Of course! I know that!"

"What you fail to grasp is that not all deaf people want to be hearing, Kate. Not all deaf people need to be hearing. I am proud of who I am, proud of *what* I am!"

"Vivian, so am I. I'm proud of who you are. It was a stupid ide—"

Without warning, Vivian's face changed. "Oh. Of course."

"Of course what?" Kate asked.

But Vivian was no longer looking at her. Instead, she stared off into the distance, her hands clenched. Then she brought her focus back to Kate.

"You're just like the rest of them. Just like my mother. That's why you never bothered to learn sign, isn't it? What's the point when you could just fix me instead?"

"I don't want to fix you. You're not broken!" Kate was shouting now, her voice shrill. "I was only trying to help. How can you think I meant any ill will? I thought I was doing a good thing, making your life easier, just like you want to make my life easier by helping me financially. I wanted to take some of your burden."

"And why do I have to change, Kate? Why can't I ever be enough?"

"Viv—"

"Just me, as I am." Vivian searched Kate's face. "Don't you love me, Kate?"

"Of course I do! Viv, let's talk about this."

But Vivian was backing away, shaking her head. "How? Charlie isn't here, Kate. Shall we play a game of Charades?" She laughed, but there was no humor in it. "Go ahead. Talk. Use your hands. Tell me what you're thinking."

"What the hell?" Kate cried. "I thought we were communicating just fine. If you wanted me to learn sign faster, why didn't you just ask?" But even as she said the words, she flashed on Vivian's frustrated expression during conversations, how she turned to Charlie whenever she wanted to tell a story. Why hadn't she put two and two together?

Vivian smiled sadly. "I shouldn't have had to."

"Viv, I'm—"

"Kate, I need you to go. I need you to pack up your things. I need space and time to think. Please don't be here when I get back."

"Vivian!" Kate cried, but Vivian had already disappeared up the stairs and out the door, her final words echoing in Kate's mind.

Please don't be here when I get back.

She felt empty inside, the loft cold around her. It was a familiar feeling. She thought of all the times a social worker had appeared at the door of her foster home to move her to a new situation.

Should she wait to see if Vivian would change her mind? No. She had told her to go, so she would go. Deep down, she had known it would eventually end. She had forgotten that everything was temporary. She had been enjoying her life so much that she had forgotten to be prepared for the end. She should have enjoyed this for what it was, but she had begun to settle in, to plan, to want something more.

She didn't want to leave. She liked this life...this life with Vivian. And now it was over. How did it always happen so fast?

What the hell was she going to do now?

Chapter 26

She picked up Max from the ice rink and brought him back to their apartment, which now felt cold, drafty, empty—and foreign. She had no idea how to tell him what had just happened.

I'm sorry, kid. I brought someone into your life who didn't stay. I put myself first and dated, even though I knew you might get hurt.

"Okay, Max," Kate said with false bravado. "It's past your bedtime. Brush your teeth, please."

"Okay, Mommy." He headed to the bathroom but turned around halfway there. "Viv'n tomorrow? Like she said?" he asked hopefully.

Kate shook her head. "I don't think so, Max. I'm sorry."

"Day after?"

"I'm sorry, Max. I'm not sure when we'll see Vivian next."

"Why?" Max started to cry.

She went to him and scooped him into her arms. Now she was crying too. "I'm so sorry, kid. See, Vivian and I had a fight."

"Say you're sorry!" he cried.

If only it were that simple. "Max, she loves you, even if you don't see her for a while."

"But she said, she said—" His body shuddered, and he broke out into a heartbreaking sob.

"I know it's confusing, Max, but..."

Max sniffled. "But she said tomorrow."

"I know, kid. I know."

Max's face rubbed into her shoulder.

She should have protected him from this.

With a few more hugs, and because there was nothing else they could do except start this new life in Chicago without Vivian and Charlie, she sent Max to brush his teeth.

When his sobs had finally stopped and he had been tucked into bed, Kate stood in the middle of her living room, feeling fully alone for the first time in weeks. She looked around, finally sitting on the couch as if it were a dirty seat on the L. Vivian's words rattled around in her mind. Yeah, there had been times when they had struggled to communicate, but it had never been that bad—had it?

Then again, if she loved Vivian, why hadn't she worked harder to learn ASL? She had acted like a tourist in Vivian's world, picking up just enough to get by. She had thought that it was enough. But a real partner would have begun learning her language. If it had been a spoken language, she wouldn't have hesitated. Then, when Jacqueline had suggested the implant and she jumped on it, she had sent the message that she didn't accept Vivian for who she was. Vivian deserved better than that.

But so did she. She had thought Vivian was different, that Vivian would never throw them away.

Kate wanted to believe that Vivian needed her, loved her as much as Kate did.

It was a dangerous thought, but first she had a few things to fix.

She grabbed her phone and typed out a text message.

I want to learn ASL. Can I take lessons from you? – K

The response from Charlie was immediate.

It's about damn time. – C

Chapter 27

KATE'S THIGHS HIT THE TURNSTILE, causing the paper to-go cup in her hand to buckle in on itself from the abrupt stop. Coffee splashed over her gloved hand and across the front of her jacket. The approaching train rumbled overhead. She frantically swiped her L card and took the stairs two at a time. "Hold the door!" she shouted as she vaulted onto the platform just in time to watch the train move on without her.

"Shit."

She was going to be late to her first ASL lesson with Charlie.

Frustrated, she tossed the now-empty cup into the trash, ignoring the sympathetic looks from the others on the platform.

She needed this lesson. She needed to see Charlie. She needed to see someone from the life she had been living.

It had been four days, and she had heard nothing from Vivian—not that she had expected to. Now she was late and covered in coffee.

The last few days had felt a lot like this. Everything was slightly *off*. She felt lost in the city she had come to love, as if it had turned against her, as if she had been swallowed alive. Urban sprawl had never intimidated her before, but as her support circle shrank, the city seemed to grow, filled with jagged angles and packed sidewalks too busy for her. Try as she might, she couldn't seem to get back on track.

Why are you even going to this lesson?

She still didn't have an answer. Why learn ASL now? She should be focusing on Max, Lyric, Louisville.

Kate checked the time and sent Charlie a quick text:

Missed the train. Covered in coffee. Be five late. – K

Fine. – C

Kate shoved her phone under her jacket and into her jeans pocket roughly, wincing at Charlie's tone. She felt the phone slip through the hole in her pocket and into the pant leg of her skinny jeans. Cursing, she jumped in place and shook her leg, trying to work the phone down to her ankle, pulling it out just as the train arrived. It was packed, leaving her standing for the next hour. As the train picked up speed, she shifted to keep her footing.

Oh well. At least she was on the train.

She arrived at Charlie's only two minutes late, her jacket smelling of wet coffee.

After they settled on the couch, the first words out of her friend's mouth were, "Look, let's not talk about it, okay?"

Kate was disappointed, but of course Charlie had to take Vivian's side. Maybe she should have asked for lessons with someone else.

But Charlie was nothing if not focused. Every time Kate started to stray to any topic that was not sign language, Charlie reeled her back in. She was all business, and Kate hated it. She wanted her friendship back.

After struggling through a series of words, Kate laughed uncomfortably. "You make this look really easy, but it's not."

"Didn't you take French in high school? ASL is based on the French language."

She tried again, but Charlie interrupted. "No, that's not the proper order. Haven't you been paying attention at all? Do it again."

Kate dropped her tired hands. "Char, I hate this. Come on, we were never like this."

"Kate, I'm not going to talk to you about Vivian!"

Kate glared at her. "I'm not asking about her! Let's talk about *our* friendship. I didn't do anything to you."

Charlie scoffed. "You didn't do anything to me? You broke my best friend's heart!"

Kate had replayed her last fight with Vivian a million different ways over the last few days, trying to figure out what had gone wrong. "I wasn't trying to change her, Charlie! I honestly thought that it would make her happy! She even said to me on Christmas Eve that she wanted to be able to *hear* me. Is it really so fucking weird that I thought that meant she wanted to hear me?"

"Why are you even here?" Charlie asked. "Is it just to talk about her?"

"No! I want to fix this. I want Vivian to be with someone who can speak with her in her language. Why do you think I'm here?"

"I don't know!" Charlie shouted. "You tell me! I don't fucking understand you, Kate!"

Kate sighed. "I messed up, Char."

"Yeah, you did," Charlie said, her voice softer now.

"It never occurred to me that I should be signing. What's *wrong* with me? I just…" She paused, unsure how to express her guilt. "I never noticed us struggling to communicate."

"Well, yeah!" Charlie snorted. "It was like you couldn't talk to her on her terms. She was always lip-reading with you or asking me to interpret, if I was there. She could never be silent. Don't you get that Vivian's natural state is silent? Maybe that's not true for all deaf people, but for Vivian it is."

"Why?"

"Because someone is always expecting her to talk! Someone is always telling her she needs to be more hearing."

Kate nodded. "Like her mom."

"Like you."

Kate startled at this revelation, but Charlie continued before she could respond. "She's more comfortable silent because that's when she can just be herself."

An argument immediately sprang forward. That wasn't fair. That wasn't right. It dried before she could say it. Kate dropped her head into her hands. She hated it. It was true, and she hated that. "Where have I fucking been?" She didn't want to be like Vivian's mother. She wanted to be the place where Vivian could go for peace and comfort.

"You look like crap," Charlie said out of nowhere.

Kate snorted. "Going through a breakup will do that to you."

Charlie pulled her legs up onto the couch and turned to face Kate. "Breakup? Viv didn't say it was a breakup."

Kate shrugged. "Of course it was. I can't even blame her."

Charlie shook her head. "I don't think so. I think she needs time. You hit a sore spot."

She tilted her head at Charlie. "You really think that she didn't dump me?"

"Vivian says what she means, Kate. If she didn't say 'we're over,' it's not over. But, dude, do you *get* why this was so bad?"

Kate considered. "I offended her. I made her feel like she needed to change."

"Yeah, but it's more than that."

Kate looked at Charlie. "What am I missing?"

Charlie leaned in. "You proved that you don't know her at all! When you were looking up the implant, were you looking on YouTube?"

Kate nodded.

"Yeah. Watching videos of babies hearing for the first time is really misleading. What you're not getting is that Vivian is *morally* opposed to having the damn implant."

"But getting the implant wouldn't change who she is, would it?"

"Kate," Charlie said, shaking her head.

"I'm serious! How am I supposed to know? I never even heard of it until Jacqueline told me. You two never talk to me about anything! You just share these silent looks that I'm not part of."

"What do you expect, Kate? It's been just the two of us for twenty years." Charlie looked Kate in the eye. "This isn't just about whether or not Vivian can hear. This is about the *culture* she's part of. This is her *world*, a place where she doesn't need to be *changed*. No one should force someone else to change who they are! If someone wants the implant, that's their choice, but no one should be forced into getting it just so other people feel more comfortable. If she got it, it wouldn't be for her, it would be for her fucking mom!"

"But—"

"Do you remember when we were teenagers and they identified a gene that they thought would explain why people were gay?"

Kate recoiled. "Of course. It was scary as hell."

"Why was it scary?"

"Because if they found a cause, they could eliminate it."

"And it gave the impression that being gay was a defect, right? That there was something wrong with gay people that could now be fixed."

Oh.

Being pansexual was not that hard. She liked the fact that she could care for anyone she felt a connection to. But sometimes other people reacted badly, and she was forced to defend who she was, to defend pansexuality in general.

Kate stared at Charlie as realization dawned. It was the same for Vivian, wasn't it? It wasn't being deaf that made Vivian's life difficult; it was the way others treated her.

Charlie continued. "And it's more than that. Deaf children are pretty much forced these days to get the implant as soon as they can, like it's going to magically erase the fact that they were born deaf. But it doesn't. CIs rarely work like an actual eardrum. The kids have to go through therapy to understand these weird new sounds they're hearing. And on top of that, a huge part of their identity has been taken away. They don't really fit in anywhere anymore. So it's not just that Vivian can't hear. She risks losing the culture that she's part of and that she loves. She shouldn't have to give up that part of herself so others will feel more comfortable with her. She doesn't need to be fixed, Kate."

She had never thought Vivian needed to be fixed, but now she could see that it looked that way. "All this time I thought she hated being deaf."

Charlie shook her head. "No, she doesn't. Maybe it's you who hates that she's deaf."

"No! I don't! But—" Kate dug deep for the truth. All this time she had thought that Vivian was missing out. "Oh God. I totally rejected her for who she is."

"Yeah. I think you saw her deafness as a disability—"

"—and it's not," Kate finished.

"Nope." Charlie popped the P. "It's who she is. Her community. Her culture."

"I have to fix this."

Charlie smiled. "You l-o-o-v-e her."

Kate laughed, and it felt so good that she laughed again. She had messed up, but Charlie didn't think Vivian was gone forever.

"I do. I do love her. But I don't understand why no one told me any of this before."

"You could have inferred it. You've seen how much Vivian *loves* her community. She's always going to events and fundraisers."

Was she? Kate thought back. Had she seen her go to any other than the Gallaudet dinner? "When? She never told me about any."

Charlie snorted. "She's constantly going."

When? What had she been missing? "You know what?"

Charlie narrowed her eyes but didn't answer.

"She told me right off the freaking bat that she didn't date hearing women. Like, she made that so clear. But at the same time, she came after me so hard."

"Yeah, she really did." Charlie let out a snort.

"But it's like she always kind of didn't trust me because I was hearing. I mean, I never heard about these events, like I wasn't welcome." That thought disturbed her. "Do you think it was that she didn't want me there?"

"No, I don't think so. I mean, maybe a little." Charlie chewed, her face thoughtful.

They sat in thoughtful silence. Finally, Kate said, "So how is she?"

Charlie shrugged. "She's a mess too."

"Oh."

"The thing about Vivian is she has this really tough game face, right? But I think she's just fucking tired of losing because she's deaf."

"Right."

"I don't know. As her best friend, I think I can say she's super tired of fighting for things."

Kate sighed, running her hands through her hair. "The thing is, no one has ever really tried to get to know Vivian in her world or fought for her, you know? Not even you, Kate."

"But she never even bothered to explain any of this. It's like she was waiting for me to prove that I was just another clueless hearing person, and once she had the proof, that was it. I made a mistake. I get it now. At least I *think* I do."

"But she's losing you anyway, right? You're moving to Louisville. You think you can still date from five hours away, but we both know it's not the same. She's losing you, plus she's losing Max. That makes it so much worse. She loves him just as much as she loves you."

Kate sighed. "What am I supposed to do? I have to go."

Charlie shrugged. "No, you don't."

Kate laughed, thankful for the joke. Only, Charlie's face didn't show any humor. "Wait, you're kidding, right?"

"I'm not kidding. You could have a perfectly legit career here. You just don't want it."

"You *can't* be serious."

Charlie shrugged again, and Kate really wished she would stop. "I see people do it all of the time. You gotta admit that you move so much because you can't settle down."

Fury, red hot and burning, ripped up Kate's spine. She *wanted* this? That was complete and total crap. She didn't want this. She wanted a life. "That is *not* fucking true. What the fuck?"

"Hey, don't get mad at me!" Charlie jabbed a finger in her direction. "We're living in the land of fucking opportunity for music. The next gig will always be there. Something will always come along here. This is Chicago. And okay, whatever, yeah, you might need to get it out of your mind that you should be playing in an orchestra, but frankly, you don't even fucking want to be. You like playing with the opera. You practically come every time you hear the word Lyric."

Kate swallowed. It was true that part of the reason she had been so excited to begin with WCCE was that the hall was only blocks from the Civic Opera House, home to Lyric. She loved to be in the pit, loved bringing a beautiful story to life. But that was a pipe dream.

"Just because the classical world tells you that you need an orchestra job doesn't mean that you do," Charlie continued.

Kate stared at her. She had no idea what to say. There were so many things wrong with that. Her mind worked. It was true: there was this attitude in her career as though anything other than a job with the CSO was irrelevant.

"I know it's not easy, Kate. But you also keep saying you don't want to move all the time. And yet you have every reason to stay here."

Kate looked at Charlie, considering.

"Besides," Charlie added, "you have people here. I'm here."

"What do you mean?"

"What, you think because you and Vivian are having issues that we're not friends anymore?"

Yes, she had assumed that if she and Vivian had broken up that Charlie would disappear. After all, Charlie was Vivian's best friend. "You haven't exactly been acting like my friend the last couple of days."

"Just because you two are having problems doesn't mean we're not family. Sometimes family needs a break. Doesn't mean things are over. In fact, I think Viv was hoping you would come after her. You know, as part of that no-one-has-ever-really-fought-for-her thing."

Then like flipping a switch, Charlie asked Kate, "So when can I see Max?"

"Will you listen to my audition pieces?"

"Deal."

As Kate settled in for the long ride back to her apartment, she took out her phone, opened her browser, and typed *why do Deaf people dislike cochlear implants?*

The pages that came up startled her.

Cochlear implants are a threat to Deaf culture.

Why Deaf people vote no on the implant.

Deaf culture and the implant.

As the train clacked across the tracks, she read and she learned.

Chapter 28

You're going to crash and burn.

Kate popped her neck and stared at the beautiful black dress hanging in her closet. If she could have gracefully gotten out of the solo piece Jacqueline had arranged for her to play at the WCCE board's New Year's party, she would have in a heartbeat. But her name was listed on the program. There was no getting out of it.

"It's a good dress." Stephen had hightailed it to her apartment when Kate called in tears, asking for his company. He was sitting behind her now.

"It *was* a good dress," she said as if the dress had died.

"And what did Mommy Warbucks say again exactly?"

"'We both know it would be to your benefit to attend tonight,'" Kate repeated.

Stephen nodded. "You'd probably lose your benefactor if you didn't."

"I know. But maybe that's a good thing?" She looked back at him hopefully, but it was clear from his expression that he didn't think so. "Stephen, she completely used me. She knew what Vivian felt about getting a cochlear implant, and she got me involved anyway."

He scratched his chin thoughtfully. "You know Danny, the sub cellist?"

"Mm-hmm," Kate mumbled, picking a piece of lint off the dress.

"He tried to get a spot in the Lyric audition, said they all but laughed at him."

"Assholes." But she got his point. Jacqueline may have set her up with Vivian, but she was still giving Kate opportunities that most musicians didn't have. "I don't know. Maybe I don't really want the audition anymore anyway. It's not like I'm gonna win." Even as she said it, she knew she did want it.

"Oh, bullshit, Flynn. Of course you do. Everyone wants that job, or at least a job like that. You would be salaried…as in steady paycheck…steady *good* paycheck, whether you play or not. Max needs that. You want the job. Your dreams haven't changed."

Her dreams had always been something she had held close to her chest. The answer used to be simple: a job with Lyric and a home.

Had that changed?

"I just want them to stop giving me stuff."

Stephen rolled his eyes. "She took you on. She's your benefactor. I'd kill for that, Flynn."

She ran her fingers through her hair. "You're right. I'm being childish."

"Little bit," he said kindly.

She turned back to look at the dress. It was so elegantly cut, so beautiful. "You know what Charlie told me?"

"Hmm?"

"She told me that the only reason I'm going to Louisville is because I can't settle. I told her she was nuts, that I had to go where the job is." She glanced at Stephen's face in the mirror. "I mean, that's the job. Right?"

Stephen casually played with a snag on her bedcover. "Vivian said something similar, right?"

Kate nodded. Everyone, it seemed, had ideas about how to play out her career, yet no one seemed to understand. What if that next gig didn't come? What would she do then? Just deciding she was going to gig and somehow make it was a huge risk. And even if it did, would she just end up in a dead-end job with no possibility of advancement? How would she ever get better? How would she ever find that endgame job? "But how would my career advance if I stay here playing gigs? I'll never get that job that lets me stay in one place and give Max a real home."

Stephen shrugged. "The job is all about being the best, right? But there's also no such thing. I mean, there's always something better. That's kind of what we do, right?"

It was true. There was always a better orchestra, a new company gaining prestige, a country that carried a different sound, your own personal best to beat.

"It's a hard job, Kate. No one told us how hard it was going to be when we were in school."

Kate chuckled. In fact, *everyone* had told them how hard it would be. But when she was young, she had been sure she was invincible and that she would be the person who beat the odds. And she hadn't had a small person to take care of either. That had changed everything.

"Well, that's why we can't turn down a contract if we're offered one, right? That's why we always have to go."

"No 'we' about it, Flynn. I extended my contract a month ago."

Kate turned to look at him. "You what?"

"I thought you two were staying. I didn't know you were planning to go to Louisville. When the guy in line for my job backed out, they offered me another year."

"Why didn't you tell me?"

"Because we were supposed to *talk* at some point."

The frustration in his voice lashed out in a small laugh, his shoulders slumping again. The waiting had been really hard on him, she realized. Yet, he hadn't said anything, not wanting to rush her with all that had happened. Touched, she sat down on the bed beside him.

"You know how this works," she said. "I have to go."

"So you've decided, then?"

"I don't see how I can avoid it. Max needs stability."

"And what about me?" he asked with a hint of anger in his voice.

"What—"

"I can help you. Come on, Kate. I at least owe you child support. You let me walk away like this huge thing wasn't happening, and I left you to do it all by yourself. So let me help now."

"Are you criticizing me for—"

"No!" Stephen crossed his arms over his chest. "But it's kind of par for the course for you. It's what you do. I don't get you, Kate. How can you be so full of fire but then just let things go?"

"What? That isn't what happens. Things end because they end. That's life."

"C'mon, Kate!"

"Hey, don't blame me because you weren't ready!" she snarled.

"I'm not! I don't!" He threw up his hands in surrender. "I just mean that I've noticed you have this expectation that people will let you down or leave you, so you just let it happen. You did it with me. And maybe you're doing it with Vivian too. It's like you can't rely on anyone too much because if you do and they don't follow through, then what?"

Then what? Then *pain*, that was what. "Do you have any idea how hard it is to have something and then lose it? I mean, look at how things are with Vivian!"

"Yes, I do have an idea," he said, his face turning red. "I do. You haven't lost Vivian. You two are fighting is all. But I'm about to lose Max. And you too. But maybe you don't really have to run off to the next job. Maybe you could stay and let those who love you help. No one wants to walk out on you. Don't you get that?

"Vivian asked for a break; she didn't break up with you. But you're a flight risk! As much as we try to keep you in our lives, you're so sure of future heartbreak that you won't even consider it."

"That's not true!"

"Charlie told me Vivian offered to help financially. I can help too. I owe it to you. But it isn't about that, is it? It's about being scared. You're so scared of losing things in your life that you don't even fight to make sure you keep them."

"That's crap!" She wasn't being scared. She was being safe. She had grown up losing everything that was ever hers. That was why she only relied on herself. It was the best insurance. And she was going to fight to keep Vivian, Charlie, and Stephen in Max's life. She would drive back and forth from Louisville to Chicago as much as she could.

She had fought for her relationship with Vivian, hadn't she? She had fought for them as a couple. She *had*, after all, made a real effort to be heard, hadn't she? Begged for Vivian to explain what she had done wrong?

No, she hadn't. Stephen was right. She had just accepted it. In fact, all she remembered thinking was that she knew it would end.

She had always assumed that everyone would let her down eventually.

Why did she always expect the worst?

All Vivian had said was that she needed some time, and yet, Kate had been convinced it was over. Just like with Stephen, she had accepted rejection and moved on.

Maybe that was why it never occurred to her to learn ASL. What would be the point if her relationship with Vivian was only temporary? Why learn local customs when you knew that one day you would return to the life you knew before?

She didn't like this line of thought at all. Was she really that person, so damaged from her past that she couldn't trust? No, she had lived a hard life and had always been on her own, but she had adjusted well, moving through her pain without consequence.

Right?

Right?

She understood at last. "How can anything last—"

"—when you have one foot out the door?" He shrugged.

She owed Vivian an apology. She should have started learning ASL the moment they became more than friends. She should have learned about her world. She shouldn't have held back, too afraid to settle.

"I don't want you to go, Kate. Max is my son. I know I have no legal rights, but I'm just getting to know him. Can't we talk about this, Kate? Please?"

She hadn't thought through what might happen when she allowed Stephen into Max's life, even in the best-case scenario where they got along. They were both supposed to be leaving when the WCCE contract ended. Stephen wasn't supposed to have found a way to stay. He wasn't supposed to ask for more.

"Look." He pushed himself up on his elbows. "Focus on tonight, Flynn. Vivian will be there. Look your best and act like you have your shit together. She *will* want to talk to you. You're pretty awesome, you know?" He gently shoved her off the bed. "Go get in the shower, Katie. Do your hair and makeup. Then we'll see what happens next. And we'll talk later. Okay?"

"Okay. Yeah, okay."

She paused just outside of the bathroom door. "Hey, Stephen."

He looked up, his eyes stressed.

She shrugged a little. "I'm glad you're back in my life."

While Kate showered, she tried to think things through.

Everyone had always let her down. It was what she expected now.

But did she want to be that person?

She was pretty sure she didn't.

It wasn't healthy, and it wasn't a mentality she wanted to pass on to Max.

The Loudest Silence

She blow-dried her hair, shaping her curls into a wild lion's mane. She listened to Max and Stephen playing in the living room as she applied makeup for the evening's black-and-white theme. She dusted her eyes with dark gray shadow and drew her lids out in thick, black cat eyes. She shadowed her cheeks with a soft black blush and applied black lipstick. When she was done, she stepped back.

It wasn't perfect, but it was beautiful body armor.

Her face said she was ready. She wasn't, though. Not really. She wasn't ready to play for the elites of Chicago. She wasn't ready to deal with Jacqueline, and she really wasn't ready to see Vivian, as much as she wanted to.

"Well, it's the best I've got," she said to the mirror. She pulled on the sleek black dress and heels, then stepped out into the living room.

Stephen whistled.

Max opened his eyes wide. "Mommy, it's not Halloween!"

For the first time in five days, she smiled. "No, it's not, buddy. How do I look?"

"Awesome!" he said, using the term that he had recently picked up from Stephen, and she laughed again.

Kate clutched the door handle of the car Jacqueline had sent to pick her up, then slid out of the vehicle. It had been hard enough to attend an event like this on Vivian's arm. Now, on her own, she felt naked and alone.

The WCCE New Year's party was at the same theater as the Halloween gala, but instead of Halloween decorations, the ballroom was covered in black chiffon. Elegant party masks lay on the dining tables, and flutes of golden champagne were everywhere. The black-and-white décor reminded her of Vivian's loft before she had it painted for Kate and Max.

She took a champagne flute from a passing server and began to circle the room.

"Ms. Flynn." Mr. Altman appeared beside her. "Lovely to see you."

"Mr. Altman. How are you?"

"Fine, fine. Congratulations on your win."

"Thank you."

"Does this mean we should take your name off the audition list?"

Kate studied him. That wasn't how it worked, and he knew it. "Of course not. I plan on taking the Lyric audition."

"That's what I wanted to hear." With a final nod, he allowed himself to be distracted by another guest.

She smiled and sipped her champagne. He *wanted* her to audition.

Kate continued circling, surreptitiously keeping an eye out for Vivian. When she felt a gaze on her, she looked up. Jacqueline was watching her with a look of amusement. Just as Kate was about to look away, Jacqueline nodded toward the left side of the room, and Kate glanced over to see Vivian dressed all in white, smiling stiffly as she shook hands and mumbled polite greetings with patron after patron.

Looking surprised, her mouth shaped Kate's name. Then she blinked and turned back to the person in front of her.

Kate made her way through the crowd and waited until Vivian said goodbye to the person she was talking to. Then she cut the line and stepped directly in front of her, forcing a smile on her face.

Vivian looked to the right and to the left, everywhere but at Kate. After a minute, Kate gently cupped Vivian's chin.

Vivian pulled her chin away. "Please don't touch me."

"I'm sorry. But would you look at me, please?"

"I wasn't sure you would be here."

Kate shrugged. "Kind of had to be. I hope it's not too much. For you. Me being here, I mean."

"Thank you for the consideration."

"No problem." It hurt to be so near to Vivian, feeling the tension between them, and yet reading the coldness in her eyes.

Vivian looked Kate up and down. "You look beautiful, Kate."

"So do you, as usual."

Vivian nodded, politely thanked her and then excused herself, stepping past Kate to the waiting silver-haired gentleman.

"Just give her time." Jacqueline's voice behind her broke into Kate's depressed thoughts. "She has always been a very headstrong woman."

"Jacqueline," Kate said stiffly, turning to face her.

"How have you been, my girl?"

How the hell did Jacqueline think she was doing? "Not great."

"And Max?"

She thought of Max standing beside Stephen as she left, his thumb in his mouth. "Worse," she said. No reason to pull punches. Then she asked, "Jacqueline, why did you do it?"

"I'm sorry?"

"Why did you use me? I thought that you cared about me, about her. About *Max*."

"Don't be sil—"

Kate was too tired for any bullshit. "Look, I don't mean to be rude, but please leave me alone."

"Katelyn Flynn, after *all* that I have done for you."

"You're right. You've done a lot for me," Kate snarled, "including interfering with my relationship with your daughter!"

"But, Kate, *our* relationship has not ended!" Jacqueline said. "Vivian may have ended your relationship, but that has nothing to do with our professional relationship. I expect you to perform tonight, and I expect you to arrive promptly at the gigs I have lined up for you."

"You can't just—"

"Katelyn Flynn!"

Kate's jaw snapped shut.

"I may have become involved in your life in a way you did not desire, but that does not mean I don't have things to offer you. Surely you understand all that I can do for you."

"Fine. But that support ends the moment I leave Chicago."

Jacqueline nodded smugly. "Agreed. As soon as you leave town."

Kate turned to walk away but turned back when Jacqueline called her name again.

"I do regret what happened."

Kate spent the rest of the evening dancing with whoever asked her, all the while glancing surreptitiously at Vivian until it was time for her piece. As she finished and laid her cello down, she saw Vivian watching her intently and walked over to her. "Vivian, please. Can we talk? I have so much I need to say to you."

Vivian's cold eyes defrosted as she looked at her, letting through a shimmer of pain. "Charlie told me about your conversation. Thank you. And we will talk, Kate, I promise. I just…I don't know yet."

Kate watched her walk away, her heart breaking all over again.

Maybe it was time to move on. Maybe Louisville would be better for her.

The only problem was that Kate loved Vivian, and she wanted to be better for her. She wanted to be all that Vivian deserved. She wanted to fight for the woman she loved.

The countdown to midnight began, voices chanting. "Ten—nine—eight—"

She crossed the room to where Vivian stood in the corner.

"Seven—six—five—"

She didn't allow herself to think.

"Four—three—two—"

She moved quickly.

"One! Happy New Year!"

She reached Vivian on the last count and pulled her close, wrapping her arms around her in a tight embrace. Then she leaned back so Vivian could read her lips. "One of my foster mothers told me once that if you kiss the person you love at midnight on New Year's, it's a promise from you to them that you will kiss them every day for the next twelve months. I love you, Vivian, and I want to make good on that promise. Please…" her voice broke, "please let me."

She leaned in, her lips hovering just over Vivian's, waiting for the signal.

Vivian's lips parted, and Kate gently pressed her mouth to hers, hungrily exploring the oh-so-familiar mouth, kissing her long and hard. Then she turned and walked away.

Chapter 29

"And the tension in your elbow?" Jacqueline asked like a physician quizzing a patient.

Kate dropped her bow arm and then flexed it, feeling it out. As much as she hated to admit it, the massage therapist was helping. The soreness was gone after the session the night before. "It's better."

Jacqueline smiled and nodded. "Good."

Kate thanked her again. She had finally given in and accepted the things Jacqueline offered.

Jacqueline was studying the sheet music Kate had received in the mail the day before. "I do wish they would tell me what they were going to ask for."

"Yeah, it's almost like they were worried you would tell someone taking the audition," Kate mumbled, only catching herself as the words were already out.

To Kate's complete surprise, Jacqueline stared up at Kate, then laughed long and hard.

Kate gaped, her mouth hanging open.

It had been a week since the New Year's Eve party, a week since she had put the ball in Vivian's court. Except for two brief text message conversations, she had heard nothing from her. On the other hand, she had seen Jacqueline three times.

And the Lyric audition was in days.

Kate had never been more prepared for an audition. With no relationship to speak of and Max having joined the Cub Scouts at Stephen's suggestion, she had plenty of practice time. And Jacqueline was like a drill sergeant in a

Gucci dress. She broke down every note that Kate played, and damn if she didn't sound better.

"Fine. I don't know which one they are going to ask for, but I do know that this one is your weakest." Jacqueline handed Kate the sheet music.

"It was one slip."

"Then let's make sure it doesn't happen again."

"Yes, ma'am."

She began to play, but feeling Jacqueline's scrutiny, her arm twitched. She looked up to see Jacqueline's I-told-you-so look. "Yeah, yeah, yeah," she muttered, and began again.

Kate played the piece through again, but she was more focused on her plans for that night.

She was going to an event in the Deaf community, her first one since the disaster with Vivian. This time she was going as a hearing person who was learning ASL. She was determined, but she was nervous too.

She finished the piece and rested her bow arm on her leg.

"Brava!" Jacqueline exclaimed. "I think you're going to do wonderfully."

Kate smiled. "Thanks."

"And what are your plans for the next seventy-two hours? Relaxation and meditation? Meditation will do wonders for your pre-audition jitters."

Kate nodded. "I know."

"Tell me you're going to *at least* take it easy."

Kate answered with a fake smile.

"Oh, Kate."

"Actually"—an idea popped into Kate's head—"there's this event at a bar tonight you should come to."

"Thank you, Kate, but I think it would be inappropriate for me to join you for drinks with your friends."

"*Not* exactly what I meant. It's a Deaf event."

"Oh?"

"Yeah. I'm going to spend some time in the Deaf community. It'll give me a chance to practice ASL. You should come with me. Think how much it would mean to Vivian if we were both learning ASL. We could be study-buddies."

"I see."

Kate pressed on. "It's not Vivian's job to make things easy on us, you know? Not if we love her. Not if we really don't want her to change to fit into the hearing world."

Jacqueline smiled stiffly. "Thank you, but no. I have so many things I need to do tonight." She looked at Kate curiously. "So you're still learning her language despite the fact that you might be leaving the area soon? Does that mean there are plans for a long-distance relationship? Have you two made up?"

"No." Kate sighed.

A knock on the study door interrupted them. Leigh poked her head in the door. "Don't forget you have a meeting in half an hour."

Jacqueline nodded, then turned back to Kate. "Now, Kate. I won't see you again before your audition, so best of luck. I want you to win. Do you hear me?"

"Loud and clear, ma'am."

"Good. Play beautifully, my girl."

"Screech! Bew! Vroom. Roar! Crash!" Max was in his PJs, driving his new monster truck across the living room carpet.

"Max," Kate said. "It's quiet time, remember?"

She pulled her shoulders back and looked at her reflection in the mirror. With stiff movements, she practiced the short sentence Charlie had recently taught her. She pointed at her reflection, let her closed fingers slide over her face, then opened them like a flower blossoming before closing again.

She could do this.

"Vroom, vroom! Screech! Pow! Roar!"

The sound effects abruptly stopped. "Mommy?"

"What's up, kid?"

"Can I hang up glow stars in my new room in Loussville?" Suddenly the room felt cold. "What do you mean, buddy?"

"After we move. Can I?"

So he knew they were moving. "Of course, buddy," she said, her voice tight.

"'Kay. Can Viv'n see me there too?"

What could Kate say to that? "I-I don't know, buddy. I hope so."

"Charlie?"

What could she say? The answer was probably not. "I hope so."

"'Kay." He slowly inserted a thumb into his mouth, his new truck momentarily forgotten.

God, were they really going to move again? *Of course* they were. And they were lucky that they could. If they stayed, her contract would lapse and she would be out of a job. She had no choice.

Or did she have a choice? Vivian had said that Kate was bleeding money every time she moved. Stephen had offered to pay child support. Charlie insisted she could live in Chicago and still have a career.

She grabbed her laptop, clicked on her banking website, and tapped the link for statements.

Thirty minutes later, the numbers scribbled on the back of old sheets of practice music spoke a very clear message.

She thought Vivian had been wrong when she had told her that moving expenses were keeping her in the red. Yet there was the answer, plain as day. The moving expenses from the last move were paid off now, but only thanks to a couple of gigs Jacqueline had recently sent her way.

So Vivian was right, and that meant Charlie was right too.

Which meant that Charlie was right about something else.

Was she afraid of staying in one place? She had never done it, not as a kid or an adult.

But if she stayed… If she committed to staying…

Somewhere along the way, she had built a foundation here: Stephen. Charlie. Neither of them had stepped away from her.

She wasn't alone here.

That meant it was possible to have a home in Chicago.

The thought still filled her with dread. Freelancing. Gigging. It was all so precarious. But that could be a good life. Maybe. Perhaps.

"Hey, Max?"

He looked up from his truck driving. "Yeah?"

"Do you want to go to Louisville, buddy? Do you want to move?"

There was no pause on his part. His look changed, little lip shivered, his eyes going wide. He let go of his toy to pop his thumb into his mouth.

Kate watched him begin to suck in surprise and discomfort.

In that open honesty that young kids had, he had answered without having to answer.

Not that Kate had thought anything else.

Still, his voice shaking a little, Max spoke. "No. I don't want to."

Kate paused on the street corner across from the bar. "She what?"

"Oh yeah." Charlie's laugh crackled on the other end of the phone. "She got all blushy and then cussed me out in sign when I made fun of her."

"Yes!" Kate punched the air, oblivious to the people walking around her.

"Apparently, you swept her off her feet. She compared you to Fred Astaire. So nice going."

She heard Stephen's barrel laugh and Max's giggles through the phone.

"Yeah, Katie, she was speaking in sign, and I could still tell she was talking about you. Her eyes got all distant and—"

Max let out a shriek and Stephen cried out, "Uncle! Uncle." Laughing, Charlie called something in Chinese.

Kate checked the street for traffic, then crossed. "Char, what if I look like an asshole at this event?"

"Oh, you will."

"Gee, thanks" Kate said, but somehow Charlie's words made her feel a little better.

"There's some awesome people there," Charlie said, "and they'll help you learn, okay? Do the best you can."

"Okay. I will. Thanks."

"Love you, Kate."

Kate paused just outside of the bar, taking that in. "Love you too."

It was sink or swim time now. She put her hand on the door handle, wishing desperately she had started learning ASL sooner.

She stepped inside. The overwhelm hit like a pipe to the gut.

Someone tapped her on the shoulder. Kate turned.

"Hi, I'm Gabby. Ve/ver/vis." The person greeting her was tall with long black hair pulled back and full lips shaped into a welcoming smile.

Kate smiled, her heart pounding. "Hi, I'm Kate." She wanted to add her pronouns, only she didn't know the actual signs. She looked at Gabby and said, "She/her," hoping ve could read her lips.

Gabby's hands began moving in a blur, and Kate's mind went blank. A siren went off in her head. *Warning. Warning. T-minus three seconds to full mental shutdown. Warning. Warning.* It was the same feeling of drowning that she'd had at the dinner with Vivian.

Slowly, she lifted her hands and signed, "Can you slow down, please? I'm still learning."

Gabby laughed and signed again, more slowly this time. "Have you been here before?"

Kate shook her head.

"Good for you." Gabby patted her arm. "I'm running this here barn dance, so let me know if you need anything," ve said in an exaggerated Southern accent.

Kate sighed in relief at the spoken voice. "This is a lot," she said. Without thinking, she had stuffed her hands in her pockets.

"Uh-uh, honeychild." Gabby shook ver finger and pointed at Kate's hands, still in her pockets.

"Right." Kate brought them up.

Gabby winked and disappeared back into the crowd.

All right, her first interaction had gone well. She could do this. Now if only her stomach would stop turning somersaults. She headed toward the bar and ordered a shot of whiskey.

She spent the next hour and a half attempting to converse. Every time someone corrected her, her cheeks burned, but it never felt as if she was being made fun or criticized in any way.

A hand waving beside her caught her eye, and she turned to see Gabby smiling at her. "How's it going?"

Kate huffed. "No one ever told me how sore your hands can get." She didn't know how to sign most of that, so she spoke and signed the word "sore."

Gabby nodded. "When I was first learning, my partner at the time rubbed my hands every night. It gets better. So why did you begin this journey? Are you planning to become an interpreter?"

Kate shook her head. "No, I had been dating—am dating, maybe—a Deaf woman," she said, interspersing her words with signs.

Gabby signed the words Kate had spoken and waited as Kate copied, was corrected, and copied again.

"Oh, I see. That's something we hear a lot. Can I give you a tip?" Gabby cupped ver hands, stretching ver fingers. "Try not to be so stiff. It's a little like talking in a tense voice. Understand? Shake it out, girl. Shake it out." Ve gently shook Kate's shoulders. "Now..."

But Kate was no longer paying attention. She could feel a gaze on her. She glanced to her right and froze.

Vivian was dressed in a business suit, as if she had come straight from work. She glared at Kate.

Gabby snapped ver fingers to get Kate's attention. "Are you all right?"

Kate turned and blinked at Gabby. "I am. Sorry."

"Let me guess, honeychild. *That* would be the not-ex?"

Kate nodded.

"Mm-hmm. Then go get her." Gabby disappeared into the crowd.

Kate turned back to Vivian. The ice queen was burning cold in her eyes. "What the hell are you doing here?"

The sign Kate had practiced—*I want to be part of your world. I'm sorry I didn't do this before. I love you so much*—was instantly lost in a fog.

Instead, she lifted her hands and carefully signed, "You're beautiful."

Vivian started, as if Kate had bitten her instead of signed. "This is *my* world. What the hell are you doing here?" Vivian pressed a hand to her stomach.

Kate gently pulled Vivian's hand away. "You don't need to be nervous. It's just me."

"That's exactly why I'm nervous," Vivian spat. "Because the one event I did take you to went *so* well."

"I'm so sorry, Vivian."

"So what are you doing here?"

"Learning!" she fired back in ASL, though her hands felt as if they were moving through molasses.

Vivian blinked. "Right. *Now* you're learning ASL. *Now* you're learning my language."

"I just... All of those things I said on New Year's, I just thought... I don't know what I thought."

Vivian lifted a single eyebrow. "I have to go."

Head hanging, Kate went back to the bar. What had she expected Vivian to do when she realized Kate was learning ASL? Jump back into her arms? Was that why she was learning? She didn't think so. As she watched Vivian across the bar, she was filled with sadness. She was just as radiant here as she had been the night of the Gallaudet dinner, so different from the woman she saw at work.

Kate was miserable. Max was miserable. And for what? The next job? The next new city?

It seemed pointless when happiness was *right here*. Everyone had told her that she and Max were wanted here. But how could she believe them when her past had taught her not to trust promises of family?

Family. They had become her family. Wasn't that what she had wanted her entire life? Could she trust that even if it scared her?

Of course Vivian hadn't jumped into her arms. Why would she commit to a long-distance relationship if it meant she was alone most of the time? Why would she if she wouldn't see Max grow up? And on Kate's current career track, she probably wouldn't stay in Louisville for long anyway.

So get off the fucking track, Kate!

She wanted off the stupid track. She wanted Vivian and Charlie and Chicago—and, hell, she even wanted Stephen. She wanted a *life*, a family.

And at that moment, the loneliness suddenly washed away.

She wanted to stay.

She had to trust Vivian. After all, who knew better about living and gigging in Chicago? And if she couldn't make ends meet, would it really be so bad to let Vivian help? Would it be the end of the world if Stephen paid child support?

She didn't want to go to Louisville. Max didn't want to go.

She wanted Vivian.

She wanted this new family.

That was why she was learning ASL. That was why she was at this bar, this event. She wasn't ready to give up. She wanted to fight for her life with Vivian.

She made her way through the crowd until she found Gabby.

"Excuse me. Would you please show me how to say something in ASL? How do you say, 'I want to fight for us?'"

Kate reached out to touch Vivian's shoulder. Vivian turned, her eyes still shining with the laugh she had just shared with the person she had been speaking to. She stiffened when she saw Kate.

Kate steeled herself. "Will you take a walk with me?"

Vivian studied her face. "All right. Let me get my coat."

"So," Vivian said, glancing at Kate as they stepped outside, "Lyric is coming up. My mother says you're doing well."

"Yeah, well, she would know."

"Will Stephen be staying with Max?"

Kate shook her head. "Nope. Stephen has rehearsal, and Stacey has a class. I'm gonna have to look for another babysitter tomorrow."

Vivian's hand bounced in an "I see" gesture. Then she said, "I have a board meeting in the evening, but I could watch him during your audition."

"You could?"

Vivian nodded. "It's a big day for you. And I know he gets nervous when you have an audition. He was a mess when you were in..." She looked away. "Anyway, the last thing you need to worry about is finding a new sitter."

Kate opened her mouth to protest, as was her habit. She never wanted to put anyone out, least of all Vivian. Except she was trying to be different. "Okay."

Vivian's eyes popped wide. "Oh. Okay. Thank you for that," Vivian said, a small smile on her lips. "So where are we going?"

She took Vivian's hand in hers and pulled her forward, grinning. "Come on. You'll see."

They turned one corner after another, twisting and turning through downtown until they emerged onto the Magnificent Mile. It looked exactly the same as the first night they had gone out together: people were walking in glamorous clothes; the bars were crowded and loud.

"I don't know if you remember, but—"

"Of course I remember, Kate." Vivian pulled on Kate's hand until she stopped. Then she started off again, this time pulling Kate behind her. "This way, if I recall." And they continued down the sidewalk.

Chapter 30

THEY MOVED IN COMFORTABLE SILENCE through the busy city, occasionally glancing at each other. The bustle of the city reminded Kate of that first night when she had listened to the muted scat of a single trumpet. Now, as then, having Vivian beside her made everything feel better, like a confirmation. No, she didn't want to leave this behind.

"We have so much to talk about." She looked over at Vivian, and when she saw she was looking in another direction, she waved her hand as she had seen Charlie do so often. Vivian turned her head, looking at Kate questioningly. "We have so much to talk about. And I wish—" She took a deep breath and blew it out in frustration. "I wish I could say it all with my hands, but I can't yet." Vivian opened her mouth, but Kate held up her hand. "I'm working hard, Viv. I don't want things to be like before."

"I can see that." She smiled at Kate. "Come over here," and she pulled Kate to sit beside her on the stone bench beside The Bean.

"I have so many things I want to tell you. On Christmas, God, I messed up. I had no idea what Deaf culture meant to you, what offering you the implant meant. I didn't understand how much a part of your identity being Deaf is. I'm sorry if I made you feel that you need to change, Viv. You don't."

"And now?"

"I did a lot of things wrong. But there were things you never told me. Why didn't you ask me to learn ASL?"

"The truth?" Vivian said. There was a shadow in her face, pain that Kate wanted to help release. "It never occurred to me to ask you." She looked out at the people milling around them as if asking for validation. "The world sees those with disabilities as responsible for bridging the gap. I simply didn't think to ask you to learn. I've always managed by accommodating the people around me. It's not entirely your fault, Kate."

"I don't—"

"But it's not what I want to do in my own home. And the more I thought about it that way, the more I realized that I deserve at least that much."

"You do!"

"And you're learning, Kate, but you're hearing. I'm so afraid you will never understand my world."

"Just because I wasn't born into it doesn't mean I can't be in it with you. Will you teach me about your world? Please?"

Vivian looked off into the distance.

Kate tapped Vivian's shoulder to bring her attention back. "I learned something about myself on New Year's. Something that I don't like."

"Oh?"

Kate told Vivian everything she had discovered in her talk with Stephen. She told her about the patterns she hadn't realized she'd been following, of Stephen's hurt when he realized Max would be leaving. She told her what she had learned from Charlie. "I don't want to be that person, Vivian."

"Of course you struggle to trust people. You all but told me that on Christmas when you said you were scared, and I didn't understand."

"What?"

"You made a comment about people who stopped giving what they had been offering. At the time, I thought you were just angry, but now it makes sense. I hope you know that I don't work that way."

"The money you offered—"

"It was offered because I care and wanted to help. Just like you would have wanted to help me if our situations were different." Vivian shifted to get closer to Kate.

"I think we're both guilty of expecting the worst. You're right, Kate. I have this whole life that I live by myself. I never invited you to come with me when I met with my Deaf friends. I have had to come to terms about my own behavior. I held you at arm's length until I completely pushed you away. I think I was scared."

"Of what?" Kate asked.

"Of being rejected. Of not being enough."

"You are enough. You've always been enough. I'm so sorry I ever made you feel that you weren't." She paused. "We made quite a pair, didn't we?"

"*Make* quite a pair," Vivian corrected.

They sat quietly, hand in hand, watching the people around them for a while. Then Kate reached up with her free hand to turn Vivian's head to face her. "I'm staying."

"What do you mean?"

"I mean, I'm turning down Louisville. You're right. I can stay here. It won't be easy, but I want to stay with you, Vivian."

"Kate—"

"No, wait. Please listen." Now that she had started, she had to get it all out. "We can do this better. We understand each other so much more now, but we also know that we need to *talk*. This whole mess could have been avoided if we had just talked about what was scaring us. So I'm all in. I'm staying, and I'm talking. We're going to make it work. But I need to know that you're all in too."

She continued, barely stopping to breathe. "I've spent my whole life in the same pattern, Vivian: I go somewhere new and I feel welcomed, maybe even wanted. And then over time, something changes and I leave. No one misses me, no one thinks twice about me after I'm gone. It's like I was never even there. I can't disappear again, Vivian. Neither can Max. He's been a mess since you left. He's back to sucking his thumb."

"Kate, I didn't leave. I—"

"But it felt like you left. We can't do that again, Vivian. You're everything to me, and you're everything to Max. And I'm learning."

"But we're from different worlds, Kate. Can you ever really understand who I am? And why would you want to when you could find someone who's easier to be with?"

"Easier because they aren't Deaf?"

"Yes."

"Viv…" Kate squeezed Vivian's hand. "I love you exactly as you are. I love you, and I want us—you, me, and Max—to be a family."

Vivian was silent, and for a moment Kate thought she had overstepped. Then Vivian said, "I want to be your home."

"What?"

"You've never had anywhere to call home, Kate, not really. I want to give you that. And I need that too. I want to be a part of your home. I want to *be* your home." Vivian reached up to stroke Kate's face. "I do want to be with you and Max. No back door, no running, just us and this makeshift little family: you, me, Max, Charlie, and even Stephen. Oh, Kate, I'm so sorry. I got so scared when you brought up the implant."

Kate cupped her cheek. "Vivian, I'm sorry too. I understand better now. And I love you. I love you so much."

Vivian's smile was wide, beautiful, filled with joy. Seeing it soothed the last bit of pain in Kate's chest.

"I want to see Max. I want to ask Max."

"You want to ask Max?" Kate asked.

"I do. I want to ask him if we can be a family. And I want…I want to tell him I'm sorry."

"Okay. Let's ask Max."

"Good." Vivian stood up and turned in the direction of the L.

Kate stopped her. "Viv, it's the middle of the night," she said in sign.

Vivian stared. "You signed."

Kate grinned. "Come on." She pulled Vivian to her feet and into her arms, and they hugged under the city's reflection in the sculpture.

"Mm." Vivian breathed against Kate's lips. "That's nice."

Kate leaned her head back until Vivian opened her eyes. "You know what would also be nice?"

"Being inside where it's warm?"

"Yup."

Vivian laughed. "Come on, you."

They waited silently for the elevator under the watchful eyes of the security guards, then stepped inside before the doors had even fully opened.

"So we're really going to do this?"

"I'm all in," Kate said.

"Then can I ask you for something?"

"Anything."

"Will you kiss me?"

Kate didn't have to be asked twice. She had meant to move in sweetly, maybe brush Vivian's cheek with her lips. Instead, she moved eagerly.

Vivian seemed to like it.

And kissing Vivian didn't soothe her fire but instead fanned the flames. She reached one hand behind Vivian's neck while with the other she cupped the back of her thigh. Vivian molded herself to Kate's body.

The elevator door opened, but Vivian pulled Kate even tighter against her with one hand. With the other, she reached under Kate's shirt, stroking her stomach, her back, and her breast while Kate trailed her mouth down Vivian's neck, sucking and nipping, relishing the taste, the scent of Vivian's perfume. God, she had missed this!

They were interrupted by an incessant beeping. Kate pulled back and said, "We should probably get out of the elevator."

They stumbled out, still entwined, their lips hungry for each other.

Vivian broke away long enough to ask, "Can you stay?"

Kate nodded. "Charlie is staying with Max tonight."

And with that permission, Vivian took Kate's hand and, groaning, pushed it under the waistband of her pants.

Kate moved her hand downward, her knees weakening when she reached the wetness between Vivian's legs.

Vivian gasped. "Oh, I've missed you."

"I've missed you too."

Reluctantly, she freed her hand from between Vivian's legs and signed, "Upstairs."

Vivian shook her head and instead pulled Kate down where they stood, yanking her pants off and kissing her again, this time lightly, gently.

"I love you."

"And *I love you*," Kate signed.

Vivian stripped the rest of Kate's clothing from her, kissing across her body, stroking her belly and her hips before slipping between her thighs and taking her into her mouth. Kate cried out softly as she stroked her fingers through Vivian's hair, then cried out again, louder this time and without restraint.

At last spent, Kate pulled Vivian up to her, clutching her tightly. They rocked together, skin against skin, their legs intertwined, holding each other as if they would never let go, until they came together, murmuring each other's name. And still Kate wasn't satisfied, so she twisted them again, and they sought one another once more until, exhausted, Kate rolled atop Vivian, kissing her again and again. They lay side-by-side, resting their foreheads together and falling into peaceful sleep.

The next morning, Kate yawned and rolled over to face Vivian, who was still asleep, snoring as though she hadn't slept well in weeks.

It was perfect.

Kate watched as the sun brightened the room. She breathed in the scent of the loft.

She was home.

She waited for the thought to trigger the usual fears. Instead, Kate felt happy—too happy to let Vivian sleep any longer.

She leaned in, kissing Vivian's nose, her cheeks, and her eyes until she awoke, stretching luxuriously. When Kate was sure she fully conscious, she asked, "What do you think about talk therapy?"

Vivian frowned. "What?"

"For me. Maybe I should check it out. I don't want to be someone who is as afraid as I've been."

"Therapy is always beneficial. Perhaps I should do it too. We've both learned so much about ourselves recently."

"That's for sure." She leaned in for a kiss, but Vivian flipped her without warning.

"I've missed you in my bed."

"I've just missed you."

"You're nervous," Vivian signed as they approached Kate's apartment.

"I don't know why, but I am," Kate answered.

"Do you think he'll say he doesn't want me?"

Kate lifted her hands to respond, but Vivian charged on. "I shouldn't have disappeared like that. I should have kept coming to see him. I should have taken him to parks and museums and been his friend."

Kate reached out and grabbed her hands. "Kids forgive a lot. Just...just don't do it again."

She opened the door to hear a movie blaring from the TV and voices that appeared to be in some form of combat.

Kate and Vivian rounded the corner in time to hear Max shout, "No fair, Aunt Charlie!" Charlie had covered him in pillows and thrown herself on top of him.

"Aunt Charlie?" Kate asked.

Charlie looked up. "Jesus, you don't tell a person that you're here? You gave me a—whoa." Charlie looked from Kate to Vivian.

"Who is it? Who is it?" Max burst out from under the pile of pillows and looked to see who had come in. Then he froze, his mouth in a perfect circle.

Charlie cleared her throat, pushing herself into the far corner to give them privacy.

Vivian crouched down at the couch. "Hi, buddy," she signed.

Max's eyebrows drew, his hand uncertainly going to pull on his ear.

Kate watched, worried.

His thumb traveled to his mouth, popping in. He didn't look at Vivian, but instead at the floor right beside her.

"Max?" Kate tried. "Look who's here."

Max didn't respond. Instead, he took a dragging step forward and then, his eyes still downcast and his thumb still in his mouth, went to Vivian and wedged himself into her embrace.

Vivian scooped him up and cradled him to her.

In her arms, he began to cry.

"Shhhh." She smoothed his hair and kissed his forehead as she rocked him.

Kate watched, somewhat startled and yet not startled at all as tears began to slip down Vivian's face as well.

"You said the next day!" Max wailed. "You said the next day, and it wasn't the next day!"

Kate wasn't sure if she should interpret for her or not since his face was in her chest, but it seemed it wasn't needed.

Vivian rocked him back and forth, her arms tight around him. "I'm here, my love. I'm here. I'm not going anywhere," she crooned into his hair.

It took a long time for Max to calm, and even longer before he was willing to sit up in her arms, though no amount of persuasion could get him to sit next to Vivian instead of on her.

They both looked like drowned rats by the time they were laughing again.

"You've grown a foot, I'm telling you."

"Nu-uh, Vivian!" Max giggled.

"Oh no?"

Kate staggered. Vivian, not Viv'n, but Vivian.

"Hey, Max, Vivian and I, we have a question for you. Do you think we can ask you?"

Max's bright eyes opened wide, his expression suddenly alarmed.

"It's nothing bad," Vivian said.

"Okay." His thumb tried to get back to his mouth, but carefully, Vivian took his hand and cupped it in hers.

"So, Max..." Kate started and then stopped. She had no idea how to ask. She glanced at Vivian for help.

Vivian looked as if she was going to be sick. "Max, honey. Your mom and I were wondering, well, your mommy, she asked me if I would be part of your family."

"Like, adopt you?" Max tilted his head to the side.

Kate chuckled.

"Something like that, Max, yes."

"You gonna be my mommy?" Max asked, his voice small. "My *other mommy*. I'll have *two* mommies."

Kate swallowed. For a swimming second, all of her old fears came flooding back. What if Vivian slipped away? How would Max handle that? How would she?

She looked up and saw that Vivian was already looking at her with a small smile on her face. With her free hand, she reached over and intertwined her fingers with Kate's.

Like ice on a burn, the fear soothed.

Trust. She could trust.

And she would make that first appointment as soon as she could.

Watching her, Vivian smiled before turning back to Max. "If you want me to be."

"What do you think?" Kate asked, rubbing his back.

He worked his hand out of Vivian's and popped his thumb back into his mouth, making Kate groan internally. He looked at Kate, then at Vivian. Slowly, around his thumb, he began to smile. "Yeah!" he shouted. "Yeah! Yeah! Yeah!" He sprang up and jumped on top of Vivian, tackling her back against the couch.

She yipped and yelped as Max's bony knees and elbows jabbed into her. Unable to help it, Kate reached out and tickled her exposed side.

Vivian gave a yell, and together, she and Max rolled to the floor, laughing and screaming and beaming brightly.

Chapter 31

IF KATE THOUGHT SHE WOULD wake the morning of the audition calm, cool, and ready, her stomach knew otherwise. She had dreamed that night of playing her cello before the judges, but the only sounds she could make were squawks and groans. The judges had run from the room with their hands pressed over their ears while Jacqueline screamed from the audience seats that she was not good enough.

Kate rolled over and groaned into her pillow, oblivious to the fact that a beautiful woman shared her bed.

The audition was tomorrow.

She jumped up from the bed and dashed into the bathroom.

Max appeared from around the corner. "Are you sick, Mommy?"

"No, buddy." Kate smiled weakly. "I'll be okay. Go watch cartoons, and I'll join you in a minute."

"Kate?" Vivian had appeared in the doorway.

She groaned into the bowl. "Go away. This is gross." Kate waved her away, then heaved again.

"Are you sick, or is this just nerves?" Vivian used her voice since Kate wasn't watching.

Kate pushed herself up from the toilet and faced Vivian. "Nerves."

"Oh, baby. Come on, let me take care of you." Vivian helped her to her feet and filled a glass with water. "Rinse."

Kate swished the water through her mouth, then washed her face and brushed her teeth.

"Come on, baby." Vivian handed her a well-worn sweater.

She laid on the couch to watch cartoons with Max, her head in Vivian's lap, but after a while, she couldn't stay still anymore. She got up and paced the living room, trying to imagine herself stepping confidently up on stage. But instead, she tripped and fell heavily on her cello, shattering it and ruining her chance at the audition and ending her career in one fell swoop. Or she imagined getting halfway through the first piece and forgetting everything that followed. Or she visualized herself playing better than she ever had in her life until the strings sliced her fingers open. Over and over, she imagined every possible version of failing.

She rushed to the bathroom again.

She had never done an audition this important, where the odds were stacked so perfectly against her while also being stacked in her favor. That was the problem. If she was taking this audition with no hope of winning, she wouldn't be nervous at all. But she was in the best shape of her professional life. She actually stood a chance. Not for the first time, fear learned so long ago slithered in like a snake hissing in her mind that if she didn't get the job then she was screwed, that she would have nothing, no resources.

She fought the learned behavior down before she rushed back to the bathroom yet again.

Finally, she gave in and tried Jacqueline's meditation for audition stress. It worked to soothe her thoughts and her nerves until Mary called to wish her luck, inadvertently reminding her of how big a deal this audition really was.

At noon, Vivian left for a meeting. Around dusk, someone knocked on the door. She answered it, her fourth Smart Water of the day in her hand.

Stephen held a bag of takeout. "Wow, you look like hell, Flynn."

"Thanks."

He scooped up Max, who told him, "Mama threw up."

"Are you sick, Kate?"

"No. Not sick."

"Ah. Worried about tomorrow?"

"No," she lied, and rushed back to the bathroom.

She would have kicked him out, but his appearance turned out to be a blessing. He made her laugh. He force-fed her Chinese food and then kept her giggling so she would keep it down. Then after helping to put Max to bed, he tucked her into bed as well.

"There is no reason to be nervous. Look at it as an opportunity. Stop worrying."

Kate scoffed. "Easy for you to say."

She couldn't sleep after Stephen left until Vivian got home around ten. Then she finally drifted off.

Kate woke up the next morning slightly thirsty after the previous day, but otherwise she was calm, she was cool, and she was *ready*.

She sat up in bed, half-expecting to be sick again.

"Are you all right?" Vivian asked. She handed Kate a small plastic trash can. "Just in case."

"Actually, I think I'm okay."

Vivian nodded. "You are."

She washed up and pulled her hair up into a ponytail. This was it. Win or lose, the audition would be over today, and she was glad.

She ate a light breakfast, kissed Max on the cheek, and picked up her cello case.

"Don't be nervous," Vivian said. "Whatever happens, it will be all right. It's just another audition."

"Right."

"And no matter what, you have me."

"I have you. I have you. I have you." Kate repeated the words like a mantra.

"And Max."

"And Max."

"I love you."

"You love me."

"And you love me too."

"Whatever happens, it will be all right," Vivian said, using her free hand to sign.

Kate nodded, her fingers clutching perhaps too tightly to Vivian's. "Right."

"It's just an audition, Kate."

"Right." Kate huffed out.

Despite the fact that Lyric was off on an entirely different L stop, neither had wanted to part that morning. Now as they approached Lyric, Kate's stomach was bubbling, only calmed by Vivian being near.

Could she bring her in as a good luck item?

"No matter what, we have you."

"You have me. You have me. You have me." Kate repeated the words like a holy mantra.

"And Max."

"And Max."

Vivian's smile pulled the corner of her lip up in that way that Kate loved. "I love you."

The words sent a trickle of delight up her spine. "You love me."

They both looked up at the hall.

She loved her. That was all that mattered.

"I love you too."

Kate walked into the legendary Civic Opera House forty-five minutes before her actual audition time, which was perfect. That gave her enough time to find where she needed to go and warm up before it was her turn.

She pushed past the heavy doors and paused inside of the lobby. The grand pillars, the crimson staircases, the huge space, at the moment vacant of patrons, gave her a small thrill. She loved old opera houses like this one.

The floor was a stark white with systematically placed tan patches; the lamps on each white pillar looked like hung torches and brought out the red of the stairs and the walls. Her mind wandered as she stared up at the two-tiered chandelier, wondering what it would be like to come here every day for work. The thought of getting to know this building, of memorizing its scent, of the way her shoes sounded on the floor, of which coffee shop nearby was best was exhilarating.

She caught herself before the thoughts could run away with her, swallowing them down, hard.

"Kate!" someone called before Kate could take a step.

Beside the door stood Jacqueline, for once looking less poised. Her hair was pulled back in her usual dancers bun, her dress pressed, but there was an excited nervousness in her eye that Kate had never seen before. Jacqueline rushed forward and pressed a to-go cup into her hand.

"Gah!" Kate pulled away as the minty smelling tea burned through the cup. "Hot, Jacqueline, that's hot."

"What? Oh, I'm sorry, dear." But she didn't stop pressing, looking over Kate's shoulder at the welcome desk. "I asked if they would let me come in with you, but they refused. Can you imagine that nonsense? I asked them if they knew *who* I was, but they didn't seem to."

Kate stared. For the first time in twenty-four hours, her stomach stopped rumbling. Jacqueline seemed far more nervous than she was.

"Imagine that. Someone in the arts in Chicago not knowing *my* name. Why, it's preposterous!"

"Shit!" Kate whimpered as Jacqueline twitched in agitation and the tea spilled onto her hand. "Okay, okay, whoa." She took the cup and put it on the floor. "Jacqueline."

"Hmm?" Jacqueline looked up, still half-distracted.

How had Kate never noticed exactly how *small* she was before? She barely came up to Kate's nose.

"What are you doing here?"

"Oh." Jacqueline smiled, smoothing Kate's collar. "I came to wish you luck."

"Like…because…" Of *course* Jacqueline would want to hear if all of her hard work had paid off.

"No, no, dear, just…" And Jacqueline Kensington shrugged. Jacqueline Kensington, the mother of all of Chicago arts, actually *shrugged.*

The world felt as if it had been knocked off its axis. Had she been body snatched?

"You care."

Jacqueline's eyes rolled as if the idea were an obvious one, as if Kate were a silly child. "Now." She spun Kate around and gave her push. "March."

Amazed, and somehow with her stomach warm, she did.

"Name?" the woman behind the table asked without looking up from her index cards.

"Her name is Katelyn Flynn," Jacqueline announced for her.

The Loudest Silence

Kate flushed. Was it dumb if she felt a little proud?

"Okay, Miss Flynn. Number forty-eight. Here is your preliminary list, and you are in room 3C. If you follow Deshi, he will show you to your room."

"Right. I gotta—"

Jacqueline nodded, her hands clasped under her chin. "I'll be so disappointed if I hear you did not play well, Kate."

Kate laughed, turning to follow the man. Now *there* was the Jacqueline that she knew.

Her nerves set, and she followed the volunteer to the small greenroom beside the series of practice and warm-up rooms.

Kate's mind was roaring a tribal war cry as she bounced on the balls of her feet, pumping herself up until the personnel manager appeared at her door again with a professionally blank smile and led her to the stage door. Again, her nerves fought to free themselves from the cage she had shoved them in, but she had locked them away too well.

"Number forty-eight?" the union representative just inside the stage door called out.

"Yeah." She shook her hand but was distracted from other polite conversation by the typical audition setup. A large white scrim cut the gigantic but bare stage off before the apron. On her side of the partition was a small stand for her music, a single chair, and a series of mats leading from where she stood to where she had to sit.

The sight of the empty stage sent a course of adrenaline through her bloodstream, hardening her to the core. For the first time, she felt a shiver of excitement.

With a stiff nod to the union representative, she walked to her seat and settled in as best as she could.

"Candidate number forty-eight," the representative behind her called to the unseen committee and gave her a nod.

"Right," Kate whispered to herself and felt a moment of delight as her mind closed around itself, shutting out anything other than what she needed to do now.

She played a few notes, listening to the sound of the hall and double-checking the tune of her strings. It was bliss and it was terrifying. She had always been told the acoustics of this hall were some of the best in the world. Apparently, that was true.

Taking a final deep breath, she began to play.

It wasn't perfect, not by any means, but she let herself sway as she folded into the music, waiting for the moment someone would stop her and tell her they had heard enough. Only no one did. She played through each required piece, breathing perhaps a bit shallowly, and when she was through, she stopped, awkwardly unsure of what she should do now. Had she ever been to an audition where they let her play the whole list? Was that a very good sign or a very bad one? It was unprecedented.

Papers rustled behind the partition. "Thank you."

The union representative was at her elbow then, smiling the same unreadable smile that would be used for the very best player to the very worst. "If you could return to the greenroom. Thank you."

Kate nodded unsteadily. Next came the first in a series of hard parts: all she could do was wait.

She opted to slip her headphones back on and watch a silly comedy on Netflix instead of continuing to practice, saving her muscles.

The adult cartoon was helpful, but her nerves were starting to get the best of her again when the personnel manager finally appeared, four twenty-five-minute episodes later.

He cleared his throat, but there had been no need for him to call attention to himself; the moment he had arrived, the room had fallen instantly silent as death.

"Lyric Opera company would like to extend a large thank-you to each and every one of you for being here today," he began. "As musicians ourselves, we know how strenuous an audition can be, not to mention the time commitment involved. For those of you who advanced to the second round, congratulations, and for those who did not, we wish you better luck next time and thank you for your interest." He paused dramatically.

Everyone held their breath.

"If your number is called, please remain here. If not, you are free to go. Two, five, sixteen, twenty-seven, thirty-three, forty-eight, fifty-two..."

Kate had been sipping her water. When her number was called, she choked. Her lungs protested the fluid and contracted tightly.

No one looked toward her, though, all eyes fixed on the manager.

Once her coughing fit was through, she jumped to her feet, bouncing and stretching like a boxer, her eyes still streaming.

She had made it. Okay. She had made it.

"A short lunch break will be taken now for the committee, as well as yourselves. Please be back in this room at a quarter to one."

Kate stared at the man and deeply hoped he was kidding. Food was the last thing she—and probably everyone else in this room—wanted.

Despite the fact that this break was routine, she was always surprised by it. It was a cruel form of torture.

She ignored the grumbles and moans of the people around her either packing their belongings to dejectedly leave or shuffling around and debating what to do during their unwanted break.

Pulling out her phone, she began to type an update to Vivian.

Hours later, Kate couldn't have been prouder of herself as she closed the last note of the final piece in round two. There was no such thing as a perfect performance; it wasn't possible, but if it were, then she would have very nearly achieved it.

She knew she had advanced before her number was even called an hour and a half later. She didn't cheer or swoon as a few others did, she just nodded, determined and ready for the final round, wishing it would hurry up before she lost this killer edge she was riding.

This time, she was sure that she was going to vomit. There was no stopping it. The disgusting part was when her nerves finally took over and she rushed to the bathroom; she was not the only one in there.

She avoided eye contact with the person at the sink when she exited the stall, washing her face and hands. "Some job, huh?"

The woman laughed with only a touch of bitterness to her voice. "Yeah, some job."

Kate had more time in her warm-up room than the last two rounds. She took full advantage, practicing the music for the last round diligently, ignoring the cellos in other rooms that were doing the same.

Her thoughts were starting to turn against her. This was the final round, which meant that during this performance, they would remove the scrim and she would finally see the committee. That was terrifying. There was a solid chance that she would know someone seated at that table.

"Ms. Flynn, we're on the person before you."

"What?" She nearly dropped her cello. She had been daydreaming instead of practicing.

Heart pounding, she stood and readied her cello. She wanted to run for the hills, but instead she followed the personnel manager.

Nausea washed over her, thick and saccharine. Her tongue was sticky and sour, her throat bobbing. Before she could stop herself, she lunged for the small garbage can ahead of them and was sick yet again.

She squeezed her eyes closed and willed her stomach to settle, mentally swearing. In that moment, she wished she could be anywhere but there. Her eyes stung with humiliation as she emptied herself. "I'm so sorry," she squawked, hanging on to the trash can for dear life.

The man had jumped back when she had rushed for the garbage. "It's quite all right. To tell you the truth, it has happened before. We have a janitor on hand."

"That...that doesn't make me feel better."

"Are you ready to move forward? We could wait for another minute."

Her stomach pitched again, but she swallowed. "No, I'm okay. I'm, ugh, I'm sorry."

He shook his head and led her the rest of the way down the hallway.

They stopped at the stage door. "You sure that you are ready? There are no trash bins on stage."

Kate cleared her throat, not really appreciating the joke.

"Here." From his pocket he produced a breath strip.

That she did appreciate.

"Okay. Good luck."

The door swept open with a crash, and Kate stepped inside the massive hall.

The Loudest Silence

With the screen gone, the house easily quadrupled the size of the hall where Kate normally worked, which was saying something. She had known of the hall's grandeur, of course, but seeing it in all of its vast glory from this view was stunning. The group of people were tiny among the seats, seeming both very far away and too close.

"Forty-eight?" the man at the table asked.

Kate jumped. She had frozen a foot into the room. "I'm sorry. Number forty-eight, Katelyn Flynn."

"Take a seat please, Ms. Flynn."

She nodded, breathing only slightly easier now that she had only seen one familiar face lingering among the strangers. She did, however, recognize the principal cellist for the opera company, which made her stomach somersault.

She sat, stiffly trying to relax.

"Ms. Flynn, we would like you to begin with the Humperdinck, scene two, please. Whenever you're ready."

She slowly let her bow rest on her strings, amping herself as much as possible but…she couldn't. She tried to reach for the reservoir of strength and energy and found it suddenly gone. "I'm sorry, can I have a second?"

"Take your time."

She stretched, taking a few deep breaths and shaking her head gruffly. She didn't have time for nerves. She closed her eyes and pulled in a shaky breath. She had already achieved something by making it this far in the audition. Now it was simply time to enjoy herself.

With another shaky breath, she opened her eyes and looked out into the darkened house.

She thanked them again and this time, when she set her bow on the strings, she began to play.

The first piece…was not a success. She could feel it in her bones. She blinked fast, tears burning. She couldn't cry.

She swallowed hard.

"All right." Barely looking up, the man at the desk sighed, flipping through papers. "Can you try that one again and focus on the allegro?"

She focused harder, tried to bring even more musicality into the notes, and though she knew she played it well, it didn't matter. She was screwed. It hadn't been good enough.

She couldn't believe it.

They named the second piece and she played it quickly and efficiently, complying when the people behind the table scribbled their notes and asked her to play something again more quickly or more loudly.

"Okay, the last thing we would like you to do is play through the Bizet again with Andrea."

The principal cellist nodded and stood.

Kate watched her approach mournfully, wishing this all could just be over and she could go home to Vivian. She got it. Everyone who passed a certain point in the audition needed and deserved a full chance, but she didn't need the casual nicety. She didn't need to make a fool of herself with someone she would never play in a section with, someone who hadn't tanked this audition.

It was all right, she reminded herself. She was so lucky. She and Vivian were together again. They were going to be happy.

Her friends wouldn't let her fall.

Kate was surprised how fun it was to play with the section leader. It was like driving a finely tuned race car down a beautiful curvy road. They flowed together. They bent and twisted with the curves of the music, anticipating each other and meeting easily in the middle. Though Kate knew she hadn't won the audition, she was smiling when they dropped their bow arms in unison.

She turned her grin on Andrea, happy to receive one back.

"Thank you," the man said from the audience, just as blankly as the last two times, which popped Kate's bubble.

She sighed deeply and shook Andrea's hand.

She considered leaving as she reentered the greenroom. She wanted to crawl away and hide in Vivian's arms.

So she paced for a full hour. She needed to move. As she did, she played a game with herself, picking out who she thought had won.

A man across the room was sitting back, his legs crossed, his arms flopped over the back of each chair beside him. He gave off a distinctly douche-y, this-is-no-big-deal vibe. She hated guys like him. They were always tools, and yet they always won everything.

A few feet away from him, a woman was spreading on a new thick layer of nude lipstick, so thick it no longer looked nude. Her clothing was tight, her hair perfectly styled. Kate wondered if she should have dressed up too.

She supposed that in the end, she still would have ruined those notes.

Kate didn't feel nauseous when the personnel manager entered the room again.

"Again, we want to thank you for spending your day with us at Lyric. I know you are all very anxious so I will get right down to it. The runner-up today is Mr. Matthew Vargas. Matthew?"

The douche-y man's leg uncrossed and fell to the floor with a smack, face set, obviously hiding his outrage.

Kate's heart sank. She had thought he would be the winner.

It was a huge honor to win runner-up at an audition like this one. It opened so many professional doors. Of course, in the end, runner-up was not the winner, but she was surprised by the dejection she felt as she clapped politely. She had been hoping that by some miracle she would at least be runner-up. If the runner-up was in town, they would more than likely get called at least once to sub for someone who was out sick.

She slung her packed cello over her shoulder, hovering by the door, pulled out her phone, and sent a text to Stephen, letting him know that she would be able to make it for the second half of rehearsal if Mary still wanted her to.

"And the winner of today's audition is..."

The three of the four people still waiting held their breath in sync.

"...Ms. Katelyn Flynn."

Kate's phone hit the floor with a crunch that reverberated through the silent room. She wasn't sure, but she thought that was her name. It sounded strangely familiar.

The people around her clapped politely for a second, a few slapping her companionably on the back, but Kate stared around.

"Me?"

"Number forty-eight. The woman who vomits."

Chapter 32

Kate entered the WCCE stage door to join rehearsal, her heart still pounding.

She pulled her cello out of its case, unsure if she could even play anything but disjointed scratches.

The moment she stepped onto the stage, the room exploded.

Someone took her cello and bow out of her hands while her fellow musicians surrounded her from every side.

"You did it, Flynn! You fucking did it! I knew you would do it!" Stephen pushed through the crowd to get to her.

Kate had managed to keep all her excitement inside, but now, in front of the guy who had become part of her family, she launched herself into his arms.

He laughed and swung her around. "I'm so proud of you! Congratulations!"

"How do you feel, Ms. Newest Member of Lyric?" Mary asked, grinning from ear to ear.

"Dizzy!" Kate admitted. "I can't believe it. I keep thinking I'll wake up and realize it was all a dream and I haven't even done the audition yet."

She turned at the clicking of heels behind her and had just enough time to open her arms before Vivian pulled Kate into a tight embrace. "You did it!"

And with Vivian's words, it finally hit home, igniting like a bonfire inside her. "Holy shit, I did it!"

"I'm so proud of you, my love. Come on. We have some celebrating to do."

The Loudest Silence

"A shot of whiskey for the lady!" Stephen demanded the moment they walked into the bar. "We're celebrating!"

"Oh yeah? Celebrating what?"

"Meet the newest member of Lyric Opera!" Stephen told him.

"No shit! Here, this one is on the house, lady."

A few minutes later, Charlie walked in, screeching like a banshee. She launched herself at Kate, wrapping herself around her like a sloth. "I can't believe it! You're staying!"

"I was already staying."

"Yeah, but now you're *really* staying! You're staying forever!"

Stephen smiled at the bartender. "Can I just tip you now so you don't throw us out tonight?"

"I'll pitch in for that." Kate reached for her wallet, but Stephen slapped her hand away.

"Your money's no good here tonight, Flynn! You can take us all out after your first show."

"Deal!"

"I can buy a house!" The thought suddenly emerged from the haze of alcohol. "Do you have any idea how long I've wanted a house?"

"How long?" Charlie asked.

"Since I was six! Since I was six, I've wanted a house that stays in one place, in one city. I can give that to Max now!" She looked at Vivian. "Do *you* want a house that stays in one place and doesn't move around?"

Stephen snickered. "As opposed to houses that don't stay put?"

"Wait." Kate reconsidered. "Should I buy a house?"

"We, baby," Vivian said. "We're a 'we' now."

"Or should I buy a condo?" Kate continued as if she hadn't heard. "Isn't it all about condos now? Except I don't want to live in Skokie."

"You will not be moving to Skokie, Ms. Flynn, at least not if you want me to go with you," Vivian stated firmly.

"Okay."

"Besides, I already have a condo," Vivian pointed out. "And I don't think it's a good place to have babies and raise children."

Babies.

There were babies in their future.

"We can get a house and a dog and a swing set. Max would love that! And we can ride bikes and have a room just for the *babies.*" She paused, a scowl on her face. "But who is having these babies, because I already had a baby."

"Ah, Ms. Kensington."

Kate turned at the voice of Zachary King. She glanced at the board members sitting around a corner table.

"Your mother is looking for you."

Vivian looked to Charlie, who quickly signed his words.

"My mother?"

Stephen stood up abruptly. "I've been meaning to talk to her about those violin lessons. This is as good a time as any to get to know Grandma, right?"

"Stephen, no!" Vivian grabbed his arm.

"I'll stall her, but hurry up."

"He headed toward the front, stopping at the bar for two champagne flutes, then turned and winked and disappeared outside.

"Kate?"

"Hmm?"

Vivian looked back at the door where Stephen had disappeared. "Did he just take on my mother for no reason other than to give us time?"

Kate nodded, impressed.

"That was a power move right there," Charlie sighed.

"If we're going to do this…" Vivian started, her eyes finally coming back to Kate.

"Which we are," Kate inserted.

"…then I have some say in Max's life, don't I?"

"That's the idea. If there are going to be babies, then we'll be coparenting."

"So I was thinking: perhaps it's time to tell Max about Stephen."

"You mean…?"

"He's a good man, isn't he? Anyone who braves my mother because they think it will make someone else happy deserves to be forgiven for past wrongs."

Stephen reappeared with Jacqueline at his side.

"Congratulations, Kate," Jacqueline said. "Brava. I came to congratulate you, but I was also hoping we could talk. Would you walk with me, please?"

"Mother?" Vivian frowned.

"Don't worry, Vivian. I have my pepper spray."

"Not what I was worried about," Vivian muttered as Jacqueline left with Kate.

It was freezing out, the air heavy with the promise of more snow, and Kate wondered why Jacqueline wanted to walk outside. She shivered and wrapped her jacket tighter around herself.

"I just wanted to tell you how very proud of you I am, my girl." Jacqueline said.

"Thank you," Kate said.

Jacqueline glanced wistfully into a restaurant as they passed. "Oh, isn't that nice."

Kate saw the family Jacqueline was looking at. It had to be the grandmother's birthday. Family members were singing around an older woman with a cake in front of her. It was a perfect picture.

Jacqueline's look was wistful.

"You okay?"

Jaqueline gave a start, her smile popping on her lips as if it were on an automatic switch. "Of course. Beautiful cutlery, did you see? I'll ask Leigh if she can find out what the design is."

Kate wasn't fooled for a second. "You know, you're not as hard as you think you are."

Jacqueline looked askance at Kate. "What do you mean by that?"

"You seem to want what we just saw. All of us, a family."

Jacqueline smiled slyly. "I thought I noticed a new spark between you two."

"Yup," Kate replied. "Vivian's talking about babies."

Jacqueline looked as if she had been slapped. "Oh." She picked up her pace.

Kate hurried to catch up. "What is it?" she asked.

"You'll have children I won't know, children I'll never be allowed to see."

"Whoa." She stopped walking and caught Jacqueline's arm.

"If you don't mind, Katelyn." She yanked her arm away. "She thinks I'm a bad person. No matter what I do, no matter who I try to be. She just—"

Maybe it was the alcohol in her system that loosened her tongue. "That's because you're doing the wrong things!"

Jacqueline glared at Kate. "Why, you ungrateful little—"

Kate raised her hands. "Stop. Just stop for a minute. You have done a lot for me. And I love you a little bit, I think. So let me do something for you." It was too late to stop now. In for a penny, in for a pound. "You refuse to speak to her."

"I do not!" Jacqueline raised her hand to her chest, ever the shocked matriarch.

"You do! I'm sorry, Jacqueline, but you do. I didn't get it at first. I just let things roll along on their own, refusing to learn sign, and it ended up making her feel like she wasn't important. I might as well have refused to speak to her."

Jacqueline opened her mouth to speak, but again Kate held up her hand.

"You know she's not going to get the implant, and she shouldn't have to. You're her mother. You're supposed to love her for who she is, not spend twenty-five years trying to change her. Trust me: she needs you. Everyone needs a mom. I know that from experience. And frankly, you need to get to know your daughter. Think about her future and whether you want to be part of that. If you do, then you need to learn her language because it will be your grandchildren's language too. You'll be the odd one out, not us. You'll be like a stranger to them. And that would be so messed up because I *know* you have so much to give."

When Jacqueline didn't respond, Kate continued. "I'm taking lessons with Charlie. And I think…I think maybe you should too. I mean, if you love her, then why not?"

Epilogue

Boxes had been packed, only this time, the boxes holding her and Max's lives weren't thrown haphazardly into the back of the car but were labeled for each room before being loaded onto the moving van. Kate's furniture had been evaluated and replaced as needed with pieces that better fit the new house.

So far, Max had only seen pictures of the newly remodeled Tudor deep in the heart of Evanston, and Kate was convinced he would explode before they arrived.

The movers were still unloading when they pulled up.

"Wait!" Kate held Max's collar so he didn't leap from the car before it had come to a full stop.

"Mom! Let me go!"

She turned the ignition off and released the squirming boy. He shot out of the car like a horse in a race and ran toward Vivian, who was waiting on the sidewalk in front of the house.

"Mama!"

It had been a smooth transition from *Vivian* to *Mama*, not that Kate was really surprised. Vivian had begun that role the moment she had picked him up that day in the park. Was it only a year ago?

I'm going to marry her. The thought never got old, never lost its shine.

Vivian looked up and smiled. "You're late," she signed.

Kate held her hands up in surrender, then slowly signed, "Max needed the bathroom."

"Watch it, Flynn," Stephen said as he picked up a box. "She just nearly ate one of the movers alive."

Vivian's mouth dropped opened. "I did not."

"She did," Stephen mouthed at Kate.

"I can read lips, Stephen!"

Stephen laughed, then headed inside with his cargo.

"Hey, Dr. Dilaney would say she is just using her best tool to incite change!" Kate called after him.

"That's right," Vivian agreed.

Kate had only had a few sessions with Dr. Dilaney, but already she could tell it was exactly what she needed to heal. Vivian, too, had begun meeting with a therapist. It was going to be a long haul to their best selves, but they both were committed.

"You made it!" Vivian's friend Amelia and her partner, Leslie, stepped out of the doorway and waved.

"Have you seen your bathtub, Kate?" Amelia asked, her hands flying.

"Nope. Vivian's been keeping me busy. She says it's big enough to swim in."

"Big enough," Leslie corrected, and Kate copied. It no longer bothered her to be corrected.

"Mommy, can I go look?"

"No way! I'm going to go first!" She sprinted around Vivian and dashed for the door. Max flew after her, giggling, and they scrambled up the center staircase toward the bedrooms, stopping at the first door. "What about this one?"

"No way! It's a bathroom!"

"I thought you wanted to sleep in the bathtub!"

"This one! This one!"

Kate followed him to a huge empty room with a window seat and a window that looked out the front of the house to a giant tree.

"This one?"

"Yeah! Look, I can see the whole block!"

Stephen entered behind them and whistled. "This looks like the perfect room for you, sport."

"Yeah!"

"Sorry, Max," Charlie said, appearing beside Stephen, "but this is gonna be my room."

"No!" Max cried, suddenly indignant. "This is *my* room!"

"Nope. I think Stephen and I are gonna take it. You can sleep in the tub."

"Nuh-uh!"

"Okay, Max. She's just kidding." Stephen chuckled. "Come on, let's go downstairs and tell the movers to bring your boxes up here."

Max took Stephen's hand. "Stephen, are you and Aunt Charlie married?"

Stephen looked puzzled. "No. Why do you ask that, sport?"

"'Cause you're always with her when you're here."

"I'm always…"

It felt as if all the air had been sucked out of the room. Kate traded a glance with Vivian. Was this the right time?

Stephen laughed nervously. "It's because we're all friends, right?"

Kate looked at him. "Yeah, we're all friends."

It *was* the right time. "Max, come here." She pulled him next to her on the loveseat. "Max, Stephen isn't around all the time just because he's our friend."

"He's not our friend?" Max asked.

"No, he is. But he's more than that." She glanced at Stephen. "Max, Stephen is your dad. That's why he's always around. He wanted to get to know you."

Max drew his eyebrows together. He looked at Stephen, then back at Kate. His face relaxed. "Oh. Okay. Can we keep doing Cub Scouts?"

Stephen stared at Max, his mouth doing the perfect impression of a goldfish. "Yeah! Of course, Max."

"Okay!" Max hopped off the window seat and tore out of the room.

"Be careful of the stairs!" Kate and Stephen called out in unison.

"I have so many parents!" Max cried out as he raced down the stairs.

"Jesus wept, that didn't go how I thought it would." Stephen collapsed next to Kate.

"That's kids for you, though."

"Want to see our room?" Vivian signed to Kate.

Stephen stood up. "I'll go downstairs and help Max."

The master bedroom was wide and open, the polished wood floor reflecting the sunlight. They walked through the French doors out onto the large patio that overlooked the huge lawn. The moving men were grumbling as they set up the swing set.

"Any regrets?" Vivian asked.

"No. No regrets. Stephen has really stepped up. I never thought it would go so well with him and Max."

"And no regrets about other things?"

"About the house?" Kate asked.

"Among other things."

Kate pulled Vivian close and kissed her. "Are you freaking kidding me, woman?"

After a moment, Vivian pulled away. "Let's not give the movers a show, darling."

Kate hooked her finger into Vivian's belt loop so she couldn't get far. "Or maybe we should." She kissed her again.

"I love you, you know," Vivian signed when they came up for air.

"I do. I do know." And she signed back, "I love you too."

"Come on. Let's bring some boxes up before Amelia begins unpacking for us."

At last, the family had their new home to themselves. Kate clicked on the JBL speaker, increasing the volume to a level that would have been forbidden in her apartment. She and Vivian began unpacking the boxes stacked on the kitchen island. Vivian picked up the speaker and was soon dancing. Kate put down the plates she had pulled out of the box and wrapped her arms around Vivian from behind. Pulling her closer, she began to tap the beat onto Vivian's breastbone with one finger.

"How far we have come," Vivian said.

Their dance was interrupted when Kate heard Charlie. "Anybody home? Hello?" She appeared in the kitchen holding a takeout bag.

"Thank God, I'm starving. Where have you been all day?" Kate signed. She went to the foot of the stairs.

"Okay, Mommy!" Max yelled back in response to her call up the stairs.

At the same time, Stephen yelled back "Okay, Flynn."

She turned and stopped, shocked when she reentered the kitchen. Vivian had frozen, the glass of water in her other hand pausing halfway to her lips.

Even Max, who came running pell-mell down the stairs a few seconds later, froze.

The magnitude of that moment sank under the weight of the one that was already happening.

Looking around the kitchen, Max grew quiet too.

Jacqueline stood, looking almost shy behind Charlie. She smiled and held out the potted plant she had brought.

Charlie had said nothing about bringing Jacqueline, of all people.

"Mother! What are you doing here?" Vivian's voice cracked slightly. She used her voice less and less the more proficient Kate became at ASL.

Jacqueline smiled and handed Charlie the plant. She picked up her hands and signed a single word. "Vivian."

Vivian dropped the plate she was holding, and it shattered on the floor.

Jacqueline hesitantly continued signing. "I thought…your new home… could use some flowers." The words were awkward, but they were in the language they had never seen her use before.

Vivian's eyes widened. "Mother?"

Jacqueline dropped her hands. "I don't know very much yet. It's only been a few weeks. Why didn't you ever tell me how difficult it would be to learn the language?"

"She practiced that!" Charlie announced, her hands picking up what Jacqueline couldn't sign.

"You're learning sign?" She looked at Charlie. "You're teaching her sign? But you hate each other."

Charlie shrugged. "We're working on it."

Jacqueline stepped forward and, picking up Vivian's hands, kissed her knuckles. "After Kate passed her audition, she told me it was time. I finally decided she was right." Jacqueline took a deep breath. "I was just trying to help in my own way. I never meant… Maybe I did, but not in the way… I don't know." She dropped Vivian's hands, suddenly uncomfortable.

"Kate did this?"

"She…she helped me see some things I hadn't seen before. She helped me realize that things could be different and they needed to be different. I make no promises, Vivian, but I'm here, and I want to try."

"Kate?" Vivian's eyes were quizzical, round, and full of astonished wonder. "You did this?"

Kate scuffed her shoe a bit and pulled her face into a small sideways grin.

Other Books from Ylva Publishing

www.ylva-publishing.com

The Music and the Mirror
Lola Keeley

ISBN: 978-3-96324-014-0
Length: 311 pages (120,000 words)

Anna is the newest member of an elite ballet company. Her first class almost ruins her career before it begins. She must face down jealousy, sabotage, and injury to pour everything into opening night and prove she has what it takes. In the process, Anna discovers that she and the daring, beautiful Victoria have a lot more than ballet in common.

This age-gap, workplace lesbian romance is a sizzling, award-winning page-turner, whether you're into ballet or not.

Never Say Never
Rachael Sommers

ISBN: 978-3-96324-429-2
Length: 220 pages (75,000 words)

Ambitious Camila might have lost her marriage but she doesn't need love to build a TV empire and raise her young son. What she does need is a nanny.

Enter Emily—bright, naive, and new to New York City. Emily is everything Camila is not and that's not all that's unsettling.

Surely she can't be falling for the nanny?

An age-gap, opposites-attract lesbian romance with a puddle of melted ice queen.

Hotel Queens
Lee Winter

ISBN: 978-3-96324-457-5
Length: 319 pages (104,000 words)

An opposites-attract lesbian romance as layered, sassy, and smart as its characters. At a Vegas bar, two powerful hotel execs meet, flirt, and challenge each other—with no clue they're rivals after the same dream deal. What happens now they've met their match?

Paper Love
Jae

ISBN: 978-3-96324-066-9
Length: 222 pages (89,000 words)

Susanne Wolff isn't thrilled when she's sent to save her uncle's stationery store from bankruptcy. Paper Love's employee Anja instantly dislikes the digital-loving snob who's her fill-in boss.

But thanks to a meddling cat, a stationery road trip, and an armada of origami boats, Susanne discovers how sexy pens, notebooks, and certain stubborn employees can be in this sweet lesbian romance.

About Olivia Janae

Olivia Janae has been a life long writer. Growing up in California, it was always her dream to one day see her name on the cover of a book ever since she scribbled down her first story in a notebook at the age of eleven. To this day, she can't believe that her dream has come true.

Now, Olivia is living outside of Chicago with her classical musician wife, son, and three cats.

Outside of her love of writing, Olivia is an avid movie buff with an obsessive love for cooking, candy making, 'Buffy, The Vampire Slayer', and Stephen King.

CONNECT WITH OLIVIA
Facebook: www.facebook.com/Oliviajanaeauthor

The Loudest Silence
© 2022 by Olivia Janae

ISBN: 978-3-96324-699-9

Available in e-book and paperback formats.

Published by Ylva Publishing, legal entity of Ylva Verlag, e.Kfr.

Ylva Verlag, e.Kfr.
Owner: Astrid Ohletz
Am Kirschgarten 2
65830 Kriftel
Germany

www.ylva-publishing.com

Second revised edition: 2022

No part of this book may be reproduced, scanned, or distributed in any printed or electronic form without permission. Please do not participate in or encourage piracy of copyrighted materials in violation of the author's rights. Thank you for respecting the hard work of this author.

This is a work of fiction. Names, characters, places, and incidents either are a product of the author's imagination or are used fictitiously, and any resemblance to locales, events, business establishments, or actual persons—living or dead—is entirely coincidental.

Credits
Edited by Sandra Gerth, Julie Klein, and Michelle Aguilar
Cover Design and Print Layout by Streetlight Graphics

Printed in Dunstable, United Kingdom